# SHADOW OF A CENTURY

## JEAN GRAINGER

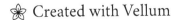

*For my dad, John, who always told us stories.*

*...For all that is done and said.*
*We know their dream; enough*
*To know they dreamed and are dead;*
*What if excess of love*
*Bewildered them till they died?*
*I write it out in a verse –*
*MacDonagh and MacBride*
*And Connolly and Pearse*
*Now and in time to be,*
*Wherever green is worn,*
*Are changed, changed utterly:*
*A terrible beauty is born.*

'Easter 1916'
~William Butler Yeats

# CHAPTER 1

S carlett set the alarm on her new cream Mini Cooper. It emitted a satisfying beep as she crossed the underground parking lot of the *Globe Messenger* Building. She felt a surge of pure joy: For the first time in her whole life, everything was perfect. She looked great – an expensive new wardrobe saw to that – and she knew that she was unrecognisable from the insecure girl she had once been. The elevator doors opened and she stepped in. The young cub reporter from the sports desk nodded, then stared at the floor. She smiled to herself. She didn't intend to be intimidating, but she was now senior staff. The kid probably didn't know what to say to her.

As the elevator ascended to the fourteenth floor and the editorial suite, she had to remind herself once more that this was really happening. Her years slaving for Artie on the *Yonkers Express* were behind her, and here she was – a senior political correspondent for the *Globe Messenger*, one of the biggest nationals in the country.

She glanced at her iPhone. It was odd that Charlie hadn't texted; he usually did, to check that she had got up. He was always gone by 5 a.m. on the nights he stayed, but last night he couldn't make it. She understood. In his position, his time was rarely his own. She smiled as she thought of the private messages he had sent her on Facebook last night while he was supposed to be deep in discussion on a video conference call with a senator in charge of a powerful lobby group for tax reform. Ron Waters was a crashing bore, according to Charlie, and a Republican through and through. He was never going to vote for Charlie or his party anyway, but he had to be seen to show willingness. He promised he was trying to get her some face time with the guy for another high-profile *Globe Messenger* piece.

The elevator door opened and the bright, modern, busy newsroom buzzed in front of her. Hundreds of screens flashed images, and lots of reporters, IT people and administration staff seemed to teem constantly from all directions. She breathed deeply, almost inhaling the atmosphere, and not missing Artie and his chain-smoking ways one little bit. She made her way with enthusiasm to the office of Carol Steinberg, the editor-in-chief.

Scarlett could hardly believe she was heading into her eighth month of working here. The time had flown by, and her star was definitely on the rise. The *Yonkers Express* piece she had done on the extremist Islamic mullah on the Lower East Side had garnered a lot of attention, and was why she was offered the job on the *Messenger*. Her pieces on Charlie now were also getting her a lot of column inches, much to the chagrin of many other journalists in the city.

Carol's text – *Get here ASAP* – came through as she was driving into the office anyway. She was looking forward to the meeting, especially since the text's urgency suggested some exciting development. Scarlett knew Carol's reputation as a ball-breaker, and that she intimidated almost all of the staff, but Scarlett admired her. She had to be tough to get where she was, and one day, Scarlett intended to hold a similar position.

Was she imagining it, or did the noise in the

office, usually deafening, suddenly drop to a murmur? The political team were standing together at their corner by the bank of flat-screen plasma TVs. She wasn't imagining it; they had all stopped talking and were staring at her. *They must be really ticked off about the mullah story*, she thought.

She pushed open the opaque glass door of Carol's office and entered the sumptuous surroundings. The TV beside the desk was live paused, and Scarlett instantly recognised Charlie's handsome features, stilled in mid-sentence.

'I'm assuming you've seen this?' Carol's voice was quiet, but lacked her usual warmth.

Scarlett was confused. 'No, is this from today? I haven't seen –'

Carol interrupted her by pressing Play on the remote. Charlie was unshaven and tired looking, as if he'd slept in his shirt. His familiar voice filled the office.

'Words can't express my regret. I have offended my party, the good people of New York who elected me, and most painfully of all, I have let my family down. I feel deep shame and embarrassment at my reckless and unprofessional behaviour, and though I don't deserve any special favours, I would ask you, ladies and gentlemen of the press, to restrict your interest to me and to leave my family out of this. They are innocents in this whole thing, and are suffering enough at this time. Thank you.'

Charlie turned away and went back into the offices behind him in a hail of questions and flashing cameras.

'I don't understand.' Scarlett's voice cracked. 'What happened?'

Carol gazed at her with thinly veiled fury. 'Last night, Charlie Morgan was in a video conference meeting with Ron Waters, the Republican senator. Morgan was sending him some data to support a point he was making, but he inadvertently sent him a message of an explicit sexual nature, clearly intended for someone else. The message also mentioned *this* newspaper by name. To add insult to injury, the message went on to outline how boring and stupid Morgan thought Waters was. Waters immediately reacted and exposed Morgan, who has, about an hour ago, admitted that he is having an affair with a journalist, the person for whom the message was intended. In addition, he has told the world who that journalist is.'

Scarlett felt nauseous. Blood thundered in her ears. This wasn't happening, it couldn't be.

Charlie would never do anything like that to her. He couldn't – he loved her.

'I took a chance on you, Scarlett. You are only twenty-six, very young to hold the position you did.' Scarlett heard her use of the past tense and every fibre of her being prayed that this wasn't happening.

Carol went on, her voice icy. 'I appointed you over others who have more experience, and who felt they deserved it more than you. I thought you had something – that's why I convinced the board to take you on. I'm at a loss for words. How could you throw everything away, everything you've worked for? And more to the point, how could you have dragged us into this mess with you? We pride ourselves on the highest standards of journalistic integrity here at the *Globe Messenger*. You have let us down, very badly. For someone in your position to have an affair with a politician is to relinquish all moral and professional authority.'

Carol's tone conveyed nothing but disgust. 'Your in-depth interviews with him that we printed make us look as foolish and corrupt as you are. But to be involved with a married politician, especially one whose unique selling point is his position as a family man, something you wrote about with such empathy… Words escape me, Scarlett. I'm so disappointed in you. I thought you were much better than this. Get your things now, rather than coming back for them, and try to get away without the gathering press outside seeing you leave, though they are already circling the wagons.'

She paused, and then added coldly, 'And Scarlett, if you give any interviews about this, I'll drag you through every court in the country. Do I make myself clear?'

Carol got up and, without a backwards glance, left the room.

\* \* \*

'THERE SHE IS!'

'Scarlett!'

'Scarlett, over here!'

'Just turn around!'

'C'mon, Scarlett…'

Scarlett emerged from the car and pushed her way up the steps to the front door of her brownstone, blinded by the incessant cameras flashing as she pushed through the heaving mass of bodies. Every hack journalist in New York was out in force, circling like vultures. News anchors smugly did their pieces on camera down the street. The fact that the target was one of their own obviously made the story even more tantalising. Many had resented her growing profile, feeling she was too young, and came out of nowhere, so they were thrilled to see her crumble. *No such thing as loyalty in this business,* she thought, while trying to keep her face immobile.

She fumbled for her keys in the bottom of her new Prada handbag as the reporters jostled and pushed to get closer. Her red hair was escaping from the chignon she had hastily tied up in the car, and she could feel the make-up sliding from her face as she began to sweat. Despite her best efforts to look calm and collected, she was cracking. She couldn't find the damn key! Her hands began to shake badly as she gritted her teeth, determined not to cry, refusing to show any weakness. *They'd love that.* Not that anything could make this situation any worse, but to have her tear-stained face splashed all over every tabloid and gossip show in town would be the final straw.

'Come on, Scarlett, just one shot. At least this way you get to look good!' There was a collective cackle.

Would she have been any different if it were

one of them? If she were honest, probably not, except that salacious sex scandals were not really her thing. Mercifully, she finally found the key, and despite her shaking hands, managed on the third attempt to get it into the lock. She quickly slipped inside and slammed the heavy door shut, leaning her back against it, her eyes adjusting to the relative gloom of the hallway. Relief flooded through her. Everything was as she left it this morning. The highly polished mahogany staircase gleamed, its snow-white carpet runner fluffily breaking the austerity of the architecture. The house smelled exactly as it always did – of lilies and cleanliness. An oasis of serenity.

She went into the kitchen at the end of the hallway and immediately shut the blinds. Alone in her beautiful new home, she disintegrated into wracking sobs. The strength that held her together for the past two hours suddenly drained out of her. The paintings, mirrors and everything else she had gathered so lovingly over the years were invisible to her now. That was it – it was all over. Her life was over. This just couldn't be happening. That press conference played over and over in her head.

*How could Charlie have hung me out to dry like that?*

Dreading what she was about to see, she typed 'Charlie Morgan confesses all' into YouTube. She watched in horror as he explained that he was a weak, foolish man who loved his family, and he deeply regretted his inappropriate liaison with political correspondent Scarlett O'Hara.

Facebook, Twitter and bloggers were already on the puns. Torturing herself, she scrolled through 'Charlie's Scarlett Woman,' 'Morgan Really Has Gone With The Wind,' 'Frankly, My Dear…' It went on and on and on.

Scarlett hated her name. She used to dread meeting new people and enduring their shocked expressions – the attempts to hide a smirk, or the all-too-common 'Did you know there was a movie…?' When she met Charlie, he told her he wanted to be her Rhett Butler. The memory brought forth a sharp stab of pain. Normally, anyone who said such a thing would have felt the sharp end of her tongue, but he was different. Even though he constantly joked and teased her about it, she forgave him. She forgave him everything…and then he betrayed her.

# CHAPTER 2

*S*carlett sat on her Roche Bobois oatmeal sofa that had cost almost a month's salary. She fought back panic at the thought of her mortgage and credit card bills, now that she was unemployed. She had some savings but not enough to last for very long, and who would employ her now? Nobody, that's who. She could hear the raucous laughter of the journalists outside the door fade in and out. She longed for someone to help her, somewhere to go, but she realised that, in recent years, she'd had no time to keep up friendships. She avoided her mother, and she had no other family. Charlie took up any spare time she had: waiting for him to call, or grasping precious moments with him.

Without him and her job, she had nothing. Absolutely nothing. A feeling of hopelessness, something she had not felt for so long, came creeping in.

Scarlett was drawn back to another time, another sofa, in a dingy, run-down apartment in Yonkers. The familiar feelings of terror threatened to choke her as she remembered sitting on her mother's lap, in the calm after the cops picked her father up yet again. She could only have been four or five, trying with her little hands to stem the blood from a cut on her mother's face, or holding frozen peas to a swelling injury. Scarlett would say prayers to the many Catholic saints represented on the damp walls of the room that her mother wouldn't die.

Lorena took her faith seriously, and the only thing that equalled her faith was her love of movies. She would tell Scarlett how she was named after the most beautiful woman in the world. When it was safe, her mother would draw out her battered cookie tin from under the table and show her the pictures from her old movie magazines. To Scarlett, the names of Vivien Leigh, Fred Astaire and James Dean were as real as her mother and father. Unfortunately, Lorena's fascination for movies was one of the many things about his wife that drove Dan O'Hara mad, and when he was mad, he was terrifying.

Scarlett remembered the titters from the other children, and the outrage from Sister Teresita in St. Peter and Paul's Elementary, when she announced that she was not, as was Catholic tradition, named after a saint, but instead after the most beautiful woman in the world.

As she became a teenager, though, she learnt to hate her name. The childhood innocence was laughed out of existence by bullies and teachers who jeered and mocked. She tried several times to shorten it, and did everything she could to get a nickname, but nothing stuck. She was born Scarlett O'Hara, and Scarlett O'Hara she was going to stay. She was teased mercilessly.

Dan O'Hara, Scarlett's father, was regularly seen staggering drunk around the streets of Yonkers, bellowing abuse at passers-by and scaring kids. As a young man from County Mayo in Ireland, he had come to the United States full of dreams and ambition. Life was going well for a time, and he met and married Lorena, a fragile hothouse flower from Georgia, whose southern charm beguiled the young Irishman. But things soon turned sour. Dan was a charmer, good looking and smart, but work shy. He always wanted to make a fast buck, but never did any actual labour. He had a friend in construction who offered him job after job, but Dan would scoff, claiming that manual labour was 'for fellas too thick to do anything else.' He always had a scheme going – some kind of a scam to get rich quick. He convinced several people to invest in his so-called *business opportunities*, and to a man, they lost their shirts on them. Eventually, he was an outcast and started drinking. Unwelcome in the more respectable establishments, he hung out in grotty, smelly bars, and over time, he was even barred from them.

The blame for his failure was never his own. No, it was Lorena and Scarlett's fault. They were holding him back, he used to snarl. If he didn't have them hanging on to him, he'd be making a fortune out West. His disappointment with life was expressed by using his beautiful young wife as a punchbag. Scarlett hated him.

When Lorena opened the door to the police, the winter Scarlett was fifteen, they told her Dan had walked in front of a truck. She watched her mother try her best to compose her face into that of a grief-stricken widow. Sergeant Kane, who'd been coming to arrest Dan for all sorts of offences over the years – not the least, battering his family – sent the other officer to wait in the car.

He sat down in the tiny living room and said, 'That's it, Lorena. You and Scarlett are safe now. It's over.'

Lorena looked as if a huge weight had been removed from her, though she was in a daze of disbelief. Scarlett remembered Sergeant Kane explaining that her father had been killed instantly; he would have known no pain. Witnesses said he seemed to be very unsteady on his feet as the truck approached.

'What kind of truck was it?' she asked, only mildly curious.

The sergeant tried his best to remain composed, professional, but he'd known this misfortunate family a long time. Though he normally hated bringing news of this nature, in this case, it was a blessing. Fighting a smile, he said, 'A Guinness truck.'

Scarlett's abiding memory of her father's untimely death was of her mother and Sergeant Kane weeping with uncontrolled gales of laughter.

Life got much easier after that, in lots of ways. Lorena, who became even more zealous about her Catholic faith as the years progressed, gave the teenaged Scarlett enough freedom to do as she wished. Lorena had been raised Baptist, but Catholicism appealed to her dramatic nature, so she had converted when she married Dan. She loved all the pomp and ceremony, and every spare wall of the apartment was adorned with icons and statues and holy pictures. Prints of sad looking nuns with brown habits and angelic faced men gazing longingly to the heavens occupied every spare space. The apartment was a source of cringing embarrassment, but since she wasn't that close to anyone anyway, she didn't have to endure kids from school seeing the bizarre décor of her home.

School was fine. She loved English, and had a great teacher who inspired her to think for herself. He often lent her books, or printed out articles about world events for her to read. She wished she had blond hair and tanned skin. Failing that, she would have really liked to look like Gloria Estefan, but her Irish heritage gave her flame-red hair, alabaster skin and emerald-green eyes. Boys tended to steer clear – their parents warning them off because of Dan – so she kept herself to herself. One guy asked her to the prom, but she declined. He was good looking and seemed nice, but there was no way she was having him come to the house. Scarlett remembered her mother's disappointment when she said she wouldn't be attending. Lorena had bought her a dress, but Scarlett couldn't face going, nor could she explain to her mother why, so she sat in her room and read instead.

She loved travel books, especially those by the *BBC World News* editor John Simpson. He wrote with empathy and intelligence about places Scarlett could only dream of: Afghanistan, Iraq, Russia. She devoured his books and fantasised of one day visiting those places.

In her final year at school, she signed up for a trip with her political science class to hear a Bostonian congressman who was touring high schools in the tougher areas of New York. A noted self-serving public servant, it looked good for the electorate that he cared about those less well off. He was part of a national education taskforce that was allegedly asking students what they thought should be done to improve educational standards in disadvantaged school districts. He was a pompous ass, as she recalled, and patronised and flirted with the girls in her class. He tried to flatter her during the coffee break, asking her questions – while all the time ogling her breasts. He repulsed her.

At the end, the girls were given an opportunity to ask him any questions. The teacher, Miss Fletcher, was obviously a fan of the congressman, and giggled and fawned whenever he addressed her. She'd prepared a long list of sycophantic questions and distributed them among the students, giving him ample opportunity to explain just how wonderful he was and how marvellous it was that he would ask their lowly opinions.

For no reason other than to knock him off his stupid perch, Scarlett raised her hand to ask a question – not one on the card distributed by Miss Fletcher.

'Where do you stand on the subject of gay rights?'

It was 2007, and the St Patrick's Day parade in the city was drawing the usual controversy by continuing to ban gay, lesbian, bisexual and transgender groups from marching. Scarlett had read about it in the paper that morning over breakfast.

Miss Fletcher went pink and stammered, 'I-I'm sorry, Congressman Bailey. That was not an authorised question...' She glared with unconcealed horror at Scarlett.

The congressman gave a slimy grin and said, 'That's quite all right, Deanna... I mean Miss

Fletcher.' The teacher had blushed and giggled again. 'I'm sure this little lady didn't mean any offence.'

He turned towards Scarlett. 'Now then, my dear, a nicely brought up girl like yourself need not concern herself with such things. I'm sure that nobody at St. Peter and Paul's wants its young ladies discussing a matter that is, after all, a mortal sin. The Church is very clear on its position on that subject, and as a devout Catholic, I would vote with my conscience.' His smug, self-satisfied smile made Scarlett want to punch him in his stupid fat face.

That was the day Scarlett decided she would be a journalist.

# CHAPTER 3

She walked into her beautifully decorated bedroom. The king-size bed dominated the sunny space, and dust mites danced in the shaft of sunlight that streamed through the glass doors leading to a small balcony. She caught a glimpse of her reflection in the full-length mirrors that formed the doors to her walk-in closet. She looked awful – pale and dishevelled eyes red from crying. Though the room overlooked the little communal garden at the back, she quickly closed the blinds in case one of the photographers managed to get in and perch themselves in a tree, waiting for the perfect shot with their long-range lens.

She sat on her bed and held a pillow up to her

face. It smelled of him, of his faintly spicy cologne. How often had she gone to sleep in his arms, only to wake alone? Always the same story. She was transported back to the early days of their relationship, before she became used to his early morning disappearances…

Scarlett recalled vividly how the alarm of his cell phone cut through the darkness. She stirred, wrapping her legs around him, willing the piercing ringtone to stop with her face buried in the back of his neck, her arm around his chest.

Charlie groaned and gently removed her arm. 'I have to go.' He kissed her palm as he tucked her arm under the sheet.

'But it's only –' Scarlett picked up her phone '– 2 a.m., for God's sake.'

Charlie ran his hand through his tousled brown curls. 'I know, but I said I'd take C.J. to school. First day, and all that. I can't just rock up at 7 a.m. You know that.'

'What will you say?' Her voice was steady, betraying none of what she felt.

'Oh, a meeting ran on – something like that. Don't worry about it. I'll try to call later.'

He padded into the shower, washing all traces of her and her house from his skin. He had asked her not to wear perfume in case Julia smelled it on his clothes, so even the shower gel she bought was fragrance free.

Feigning sleep, she heard him slip out. He'd walk the two blocks to the subway and take a cab from there. Despite his passionate nature, Charlie Morgan was very careful. She tortured herself by imagining him slipping into bed with Julia, she all concerned that he worked so hard. Then she'd wake in the morning, looking fresh as a daisy, and prepare their two adorable children for school.

Julia was beautiful in a really natural way – no Botox or plastic surgery. Her hair was naturally blond, and her skin tanned to a golden brown since she played often on the beach with the kids. She was on several worthy committees and was always in the papers. The perfect politician's wife.

Scarlett lay down on the bed and pulled the covers over herself, glad of the warmth. Though filled with self-loathing, she tried think. It wasn't all her fault – she had never intended for things to turn out like this. She had been doing a profile piece on him in the run-up to the election and met him and Julia at home. Carol was amazed and delighted that she had managed to secure a feature interview. He was notoriously private about his family, and Scarlett knew it was a really good mark for her, especially since she had only been with the *Globe Messenger* a few short months. He repeatedly explained to the media that his children and his wife did not run for election, and so he wanted them to have as normal a life as possible. This 'family comes first' attitude had won him lots of votes in a world, where most politicians used their kids to further their own campaigns.

During the interview, the Morgan children, then aged five and seven, had played angelically with educational and sustainable wooden toys while munching happily on carrot sticks and hummus. Julia sat on their large comfortable sofa beside her husband. If you had to draw the perfect American family, the Morgans were as close as you could get. The perception was that Charlie Morgan was a powerful man, unafraid to do what was right, but despite that, an all-round good guy.

Scarlett was terrified at the time, but managed to hide her nerves as she asked intelligent and pertinent questions. Artie had set the interview up for her, but made her promise to take the credit. Her old editor was more like a father figure to her, and though he made out like he was insulted that she had left him and got the job at the *Globe Messenger*, she knew that really, he was proud of her. He was acquainted with Charlie Morgan's father from years ago, so he pulled in a favour.

The interview was wide-ranging, sounding Charlie Morgan out on issues from abortion to gun control, and he presented a compassionate yet realistic case for everything. Broadminded and liberal, he appeared to have his feet very firmly planted in the realpolitik of twenty-first century America.

So impressed was she with him that she wrote an uncharacteristically flattering piece, admitting that she had been looking for flaws, but there just didn't seem to be any cracks in the image he presented to the world. All really was as it seemed. Of solid New England stock, he had graduated from Harvard and chose to leave the family business to his brothers and entered politics. Julia was his childhood sweetheart and they seemed happy. As he sat in the sunny living room of his Montauk, New York, home, he looked handsome and relaxed – not slimy or aggressive or sexist, or any of the other traits she associated with politicians. His brown, slightly curly hair was well cut to look casual, and the light-blue linen shirt and Levi 501s fitted him perfectly. His skin was tanned dark-brown from a summer of sailboarding with his children.

It was at moments like that, as she mixed with the powerful and successful of the city that it struck her how far she'd come from the cowering kid of a crazy alcoholic Irishman and poor old Lorena. She had kept her promise to herself and studied hard for her last year at school and graduated, then went to the local community college to study journalism. There was no way Lorena could have afforded to send her to one of the big colleges.

She did well and managed to get a job on a local Yonkers newspaper, writing about local charities and reporting on town council meetings. Artie Schwitz, the editor, was a small old Jew who liked the spark he saw in Scarlett. He remembered Dan from his days of drinking and roaring around the streets, and decided to give his daughter a chance. She was tenacious and dogged in her pursuit of stories, often scooping the bigger publications, and it was through her persistence she managed to increase the circulation of the *Yonkers Express* to record numbers. The interview she did with the mullah from a radical Islamist mosque on the Lower East Side, who had refused all interviews before, plucked her from obscurity. In a letter that she was sure was correct, written in his native tongue, she'd told the old man from Iraq how she had gone to night school to learn Arabic. He agreed to talk to her and explained the despair and fear in Moslems in New York in the wake of 9/11. It was an unimaginable scoop for their small paper, and led to a huge surge in circulation.

Her coverage of 9/11 continued to be very well received, and when she wrote a feature on the reaction of the Islamic community of the city to the terrorist attacks one year on – with the blessing of the mullah – she won the prestigious Carter Award for Journalism, the youngest ever recipient. She knew she was on the rise, and when she saw Carol Steinberg at a press event, she approached her and asked her for a job. Carol had smiled politely and suggested that she email her resume to the *Globe Messenger* office. Two weeks later, she had an interview. Life since then had been a whirlwind. She bought a small house, a car and a whole contemporary wardrobe on the strength of her new salary and the money she had saved over the years working for Artie. She was on top of the world.

Charlie made no reference to the fact that his father had asked him to do the interview as a favour to Artie, and she was grateful to him for that. In the months that followed, they would meet at events, and they were always friendly. Then one night in Atlantic City, after a Democrat campaign meeting, they found themselves staying at the same hotel. He invited her for a nightcap in his suite which had an office attached. She'd been there earlier to collect some briefing documents and it was a hive of activity, and not realising his staff had gone for the night, she agreed.

They talked and laughed until the early hours, and she found herself telling him about her father. Not used to drinking, she poured her heart out about the violence and fear that overshadowed her childhood. Her anger at her mother for not leaving, for not keeping them safe from him, and her anger at Lorena for giving her such a stupid name – it all came out. Charlie said he loved that she was called Scarlett O'Hara and that she was every bit as hot as Vivien Leigh.

He listened without judging and congratulated her sincerely on how far she'd come. Undoubtedly the whiskey played a part, for she had never told anyone about her past, but Charlie was easy to talk to. She felt she could trust him. They met a few more times after that night, both knowing an affair was inevitable. And so it began, she was his mistress – the other woman. She looked at herself in the mirror some mornings and said that to herself, but those sordid, dirty little words just couldn't be applied to what she and Charlie had. With him, it was honest. It was love.

She had tried to block out Julia and his children, the eldest now about to start middle school. If the relationship was good, he wouldn't be seeing Scarlett. That's what she told herself. He never gave her any of the standard lines – that his wife didn't understand him, that he was only staying for the sake of the kids, that they'd be together properly when the kids left school. He simply never discussed it. His life with Julia was one thing, his life with Scarlett something else completely, and never the twain shall meet.

She pretended that it suited her, that she was so taken up with her career that a full-time relationship would be just too restrictive. But as the months went on, she knew she was lying – to him and to herself. She never raised the subject with him… Probably, she told herself, because she wasn't at all sure of what his reaction would be. He told her all the time that he loved her, that she was not like anyone he'd ever met, that she was gorgeous, but still she was not convinced. If he had to choose, would she be the one? He used to joke that she was his Vivien Leigh and always signed his texts 'Rhett', or just 'R'. She thought it was cute, though she wished he could have chosen something other than her ridiculous name to make jokes about. In the cold reality of what had happened, she realised that he wrote 'R' in case anyone found the texts. Charlie was protecting himself.

And now, the worst possible thing had happened. She'd destroyed everything she'd worked so hard to build.

# CHAPTER 4

The phone rang again – for the hundredth time since she got home. She looked at the screen: Lorena. She would just keep calling, Scarlett knew that, but she couldn't face it. She let it ring out. Journalists and lots of unrecognised numbers were calling all day, trying to get the scoop.

Moments later it buzzed again, with a text from Lorena. Scarlett sighed. Her mother couldn't text properly despite Scarlett showing her about a hundred times, so reading her messages took a lot of guesswork.

*Scar let. I wil come over to your hoof rite no if you do not an sser me.*

Scarlett groaned. A visit was the very last

thing she needed right now. Reluctantly, she called her.

'At last!' Lorena never lost her southern drawl, and she spoke with the breathy hesitancy she considered attractive.

'Hi, Mom.'

'"Hi, Mom!" Is that all you have to say? Scarlett! I have been calling and calling. What on earth is going on? They are saying the most terrible things on the TV! Tell me none of this is true.'

Long seconds ticked by, the silence between them deafeningly oppressive in the shadowy kitchen. She knew what Lorena would think. That she was an adulterer, a homewrecker, that she'd committed a moral sin and had destroyed everything she had worked so hard to build. She had no credibility now – political or personal – and she would never have it again. Her readers and followers really had believed she was a decent, honest analyst of the political landscape. They had trusted her to tell them the truth, often even when the truth was something they would rather not hear.

The thought of them reading about her in the daily tabloids made her feel nauseous. The hacks would no doubt fill whole articles with salacious titbits about her and Charlie's affair. She sighed. 'I wish I could, Mom.'

'So, my daughter is a fornicator, an adulterer? Is that what you're telling me?'

'Yeah. All of that.' Scarlett was exhausted. She didn't have it in her to defend herself, even if there was something she could say.

'Scarlett, apart from the fact that you have destroyed your career, did your eternal soul not enter into your head? You have committed a most grievous and mortal sin! When I think of his poor wife and the little children… So now what? Does he want to leave his wife and marry you? Is that it?'

She stared into space, barely hearing her mother's diatribe. She had no plan. She and Charlie had never discussed what would happen if they were found out, never considering it as a possibility. She really had been that stupid, believing they could continue indefinitely in their own little cocoon, untouched by reality.

'No,' was all she could manage, and the word sounded like someone else's.

'So, that's it, is it?' Lorena's voice was rising in frustration and disappointment. 'You had an affair with a married man. You have destroyed everything you've achieved. You do know that, don't you? People trusted you. They believed you when you told them what was really going on behind the closed doors of power, and it turns out you are just as bad as those you helped to expose over the years. To add to that, as if that wasn't enough, tonight there are two children whose lives have been devastated by these revelations of their father's sordid sex life. You of all people know what it means to have a father you can't trust, and yet you could do this...'

Scarlett knew everything Lorena was saying was true. She had nothing – no way to try to justify what she'd done.

She walked to the living room and flicked on the TV while Lorena went on and on. The news anchor was discussing, with a child psychologist, the impact that revelations of infidelity have on children. The ticker tape along the bottom of the screen burned into her brain: *Senator Charlie Morgan admits to an extramarital affair with political correspondent for the New York* Globe Messenger *Scarlett O'Hara.*

She changed channels, only to be confronted with the face of Sam Winters, Charlie's publicist. He would have convinced Charlie by now that the only way to salvage anything at this stage was to come out contrite and honest. The whole 'I am an ordinary man, flawed and sorry' kind of line. Sam wasn't the best campaign strategist in the business for nothing. He knew the electorate, and was aware of what they would take and not take. After the Clinton debacle, Charlie had explained to Scarlett over beers one night that the American public can forgive most things, especially if the person needing forgiveness was once loved, but a direct lie to their faces when asked a straight question was the tipping point.

'Do that,' he explained, 'and you are dead in the water.'

Charlie had carefully built an 'ordinary Joe' image. Now he was an ordinary Joe who made a mistake. In time, they would take him back – perhaps even Julia would. He could go on *Oprah*, explain he was a sex addict or some other such crap, shed a few tears and the nation would melt once again to the charms of Charlie Morgan.

The other woman, on the other hand, is damned forever. And if that woman made her living out of being an honest journalist, well... She was under no illusions. She was finished.

'What do you want me to do?' Lorena's voice was quiet now, and Scarlett tried to focus on it. She muted the TV but left it running. She deserved it. The footage of her fumbling for her keys half an hour before was now emblazoned on the screen. She could just imagine the anchor's voice as he explained with velvety tones who she was. The puns on her name would abound, and his glee at her demise would be very thinly concealed.

'Nothing. There's nothing you can do. I'll call you in a few days.'

Scarlett summoned her remaining strength to talk Lorena out of coming over to the house. 'Honestly, Mom, there's nothing anyone can do at this stage.' Her voice was monotone. 'I'll get away, I think. Go somewhere for a few months…'

The idea was forming in her head as she said it. She had to keep Lorena away for now. She was barely keeping it together as it was. Adding a hysterical Lorena – invoking saints, and asking her over and over how she could have committed such a grievous and mortal sin – would be just enough to push her over the edge.

'Ok, Scarlett. I'm so worried about you. I'm going to ask Fr Ennio to say a Mass for you, right this minute. I need to get off the phone now so I can call him.'

'Fine, that would be great. Thanks.' Scarlett hung up before her mother could start on another rant.

She leaned back on her comfortable lounger and stared at the ceiling. The bespoke chandelier that she had spent ages planning for? Invisible to her now. The TV, silent, flashed images of Charlie's house in Montauk, his children's school, his wife, like an endless roll of torture. She knew she should turn it off, but she couldn't.

Suddenly, she saw him driving his car out the driveway of his home, unshaven and crumpled looking – an appearance no doubt carefully designed by Sam. She was sure he was going to drive away, and then realised he was slowing down. As he lowered the window to speak to reporters, she scrambled for the remote to raise the volume.

'…understand it's a story, and you have a job to do, but my wife and children are innocent in all of this. Go after me if you want, but please, keep them out of it. I'm truly ashamed of myself and my actions, and I will answer for them, unreservedly. But I'm asking you to spare my wife and children…' Tears glistened in his eyes – the eyes that had so often twinkled at her across a crowded room, or bored into her soul as they made love.

He made to put up the car window when one of the reporters asked, 'What about your girlfriend, Scarlett O'Hara? Is she just an innocent in all of this as well? Is that where you are going now?' He stuck a microphone in the car window.

Charlie ran his fingers through his hair – a learnt gesture, surely, since she'd never seen him do that before – and he rubbed his face. The performance had Sam written all over it.

'Look, I'm not denying the indiscretion; it was wrong and stupid of me to risk my beautiful family. I'm truly, truly sorry –' His eyes shifted to the camera. 'Ms O'Hara is very familiar with the world of politics. She understands how it works, but not my wife and family. No, I'm not going to Ms O'Hara. She and I have had no contact, and I won't be seeing her again.'

He put the car window up and drove away as the cameras flashed and whirred. Scarlett just made the sink in time as she vomited the entire contents of her stomach. Tears and mucus covered her face as waves of nausea gripped her, and she could do nothing to stop the retching.

After what seemed like hours, the heaving in her stomach subsided, and she slid down the kitchen cabinets and sat on the tiled floor. Sitting there for what might have been minutes or an hour, she was interrupted by yet another message on her phone.

*I'm so, so sorry. You know I had to do it. I had no choice. Talk soon. R xx*

She crawled to the couch and covered herself with a woollen throw she'd been given as a gift by a woman and her sister on whom she'd done a story. They ran a shelter for battered wives in Brooklyn. What must they think of her now? She drifted off into a dreamless sleep.

# CHAPTER 5

Scarlett's phone buzzed on the coffee table: Charlie again. Outpourings of sorrow at what he had done. Texts telling her how much he loved her, and how she must understand that it was the only option. Waters was going to break the story anyway. He had got distracted during the meeting and started sending her messages and inadvertently pressed Send to the Republican instead of Scarlett. He begged her not to speak to anyone.

She longed to see him. He would never deliberately hurt her, and she believed him when he said he wished it were different. She knew they were both being watched like hawks, so trying to meet up would be just impossible. She hadn't replied to any of his texts. Lorena called constantly. Scarlett answered one in ten of her calls to keep her from coming over. Apparently one Mass wasn't enough to exonerate her terrible sin, so Fr Ennio was saying a novena as well in Lorena's living room every night. Lorena was begging to visit.

She'd had other emails and text messages of support from a few colleagues and acquaintances, but mostly they were reporters wanting to 'give her a chance to tell her side of the story,' or strangers venting abuse. This morning a text message, from a number she had never seen before, went on for ages about how she was clearly possessed by the devil, but if she paid just $5,000 dollars, she could be exorcised. It had made her smile for the first time since the whole thing happened.

The doorbell rang constantly. She never opened the door and refused to open the blinds. Lorena had tried to get in a few days ago, but was intimidated by the army of reporters outside the front door. At least they were good for something she supposed.

Scarlett picked up her phone and opened the text message. Perhaps her evangelist 'friend' was offering further de-devilling.

*Answer your goddamn phone you stupid broad!*
*X A*

She closed the text and the home screen of her phone flashed: 156 missed calls.

She knew Artie had tried calling her a few times, but she'd ignored him. Unlike all the other calls she ignored, though, she felt guilty about his. He was her first editor. He gave her a job on the *Yonkers Express* when she was just a cub reporter, and when the time came for her to move up in the world, he let her go, albeit grudgingly…

'O Miss High and Mighty, so we're not good enough for you any more, that it?' he had rasped, the ever-present cigarette dangling from the corner of his mouth.

'C'mon, Artie, don't give me a hard time about this. You know what a job on the *Globe Messenger* can do for me,' she had pleaded guiltily. She knew there was nobody of her calibre on the staff of the little paper, and that her work had been making the *Express* profitable for the first time in years.

'Yeah, yeah, kid. Whatever,' he growled, sucking furiously on a cigarette. If Kathy, his wife, caught him smoking, she'd kill him, so he smoked incessantly at work to make up for not being allowed to at home. A heart attack earlier in the year made his wife of thirty-five years put her foot down. 'It's time you moved on, I guess. Just don't screw it up, ok? You're a good-looking woman – use it, but don't let it be all about that, you hear me?'

So she had moved to the *Globe Messenger* as a senior political analyst, ahead of several older men, and loved her job. Her salary package was quadruple that of the *Express,* and she was enjoying life, covering New York politics in the run-up to the primaries. She even got to meet John Simpson, whose books she'd read voraciously as a teenager. They talked about the conflict zones of the Middle East, and she really felt like she had arrived.

Artie had trained her well. She had an uncanny knack of finding the right people to talk to, giving a human dimension to the issues. She never flirted or was coquettish, like so many of her female colleagues, and she was riding high in the polls for a journalism award later in the year. She kept in touch with Artie and met him for a few beers in the bar at the end of his street most weeks, where he told her how her latest piece was too soft, or that she could have done better with a story, but she knew that deep down, he was proud of her. In lots of ways, Artie Schwitz was the father figure she never had.

She should call him. Artie was abrasive at the best of times, and she knew she was in for some earbashing. The phone rang once and he answered, 'Yeah. Now she calls me!'

'Sorry, Artie, I just couldn't –'

'Whatever. You screw who you like. It was dumb, though. Even for you,' he growled.

'Agreed. Did you just want to tell me that?' Scarlett sighed.

A wheezy chuckle sounded in her ear. 'No, not just that, though I never trusted him, that Morgan jerk. Too squeaky clean – you shoulda known that. You don't get to the top by playing nice all the time. Women. You're all the same, letting your heart rule your head…'

Scarlett fought the urge to pick him up on his sexist remarks, but knew she just had to take it. She deserved it, anyway.

'So what was the other thing?' She was barely controlling her frustration. He was her friend, she knew that, and he'd been good to her over the years, but…

'I gotta job for ya.'

What was he talking about, a job? She couldn't take a job now with everything going on. Maybe he was losing it. He wasn't getting any younger.

'Thanks, Artie, I appreciate it, but I'm not really –' She was determined to stop him before he said another word.

'So what you gonna do, eh? Sit in your house all day, scared to come out? You turnin' chicken after all these years?' The wheezy chuckle sounded again.

'No. It's not that. It's just that I'm going away. So I can't –'

'Where?'

Silence ticked as she tried to think of somewhere. 'Fiji,' she blurted out in desperation as her eye caught the spine of the DVD *The Truman Show*.

'Why?' His voice cut through the silence like a knife.

'Erm… To recover, to relax and let all this die down…' she mumbled.

'To hide. That's what you're doing – hiding. So you must be chicken after all. Don't be a schmuck, O'Hara. So you slept with the wrong guy, and now his wife and kids are all over the front pages and you look like a bitch. So the hell what? You're a regular Mata Hari, but you locking yourself up like this is becoming a story in itself. You've done too much to have this be the end, to have this be what they remember about you.' His voice was softer now.

'I can't, Artie. I just can't face it.' She tried to hold back the tears.

Artie's voice lost some more of its gruffness. 'C'mon, Scarlett. You're Dan O'Hara's kid. You shouldn't have amounted to anything, but here you are. If you let them win, then you might as well have never pulled yourself out of that crappy childhood. Look, I know you're scared, but suck it up, ok? Meet me at the office. I'll tell you my plan then.'

Scarlett held the phone to her ear. Artie had finished the call without any goodbye, but then that was standard practice for him.

She couldn't stay cooped up in the house forever, but the thought of going out, facing them all baying for blood, was terrifying. She stood up and examined her face in the oval mirror over the fireplace. She looked pale, but ok, her wavy red hair curling softly down her back and her green eyes shining. Artie was right. This was no way to live. It was time.

# CHAPTER 6

'A burglary.' Her voice was flat. She knew she should be more grateful, but it was such a comedown.

'A series of burglaries, actually, in Queens. Look, I know it's not what you've been used to, kid, but it will put bread on the table. You were staff, but only freelance on the *Globe Messenger,* so they ain't gonna give you a red cent. You're lucky they ain't suing your skinny ass for dragging their name through the mud.'

Artie was still smoking, and the air between Scarlett and him was tinged blue. Old editions of the paper were piled on every available surface, and used coffee cups were all over the tiny office.

'It's not that I'm not grateful, Artie, but

coming back here, after everything… Also, this place is filthy, and a health hazard. You should clean it.'

'I like it like this. Stop!' he yelled as she tried to gather up the cups with the dregs of coffee in them. 'Stop touching things. Just leave it!'

'It's not like you're going to get any better offers.' Artie smiled, locating an ashtray under a heap of yellowing newspapers.

'Thanks for pointing that out,' she said sarcastically. 'I don't know. I don't really do human interest stuff any more…'

'You don't "*do*" human interest, huh? Well, from where I'm standin', sweetheart, you don't "*do*" politics any more either. Maybe you shoulda thought about what you should and shouldn't "*do*" before you hooked up with a married politician.'

Scarlett was miserable. She'd battled her way out of her house amid cameras and reporters shouting and laughing at her. She realised how stupid she had been, to think that two high-profile people could conduct an affair and that it would never come out. 'The truth will out.' It seemed the old adage was right. She deserved no sympathy, she knew that, but she just wanted to yell at the gathered reporters, 'It wasn't all me, you know! He pursued me! He's the one who made a promise to someone else, not me!' Thankfully, she never did, knowing how much they would love it. The endless hours spent on the pavement outside her house would be worth it for just one crazy emotional outburst. She battled her way through them and made sure her car key was in her hand this time.

She managed to lose the tail they put on her by zigzagging around the back streets, and she endured all that to listen to Artie making her feel worse than she did already. She knew her career was over. She didn't need him to drive it home so forcefully.

'Look, it's all the same to me who does it. I got plenty of young cubs out there, writing classifieds for lost dogs, who'd bite my hand off for this. I just thought you got bills to pay, you need a job, maybe somewhere to lay low for a while… My mistake. Forget it!'

Scarlett got up to leave and looked out into the newspaper offices beyond. The floor space was bright and modern, with computer screens everywhere. So much had changed since she started out here. Though he knew he had to move with the times, the dramatic overhaul of the main offices was resisted fiercely by Artie, so his office was the only thing that hadn't changed in the ten years since she walked in the door, looking for a bit of experience.

Could she do anything else? She knew the answer: Journalism was in her blood. She couldn't imagine another career. Artie was giving her a lifeline when there were no other offers on the table. She would be foolish to turn it down.

'Ok. Gimmie the address.'

Artie handed her the piece of paper and put his arm around her shoulders. Scarlett was used to gruff, cranky Artie, so she hoped he wasn't going to be nice to her. It would only set off the tears again.

'Look, kid, I know this ain't easy, with hacks outside your house and everything, but they'll get bored. And this Morgan guy, he ain't worth your tears. You deserve better.'

# CHAPTER 7

She tried to avoid putting on the TV or radio once she got home, but she had inadvertently seen the headlines when she stopped for gas and a few groceries. They were really going to town on Charlie, and her name was journalistic manna from heaven. Every pun and alliteration possible was being trotted out.

Though she had sworn to herself that she wouldn't, she had given in and texted Charlie back a few times since it all happened, but still there was no way to see each other without the press getting hold of it. He said he missed her and longed to see her, but he couldn't. The stabbing pain of betrayal was dulling to a gnawing ache, and she was at least able to breathe. She convinced herself that he didn't betray her – not really. She tried not to think of him at home with Julia and the kids. He hadn't moved out of the family home, according to the reports, and she wondered what was going on in there. She imagined him sleeping in the spare room, thinking about her and wishing he was in her house, in bed with her, instead of living with the cold disdain of perfect Julia. Both Charlie and Julia came from powerful political families, and they were experts at manipulating the press. They'd pose a united front, but surely she must have asked him if he loved Scarlett, and he would have had to tell her the truth. He couldn't lie about that to his wife's face. She knew he couldn't.

Standing at her kitchen window after the meeting with Artie, she admired the scene outside. One of the reasons she loved this house was because it backed onto a communal yard, with lovely mature trees. She watched a woman – a neighbour, presumably – playing with her children in the newly fallen leaves. She didn't know anyone in the area. She had so rarely been home since she bought the house six months before, and when she was there, she was working. Socialising with her neighbours wasn't something that appealed to her. Though, in fairness, she thought, she should contact the owners association to apologise for the intrusion of the reporters. They were always shoving leaflets under her door about meetings to improve amenities and stuff like that. She would drop them an email later.

Charlie would have been all for that kind of thing: being involved, knowing your neighbours. 'All politics is local' was one of his mantras. Charlie. There he was again. If he were here, he would have asked her for the name of the chairman of the owners' association so he could send them a Christmas card. Another of his theories – that people vote for personalities, not policies – seemed to be depressingly accurate. They would forgive him, eventually, but she would be the 'Scarlett Woman' forever. Somehow, she was sure, Sam would manage to turn this into a PR exercise.

*Charlie will be truly sorry, probably find God, and be forgiven. He and Julia will appear on some chat show, where he will look contrite and grateful, and she'll be stoic and kind – 'love the sinner but hate the sin' garbage.*

*How often we laughed about such turnarounds in others who fell from grace. The nation will love Julia even more for standing by her man. The word 'vows' will be mentioned more than once in the interview, and God will, of course, be invoked, and everything will be fine. They will be stronger as a couple because of it.* She could almost write the script.

She, on the other hand, would be left to burn in the fires of hell for all eternity, to use her mother's language. Julia wasn't who he wanted – she knew that in her heart. Charlie loved her. She knew he did and she loved him. His last text had said he had to do this for America. It was a bit corny, but she knew what he meant.

Lorena had, mercifully, stayed away after that first failed attempt to get in the door. The daily prayer, seeking forgiveness from God, as a text message, was quite enough. Lorena in real life would be more than she could bear. It was bad enough to be facing humiliation and unemployment without adding her hysterically Catholic mother into the deal.

Scarlett only had one option now, and that was to do something with this burglary story.

The name she had been given for one of the victims was a Mrs Eileen Chiarello, and she lived on a side street in the Richmond Hill area of Queens. The cops had told Artie that the burglars were targeting older people, so the piece was to serve as a public service announcement to the elderly to be more conscious of security. They were approaching local newspapers in all five boroughs to try to promote safety in the home for older people.

Scarlett smiled. She had forgot just how much public service was a part of local newspapers. It was a long way from the cut and thrust of political analysis.

She called and spoke to a woman, who sounded old and a little distracted, and arranged an appointment for the next day. She urged her to call the newspaper office to verify she was who she said she was, and when she gave the woman her name, she waited for the inevitable comment about it. Mrs Chiarello made no remark. Was it possible that someone in the world had not seen that stupid movie?

She had considered changing her name a while ago, but as she climbed the ladder, she realised her name had become a brand, much as she loathed it. She'd heard all the jokes a hundred times, and if she had a buck for every smartass man who said, 'Frankly, my dear, I don't give a damn', to her, she'd be a very wealthy woman. How people reacted to her name often told Scarlett a lot about them.

# CHAPTER 8

*S*he dressed in jeans and a shirt, her power wardrobe of no use to her now. Over the years, she'd grown to accept her distinctly Irish colouring and stopped trying to change it. Her hair was the first thing Charlie said he noticed about her. He used to say she reminded him of a Celtic goddess. She remembered one time he bought her a beautiful miniature painting of an Irish queen, called Gráinne Uaile. He said she was a sailor or a patroness of the sea or something from Ireland.

As she drove to the address Artie had given her, she spotted a guy drunk and shouting on the sidewalk. A kid stood at one side of him, and she was instantly transported back to her childhood.

Her heart went out to the little boy. She knew exactly how he felt: embarrassed, frightened and worried.

She remembered what it was like when she was young… Usually running – to avoid Dan in one of his rages – to Andrus Park, where she would sit on the swing until it got dark. Lorena always knew where to find her, and had taught her to run from her father as soon as she was old enough. She would swing, singing hymns to herself to block out the thought that maybe this time her mother wouldn't come. That Dan would kill her.

She wondered what would have happened if he had killed her mother. She was seriously injured so many times that it seemed unlikely that she would survive. He didn't often hurt Scarlett, but watching him batter Lorena was enough. When she was very small, too young to run to the park, she would hide under the table and close her eyes tightly and put her hands over her ears. From her hiding place, she would see what was left of their crockery smashed, movie pictures torn from the walls. One time he tore the leg off a kitchen chair and laid into Lorena with that. She was in hospital for about three weeks that time, and Scarlett went to a children's home in Queens.

She remembered that home as really lovely, with kind people working there. The food was delicious and the other kids were fun. One day, they were even taken to Coney Island. It was the best day of her life. The day Lorena came to get her, a few weeks later, with the bruises on her face a horrible purpley-yellow and limping badly, Scarlett wished she would just go away. She wanted to stay in that home forever. That day she swore that when she grew up, she'd buy a lovely house in Queens.

The place always meant something to her, so when she was at last in a position to buy a house, she chose that borough without hesitation. Charlie laughed at her selection, claiming she was more of a Manhattan chick than someone who belonged in a solid blue-collar, hardworking-but-not-particularly-glamorous community. But Charlie never understood: Queens, to her, meant safety. She was surprised to realise that Mrs Chiarello lived very near that children's home.

Scarlett pulled up outside the small neat bungalow. Richmond Hill bordered the affluent Forest Hills area of Queens, and while it was not as upmarket an area as its neighbour, it certainly wasn't the projects. This bright, well-maintained little suburb looked like it was home to lots of older people, and couples with small kids who were no doubt out at work all day. A perfect target for burglars.

Richmond Hill was also firmly in the commuter belt, so Scarlett surmised that people parked their cars here and caught the subway downtown to avoid the extortionate parking rates in the city. Vehicles coming and going wouldn't be noticed. Old men and women shuffled along the sidewalk with their newspapers and little dogs, it being a Saturday, and kids rode their bikes and hung out on street corners. All around Scarlett, people walked, jogged, rollerbladed by, music pumping from their iPhones through expensive headphones.

She was surprised at the sudden rush of affection she felt for her city. Queens was like a little snapshot of life in this big, noisy, rude-but-exhilarating metropolis. You had everything in New York: The best and the worst of existence all pushing forward together. You could be forgiven for thinking no one cared about anyone else if you were to shove your way onto the subway during rush hour, or try to get served at a lunchtime deli without elbowing and jumping ahead. But then 9/11 changed all that.

The horror of the attack touched every one of

the 8.3 million New Yorkers. No matter what age, ethnicity or social class, the people of this iconic, world-famous city were shaken to the core by the terrorist attacks. Ironically, the strikes had the effect of making New Yorkers feel closer to each other. Artie always used to say, 'Nothing unites like common adversity,' and he was right.

Mrs Chiarello's house was quiet, with no sign of life. The drapes were pulled closed and there was no car in the small driveway. She fought feelings of despair at being reduced to this kind of story again as she approached the small neat house. The doorbell was a ceramic one, with a floral pattern on it, the porch filled with pots of brightly coloured flowers. Hanging baskets and window boxes offered a profusion of colour as she waited. Through the frosted glass, she could make out a small figure approaching the door.

As the door opened, Scarlett tried to sound unthreatening. 'Good morning. Mrs Chiarello?'

The old lady shook her silver head. She seemed frail and furtive. 'I don't need anything, dear.'

As she started to close the door, Scarlett realised the woman was even older than she imagined. 'No, ma'am, I'm not selling anything. I just –'

'I'm a Catholic all my life,' the woman went on, 'so I see no reason to change now. If you'll excuse me –'

'I'm Scarlett O'Hara. We spoke on the phone? I'm from the *Yonkers Express*.'

The woman seemed to relax and opened the door a bit wider. 'Oh, yes, of course. I'm sorry. It's just that I've been burglarised and I...' The old lady was visibly upset and Scarlett felt sorry for her.

'I would ask you in, but the place is really in a state. I need to tidy up and see what's been taken. Perhaps you could come back? I've been in the hospital, you see...'

Scarlett thought quickly. She had to bring this story back to Artie today. He considered her pathetic enough already without her showing up without the copy. 'How about you let me in and we can take a look together?'

'Well, perhaps... I don't know. You see, the police called my doctor, who insisted I go to the hospital. The person who robbed me knocked me over as he left. I banged my head and I hurt my wrist when I fell, but I'm fine. I was coming in from doing a little shopping when I disturbed him, obviously. I was very shaken, as you can imagine, so I've only just got home...and I don't even know where to start, to be honest.' Tears were forming in her eyes.

Scarlett felt such an urge to strangle the scumbag who had done this. How could people like that look at themselves in the mirror after doing such a cowardly thing?

'You could call the paper and check I am who I say I am, if you like. I'm happy to help you out. I don't have anything else to do today.' Scarlett realised she sounded a little desperate, but she really did want to help this lady. The woman eyed her keenly, weighing up whether or not to trust her. Seconds passed, and eventually the woman moved aside and ushered Scarlett into the house.

She was shown to a sunny kitchen at the back of the house, and immediately, Scarlett was struck by the mess. The house had been turned upside down. Crockery and foodstuffs were strewn all over the floor. The stand where a TV had obviously once stood was now bare, the electrical cables wrenched from the wall. The small appliances had been robbed. The burglars had emptied food and liquids everywhere, and sticky syrup was dripping from the countertop.

'They got my jewellery from my bedroom. It wasn't much, but it meant a lot to me, and my TV and... Oh, I don't know. Everything...and something else. Something I think they took that…' The old lady's voice shook as she tried to come to terms with what had happened.

'Look, why don't you sit down. I'll make you some coffee or tea and I'll start to clear this place up. Have you got house insurance?'

The woman nodded.

'Well, then, I know this is a terrible shock to get. It's a horrible thing to happen, but we can put this right, and the insurance will pay out to re-place anything valuable. You'll probably end up with better stuff.' She smiled at her little joke, trying to raise Mrs Chiarello's spirits.

'But you have enough to do, I'm sure. I couldn't ask you to –'

Scarlett raised her hand to stop her. 'My life isn't exactly full to the brim with social engage-ments right now, so I don't actually have anything else to do. And I'd like to help, ok? Now let's get this coffee going.'

Scarlett busied herself trying to find cups, but most of them had been smashed.

'Tea, please, Scarlett, if you don't mind. I never liked coffee. This really is extraordinarily kind of you. I feel terrible taking up your time like this.'

Scarlett prattled soothingly about how helpful the insurance company were sure to be, and how even though it looked awful now, they'd have the place tidied up in no time. The old lady just sat amid the ruins of her little kitchen, fighting tears.

'I wonder if your living room might be more comfortable for you,' Scarlett said. The kitchen was destroyed, and looking at the devastation seemed to be upsetting Mrs Chiarello further.

'Yes, I… Well, I went in there with the policeman, but to be honest, I was in a little shock. I think it's a bit better. I've just got back from the hospital, you see, right before you arrived. The police were asking me what had been taken at the time, but I couldn't really focus. I'm sorry – you must think I'm a crazy old lady.' She half smiled.

'Not at all,' Scarlett reassured her. 'I'd be exactly the same. It's horrible to have someone come into your home, to go through your things. No wonder you're a little disoriented. It's natural after what you've been through. I'll tell you what. Why don't we go through to the living room? You can have your tea, and when you're feeling a little better, we'll see what we can do to get this place back into how it should be. Ok?'

Mrs. Chiarello followed Scarlett into the small hallway and indicated the door on the right. The small, bright room was not as bad as the kitchen – some books and pictures taken off the walls and smashed or torn, but the intruders obviously had decided there was nothing of value in there. Scarlett guided the old lady to an easy chair beside a little fireplace and handed her the tea.

She picked up the photographs from the floor and tried to save them. They would need new frames, but they were ok. It was only as she tried to rectify the vandalism that she noticed something unusual about her surroundings.

The walls were adorned with black and white photographs of men and women in military garb, and standing in the corner of the room was a green, white and orange flag. Over the mantelpiece was a framed copy of the Irish Proclamation of Independence, and Irish memorabilia dotted every surface. With the last name *Chiarello*, Scarlett had assumed the woman to be of Italian extraction, not Irish.

Mrs. Chiarello's eyes rested on the photograph on the mantelpiece of a woman, dressed in a military uniform, which had survived the burglary. The old woman spoke quietly. 'That was my mother.'

Scarlett picked up the photograph carefully. 'When was this taken?' she asked.

'Easter Week, 1916, in Dublin. It's the only one in existence, I believe. It was found among the papers of a friend of hers, a Mrs Grant, in Ireland, when she died back in 1960, and her lawyers managed to track my mother down and send it to her. I remember the day so clearly. She stood in this room, just where you are standing now, and opened the envelope. I think Mammy must have been in her early sixties then. She was surprised at the Irish postmark. She had contact with people from there when she first came here, but less so as the years passed. There was a letter from a lawyer, saying this photograph, as well as some correspondence, were found among the personal effects of Mrs Grant. As they knew from the name written on the back who it was, they managed to locate my mother. Mammy was so choked with emotion, she couldn't speak, and she wasn't that kind of person, given to emotions. But I'll never forget that day, not as long as I live.'

'Was she involved with the revolution?' Scarlett was intrigued. She had grown up listening to Dan drunkenly roaring about the political troubles in Ireland, so the rebellion of Easter Week 1916 and the subsequent War of Independence were indelibly printed on her memory.

'Oh, yes, dear, she certainly was. She was in Cumann na mBan, the women's army - women who fought and were wounded and died right alongside the men. Mammy fought to free Ireland. Along with so many others.'

Mrs Chiarello paused. She crossed the room and took down a large photograph from a side table, and gestured for Scarlett to come and see it. Scarlett placed the photo of the woman carefully back on the mantelpiece and crossed the room, avoiding the broken glass on the carpet. It was a wedding picture, the bride clearly the woman in the other photo. She was very petite and pretty. Her hair was long and her features tiny and perfect, like a doll's. She wore a lace wedding dress and a long scarf on her head, a look Scarlett had seen before in photos from the 1920s. The bride's hand rested gently on the arm of the tall man at her side. He was in a military uniform and looked very handsome, though he looked like a giant beside his bride.

'What a handsome couple! They look very glamorous in their finery,' Scarlett remarked.

The woman smiled. 'They were my parents. They got married when my father got back from England in 1917, before all the trouble happened with the treaty. Half of the people at their wedding fought on different sides during that war… A great many of them never survived.'

She seemed to assume that Scarlett under-

stood the intricacies of Irish politics. The
Northern Ireland issue was one most New
Yorkers were familiar with in some way or another, but despite her voracious interest in politics, she was ambivalent at best about the goings-
on in the birthplace of her father. She recalled
from the depths of her memory the details about
the War of Independence that followed the up-
rising of 1916. Ireland had been colonised by
Britain centuries earlier, and in 1916, the Irish
had made a bid for freedom.

After two years of war, the British agreed to
negotiate a peace settlement, but refused to hand
over some parts of the north of the country,
which split the Irish. Some people thought it was
a stepping stone to full independence, but others
disagreed, and felt that they should have kept on
fighting.

'So your parents were patriots, then?' she
asked kindly, smiling at the pride that shone
from the old lady's eyes as she gazed at the
picture.

'Yes. Patriots... I suppose they were. Then
again, one man's patriot is another man's terrorist, isn't that what they say?' She shook her head.
'I never thought of them like that. They were
young and in love, so in love that nothing else

mattered. Freeing their beloved country and being together – that was all they wanted.'

'Well, Mrs Chiarello, I know this has been an awful ordeal for you, but at least you still have your precious photographs.'

'Eileen, my name is Eileen. That's just it, though. I have the photos, but there was something else – something Mammy held so dear to her, all her life, and I think it might be gone. I don't know what I'll do, if…' Her voice faded to a whisper.

'What was it? Maybe it's not gone. The place is in such a mess that perhaps it's around somewhere. If you tell me what it is, I'll be happy to look for it.' Scarlett spoke gently. This wasn't how she imagined her day panning out, but it felt good to have a purpose. She didn't know it, but Eileen was helping Scarlett as much as Scarlett was helping her.

'It was a sheet. Well, a flag, wrapped in a sheet. I kept it in the sideboard there, but I looked after the burglar left, before the police came, and I couldn't find it.' Eileen was devastated. 'It's of no use to anyone – it just looks like an old rag, really – but it meant the world to Mammy. I hate to think it just ended up in a dumpster when they realised it was of no use.'

Scarlett got up and went to the sideboard that Eileen had indicated. There was a canteen of cutlery in there, and some china bowls, two of which had been taken out and smashed. There was no sign of a sheet.

'Maybe they took it upstairs, to put things into?' she offered.

'Maybe.' Eileen was despondent. 'Though I can't imagine why.'

Scarlett thought for a moment. Eileen was too shaken to be dragged upstairs, and on top of that, she had no idea what state the rooms were in on the next floor. When the police came yesterday, Eileen was so shocked that she probably didn't register details. Scarlett had heard horrible stories of burglars soiling beds with excrement after break-ins, and Eileen could really do without that horror. She decided to go upstairs alone and survey the damage.

'Why don't I take a look? If I find it, I'll bring it down to you. You just rest there for a while.' Eileen nodded sadly and sat back down, lost in her thoughts.

The little house was everything Scarlett, as a child, imagined as the perfect home. Little knick-knacks were on surfaces with no fear of being smashed in a drunken rage. The carpet was soft beneath her feet, and the house smelled of lavender. If she'd had a Grandma, then she would have wanted an Eileen, she thought. When Dan was on one of his benders, she remembered wishing she had a lovely Grandma who baked cookies and had a house that looked just like this.

The two bedrooms upstairs were in disarray, but thankfully, no other damage was done. An empty jewellery box was thrown on the bed in the main bedroom, and some clothes had been torn from the closet and drawers. But as she replaced them and straightened out all the things on the nightstand she was relieved. At least Eileen would be able to go to bed tonight in relative order.

The second bedroom had the contents of the closet and the drawers pulled out also. Eileen obviously kept winter coats and extra blankets and that sort of thing in there. As she began to replace the old-style heavy woollen blankets, she saw on the floor a greying cotton parcel, around a foot square and tied with a length of silver ribbon. It could be the flag Eileen described. She finished tidying the room and went quickly downstairs.

'Is this it?' Scarlett asked hopefully.

The long-controlled tears finally flowed down Eileen's old cheeks, and Scarlett felt good about herself for the first time in ages. 'Thank you.' Eileen squeezed Scarlett's hands as unadulterated joy shone from her face.

She took the greying piece of fabric from the parcel. It had been folded with care many years ago and was frayed on the creases. She opened it out gently in case it fell apart, and she laid it carefully across the table.

Scarlett was intrigued. There was no doubt that the fabric was old, but it wasn't a flag in any sense that she understood the term. It was more like a sack of some sort, which had been ripped down the seams. There appeared to be two roughly cut holes on one end, and the fabric was darker around them. The fabric itself was soft and heavy. There were a variety of stains on it, from tan to dark-brown in colour.

Then she noticed something on the corner. In very faded, almost invisible print, were written the words *Boland's Mills.*

A memory flashed in Scarlett's mind. The name brought her back to their apartment in Yonkers, years earlier. She was in bed, and she could hear Dan roaring out on the street. It must have been in the early hours of the morning. Someone was trying to shut him up while she cringed in her bed, knowing that once he got in, he would either collapse on the couch and pass out, or else start on Lorena. The other voice was quiet and impossible to make out. Scarlett prayed it was a cop who might arrest him and lock him up overnight.

The voice seemed to be calming Dan until she heard his loud rough voice again. 'Whaddaya know about it? You call yourself Irish, but where was your de Valera when he was needed? You tell me that. Lemme tell you where he was – hiding down in Boland's Mills!'

The reference to Boland's Mills was a regular motif of her father's drunken ramblings. He considered himself quite the authority of Irish history, though his rhetoric was based much more in rabid Republicanism than on any actual knowledge of the facts.

Eileen interrupted her reverie. 'This means more to me that anything else in the world. Mammy brought it with her, you see, from Ireland. It sort of represents her life there, and everything that happened. I couldn't bear to have lost it.' Eileen touched the old fabric affectionately.

'I'm glad it wasn't taken. Now, let's see about getting this place cleared up, shall we? How about you go upstairs and lie down? You must be exhausted after everything that happened. I'll make a start in the kitchen.'

Eileen looked intently at Scarlett. 'I'm not sure of many things at this age, Scarlett. That's what happens as you get older. The black and white certainty of youth disappears to be replaced with lots of grey, but I'm sure of this: Someone sent you to me today. I can't thank you enough for everything you've done.' Eileen squeezed Scarlett's hand.

'It's no problem. As I said, I don't have much going on these days. It's nice to have a diversion.' Scarlett smiled. She couldn't explain it, but she felt a connection to this woman.

# CHAPTER 9

DUBLIN, 1913

'*J*ust leave it there, Mary. I doubt I'll have time for more than a cup of tea this morning.'

Mary Doyle placed the breakfast tray on the sideboard of the bedroom as her employer sat at her dressing table pinning her long dark hair under an elegant hat.

'Mr Larkin is speaking at the Imperial Hotel this morning, despite the viceroy's edict that he shouldn't speak in public. He is either a very brave or a very foolish man. It's difficult for one to see which at the moment – Pass me that pin there, please. Mr Grant is incensed, of course. Well, you heard him yourself at dinner last night. Threatening to lock out every single last one of the men who follow Larkin.'

'Yes, ma'am.' Mary helped her employer to fix her hat on her head. Glancing in the looking glass, she admired the older woman. Her employer must be in her early forties, yet her figure was that of a girl. She was always immaculately groomed and her hair always shone beautifully. She had intelligent hazel eyes which radiated kindness. Mary was used to Mrs Grant's regular discussions regarding the growing unrest in the city. She voiced her opinions freely to Mary, but usually just agreed with her husband when he expounded on the stupidity and danger of unions and Larkinism. Mr Grant, and many employers like him, were refusing to allow the workers to join a union – or do anything to make their appalling situation any better.

'He simply refuses to accept what is factual evidence, that's the thing. Dublin has the highest infant mortality rate in Europe – the third highest in the world, for goodness' sake! I don't know what, but something will have to be done. People are living in atrocious conditions, with no proper medical care, or even adequate nutrition.

The poor will be out with guillotines next, demanding the heads of the wealthy, and who could blame them? Tell me, Mary, has he left for the factory?' Mrs Grant turned to face her.

'Yes, ma'am, about twenty minutes ago.' Mary remembered seeing him leave by the front door. He always gave her an oily smile and tried to touch her hand as she handed him his coat. He made her shudder. It surprised her that someone as beautiful as Mrs Grant would be married to such an unattractive man. He was balding and wiry and wore what was, in Mary's opinion, a ridiculous moustache which covered a lot of his thin pale face. He never spoke to his wife with any kindness or love, and everything he said seemed to be a sneer or a cutting remark.

'Very good, then. I shall be going also to Liberty Hall, where Countess Markievicz is feeding 3,000 people a day! The families of the locked-out workers are starving, literally starving in front of our eyes. I know that some of the women down there are begging their husbands to go back to work, to accept their employers' conditions – no matter how awful, for the children if nothing else – but if they do that, well…'

Mrs. Grant walked over to the sideboard and sipped her tea.

'Perhaps you should eat something, ma'am, if you're going to be working all day?' Mary spoke quietly. It was one of the reasons she'd got the job over so many other applicants. Mrs Kearns, the cook and housekeeper, who'd interviewed her for the job three months earlier, had explained that the master didn't like loud voices, and so Mary with her soft Tipperary accent would suit them fine. The other girls waiting to be seen that day were chatting while they listened for their names to be called, but Mary remained quiet, only answering direct questions with single-word answers. She needed this job badly and was determined to get it. The others, who were discussing boys and dances and the Lockout with such enthusiasm and sometimes colourful language, seemed to think they were not being overheard.

When it came to her turn, Mrs Kearns asked her what she knew about being a maid. She explained that she had grown up in an orphanage and so was very used to cooking and cleaning, though serving at a fancy table wasn't something she had ever done. She had a nice reference from the nuns, claiming she was a good girl, hardworking and honest, with a deep faith. Sister Benedict had asked in her letter that Mary's new employer not hold the girl's lack of parentage against her, for it was through no fault of her own that she was the product of a sinful act.

Mary reddened with embarrassment as Mrs Kearns read the letter aloud in her broad Dublin accent. Up to that moment, Mary had no idea what it contained. The envelope was addressed to 'The employer of Miss Mary Doyle'. Sister Benedict had merely handed it to her on her eighteenth birthday, telling her that she was no longer the responsibility of the community, and dismissed her without a trace of affection or concern.

That day, Mary walked down the driveway, away from the only home she'd ever known, feeling a myriad of emotions. She was overwhelmingly relieved to be free. Free of the drudgery of daily hard physical work, and living under the constant knowledge that she was a nobody, with no family to give her a position in life. But she would miss the others, especially the little ones, and one or two of the nuns who were kind to her. The order had taught her to read and write, and had taken care of her physical needs reasonably well, but there was never any love or affection. She was never allowed to forget how she was the result of a sin and was therefore tainted. Starting out in the world, alone and without one single person to call her own, was daunting but liberating.

She had enough money, given to her by the nuns, for a bus ticket and a few nights' accommodation. She had never been to the capital city – or anywhere else for that matter – but it seemed like a better option than staying in Tipperary. Sister Margaret, who was always kind to her, told her to try to get a job in a big house, and apparently there were plenty of those in Dublin. She was good at sewing and mending and could cook well, and it would be fine if she got a job with accommodation.

The nun had given her the name and address of an old school friend in Glenageary, a Mrs Carmody, who might be able to help Mary find a job if she mentioned she knew Sister Margaret. The nun told Mary to say she was a friend of Kitty Kennedy's. Mary gazed in amazement at this revelation, that the kind Sister Margaret was once a girl called Kitty Kennedy. Sister told her that she would pray for her every day and asked that Mary write and tell her of her fate. Sister Margaret was a late vocation, not entering the convent until she was in her late twenties, and was from Dublin, so she was a bit more worldly-wise than some of the other sisters.

Mary had walked to Nenagh and waited for the bus to Dublin. The journey took her through lush green countryside, which eventually gave way to houses, and what looked like factories. Mary gazed with a mixture of horror and excitement at the scene before her as the bus edged its way up the quays of the River Liffey. Horses, trams, delivery carts and even a few motor cars fought for space among what seemed like thousands of people, confidently making their way about their business. She got off the bus and, after a few false starts, navigated the huge city with difficulty. She eventually made it, hours later, to the address the nun had given her.

True to her word, Sister Margaret's school friend received her in the parlour. She was pleased to hear of her old friend and asked Mary lots of questions about how Kitty Kennedy was faring as Sister Margaret. Mary tried to answer without explaining to Mrs Carmody just how little the children had to do with the nuns. Eventually Mrs Carmody said that she herself had no need of staff at present, but that Mary should go down to Mrs Grant, next door but one. She was a friend of Mrs Carmody's, and was looking for a maid.

Like most Dublin ladies, she preferred servants from the country. City girls were too forward. Her own girl was from County Limerick, she explained, and came from a large family. Apparently she was a godsend after the bold strap of a girl from the Liberties area of the city she had let go for keeping company and attending dances.

Mary noted what she said and thanked God that she would have no reason to be keeping company with men, nor had she any interest in going to dances. The nuns had told her often enough how the badness was in her blood, how it was precisely that sort of behaviour that got her mother in to trouble, and she resolved from a very young age to avoid any such occasion of sin. Mrs Carmody very kindly told her a little of what would be required of a maid in a house such as hers, then a uniformed woman to bring Mary to the kitchen for a bowl of soup and a cup of tea to get her settled before she approached Mrs Grant.

'Aren't you a scrawny little thing? The mistress says you're to have a bite before you go, so sit yourself down at the end there. Eileen, get her a bowl of soup and a bit of soda bread.'

The woman, who turned out to be the cook,

returned to her kneading on the huge work surface in front of the range, a task that had obviously been interrupted by the mistress's new arrival. Mary was in awe of her huge hands and strong arms as she bellowed out instructions to Eileen. She scrutinised Mary, making her feel like a piece of meat she might buy at a butcher shop.

'You're pretty enough then, lovely red hair. I used to have red hair when I was young, not as nice as yours, though, more carroty. You have a bit of blond and a bit of gold and brown in there as well as the red...makes it better, I think. And you've been inside most of your life, I'd say? No country girl would have that porcelain skin, I can tell you! For all that, though, there's not a pick on you. Did them nuns feed you at all?'

The Carmody cook babbled on as the serving girl placed a steaming bowl of delicious-smelling soup before her. Eventually the old cook went to the larder behind the kitchen, giving the girls a chance to talk.

'So, have you ever been in service before?' Eileen was curious. Mary was intimidated by this girl, who looked around her age but seemed so much more confident. Her dark hair was drawn up into her cap, but a few tendrils of curls escaped. She had a curvaceous figure and dancing vivid blue eyes, and her skin was the colour of people Mary had seen in pictures in the Bible – kind of a golden brown. She had never seen anyone like her. The nuns would have said she was flighty looking, but Mary thought she was lovely. Like a saint, or a *señorita* she had seen in a picture book once.

'No, not really, but I grew up in an orphanage, so I'm used to hard work,' Mary replied shyly.

Eileen said conspiratorially, 'Well, that one Mrs Carmody is sending you to, Mrs Grant, I only know her from coming here for bridge and she seems nice. She's only two doors up from here. You'll have to be on your best behaviour, though, and don't say anything about politics.' She was cutting a slice from a newly baked cake of soda bread, and Mary's mouth was watering.

'I don't know anything about politics.' Mary looked innocently at Eileen. 'Will she ask me about it?'

Mary was suddenly fearful that her one chance might slip away if she were to be quizzed. There were never newspapers in the convent, so very little was known of the outside world. Mary had nearly jumped out of her skin when she'd seen her first tram earlier this morning. The city was so big and busy and smelly that she desperately wanted to find a position. She had no idea where to try to find lodgings if this job wasn't offered.

'Aah, I wouldn't think so. She's into the union,– well, not into it as such, her husband wouldn't allow it if he knew. He's after locking all the men out of his shirt factory, you see.'

Seeing Mary's look of confusion, she asked incredulously, 'Were you living under a stone, or what? It's all anyone talks about up here – Jim Larkin and the Lockout. The men are out on strike for better pay and conditions, but your man Grant has the contracts to make all the uniforms for the British, so he's raging. He locked everyone who wants to join the union out of the factory. Tempers are running very high, let me tell you. The people who are out on strike have nothing – no money for food, or medicine, can't pay the rent. It's terrible, so it is. His missus then is a whole other kettle of fish. She's down in Liberty Hall with Countess Markievicz and the rest of them feeding the needy, but if Mr Grant was to get wind of it, there'd be blue murder and no mistake. He's a right lighting divil, they say.'

Mary was confused. 'But why do people want join a union if it means that they lose their jobs?'

Eileen sighed and smiled. 'You really are a bit

of an innocent, aren't you? Look, people up here, in Dublin, aren't like people from the country. They're living in a desperate state altogether, a lot of them. There's hardly any work and them that have jobs are only earning small money, and the most of that goes over the counter for drink anyway. So a few months back this fella – from England, I think he is – James Larkin is his name. Well, he arrived and told them that that they shouldn't put up with it any more, and they should all get together and join a union. Y'know, for better money and better conditions and the like. He's supposed to be a fierce powerful talker altogether. Well, some of them were bowled over by him, and went along with it. If they did anyway, the bosses weren't having any of it and threw out each and every fella who joined, and now they can't go to work and their families are starving. Mrs Grant is stuck in that soup kitchen with the Countess and all the women who are on the side of the workers. Mrs Carmody upstairs tells me about it when I'm dressing her. She's not involved really, doesn't really trust Larkin because her husband thinks he's a communist and against the Church, and she follows him in everything. Mrs Grant, now, she's different. She goes to meetings and down to Liberty Hall, giving out free food, but as I said, if her husband found out, well… I think Mrs Carmody kind of admires her for her gumption, though.'

Mary was trying to take in all of what Eileen had told her while eating the delicious soup and bread lathered with thick butter. Suddenly a bell rang in the kitchen, making Mary jump.

'That's only herself calling me! Lord, but you're a skittery little thing aren't you? You'll be used to hearing bells ringing after a week or so in service, let me tell you! Hold on there, till I see what she wants. Help yourself to another bowl of soup if you're hungry.'

While Eileen went upstairs, Mary took in her surroundings. The cook was busy in the pantry, so she was alone. Upstairs had reminded her of the nuns' parlour, all polished surfaces and fresh flowers, but the kitchen here was nothing like that of the orphanage. The AGA gave lovely heat and there was a delicious smell of baking and roasting meat. *Imagine working here every day, with so much food around you, able to have a slice of soda bread or a few currants whenever you like!* As far as she could see, there was just Eileen and the cook down here. She offered a secret prayer that she would be able to get a similar position. She hardly believed she could be so lucky.

Soon Eileen was back. 'You picked the right day, anyway – she's meeting girls today about the job. The master there apparently scared the living daylights out of their last girl but one, and she left. She got some city one then, from up on Francis Street, but a right cheeky piece she was, it seems. She was courting on the footpath outside the servant's door. Imagine! So she got the high road after two days.' Eileen handed her an envelope. 'Mrs Carmody said you're to give this note to Mrs Grant when you get there. You'll probably have to meet Mrs Kearns first – that's the Grants' housekeeper. She can be a bit of a Tartar, but she's all right under it all. Just be polite and answer up and don't have hair hanging in front of your face. Don't look at the floor, but don't come over too cheeky either, though there's no fear of that, I'd say. Now get yourself cleaned up – scrub those fingernails, she'll check them. There's a little bathroom down the corridor there, and then you'd better get a move on in case someone gets in ahead of you. Let your bag there in the corner. You can come back for it when you get the job. She'd be a grand woman to work for, so be sure you give a good account of yourself. Tell her you're able to do everything, and sure if there's anything you can't do, then I'll help you. I'm only a minute away. Us country girls have to stick together.' Eileen ushered Mary down the corridor with a wink.

That was three months ago. Mary could hardly believe her luck. The Grants' housekeeper seemed to think she was acceptable, and she was taken up to meet the mistress in her sitting room, where she was engrossed in a newspaper. Mary gave her the letter from Mrs Carmody.

'Well, my friend Mrs Carmody seems to think you are of good character and have been well brought up, so I think we will give it a try. The position is housemaid, as I'm sure Mrs Kearns has already explained. You will be answerable to her, and I shall also require you to help me with dressing and so on. I hope you'll be happy here, Mary. Mrs Kearns will see you get settled in. Welcome to Dublin.' Mrs Grant smiled at her and went back to reading her paper.

Mrs. Kearns had shown her to a bedroom all to herself, with a bed and a locker and a little wardrobe. There was a rug on the floor, and a Sacred Heart picture on the wall. The first few nights she found it hard to sleep, having never slept alone in her entire life before, but she soon came to love her little room. She had one and a half days off a month, and a salary of twenty pounds a year. To Mary, such a fortune was unimaginable. She had yet to spend any money since she had been given a uniform, and all her food was included. She struggled at first to fit her thick auburn hair under the cap, but Mrs Kearns showed her how it was done.

Her pale skin was getting a light glow from being outside as she ran errands for the house-keeper in the autumn mornings. She marvelled at the array of goods for sale in the shops and loved her morning adventures to the butchers or green-grocers. The only place they ever went to from the orphanage was to Mass, and even then there was a passageway from the convent into the church, so they were very rarely outside. The or-phanage boys were responsible for the cattle and hens and the farmwork, and the girls did do-mestic work inside. The Grants got most things delivered, but Mrs Kearns sometimes forgot something and sent Mary to fetch it.

She passed a sweet shop every day, and re-alised she'd never actually tasted a sweet. After a few weeks of her pay sitting in her drawer, she took a penny out and gathered up her courage to go into the shop. She bought some toffee and ate it as she walked home. It was the most delicious thing she'd ever tasted. She would have loved to have sent a treat back to the children in the convent, but she knew the nuns would never allow them to have anything like that. She had written to Sister Margaret, thanking her profusely for everything, and especially for helping her secure such a wonderful position.

It was her day off one Sunday, and she and Eileen had gone to Mass together and then for a walk in Stephen's Green despite the growing signs of winter. The poverty that she witnessed constantly shocked Mary. Children begged in the street, dressed in rags with no shoes on their feet. Men seemed to stand around in groups smoking and talking, and women pushed prams with skinny, pale babies and toddlers who looked cold and miserable. The weather was bitter and Mary was glad of the coat and hat Mrs Grant had found for her, realising she didn't have one. The police were everywhere. There seemed to be two different kinds, and people were fearful of both uniforms. They patrolled the streets, ever on alert, and gave the impression of caring nothing about the misery and starvation all around them.

Each morning, after breakfast had been served and collected and Mrs Grant had left for Liberty Hall, Mary reported to Mrs Kearns for her list of jobs. There was a lad around as well,

Jimmy, who was about fifteen. He didn't live in, but he fetched coal and chopped kindling and ran errands. Mr Grant had just bought a new carriage, so Jimmy was to be his coachman. He was a chirpy little lad, and very small for his age. He adored Mary and was always trying to impress her.

'That lad is soft on you,' Mrs Kearns remarked in disapproving tones. 'Mind you don't encourage him.'

'No, Mrs Kearns,' Mary replied dutifully. She was anxious to avoid any situation that would displease the housekeeper. Already she had been less than impressed that Mary had no idea how to bake, since cakes were never a feature of life in the convent. Sometimes parishioners would deliver scones to the nuns, and there was always a feast of cakes at Easter and Christmas, but the children were never allowed to taste them.

'Not even on your birthday?' Eileen had asked incredulously as she showed her how to make Madeira cake and currant buns on her half day. 'We hadn't much growing up, but Mam always tried to make a sweet cake for our birthdays, and sure what with there being so many of us in the family, it was nearly always someone's birthday. My mam makes the best trifle too. We used to have it on Sundays. My brother Rory, he's a year older than me, was a divil for getting into the pantry and stealing the cream off the top. Mam would pretend to murder him, but we all knew Rory could get away with anything. He always could.'

She smiled at the memory, and Mary wondered with a pang what it must have been like to grow up in a loving home with so many brothers and sisters. Eileen's eyes glittered with an idea. 'I'll tell you what, why don't we go to Bewley's on Westmoreland Street for your birthday? Their cakes are amazing. When is it?'

Mary knew she would have to confess her dark secret sometime, but Eileen was the only friend she had. She'd passed Bewley's Tea House on one of her walks around the city when Mrs Grant asked her to accompany her on shopping trips to carry bags and boxes, and the aromas coming out of the beautifully decorated café and the sight of people sitting at tables having cups of tea and cakes delighted her. It never occurred to her that she could go in.

'I don't know when my birthday is.' She spoke quietly.

Eileen looked up from her baking. 'Why not?'

Mary could feel her cheeks reddening. Maybe

someone as nice as Eileen wouldn't want to have anything more to do with her once she found out the truth.

'I-I-I don't know who my father was. My mother had me, and I was put into the orphanage. She wasn't married, you see… I was the result of a sinful act…' Mary's voice was barely audible now.

Eileen covered the ground between them quickly and put her arm around Mary.

'Is that what the nuns told you?'

Mary nodded. 'It's true.'

'Do you know who she was, where she is now? Your mam, I mean?' Eileen's kindness brought tears to Mary's eyes.

'No. I don't know anything about her. I was just told she was a sinner and I was the result. The nuns called me Mary, so I don't even know my real name, if my mother gave me one. I only just found out how old I really am. They told me three months ago that I was eighteen, and that it was time for me to leave the convent and fend for myself. Every night I thank God for sending me to you and for my job, and Mrs Grant…'

'Aah, you poor thing, that's awful. I bet your mother wishes she knew what had become of you, and thinks of you every day. I'll tell you something else: She must have been a beauty, your mam. I bet you look just like her. I'd love hair like yours, that gorgeous copper colour instead of boring auld black. And these flippin' curls will be the death of me – I can never look sophisticated with bits sticking out the whole time. You're so lucky, you know. My mam used to threaten to cut mine off every Sunday morning, and she trying to brush it for Mass.' Eileen giggled at the memory.

'I wonder, do you get your green eyes from your mam or your daddy? I bet they were a right handsome pair, the two of them, and they'd love to see how beautiful their little girl grew up. Here, I've an even better idea than Bewley's! How about next month, when it's your Sunday off, we go on an adventure? We can make it your birthday! We'll take the tram from Nelson's Pillar to Kingstown and then we'll have tea in the Royal Marine Hotel. Oh, you should see it, Mary – it's like something out of a storybook.'

Mary smiled at her friend's enthusiasm. 'You're so kind, but there's no need. My life now is so much better than it was. I have to pinch myself sometimes. You don't miss what you never knew.' Mary shrugged resignedly.

'"No need?" There's every need. A girl has to have a birthday so she has an excuse to get her finery on. No, I'm adamant. We're going to the Royal Marine for tea to celebrate the birthday of Mary Doyle, spinster of this parish.' She chuckled, nudging Mary and causing her to giggle too.

'But surely we wouldn't be swanky enough for a place like that. They wouldn't leave the likes of us in, would they?'

'Speak for yourself! Now listen to me. Before the big day out, we are going to go shopping, into Clery's, and we are going to get you a new frock and stockings and even a pair of dainty shoes. Kit you out right and proper. You'll knock the eyes out of them below in the Royal Marine. Sure, when was the last time you got a new frock?' Eileen's hazel eyes twinkled with excitement. 'You never know who we might meet!'

'I never had a new frock or a new anything else, for that matter, in my life.' Mary spoke freely to her friend, all earlier shyness gone. Eileen had appointed herself Mary's protector and adviser, and Mary trusted her completely.

'Well, all the more reason to spend a few shillings on yourself so. Sure you have three months wages got now, and only a few toffees to show for it. You never know, we might meet a young man on our travels!' Eileen giggled.

Mary suddenly got serious, remembering the

dire warnings of the nuns not to fall into the same trap as her mother. She would have to be very careful to avoid all temptation for fear she'd go down the same sorry road.

'There won't be men there, will there? I...' She couldn't articulate to Eileen her fears.

Her new friend understood her insecurities and instead of teasing her, soothed her. 'Aah look, Mary, we'll have a lovely day out, the two of us. We'll walk on the pier and have tea and ride on the tram. 'Twill be great altogether. And my brother Rory, he works at the hotel, did I tell you that? Anyway he does, and he'll escort us, so we'll be quite safe. Nobody would look sideways at us with Rory around.'

The pride with which Eileen spoke of her brother gave Mary a little pang of envy. She would have loved a brother or a sister – anyone, really – to call family. Eileen was forever telling her about her family back in Foynes, County Limerick, and her mam and daddy and how much she missed them all. Getting one whole week of holidays in the summer meant she could go to visit them, and she was so excited already and planning little gifts for them all. She sent most of her wages home to help the family, and her mother was always saying she should keep a bit more for herself. But Eileen knew how hard it was to keep the family going, so she didn't mind.

Mary had nobody to send her money to. She had thought that maybe she should have sent some back to the convent, but Eileen soon told her that she would be mad to do such a thing. Sure weren't the nuns living in the lap of luxury? They wouldn't pass it on to the children anyway, so why would she be working hard to make life even easier for them?

The work wasn't hard – not compared to the convent. She rose early and got the fire started, and the bread in the oven. She served Mr Grant his breakfast in the dining room, and that was the only really bad bit of the day. From the very first morning, he was always finding reasons for her to be near him, and never lost an opportunity to touch her. She hated being alone with him, but she would never say anything in case it meant the end of her job. Eileen warned her to give him a wide berth, but it was easier said than done. He wasn't around much during the day, thankfully, and after he left for work at his factory, she made up the mistress's breakfast tray and brought it up to her.

She loved that time the best, helping Mrs Grant to get ready. The mistress was the most beautiful woman Mary had ever seen. Mary loved the way her wavy chestnut hair flowed down her back in the mornings, and was getting quite good at pinning it up for her each day, as she had been shown. She watched Mrs Grant in the mirror as she applied powders and creams to her flawless porcelain complexion while Mary laid out her outfit for the day. Though she was undoubtedly much older than Mary, she had the figure of a girl. And looking every inch the lady, she was feisty and spirited and very opinionated. She had such beautiful things: jewellery, hats and so many shoes. She had dresses and costumes and coats in every colour and style imaginable, and yet she went shopping at least once a week. She often gave Mary little things – gloves or a scarf when she tired of them. But while they were beautiful, Mary never wore them. She would have felt a fraud going around Dublin on her half day done up like a lady.

# CHAPTER 10

The girls giggled as they bought a bag of sweets for the journey. It was a cold breezy November day, but the sky was clear and the sun shone brightly. Mary found it hard to resist looking at herself in the shop windows as she hurried to Nelson's Pillar to catch the tram to Kingstown. How Sister Benedict would have given out about the sin of pride, but she had never owned anything so pretty. The new dress Eileen had picked out for her really was the nicest thing Mary had ever seen. It was in the sale in Clery's and cost three shillings and sixpence, ankle length and cornflower-blue, with long sleeves and a pale-blue collar. A row of pearl buttons went down the front. Mrs Grant had demanded to see her modelling it when she told her that she had been shopping.

Mary remembered the acute embarrassment she felt going upstairs dressed like a lady rather than a maid, but even the dour Mrs Kearns seemed impressed as they both climbed the stairs to Mrs Grant's sitting room.

'Oh, Mary!' Mrs Grant exclaimed. 'You look absolutely lovely, my dear. Doesn't she, Mrs Kearns?'

'She does indeed, ma'am,' Mrs Kearns replied sincerely.

'Just stay there now, I have just the thing!' Mrs Grant went to her adjoining dressing room and opened her enormous closet. She ran her fingers over the rows of beautifully pressed coats and dresses. Withdrawing a cream-and-blue ankle-length coat and cream wide-brimmed hat with a silk forget-me-not stitched to the band, she announced, 'This never suited me, but it will be simply beautiful on you, Mary. Your waist is so tiny and it cinches in perfectly. Here, let's try it on...'

'B-b-but, ma'am, I couldn't...' Mary was nonplussed.

'Nonsense, of course you can. I never wear it and Mrs Kearns tells me you are going to have tea at the Royal Marine with your friend to celebrate your birthday. Consider it a birthday present from Mr Grant and myself.'

Mary allowed herself to be dressed and, when she stood in front of Mrs Grant's mirror, she didn't recognise herself.

'You really are very pretty, Mary. Now off you go, and enjoy your day. Happy birthday, my dear.'

Mary thanked her employer and went back down to the kitchen. It felt strange to be going for a full day out, for usually her life revolved around Mrs Kearns and the kitchen. Mary felt such affection for the old housekeeper and confided everything to her. One night a few weeks ago, as they were enjoying their nightly cocoa and currant bread, the old housekeeper had asked about Mary's mother and she'd told her the truth. Mrs Kearns told her that night that life was harder for women than men in lots of ways, and that she was a good girl to have turned out so well. She also told Mary that her only daughter would have been around Mary's age if she'd lived, but TB took her when she was just eleven years old. Her husband had died years earlier and so she too was alone. She wasn't given to softness, but there was a kindness to Mrs Kearns that her stoic exterior belied.

As Mary was leaving to meet Eileen, Mrs Kearns took a little bag out of her skirts. 'This is for you. For your birthday.' The old woman proffered the paper bag.

'But it's not really my birthday, and anyway, you don't have to get me anything...' Mary was flustered.

'Yerra, 'tis only something small.'

Mary reached into the bag and pulled out a tiny silver medal on a chain.

''Tis St Anne, the mother of Our Lady. She's the patron saint of mothers. Wherever your poor mother is, I'm sure she thinks of you often. Now, go on, let you, or that other one will be in here on top of me with her giggling.'

Despite her complaining, Mary knew that Mrs Kearns liked Eileen and was happy for Mary that her friend called for a cup of tea in the evenings when she had finished seeing to Mrs Carmody.

Tears stung Mary's eyes. Mrs Kearns must have guessed how much not having a family of her own gnawed away at her, and that she had thought of somebody giving her something so lovely was overwhelming. No one had ever given her a present before, and here were these people who were no blood relation at all showing her such kindness.

'Thank you, Mrs Kearns. I'll treasure it.'

'Get out now, will you? I've to mop this floor and you're in the middle of the way!' And she shooed her out the door, trying to hide her pleasure at Mary's gratitude.

The two girls sat side by side on the tram. A man stood beside them as the tram filled up. He kept looking at them, and Eileen nudged Mary. Mary wished he would look somewhere else and stared out the window. He smiled at her reflection and she averted her eyes and breathed a sigh of relief when he got off the tram.

'I can see I'm going to fade beside you. The lads won't look twice at me with you here.' Eileen was mock despondent as they walked into the freshening breeze.

'Don't be daft,' Mary replied, embarrassed. She hated it when men looked at her. She was sure it was because she always looked so awkward and out of place.

'I'm only joking you.' Eileen knew how her friend felt about male attention, but she also knew that Mary was going to find it unavoidable. She was so striking-looking with her copper hair and those dark green eyes. Her skin was the colour of alabaster from a lifetime spent indoors working, where Eileen's own was tanned thanks to a childhood outside, helping on the family farm. Mary had a delicate frame – which Eileen was always telling her she envied – instead of her own fine strong physique. 'Beef to the heel like a Mullingar heifer, that's me!' she always joked.

Mary knew that for all her friend's bemoaning of her own shortcomings, she had no shortage of admirers. All the delivery boys, and even a few of the men, waited outside of Mass every Sunday to try to charm Eileen, but while she joked with them in a way Mary could not, she never let it go any further than friendly chat. Eileen had told her that she used to get letters from a friend of her brother's back in Limerick, called Teddy, and while there wasn't a romance, she thought he was very nice. Mary suspected that Eileen had feelings for this Teddy Lane, but she had come to Dublin to work and to help her family out – not to be daydreaming about boys.

The Royal Marine Hotel really took Mary's breath away. She looked at the beautiful facade overlooking the harbour and thought it was the most beautiful building she had ever seen in her life. She felt a surge of anxiety when she saw the liveried doorman helping a lady down the steps to a waiting hansom cab as she emerged into the cold afternoon. Surely he wasn't going to allow them in to such a fancy place?

As the cab drew away from the kerb at the front of the hotel, Eileen squeezed her arm in glee. Any worries Mary had were dismissed as Eileen dragged her to the door.

Inside the hotel, crystal chandeliers hung from the ornate ceiling, and in front of them was a magnificent marble staircase carpeted in red and gold. The silk-covered walls were adorned with paintings – seascapes and portraits – and the lobby hummed with activity. Eileen led her into the large dining room to the left of the foyer, and immediately they were approached by a splendidly dressed waiter.

'A table for two, ladies?' he asked in plummy tones. Only the slightest raising of his eyebrow gave the indication he thought they may have been out of their depth. Eileen soon showed him how wrong he was. Mary was astonished to hear her friend address him using an accent she'd have never heard before.

'Yes, please. By the window, if possible. We are celebrating my friend's birthday today.'

Mary got the distinct impression that he would have preferred they stay at the back of the room, near the staff entrance, but Eileen was having none of that. As he held the seats out for them at a table in the beautiful bay window, he handed them menus.

'Oh, there's no need for menus. We'll have afternoon tea for two, please.' She smiled sweetly and the man nodded curtly.

'Eileen!' Mary whispered. 'Are you sure we should be in here? I don't think they want the likes of us. And anyway, how much is this going to cost? Have we enough money?' Mary was starting to panic.

'Of course we have, and anyway, it's my treat for your birthday. I've had it here once before. When Mam came up to Dublin last year to see a doctor, Rory arranged with the manager for us to have our tea here. Oh, wait till you see what they give you, Mary! Tiny sandwiches and scones with jam and cream, and even little sweets, and it all comes out on a big tiered tray. 'Tis lovely, so 'tis.'

The view of the sea fascinated Mary. She had never seen the sea until she came to Dublin, and the white horses on the waves as the sea pounded the pier was mesmerising.

Just as Eileen promised it would be, the tea was delicious. The sandwiches were so delicate with the crusts cut off the bread, and the scones melted in the mouth. Mary felt like royalty.

'Thank you so much for today, Eileen. This has been the best day of my life. Honest to God, I never imagined places like this even existed. And the idea that someone like me would be sitting here, in this gorgeous dress and coat, with a friend like you...' Mary's voice cracked with emotion.

'Aah, here, will you stop it? Sure 'tis a great treat for me too, and I think you're well overdue a bit of joy in your life. Life down there in the convent wasn't much fun, was it?'

Eileen never pried into Mary's past, knowing how her origins embarrassed her, but today Mary didn't mind talking about it. Tipperary and the convent seemed so long ago.

''Twasn't that bad. Some of the nuns were nice. I knew no other life anyway, so it didn't seem that desperate, but compared to my life now... Well, now it's just lovely. The thing I missed most was having someone of my own – you know, a brother or sister, or a friend, even. We weren't really supposed to make friends, you see. If they saw you getting friendly with someone, then you'd be moved away from her. They didn't want us talking in case we found out anything about ourselves or each other, I suppose. Sometimes, I used to look after the really small ones, but then they were usually adopted. Every few months someone would come, in a big car. One time I remember – Americans, I think they were – came and took a few little ones away with them. I don't know where they ended up, though.'

Eileen's voice was kind. 'Did you never want to be adopted?'

Mary smiled. 'I used to dream about it, but nobody ever wanted me. Others like me got adopted, so maybe it was that nobody wanted a child that looked like me when I was little, and once you grow up a bit, then there's no chance. People want babies, you see, so they can pass them off as their own, I suppose. The nuns said they even had to baptise me themselves because my mother probably didn't do it. One of the nuns let slip one time that my mother kicked up a terrible fuss and didn't want me adopted, but maybe she just said that to make me feel better. I can't imagine that my mother's feelings on the subject would have held much sway with the nuns anyway. When I was small, I used to dream that she'd come back for me some day and we'd go off together and live somewhere far away, maybe even in America.' She laughed at her own foolishness.

'Stranger things have happened, God knows. I bet that nun was telling the truth, that your mam fought to keep you. But a girl on her own with no husband to give the baby a name wouldn't have any choices.' Eileen was ever the optimist. 'I'm sure she loved you, but it would just have been impossible. I hope she had a good life, and I bet she often thinks of you. Maybe she got married and now has other children. Imagine! You might really have brothers or sisters, but you don't know it. And sure won't you have your own family some day? When you meet your husband and have your own babies?'

Mary looked at her friend, perplexed. It had never really occurred to her that one day she might marry. Life in the convent was monotonously predictable every day, and now that she was here, in Dublin, she was living a life she never imagined was possible. The idea of leaving Mrs Grant's house, and Mrs Kearns and Eileen, to go and live with some man never even entered her head.

'The look on your face, girl – you'd swear I suggested you go away with the fairies!' Eileen giggled. 'That's what happens, you know, eventually to us all. We get married and have babies. I know you're only young, but some lad will catch your eye some day, mark my words.'

Mary laughed at her friend. 'Well, there isn't exactly a hundred young men begging for my hand in marriage so far, is there? And even if there were, I wouldn't have a clue what to say to them. So it's just as well that, despite all my finery, I'm not being pursued like you think.'

She lowered her voice to a whisper. 'Anyway, sure a decent boy from a nice God-fearing family wouldn't want anything to do with me – me with no one nor nothing to my name. He could hardly bring me home to his mother out of an orphanage. No, if I can stay in Grants's forever, that will do me.'

They chatted on and on through the afternoon, with Eileen asking for a top-up of tea when it ran out. Eventually, they left the hotel and were walking along the pier, admiring a huge ship docked at the quay, when they heard a voice calling 'Eileen!'

'Ye're like a pair of whippets, the two of ye. I'm trying to catch up to ye for the last ten minutes!' The hotel doorman was panting and resting his hands on his knees, trying to catch his breath.

'Well, you must be eating too many leftovers from the kitchen so,' Eileen joked. 'There was a time when you could outrun everyone in Foynes, and now look at you, puffing and spluttering like an auld man!'

The man recovered and Mary noticed how familiar he looked. His black hair, though cut quite short, was curly, and his skin was tanned, but it was his vivid blue eyes that caught her attention. His whole face seemed to dance with what the nuns called *divilment*. He didn't look like a man who took anything too seriously. Mary imagined he must be very popular with the girls as a group of them passed, casting admiring glances in his direction. He seemed oblivious, though, and was smiling broadly at Eileen.

'Enough of your cheek! Now introduce me properly. I don't know what kind of rearing she had at all!' He winked at Mary as he stood up to his full height, towering over her.

'Mary Doyle, let me introduce my brother, Rory O'Dwyer. Rory, this is my best friend, Mary Doyle, all the way from County Tipperary and up here in the big city making a name for herself.'

Mary coloured with pleasure – no one had ever called her a friend before, let alone a best friend. Rory looked exactly like Eileen, only a male version. When Eileen said her brother worked at the hotel, Mary thought she meant in the cellar or washing pots or something, not the doorman with his beautiful uniform. In all their chatter, she never mentioned what exactly he did there. Mary was amazed at how similar they looked, both handsome and quite exotic-looking with their tanned skin and dark hair.

Rory held out his hand and she placed hers in it. 'I am delighted to make your acquaintance, Miss Doyle, and if you can have any kind of positive influence on my unruly and unladylike sister here, I'm eternally grateful to you. Now then, ladies, shall we take a walk along the pier and watch the big ships coming and going from dear old England?'

'Don't start, Rory. We're having a nice day!' Eileen warned.

'I am starting nothing, Eileen. If a man cannot remark to his sister and her best friend his feelings at being subjugated and humiliated by a foreign oppressor who seeks to dissolve every shred of dignity and self-determination a man possesses, then who can he say it to? Maybe Miss Doyle agrees with me, Eileen. Did you ever think of that?'

Eileen rolled her eyes at Mary.

'Well, Miss Doyle? What say you? Should we be good little colonists as Mr Redmond is suggesting and beg and scrape all our lives to our English betters, or should we stand up, stand strong, unite and get rid of them for once and for all?' Though his tone was jokey, Mary sensed a passion behind the words.

She was glad she had taken to reading newspapers in her little room at night after Mr Grant had finished and discarded them. She was familiar with the opinions of John Redmond and the Home Rule agenda of the Irish Parliamentary Party. Mr Redmond seemed to think that getting a parliament of sorts in Dublin, which would still be answerable to England, would be enough, but clearly Rory didn't agree. Mary found herself wanting to agree with him.

'Well, I do know that Mr Redmond says he will never support votes for women under any circumstances, so I don't think he and I are ever going to be the best of friends.' Mary felt quite cheeky mentioning such a topic, but the mistress was very passionate on the subject. And the more Mary read about the women's suffrage movement – even if most of the press coverage was negative – the more she warmed to the idea. Why should men rule simply because they were men? She would never have had the courage to voice such opinions aloud, but Rory seemed to agree, and she realised she wanted him to know she wasn't ignorant of current affairs.

'Aah, an agitator! Wonderful! You are quite right not to trust him, Mary, my dear. He'd have us kowtowing to their king forever if he could. No, the Volunteers, now – they have the right idea. Do whatever it takes and finally get Ireland free, its men and its women. An Irish Republic, for once and for all.'

'Aah, Rory, give over, will you? And don't let anyone hear you going on with all that Volunteer stuff. It's only going to land you in trouble. You know it and I know it. And 'tis I'll have the job of writing to Mammy and Daddy and telling them that you're in jail…or worse.'

'Better try and die to be free than to live in slavery, Eileen. Mary agrees with me. Don't you, Mary?'

'She thinks you are full of wind, the same as I do. Now are we going for a walk or not?'

Rory offered each girl an arm, and together the threesome walked along the pier, Rory continuing to argue the case for independence. Mary enjoyed listening to him. He was so passionate and what he said made such sense. Despite Eileen's disapproval, Mary knew she was proud of her funny, handsome brother. As they walked along the pier, Rory pointed out various land-marks to them and saluted several walkers. He seemed to know everyone.

Up ahead, a large crowd was gathered. Ini-tially, Mary thought it was just people waiting for the boat to England, but as they drew nearer, they could hear singing. The group of people – nuns among them and led by a priest – were singing *Faith of Our Fathers* lustily while a group of men were trying to shepherd large groups of small children, dressed in rags, onto the boat. The singers were forcing them back onto the quayside.

'What's going on?' Eileen asked Rory. When he replied, all trace of the earlier joviality had dis-appeared.

'The locked-out workers are trying to send their children to England, to be looked after by sympathetic families over there, but the Church is against them going to Protestant homes. They'd rather they starve to death as Catholics. They've been down there all the week, stopping the men from getting the children on the boat. They'd sicken you, so they would, the Church. For all its money, they won't lift a finger to help the poor people living in the tenements, and the places rampant with disease and TB and the whole lot. But when the families let their babies go, when they've no other choice, the Church won't let them. They think anyone who joins the union is a communist, and so they are doing everything they can to punish those that are locked out.'

Mary could sense Rory's anger at the situation, but she was shocked to hear him speak of the Church like that. She'd been brought up to bow to the rules of the Church over everything else. She never met anyone who felt otherwise.

'We'd better turn around,' Eileen suggested. As they turned, they saw several members of the Dublin Metropolitan Police approaching the crowd. They were armed with batons, and soon the entire crowd was reduced to a brawl. Children cried with terror in the midst of the fracas and were being pushed dangerously close to the open quayside. Rory ran into the crowd and pulled two little girls back from the edge. Eileen and Mary followed him, and between them they were pulling the smallest children out first. Mary's new hat was knocked off and trampled underfoot, but she was running away with a baby under each arm and two or three more holding onto her skirt. She sat them on a low wall away from the riot, giving instructions to the oldest one – a boy around seven or eight – that he was to make sure no one moved. The babies she put into the arms of two little girls with orders to not let them go.

She dashed back into the heaving mass of bodies again and extracted more children, while the men who were leading them to the ship were being subjected to violent attack by the police and the singers. Rory and Eileen had seen where she had put the others and were bringing more little ones there. Several police vehicles had arrived, and policemen were throwing agitators into the vans with no concern for their safety. In the middle of it all, a priest, in full vestments, was praying loudly for the defence of the Catholic faith against the dual evils of Protestantism and communism.

Rory shouted to Eileen and Mary to stay with the children and he would go back into the thinning crowds and try to get more out. As he ran off, Mary saw a little girl holding onto a rope who had been pushed off the open quayside by the surging crowds. She was screaming, but no one could hear her. Mary rushed forward and managed to squeeze past the many one-to-one fights that the riot now amounted to. She knelt down on the filthy ground and grabbed the little girl's arm. Eventually, she hauled her to safely. Holding the child close to her, she tried to get back through the crowd when she spotted a policeman about to hit Rory with a baton. She ran over and grabbed the policeman's raised arm. He swung around in outrage only to find his assailant was a small young woman with a child in her arms.

'Right you!' he yelled and dragged Mary and the child to the van, where they were roughly thrown in with the others. Moments later, Rory was thrown in too. Before they closed the doors, Mary told the little girl to run to Eileen, who would take care of her. The policeman guarding the van allowed the girl out and Mary was relieved to see her run into Eileen's arms. Rory managed to make a bit of space on the floor of the van and pulled Mary to sit beside him. The crush was unbearable, as at least twelve people were shoved into the tiny dark space. Rory held her hand as the vehicle slowly made its way up the quay.

# CHAPTER 11

'*D*oyle. Mary Doyle,' a guard's voice called out from the corridor outside in the early morning. Mary leapt up from her place on the floor where she'd spent the night sleeping awkwardly. Elbowing her way from the back of the overcrowded cell, she tried to get over to the thick wooden door amid grunts of protest from her fellow cellmates. The smell of urine from the bucket in the corner, combined with cheap perfume and unwashed bodies, was nauseating.

'I'm Mary Doyle,' she managed to call through the tiny spy hole in the heavy door.

'Yez'll havta do better dan tha', luv. Dat fella's deaf as a post,' a cheaply dressed woman with a strong Dublin accent advised her with a cackle that revealed several missing teeth.

'Here! Mister Curley! She's in here!' the woman roared deafeningly.

'All right all right. Jaysis, Margot, you've a voice like a foghorn, did anyone ever tell ya tha'?' The warder was checking his ring of keys for the correct one. 'Now just Mary Doyle, righ'? The magistrate is only dealin' with breaking the peace this morning. The rest of youse brassers will havta wait yer turn.'

'Dat's not wha' you said last nigh'!' Margot crowed, much to the delight of her fellow inmates who screamed with raucous laughter.

Clearly, a night in the cells was a common feature of their lives. Mary couldn't wait to get out. She'd learnt more about what men and women get up to in those long hours last night than she ever needed to know. The bawdy, graphic descriptions of the various wants and needs of the women's customers would never leave her. It was a much more worldly-wise Mary who emerged after a night with the working girls of Dublin city. She pushed past them to get out the door and meekly followed the huge prison guard down the dark, dank corridors.

Her dress was ruined and the coat Mrs Grant

had given her was torn beyond repair. Her hair hung over her face and she was absolutely filthy. There was no way she could appear in public looking like this.

'E… Excuse me, sir,' she stammered shyly. 'Do I have to go in front of the magistrate now?'

The prison officer laughed and Mary saw kindness in his eyes. 'Well, young lady, I dunno who ya are, but ya have some important friends who are making this go away for you. A Mrs Grant explained to the magistrate that ya were only trying to help the chizzelers tha' got caught up in the carry-on down at the docks. You're being collected now, but mind you don't get yourself involved in anything like this again. He might not be feeling so kind the next time, y'hear me?'

Nodding with relief, Mary followed the officer out into the public area of the jail, where Mrs Kearns was waiting.

'God in heaven, child! Look at the cut of you!' Her words were spoken in concern and she went forward and grasped Mary's elbow. 'Thank you, sir,' she said to the guard. 'I'll see nothing like this ever happens again.'

Jimmy was outside with the Grants's carriage and Mrs Kearns bundled Mary inside. All the way home, Mrs Kearns said nothing. Eventually Mary spoke. 'I suppose they are letting me go. I'll just get my few things and…'

'Well, we'll have to see what's to be done. Lucky for you, Mrs Grant is on a committee with the magistrate's wife, and so when Eileen came to tell us what happened yesterday, the mistress was able to use her influence to get you out of it.'

Mary remained quiet for the rest of the journey. How could she have ruined the best thing that ever happened to her? Getting arrested by the police! Mrs Grant was a respectable woman who couldn't have people who were in trouble with the law in her service. She wondered how Rory was. They were separated once they got to The Barracks. Thank God Eileen got away and was able to get help.

Maybe Mary could go to England? Get the boat from Kingstown. Eileen said there was loads of work over there on account of them having so many more big houses. She often said she would have gone herself for the adventure if she wasn't going to be so far from the family. Mary had no family, so that wasn't going to be a problem. Mrs Grant, or maybe Mrs Kearns, would write her a bit of a reference. Mrs Kearns was kind, and she might give her that to make her chances of getting a position a bit easier. Well, it was more than she deserved but…

Her reverie was interrupted by the sudden stop of the carriage as Jimmy drew them level with the back door.

'Let's get you cleaned up a bit before you see the mistress,' said Mrs Kearns with a sigh.

Mary ran upstairs and quickly washed her face and hands and brushed her hair. She put on her maid's uniform and tied her hair neatly under her cap. She'd have a proper wash later on, but for now, she didn't want to keep the mistress waiting.

Quaking with fear, she left her little room. Tentatively she knocked on the drawing room door.

'Come in.'

'Ma'am.' Mary's voice was barely audible, her eyes downcast.

'Aah, Mary. You're back! Thank God for that. You poor girl – what an ordeal it must have been for you.' Mrs Grant's tone was full of concern.

'Mrs. Grant, ma'am, I'm so sorry. I am so ashamed of myself. After all you've done for me…' Mary began.

'Nonsense, child. What you did was very brave. Mrs Carmody's girl – Eileen, is it? She came and told me everything. This situation with the locked-out workers' families is simply intolerable. That those women and men agreed to send their little ones away to a foreign county because they cannot afford to feed them is difficult enough, but for the priests to stand at the quayside, with their religious militia, stopping these already heartbroken families, is nothing short of outrageous. I know that you and your friends were not involved directly, but the fact that you risked your own personal safety to protect those innocent children… Well, I am so proud of you. The employers of this city, my own husband included, should be ashamed of themselves for having created this situation in the first place.'

Mary had no idea what to say. It was an incredible thing that Mrs Grant wasn't angry, but to have her so supportive was totally unexpected.

'I know people think that someone of my class should support the employers, but let me assure you, I am not unique in my views, and many more than I feel this way. We as employers have a moral responsibility to those in our employ, and under the current system, that responsibility is too often being thoroughly shirked. People are entitled to decent work – isn't that what Mr Larkin says?'

Mary was used to hearing her employer quoting Jim Larkin, the bane of the middle and upper-classes' lives. He regularly spoke and blamed them for the deplorable conditions endured by the poor of the city.

'I suppose it is, ma'am, but I just saw those little ones in the middle of all that fighting and I knew they were going to get hurt if someone didn't take them out of it. Rory – that's Eileen, Mrs Carmody's girl's brother – ran in and we just followed.' Mary didn't want Mrs Grant to think she routinely involved herself in street brawls, whatever the cause.

'Yes, I believe his employers, the Royal Marine Hotel, have seen to it that he was released without charge also. Some guests witnessed his actions and recommended to the manager there that they intervene. I'm just glad you weren't hurt, my dear.'

Relief flooded through Mary as she realised she was not to be dismissed, and that Rory was safe.

'Ma'am, about the beautiful coat and hat you lent me. I'm afraid they're ruined. I can pay you something for them now, and perhaps you could withhold my pay until 'tis paid off. I'm sure the coat was very expensive, but if you'll allow me to pay that way, I'll work very hard until…'

Mrs. Grant waved her hand. 'Not at all. As I said, it never suited me. It is a pity, though, as it was perfectly lovely on you. There won't be any need to pay it back. It was a birthday gift, remember? Please, don't think of it again. Now, Mr Grant will be home shortly, and I think it would be best if he remained ignorant of the happenings of the past day and night, don't you? So if you would run along and help Mrs Kearns now, in case he notices anything untoward. But as soon as you are able, have a bath and get to bed. You must be exhausted. And Mary, well done.'

Mary backed out of the little drawing room and almost skipped downstairs to the kitchen. Mrs Kearns looked up from her gravy and instructed Mary to lay the joint to rest on the slab on the sideboard. The next hour was spent running up and downstairs with bowls and platters. The Grants had company for dinner that night. As she stood in the corner of the room, having served coffee and petit fours, she overheard the men's conversation.

Mr. Grant and his guest William Martin Murphy were discussing the difficulties of continuing business as usual without a workforce.

'Well, there is always the option of bringing in workers from England. I'm considering it because I'll never get these contracts filled otherwise. Dublin Castle won't wait forever. They can get the uniforms made in England just as easily, and then where would I be?'

Mary could hear the frustration in Mr Grant's voice.

'If that troublemaker Larkin had kept away, we wouldn't be facing this disaster now. They are blaming us, you know – blaming us because their children are starving and disease is rife. These people had jobs, decent jobs with fair wages, and it wasn't good enough for Larkin and his ilk. He's making us out to be blood-sucking tyrants when what we are is businessmen trying to keep our enterprises afloat in what are very difficult economic conditions. He's never run a business, yet he has the audacity to tell me how to run mine.' Mr Murphy was incensed.

Mrs. Grant interjected, 'There were riots today at Kingstown, the priests refusing to allow the locked-out workers' children on the boat to England. There were terrible scenes, it seems.'

Mr. Grant looked at her with distain. 'Yes, well, what they do or don't do with their children is their own business, and we should have no part in it. In any case, like most things, it was probably overexaggerated and typically sensationalised by women. Jeremy Johnson, a captain in Dublin Castle, is a friend of mine from the club. He said the police were being set upon even by the little brats they were trying to get on the boat. They breed like rats in those tenements, and they rear the children with no respect for law and order.'

Mrs Grant caught Mary's eye and gave her the faintest of smiles.

A short while later, having seen the Murphys out, Mary cleared the remaining glasses and ashtrays from the small sitting room where the last embers of a fire were glowing. She was dead on her feet, having had virtually no sleep the night before. Mr Grant had retired for the night, but the mistress was reading a newspaper on the Queen Anne chair beside the hearth. As Mary bade her goodnight, Mrs Grant called her back, indicating that she should take a seat. Nervously, she placed the full tray on the side table and perched on the matching fireside chair facing her employer. She felt awkward sitting in the presence of the mistress. *Perhaps she has rethought her earlier generosity.*

'Mary, I have been thinking, and here is something I want to ask you. I am trusting you that it will go no further than between ourselves.'

Mary's heart thumped loudly. While Mrs Grant had always been a kind employer, and she trusted her well enough to discuss political issues, they had never had an intimate conversation.

'Yes, ma'am, of course,' she half whispered.

'Why did you do what you did yesterday?' She fixed Mary with a direct gaze.

'Well, ma'am, I don't know.' Mary was unsure of what to say next. Perhaps she had misjudged the situation earlier and Mrs Grant was not as understanding as she first seemed. 'It just seems wrong, I suppose. Those men and women – fathers and mothers – weren't giving their children away on a whim. They have to, and… Well, they were so frightened I just had to help them. None of this is their fault.'

'And what do you think about the situation here? Politically, I mean.'

Mary knew she was being tested. Eileen had warned her about this. Mr Grant was a hard employer at his textile company and notorious throughout the city, but his wife was her own woman underneath it all. One time Mary had questioned the cook on the volume of stew she was making for Mr and Mrs Grant, and Mrs

Kearns told her that the mistress instructed her to give food out at the kitchen door to anyone who needed it. As time went on, Mary noticed that the household regularly overordered from the grocer and butcher. Mr Grant paid all the bills and never questioned them, so it was his wife's way of helping the destitute of the city.

'I don't know much about it, really, but I suppose I think that each country should have control of their own destiny and not be dictated to by anyone else.'

She knew if Rory heard her, he would have been proud. The thought emboldened her to continue. 'I only know what I read, but it seems that if this situation, with the workers locked out, continues, things are going to get even worse than they are now.'

Mrs. Grant smiled. 'Quite.' She looked at Mary for a long moment, as if weighing up what she was going to say next.

'Mary, I am a member of an organisation, an organisation of women who have dedicated themselves to the Irish cause. We support the Irish Volunteers, and while we are an independent group, we seek – through force of arms, if necessary – to free Ireland of slavery. Irishmen *and* Irishwomen.'

Mary didn't know what to say. Clearly Mr Grant knew nothing of his wife's allegiance to this group.

'The young man with you yesterday, when you were arrested – do you know him?' Mrs Grant's question was direct but gentle.

'Yes, ma'am. That was, is, Rory. Rory O'Dwyer, Eileen's brother. He met us when we went to Kingstown because he works in the Royal Marine Hotel.' Mary was anxious that Mrs Grant realise there was nothing untoward going on. Fraternising with the opposite sex while in service in a respectable house usually meant instant dismissal. Sister Margaret had warned her of that.

'Yes, indeed, but what you may not know is that he is also an active member of the Volunteers. It is young men like your friend Rory who will hopefully free this country. My father, who has long since passed, was in the Land League and fought against the oppression of the tenant farmers by rack-rent landlords. It was something I didn't feel necessary to disclose to my husband when we married, and now I'm afraid we rather find ourselves at opposite sides of the political debate. As you may have gathered, there is no love, or even passing affection, between the master and me. When I met him, at a dance in Galway, he seemed so sophisticated. He was my ticket out of the countryside and up to the city. My father was away in England while we were courting, and my mother was anxious for the match, given he was so wealthy, so she encouraged it. I foolishly thought we could grow to feel something for each other, but he just wanted a son – which I am seemingly incapable of producing. So there is nothing between us. He cares only for profit, not for people...not for me. Anyway, you must be wondering why I've brought you up here and divulged so much to you.'

She paused, composing carefully what she was going to say next. 'You see, to my mind, the strike, the Lockout, all of it, is a sign, a portent of things to come. At long last the Irish are saying "Enough is enough". We will be treated as subhuman no longer. But we need manpower, and womanpower too. We can do it if we unite. I need my husband's money and influence to help the cause, but of course, discretion is paramount. If he were to find out my activities, there would be very serious consequences. He is not known for compassion. I have plans – big plans – to relieve my husband of some of his wealth and, shall we say, redirect it into channels more deserving. I need someone to be my right-hand woman. Someone I can trust to communicate with others, to represent me when I cannot be there. And Mary, due to the bravery and tenacity you showed yesterday, combined with what I know of you since you've been with us, I want you to consider being that person.'

Mary was nonplussed with the whole outlandish conversation. Mrs Grant revealing the details of her problematic marriage to a maid was shocking enough, but all this about the Volunteers and Irish freedom and the like... Mary was amazed. Earlier she had been expecting, at best, a severe reprimand for having got herself arrested and drawing the Grant household into disrepute, or at worst, to be instantly dismissed. But it appeared that Mrs Grant was asking her to get involved in something she knew nothing about, but seemed very dangerous.

'Ma'am, you see, the thing is... I only did what anyone would have yesterday. The little children were being crushed by the crowds, and they were terrified. I didn't do it for any other reason...' Mary was at a loss as to how to respond.

Mrs. Grant smiled. 'Mary, my dear, this is all highly irregular, I know. You've had a very sheltered upbringing, and while you've been taught well how to be of service, and your manners and demeanour are impeccable and entirely fitting for a maid, I imagine your experience or knowledge of the world outside of the convent is minimal.'

Mary remained silent, but nodded slightly.

'As I thought.' Mrs Grant sat forward and held both of Mary's hands. 'Mary, my dear, we are living in very interesting times. Very interesting, but also very dangerous. This country of ours has been oppressed for far too long. Britain has had a stranglehold of Ireland for so long, and they have created a horrifically repressive society where even Irishmen, such as my husband, feel it is in some way justified to reduce those worse off than themselves to still further depths of poverty and deprivation. And do you know why they do it? Why men like my husband and William Martin Murphy bleed the workers white? It is so we can live like this –' Mrs Grant waved her hand around the sumptuous room '– and you and your class can slave and enjoy no such quality of life. I may have been born into a different class than you, Mary, but I hate everything about it. In my eyes, we are all born equal and we should die that way. No one is better or worse than anyone else. We, the Volunteers and the women who support them, are seeking not simply to solve the problems of poverty and oppression. No, we want more than that. But Mary, what we seek has eluded our ancestors for centuries. We seek the total removal of Britain from Irish affairs. We want a Republic where we – and we alone, Irishmen and women – are the sole masters of our fate. Answerable to nobody but ourselves. We want to live in a country where the dignity of every man, woman and child of our state is respected and protected. A country where every child born under the Irish flag, irrespective of the economic circumstances of their parents, is cherished and protected. But we need help, and we need it from every part of society on the island. Will you help, Mary?'

Mrs. Grant's eyes glistened with emotion and determination. Mary sensed the deep conviction in the woman and was moved by it. The ideas that Mrs Grant had – about people being equal and it not being fair the way some people were so well off while others suffered – had never really occurred to her until she came to Dublin. She found herself thinking of all the children that grew up in the convent. From the moment they could understand, they knew they were worth much less than a child with parents who had a home of their own. She herself thought she was so lucky to have a job in a nice house like this, but the idea that she could – in theory, at least – be a mistress of such a house was inconceivable. The poverty in Dublin was unbearable to watch: Women wearily walking the streets with scraps of infants too weak even to cry, children barefoot and barely clothed despite the bitter cold, shoved aside on the footpath to make way for ladies and gentlemen in their finery. Mrs Grant was right, it wasn't fair. Suddenly Rory came to her mind. He spoke with the same conviction that day on the pier, before all the drama with the protests.

Mrs. Grant waited silently for her answer. On one level Mary was terrified, but her employer was asking something of her and she really couldn't refuse. She thought about her life so far, how she had never envisaged a future beyond mere survival before, but now, here were people like Mrs Grant, like Rory, telling her things could be different. The one night she had spent in prison was terrifying, and if she were to involve herself in anything that was to challenge the regime, the consequences could be much worse. She had witnessed firsthand the ferocity of the Dublin Metropolitan Police on the pier at Kingstown, and from reading the papers, she knew the British would tolerate nothing even re-sembling dissent.

'I'll do it.' She spoke quietly, but without fear. 'I don't know if I'll be good enough, but I'll try to help you, whatever way I can.'

# CHAPTER 12

The day following her visit to the old lady in Richmond Hill, Scarlett found herself thinking about the flag... How strange that the last time she heard the name Boland's Mills was years before. She doubted she would have remembered the name of it if anyone had asked her.

She began by researching Boland's Mills. The first entry on the Google search gave a Wikipedia entry. It was in Dublin – the capital city of Ireland – and the mill was one of the locations of the 1916 Easter Rising. It was claimed by Éamon de Valera, one of the leaders of the Rising for the Irish Republic, and de Valera's forces had occupied the mill at the start of the rebellion. The location was selected in order to cover the southeastern approaches to the city.

Ok, she surmised, Dan did make the right connection – at least with this Éamon de Valera guy. She remembered thinking as a kid how the name sounded more Spanish or Italian than Irish. Scarlett read for hours, refreshing her memory of Irish history, learning that after centuries of oppression of the Irish by the English, and several failed attempts at liberation, a group of disparate agitators, from shopkeepers to poets, communists to Catholics, decided to strike once more for Irish freedom. They were called the Irish Volunteers, and on Easter Monday 1916 they, along with the socialist Irish Citizen's Army and Cumann na mBan, mobilised into an army which would take over the General Post Office in the centre of Dublin, as well as other strategic locations, and declare Ireland free of Britain.

The timing was better than previous attempts due to pressure placed on England, which was, by then, heavily embroiled in the First World War. A Proclamation of Independence was issued, and the British forces in the city reacted with brutal outrage at the revolutionaries' audacity. The fighting went on for a week. The city was destroyed and the death toll rose rapidly. Eventually, the leaders had no option but to surrender. They were outnumbered, and they were no match for the resources of the largest and most powerful Empire the world had ever seen. They surrendered to the British and emerged into the streets outside the various garrisons they had commandeered during the ill-fated Rising.

Scarlett quickly trawled through the various websites dedicated to the Irish struggle for independence and realised just how much she didn't know. She found the subject interesting, and she never ceased to marvel at the conviction felt by those who, despite all the odds, take on those who oppress them. She'd read about it in the former Soviet states as they seceded from the stranglehold of the Soviet Union one by one. And she'd watched with fascination the revolutions of recent years in North Africa. The plight of woefully mismatched Palestinians as they took on the might of Israel – with its powerful and wealthy friends – even when it wasn't politically expedient to do so, was something that touched her deeply. The passion of those who fight against injustice, even paying the ultimate price, always stirred her, and those feelings began to emerge as she read about those Irish who believed that they had right on their side and cared enough, not just for themselves, but for the future generations.

Eileen had been so tired and drained when she was with her, so Scarlett didn't press her for the story, but she was intrigued by the flag and what it meant. She trawled the websites for mention of a flag. She didn't know how old Eileen was, possibly ninety or thereabouts, and this flag had been owned by her mother in Dublin in 1916, almost 100 years ago.

She would call her during the morning to check if she was ok. She couldn't explain why she had taken this old lady to her heart, but she had. She had cleaned up her kitchen and put things right in her house as best she could, and promised to drive her to purchase replacements for the items that had been stolen.

Her phone rang: Lorena. Scarlett groaned and pressed Answer on the screen.

'Hi, Mom.'

'Scarlett, I've been going out of my mind! Where are you? Fr Ennio and I were waiting for you last night to do the novena to St. Jude. Don't go crazy now, but we were thinking that maybe your recent behaviour could be explained by demons?' Lorena's voice was rushed, breathy.

'Er... demons. Really?' Scarlett sighed.

'Yes, Scarlett, demons. Just because the younger generation like to think that hell and demons don't exist doesn't mean that it's true. The devil makes work for idle hands, you know. He is moving among us, urging us to commit the most grievous sins, and sometimes we are powerless in the face of such demonic pressure. Fr Ennio and I are planning to go to Mexico, actually, to pray for strength to be God's army on earth against these forces of evil. I mean, why else would a good, God-fearing girl decide to become an adulterer, succumbing to carnal lust with a married man, married in front of Our Lord...'

Scarlett let her rant on about demonic influences without interruption. She was scrolling through the website of the Irish Military Archives, reading firsthand reports of the Irish Revolution, or 'Rising,' as it was known. There might be a great story to be told about Eileen and her flag, maybe something that would kick-start her career again. In the run-up to the centenary of the Easter Rising, there was huge interest in the United States about all things Irish.

'Scarlett! Scarlett! Are you listening to me?' Lorena's tone changed.

'Yes, yes, I am,' Scarlett answered resignedly.

'So? Will you do it?' Lorena was belligerent.

'Do what?'

'Oh, for goodness' sake, Scarlett, will you allow Fr Ennio to exorcise the demons from your body, cleansing your soul of this most terrible sin?'

'Aah. I'm not sure I can fit that in, Mom. I have to help this old lady whose house was burglarised...'

'And that's more important than your soul burning in hell for all eternity, is it? Well that's fine. You are coming here for lunch next Sunday anyway. We arranged that, so I'll be sure Fr Ennio comes too. He can perform the rite then and there, and then we can all have a nice lunch. I'll make my chicken Creole. You love that.' Lorena sounded pleased with herself.

Before Scarlett had time to object to the bizarre Sunday afternoon activity, Lorena had hung up.

She sat with her phone in her hand for a moment, thinking about her mother. She admitted she had given Lorena a wide berth for the last few years, focusing on her career. Then the whole thing with Charlie was so all consuming, and Lorena would never have understood. Maybe it was time to pay a bit more attention to her. She was clearly getting into the religion thing in a really big way.

Lorena loved all the dramatics of Catholicism. It appealed to her fanciful nature, and Scarlett was almost grateful to the Church for keeping her mother so occupied. Just lately, though, she was coming out with some really odd things, even for her. This Fr Ennio guy was featuring very heavily too. Scarlett had never met him, but perhaps it was time she did. The prospect of a lunch with her mother and her pet priest was awful, and to have some weird ritual added in for good measure filled her with dread, but she decided she'd better go and see what was going on with Lorena. How is it, she thought guiltily, that she could feel such affection for Eileen, whom she'd only just met, and yet she seemed to want to avoid her own mother like the plague?

# CHAPTER 13

Scarlett sat in her sunny kitchen, savouring the old familiar feeling of getting to the bottom of a story. She couldn't explain it, but she just had a feeling about this flag thing. Initially she had only gone to see Eileen to keep Artie off her case – and to fill the long empty days. But since she met Eileen and saw the flag, she managed to go five minutes without thinking of Charlie. She missed him like a physical pain, and checked every text promptly in case it was from him. It still hurt like hell if she thought about the whole mess, but this with Eileen was something she could do, something to get her teeth into. He had called last night, briefly, to tell her that he was moving off the political scene for a while and was taking his family on an extended vacation to get out of the media spotlight. The mention of his family sent a stab to her heart. She was silent as he explained his plans.

'You understand, don't you, Red?' he said, using his pet name for her. 'You know I'd rather be with you, but I have to try to clear this up. Julia wants to have a bit of normality for the kids, and show the country a united front.'

'Sure,' she said, knowing she sounded like a grumpy teenager.

'Don't be like that, Scarlett – all Vivien Leigh and hurt and dramatic. You know if I could be with you, I would be.'

Scarlett heard the edge in his voice. Charlie was impatient and had low tolerance for those who weren't seduced by his charm, even when he was totally in the wrong. Scarlett knew that to push the point that she felt betrayed would only antagonise him further. At least a few phone calls and texts were better than nothing. Everything in Charlie's life was made right by those around him, his wife, Scarlett, Sam. Even now they were protecting him. Scarlett wondered why people like Charlie seemed to not be subject to the same inconveniences or pain as ordinary mortals.

The press had backed off in recent days, chasing the next big scandal. A young socialite was found dead in her apartment in Manhattan three days ago, and Scarlett felt an inappropriate gratitude to the girl.

'So, Red, what are you doing with yourself these days without me around taking up your time?' he murmured. 'Entertaining yourself somehow?'

His low, sexy chuckle caused Scarlett's stomach to flip over. 'Well, I'm doing a little bit of work for Artie. Remember my old boss? And seeing my mother, that kind of stuff.' She tried to inject some breeziness into her voice. She was about to tell him about Eileen and the flag when he cut across her thoughts.

'Great. Are the reporters still camped outside?'

'Uh...no. There were one or two yesterday, but that homicide downtown seems to have taken the heat off, thank God.' She wished she could shake the niggling feeling that his concern was less for her welfare and more on how to limit possible further damage.

'Good, good. You're doing great, Red, really great. Just don't say anything to anyone and try to be a neutral as possible when you are out. You know how they can get a shot of you laughing or sad or something and blow it out of all proportion.' He paused. 'So, how about those plans you mentioned, to do a bit of travelling? Great opportunity for you now that you've no ties. No work ties, I mean,' he added hastily.

Was he trying to get rid of her? She dismissed the idea immediately. Charlie loved her – of course he did.

'No,' she said slowly, trying to decide the best thing to tell him. 'I'm kind of getting into a story for Artie – just a local thing, but it's something and so I'm gonna stay put for a while.'

His hesitation was palpable. 'Oh, right. I didn't realise it was an actual job. I thought you just dropped by and he got you to do something. Yeah, that's great, good. I'm glad.'

His words were contradicted by his tone, and she tried to tell herself she was imagining it. They were both all over the place. 'I'd love to see you.' She tried not to sound pathetic.

'Me too, Red, me too, but you know what it's like. I'm being watched 24/7. This whole thing is at a very delicate stage. How things go down in the next few weeks will decide the way the electorate reacts to the story. It's vital we play this right.'

*Weeks.* She knew how it was, but she hoped

he'd find some way to see her. The idea of not seeing him for weeks filled her with misery. She heard murmuring in the background. He surely was alone if he was calling her?

'Who was that?' she asked.

'Who?' he answered smoothly.

'A voice, like someone talking to you while you're talking to me.' There was no way he would allow anyone to hear him on the phone. She wondered if the phones were being hacked.

'No, there's nobody here. Must have been the TV. I have it on behind me. So anyway, Red, I have to go. You're doing such a great job. Just keep doing what you're doing and we'll talk again soon, ok?' She could have sworn she heard the murmuring voice again.

'And be careful of anyone approaching you. Hacks are using all kinds of stunts, but hey, who am I telling, eh?'

He chuckled, but she was hurt by the implication that she was the kind of journalist who used stunts to trick people into divulging things to her. That wasn't her style at all, but she bit back the words of admonishment. She only had a few precious moments on the phone with him every few days. She didn't want to waste it arguing.

'Ok, bye, Charlie.' She waited for him to tell her he loved her. She couldn't say it first.

'Bye, Red. Take care.' And the line went dead.

# CHAPTER 14

SEPTEMBER 1914

*M*ary watched the miserable hordes of people queuing up at Liberty Hall from a cheap café across the street. Countess Markievicz had set up a soup kitchen to feed the poor and the hungry, but even with her considerable assets, and the support of some of her gentry friends, supplies were short. The police kept records of anyone connected with the labour movement and were likely just to pick suspect people up on a whim. There was a lot of patrolling going on, so Mary decided to bide her time before trying to get into the building. The authorities knew that Liberty Hall was a meeting point for the union and watched those who entered carefully.

Mrs. Grant said that there was to be an event on in Dublin Castle this afternoon, so military presence on the street would be diminished. If Mary was stopped by the police, she was to claim that she was hoping to volunteer at the soup kitchen and thought she should go around the back. The banner across the front of the building that read 'We Serve Neither King nor Kaiser, but Ireland' always gave her courage.

As she sipped her cup of tea, she thought back to the first Cumann na mBan meeting last April in Wynne's Hotel. She'd felt so out of place in the sumptuous surroundings, but Mrs Grant had spoken so well and with such passion that she found herself gaining more and more courage with every passing minute. These women – some of them university professors and doctors, and the daughters of wealthy Protestants, but many more from the working class – were gathered to set up a council of Irish-women. They talked about getting the vote, something Mary had found exhilarating, but more importantly about how it wasn't enough for the women of Ireland to sit at home and wait patiently while the men made a bid for Irish freedom.

They would form a group, one to work alongside the Volunteers and do more than just knit socks and cook dinners. The proposals the women made were so exciting. Women could learn first aid, make stretchers, learn to drive ambulances, and raise money to equip the men with weapons and uniforms. She could recall vividly the fire in Mrs Grant's eyes when she spoke about the absolute need to remove Britain from Irish affairs. How the Irish were entitled to rule themselves, and to cherish all the children of the nation equally. Mary wished Rory could have heard it.

Mr. Grant had remained ignorant to his wife's political fervour until the day after the mistress's public speech. Though she was magnificent, Mary was worried what the master would do if he found out what his wife was involved in, something he would see as treasonous. He was as loyal to the king of England as anyone from London or Liverpool. As they went home after the speech, the mistress was so elated at the response by the women of Dublin that she gave no thought to the consequences of her actions.

Mary still shuddered when she thought about

it, and it would remain forever etched on her mind. On the day after the meeting, life in the Grant house was exactly as normal until the master stormed in the front door two hours early, almost knocking Mary aside as she polished the parquet in the hall. Mrs Grant was in the drawing room, alone. Mary heard the door slamming upstairs and then the scream. Mrs Kearns came running from the kitchen at the sound, and together they stood in horrified silence as the banging and crashing from the drawing room was interrupted only by the anguished cries of the mistress and the roars of the master.

They looked at each other as the minutes and violence ticked on, terrified and unsure of what to do. Furniture was being thrown, glass smashing, and the shouting and screaming was relentless. Should they get the police? Mrs Kearns was rooted to the spot, but Mary realised that if she didn't do something, the master was surely going to kill the mistress.

She ran – without any real plan – up the passageway to the drawing room and burst in, just in time to see him throwing his wife to the floor. He had ripped her dress, leaving her body exposed, and was about to unbutton his trousers. His intentions were clear. Mary grabbed the first thing she could see – an onyx statue of a leaping trout.

'Get away from her!' she shouted. The master turned and the mixture of shock and rage on his face sent a bolt of terror through Mary.

'You little bitch!' he roared. 'How dare you tell me what to do in my house. Get out before I...'

Mrs. Grant tried to get up, but he punched her in the face and blood spurted from her nose. Mary ran and hit him as hard as she could on the temple with the statue. He fell sideways, stumbling on the hearth of the fireplace.

He lay on his back staring up at her, his trousers open and his hair dishevelled, incredulous at her audacity.

'Mrs. Kearns is getting the constable, and I saw him pass by only a minute ago so he'll be here any second now.' Mary was amazed that any sound came out of her mouth at all, but her words had the effect of diffusing the situation.

Downstairs, there were voices.

He got up, walked right up to Mary, and stared into her face. 'You'll pay for this, by God, I'll see to it that you pay dearly.'

He marched past the women as if they didn't exist and stopped momentarily at the looking glass in the hallway to remedy his appearance. He buttoned his trousers, tucked his shirt and straightened his jacket and tie. Then he removed a hairbrush from the hall stand and calmly brushed his sparse hair into place. Once he was happy with his reflection, he placed his hat firmly upon his head, walked out and slammed the front door.

Mrs. Grant was seated on the fireside chair, her hair hanging about her face. Her dress and undergarments had been torn from her body, and she was bleeding profusely from her nose. Mary took a shawl that was lying on the back of the chaise longue and wrapped it around the lady who had shown her such kindness, feeling helpless.

'Thank you, Mary, dear,' Mrs Grant whispered as the housekeeper entered the room.

'Ma'am, Jimmy went for the constable but he couldn't find him. Should we get the doctor this time?'

Mrs Kearns hesitated. Scandal was to be avoided at all costs. As Mary caught the glance between her employer and the old cook, she realised this was not the first time this had happened.

'No, thank you, Mrs Kearns. I'll be fine. If you could just help me to my bedroom, and Mary, perhaps you could run a bath for me.' She winced as she tried to stand.

Mrs. Grant saw her pale and smiled weakly. 'No one said it was going to be easy, Mary. There are going to be battles everywhere, some with uniformed men and weapons and others in the drawing rooms of the wealthy. Either way, blood must be shed and lives lost if necessary. My husband disagrees with my ideology, but that is to be expected. What we will... No, what we must achieve will destroy everything he holds dear. It is inevitable that he would resist.'

'But ma'am, you're bleeding...' Mary protested.

'It matters not a jot, my dear. More blood than mine will be shed setting Ireland free. Now if you could help me rise, I'll try to clean myself up. I'm meeting someone later to discuss the future plans for the movement, and I can't look like this.'

'Aah, Mrs Grant, you can't go out now, not like this. What if the master finds out...' Mrs Kearns was pleading.

'We shall just have to be extra careful then, won't we? My husband cares nothing for me, we all know that, but having his wife, his property – as he sees me – publicly speaking out against the kind of tyranny he metes out, and now my stance on the Irish Republic… Well, you saw how he reacted. Someone let out a jibe about men controlling their wives at his club and he was incensed. At my actions, of course, but possibly more at the fact that I defied him. He and his cronies want everything to remain exactly as it is now. He won't want a scandal, however, so I think as long as I keep my involvement more low profile, everything will continue as it was.'

Shaking her head, Mrs Kearns went to fetch some warm water and antiseptic ointment while muttering how no good could come of this.

Left alone with Mary, Mrs Grant spoke urgently. 'I need you to be my eyes and ears, Mary, now more than ever. The freedom I've enjoyed up to now will, I fear, be severely curtailed by my husband. I daren't risk antagonising him further, not because of fear, but without my help financially, the movement will suffer. I must maintain my marriage, as it protects us, you see. The British would blanch at the idea of arresting or mistreating someone of my status, and while we, and women like us, remain free, we can achieve great things.'

'But ma'am, how can you go on? He'll kill you the next time.' Mary was anguished. Mrs Grant's face was swelling quickly, and a large clump of hair had been pulled out of the side of her head.

'No, he might injure me, but he won't kill me. He couldn't bear the scandal – police and courts and so on. Dear me, no! Now, to more pressing matters. Perhaps Mrs Kearns is right. I must look frightful, so I'll remain at home, but you can go in my stead, my dear. I need you to bring this to Liberty Hall. It's a note, and deliver it straight into the hands of Mrs Sheehy-Skeffington. Do you think you can do that? We are living in dangerous times, my dear. Exercise extreme caution, and place the note under your bodice. The police won't search a young lady, and anyway there's a ceremony in the Castle this afternoon, so many of them will be attending that.' Handing her a small folded piece of paper, Mrs Grant squeezed Mary's hand.

Mary watched the army move on towards the Castle. She left the café, skirting around the ever-growing queue for food to the back door as she had been instructed. She mounted the stairs, unsure of where to go. She had seen Mrs Sheehy-Skeffington at the first meeting of Cumann na mBan, but wasn't sure she would recognise her. As she reached a landing, she heard muffled voices behind a large panelled door.

Tentatively she knocked, mentally preparing her speech.

'Yes? Who are you?' The man who opened the door was very tall and thin with unkempt grey hair protruding over his ears. He was wearing a shirt without a coat or tie, and his trousers were tucked into heavy boots. His accent was rough and Mary quaked inside.

'I have a message for Mrs Sheehy-Skeffington.' She spoke barely audibly. She was worried how she could remove the note from down her bodice in front of this man.

'Mary!' The door opened wider and she looked up in amazement.

'Hello, Rory.' She smiled shyly.

'Come in, girl. What brings you around here? Are you joining up with the Citizen Army?' He laughed.

Rory led Mary by the arm towards a battered-looking desk where a third man sat. He was poring over a paper, and it wasn't until he looked up that she recognised the round face and bushy moustache of James Connolly, leader of the Cit-izen Army and a co-agitator with Jim Larkin during the Lockout of the previous year.

'Mr Connolly,' began Rory, 'I'd like to intro-duce a friend of mine, Mary Doyle. She and my sister Eileen were with me when we got arrested that time at the dock in Kingstown.'

James Connolly stood up and came around the desk, his hand outstretched. 'A pleasure to meet you, Miss Doyle. I have no fear for the future of our nation with yourself and young Rory here leading the way. Now, can we do something for you?'

Mary gulped back her nerves. 'Yes, sir. I'm to deliver a message to Mrs Sheehy-Skeffington.'

'Well, leave it with Rory there and he'll see she gets it.'

He spoke kindly, but she knew she was being dismissed. Connolly left the room to discuss something with the tall man. When they were gone, she tried to avert her eyes from Rory. She hadn't seen him since the day on the pier. Though she'd imagined several times in her head what it would be like to see him again, she was now burning with embarrassment. Eileen had met him a few times, but only briefly. He was very busy with the movement, she said.

'So, Mary, where's the note?' Rory smiled innocently.

'You'll have to turn around,' she was just barely able to mutter.

'What? Oh…oh, I see…' Rory grinned and

turned his back to her while she dug deep into the bodice of her dress, extracting the note.

Handing it to Rory, she gathered her courage to speak again. 'I'm glad they let you out – the last time, I mean.' She felt foolish.

'More fool them.' He grinned. 'Out to do more mischief! Well, I'm glad your Mrs Grant was able to rescue you. 'Twasn't too bad, was it?' he asked.

'No, then, 'twas fine. A bit smelly and too many women in there, but I survived.' She smiled.

'Well, at least 'twas winter time. The jails get fairly unbearable in the heat. The cold keeps the smell down, they say! Sure you're made of tough stuff, and I knew it the first time I met you. It's lovely to see you again, Mary, but I have to go. I'm only here on an errand myself, but maybe we could go for a walk on Sunday? All three of us. I mean, Eileen too?'

He looked like an eager little boy and his blue eyes twinkled in his tanned face. His hair had grown a bit longer than when she'd seen him last, but he seemed older somehow. She'd longed to ask Eileen about him, but was afraid to. She was lovely and such a good friend, but Mary had her doubts that she'd be too happy at a girl from an orphanage setting her cap at nice, respectable Rory O'Dwyer.

'That would be lovely,' she said. 'I'm off this Sunday, actually,' she continued, praying she wasn't being too forward. She was glad he suggested Eileen go as well. She wouldn't know what to say to him if they were alone.

'Oh, this Sunday I've to go down the country.' He looked disappointed. 'I can't really go into it, but maybe the Sunday after that?'

'I only get every second Sunday off,' Mary offered, trying to hide her regret.

'Well, that next Sunday so. There's a small bit of heat left in the days now and sure 'twill be something to look forward to. We could go out to Howth on the tram, or maybe even up to the zoo? Were you ever there?'

Mary suppressed the urge to laugh. No, she'd never been to a zoo, or anywhere. The nuns didn't do things like that – take them on outings or anything. They went to school and Mass, and they worked. That was their life. The idea of any entertainment, planning something, anything the children would enjoy, was laughable.

'No, Rory, I've never been to the zoo. But I'd love to go. I'll pay for myself, of course…'

'Indeed, and you will not. No, Miss Doyle, we are going to have a grand day, the three of us. We might even manage a bit of a picnic? I'll meet yourself and Eileen off the tram on Sackville Street, and we'll stroll up to Phoenix Park and have a day out for ourselves. Now, I'd love to stay, but I really must go.' He turned on his heel to go down the stairs. He stopped and turned back to where she was standing. 'I can't wait to see you again, Mary.' And he winked and was gone.

SHE COULDN'T BELIEVE IT. She lay in bed at night dreaming up ways she might run into Rory, but she knew it was just a dream. No matter how hard she tried to forget him, she thought about him constantly, but she was too timid to mention it to Eileen. She had no right to have notions about someone like Rory. They would often sit in the Grants's kitchen in the evenings and drink tea, a luxury afforded very few maids, but Mrs Kearns enjoyed listening to their chatter. Eileen popped in and out from Carmodys, whenever she got a moment, for a chat. Mrs Kearns was, Mary learnt, well aware of the mistress' politics and had covered for her on more than one occasion when the master came home to an empty house. Mary thought she would have been in disgrace for her involvement with anything political, but the truth was that in that house, political dissention got the tacit approval of the housekeeper. It was one of the many reasons Mrs Kearns liked Eileen so much. She was becoming more and more involved with the women's council, and their talk in the evenings inevitably came round to topics such as women's suffrage, or the role women could play in bringing about independence. The housekeeper oversaw the conversation and didn't allow it get too radical. She was a kind but strict woman who would tolerate no silliness or improper chatter about romance, so even if Mary wanted to ask Eileen about Rory, she couldn't without raising the eyebrows of Mrs Kearns in disapproval.

The two did go walking on their day off sometimes, but Eileen was so enthusiastic about the cause and the fight for freedom that the conversation usually went that way. She mentioned Rory often, of course. He was a member of the Irish Volunteers, and she told Mary how he'd asked her to make a uniform for him. The pride Eileen felt in her brother glowed out of her when she spoke of him. She explained to Mary that there was an official uniform made in Cork, but it was too expensive, so Eileen and Rory together saved enough money for the serge cloth in exactly the right shade, and most evenings she sat in her room and sewed until she'd produced a very good replica, complete with brass buttons adorned with the Irish harp. She kept her political opinions secret from her employers. The Carmodys were good people who treated their staff well enough, but they were firmly behind the union, with Britain. Their delight when their eldest son joined up the day war broke out said it all. When Eileen dusted his photo, in pride of place on the mantelpiece, she told Mary she silently asked him the same question every day: 'If you are so mad to fight, James Carmody, why not fight for something worth fighting for? In your own country, for your own people?'

His face beamed back at her, his face radiating pride. He was the same age as Rory, and though both boys were born and bred on this island, they were a million miles apart.

'You should have seen him, Mary,' Eileen said, eyes blazing in indignation, 'the day he left. Full of himself he was, like he was doing a great thing, going off to fight for the British king and the precious Empire. He couldn't see how he was being a traitor to his own country, not for a second could he understand – not his parents either. There they were, all standing for the photographs and his uniform all shiny and new. If they force our lads, bring in conscription, I mean, it will be a good thing you know.'

Mary was nonplussed. How could forcing young Irishmen into the British Army be a good thing? Eileen laughed at her friend's innocent face.

'See, if they force them, then it will be like a huge recruitment campaign for the Volunteers. Loads of lads are scared to join us, or forbidden to by their families to get involved for fear of what could happen to them, but if the alternative is to become cannon fodder for the king, then watch what happens! Just you watch and see. They'll come flocking to the tricolour and to the Volunteers, and then we'll have a serious chance of striking for freedom. It's within our grasp, Mary – a country of our own, where everyone is treated fairly and equally, women and girls too.'

Mary felt the passion with which Eileen spoke. The war in Europe, which was supposed to be over by Christmas, had dragged on for three months now with no sign of victory in sight. The British were going to need more recruits, and not everyone was as enthusiastic for slaughter as James Carmody, it seemed. Mr Redmond and the Parliamentary Party were advocating joining, but the Volunteers and Cumann na mBan were split on it. Mrs Grant and Eileen were vehemently opposed to helping the enemy in any way at all. And while Mary could see their point, she knew most of the boys and men that went to the front in British uniforms did it, not out of a sense of pride, but for the money. After the Lockout, many of Dublin's poor never really recovered. The workers went back, but the employers found their own subtle ways of punishing those who dared seek better conditions. The war meant an opportunity to make money, to feed their wives and children. She didn't share her friend's disdain for the men who joined up, but then Eileen never really understood what it was like to have nothing.

'It is hard for people though, Eileen,' she began. 'They come to the back door looking for scraps and they really are half-starved. You can't blame men for trying to feed their families. It's not as bad as it was during the Lockout, but people are still poor and children are still dying for the want of the doctor.'

'But can't you see, Mary, that for as long as the chains of imperialism bind us, it will always be that way? They'll never let us get strong enough to rise up. They have us where they want us, strong enough to work and make them richer, but too weak to fight for what's rightfully ours. By fighting their war for them, we're making them stronger and weakening ourselves. I do feel sorry for the poor people left with no other choice, of course I do, but joining up is only solving a short-term problem and making the bigger one even worse. No, we have to keep up the anti-recruitment campaign. Bring them into the Volunteers.'

Mary smiled. She and Eileen could talk like this for hours and she felt alive, like her opinion mattered to someone. Spotting a pair of Royal Irish Constabulary officers approaching, she rapidly changed the subject.

'How are your parents? Have you heard from them recently?'

The officers passed, ignoring them completely, but their presence alone was intimidating. The trees were shedding their foliage, and it was hard to imagine as they walked on a carpet of red, gold, and yellow leaves that such weighty matters were all around them. Mary tried not to dwell on the danger she was in if the authorities found out about her association with Cumann na mBan. While the organisation was not illegal as such, membership would not be something that the

RIC would find favourable. In addition, she gave what she could to the Defence of Ireland Fund, specifically set up to raise money for arms. Seeing police and soldiers on the street was commonplace, but it still gave her a shudder. At the mention of her parents, Eileen seemed to deflate.

Eileen told her how their parents were proud, but worried for their son's safety, and when she wrote and told them that she too was joining Cumann na mBan, her mother wrote back and begged her not to. Having her son in the Volunteers was one thing, but to have her daughter at the mercy of the British was too much for her to bear, it seemed. Her friend was visibly upset at hurting her mother and going against her wishes. Mary led her to a bench by a duck pond.

'I got this letter from my father.' Eileen took the note from her boot and handed it to Mary. The letter was short and the creases were frayed from having been read so often. Mary opened the page and began to read.

*My dearest Eileen-Óg,*

*Your mother tells me of your plans above in Dublin and I'm sure you know she's very vexed with you. I'm not a great one for writing, but I wanted to say this to you. I am filled with pride that my fine son and daughter have turned out to be such people as ye are. Ye face dangerous times, and your mother and myself and yer brothers and sisters will pray for you every night that God will keep ye safe and away from all harm.*

*God Bless,*
*Daddy*

MARY FOLDED the letter and returned it to her friend. Tears glistened in her eyes. Once again Mary felt deeply the loss of her parents. The love Eileen and Rory's parents had for them was something she never knew, and she envied her friend. Eileen put the letter back in her boot and squeezed Mary's hand.

'Someday I'll bring you to meet them. They'd be delighted with you, so they would.'

Mary had been delaying telling her friend about the meeting with Rory. She knew he had not met Eileen in a few weeks because she said he was very busy down the country, and she was dying to meet him and hear all his news.

'I met Rory last week, in Liberty Hall.' Her voice sounded rushed in her ears. Her heart was pounding, but she forced herself to go on. She was being silly, probably reading far too much into it.

'Did you? You never said.' Eileen was surprised.

'Well, I didn't like to say in front of Mrs Kearns. You know how she is if we mention boys.'

'Rory is hardly "boys," though. He's my brother. Anyway, how was he?' Eileen seemed ok, but curious.

'Oh, he was fine. I'm surprised he remembered me, actually. Sure we only met that one day on the pier, and with everything that happened after that, well, I was sure he'd have forgot me. Anyway he was in great form, heading down the country, as you said. I don't know why, obviously. He was with Mr Connolly, though, and he seemed to be very well thought of from what I could see.'

Eileen beamed with pride. 'He doesn't say. Not one for bragging is Rory, but he must be climbing the ranks if he's that close to the top brass, mustn't he? What else did he say?'

Mary knew she'd have to spit it out. 'Well, as I said, we only spoke for a few minutes, but he did ask if we would like to go on an outing three weeks on Sunday, to the zoo. All three of us, and bring a picnic maybe if it's not too cold.'

'Oh, but I can't go that Sunday.' Eileen was frustrated. 'I'm doing that extra first aid course on treating bullet wounds, remember? Mrs Sheehy-Skeffington asked me to do it, and then maybe teach a class on what I learnt the following week, so I'll have to go.'

Eileen mistook Mary's crestfallen expression as disappointment at not being asked to do the course.

'Aah, Mary, she only didn't ask you because Mrs Grant has told her how much she needs you. It's not that she thinks you're not good enough. Sure, you did better at that bandaging lesson than me!'

Recovering, Mary reassured her friend. 'Aah, sure, I know that. Mrs Grant has me running all over the city doing this and that, though I will keep going with the basic first aid. Did I tell you Mrs Grant wants me to learn to drive?'

Eileen's eyes opened wide in disbelief. 'A motor car?'

'Yes. I'm terrified! Mr Grant bought one a few months back and Jimmy learnt to drive it. Mrs Grant wants him to teach me – without the master finding out, of course. Jimmy is delighted, as you can imagine,' she added wryly.

Both girls laughed. Jimmy was always trying to court Mary, but she was having none of it. He was a harmless enough lad, Dublin born and bred, but too young for her, even if she was interested – which she wasn't. Anyway, Mrs Kearns and Mrs Grant would be appalled to think the staff were carrying on.

'But even if you do learn, what good is that going to be? You'll hardly be driving around the city delivering notes and such, and the master inside in his mill?' Eileen was confused.

'Yes, but you know Mrs Grant. She gets so excited about things. She says that when the revolution comes, women who can drive will be a real asset. So Mary Doyle is, it seems, to learn to drive a motor car. Sure maybe someday, I'll drive down to the convent and pull up outside and toot the blower thing and all the nuns will come running in case 'tis the bishop and 'twill be none other than that worthless little scrap of an orphan girl they put out a few years ago.'

Mary was giggling at the thought, but suddenly Eileen grew serious and looked deeply into Mary's eyes. 'Now you listen here to me, Mary Doyle.' She spoke with an edge of steel in her voice. 'You are not worthless. You are a great person and strong and brave and kind, and I won't hear that kind of talk. T'wasn't your fault your parents couldn't keep you, and we'll never know why. But you are as entitled as anyone else to be treated with respect and dignity. That's what we're fighting for – so nobody can put a person down because they are an orphan or they're poor or a woman. You're every bit as good as anyone else, and better than most. Do you hear me?'

Her determination and fortitude moved Mary almost to tears. 'Would you mind very much if I went with Rory to the zoo?' The words were out before she knew it.

'Aah, I see, only waiting to get me out of the way, were ye?' Eileen turned and faced the pond, her strong, handsome face unreadable.

'No, Eileen, it's nothing like that. I'd love you to come, of course I would. Forget I said anything. We might go another time,' Mary replied, panicked now that she had deeply offended her friend.

'Would you go way outta that, ya big eejit!' Eileen's eyes twinkled as she turned to look at her friend. 'He's always asking about you. I just thought you'd no interest in fellas. Go on up to the azoo, as they say here, with my brother, but mind he doesn't sweet-talk you now. He's a great knack for that. No woman in Foynes could refuse Rory, Mammy used to say. Not that he has a woman in Foynes, or anywhere else,' Eileen hastened to add.

Mary felt joy bubble up inside her. 'Don't worry. I'm sure he doesn't see me like that. It's just a friendly picnic is all it is.' Mary tried to keep the glee from her voice.

'Oh, I doubt that, Miss Doyle, I doubt that very much indeed. I know my brother, and he's got his eye on you. Maybe we'll be bringing you to Foynes sooner than we thought. Now so, we better be getting back. I've to finish the cap for your beau, though why I'm doing his stitching and you're being taken on picnics, I don't know. Myself and poor old Jimmy will be left on the shelf at this rate!' Eileen grumbled good-naturedly as they walked through the park and back to the tram.

# CHAPTER 15

NOVEMBER 1914

*T*he silence in the dining room was deafening as the Grants ate breakfast together. It was the Sunday Mary was due to meet Rory, and she was nervous and excited.

Mr. Grant rattled his newspaper. 'We've declared war on Turkey and annexed Cyprus. The Germans are on the back foot, so perhaps this wretched business will be over by Christmas after all. We'll have our boys home safe and sound, and the Kaiser on the canvas.' His self-satisfied, smug face sneered.

Mary caught Mrs Grant's eye as she served the bacon, urging her employer not to react. The master deliberately tried to antagonise his wife by referring to 'our boys' and using the term 'we' to describe the action of the British government. He was a nasty, sadistic man who thought he knew how much his wife needed him. Ever since the evening when he came home and beat her up, he had restrained his physical attacks, but his verbal ones were designed to humiliate and insult his wife.

Mrs Grant knew, however, that without her position as his wife, the help she could give the movement would be negligible, so she endured his constant jibes. People like them simply did not divorce, at any rate, no matter how miserable the marriage. He seemed to delight in antagonising her. He would crow with delight at victories of the British over the Irish, and laugh contemptuously at reports in the paper of the actions of the Volunteers or Cumann na mBan.

'More tea,' he barked at Mary as she served him bacon and eggs, locking his eyes on hers.

'Yes, sir.' Her hands shook and the cup rattled in the saucer as she poured. Weak winter sun shone through the window into the beautifully decorated room. Mrs Grant had an exquisite eye for detail, and her home was a credit to her. Fresh flowers bloomed in vases in each room, to coordinate with the colour of the décor. Blue hyacinths and hydrangeas wafted their fragrance around the elegant room, tastefully furnished in tones from pale eau de Nil to the deepest midnight-blue. The flowers were delivered each morning, usually accompanied by a note, which was to be brought immediately to Mrs Grant's room. The florist was a section leader, and each morning, instructions for the furtherance of the cause left her shop to be delivered to the parlours, drawing rooms, and bedrooms of the Dublin middle classes.

Handing the master his tea, she almost jumped when he addressed her. 'Mary?'

'Yes, sir?' she replied. She felt the terror rise in her. He had not mentioned anything about the night of the attack since it happened. In fact, he was quite lecherous, and she often found him leering at her while she served at the table.

'What do you think of this rubbish talked about Irish independence?' His moustache seemed to bristle in his thin pale face as his light-blue eyes fixed her with an icy stare.

'I...I don't know anything about it, sir.' She tried to leave.

'Come now, living in a house such as this, you must have gleaned something of the rot that threatens our world, hmmm? Where are you from?'

Mr. Grant knew perfectly well where she was from.

'I'm an orphan, sir. I came out of a convent in County Tipperary.'

'Aah, yes, you did mention something. So tell me, Mary, are you happy here?' The question was delivered pleasantly enough, but she sensed the menace that lay beneath it. Was she to be next to feel his fists? He was small and thin, but obviously strong, judging by the damage he had inflicted on his wife the last time. Mary was terrified of him.

'Yes, sir, I'm very grateful for the opportunity you've given me, sir.' Mary kept her head down, praying the encounter would end.

'Good, good. My wife, you see, would have us believe that all those in gainful employment are wretched and starving. And that we, the employers, are bleeding our employees white. You don't look starving to me, I must say.' He smirked, his eyes roving suggestively over Mary's body.

'No sir,' she murmured, mortified.

'My wife also thinks that the food that fills her belly – and the money for her fine dresses and shoes, and for every single thing that she thinks is hers by right – just appears out of thin air. The beautiful artwork and antiques that decorate our elegant and sumptuous home just dropped out of the sky. Now what do you think of that, Mary, as someone who at least works for a living and doesn't leech off others?'

Mary's pulse was pounding in her temples. She felt sick.

'I enjoy my work, sir, and I am very grateful.' Her voice tapered off. She wished she could catch the mistress's eye, but she didn't dare.

'Yes, I can see that. Now this other matter. This political claptrap about freeing Ireland from the 'yoke of British Imperialism,' I think these up-starts call it. What's your opinion on that?'

Mary swallowed quickly. 'As I said, sir, I don't know much about it.'

'Really? You surprise me. The thing is, they are all constantly under surveillance. They think we don't know who they are, and what they're up to, but we do. And we will strike when we see fit. A bunch of Leninist writers for rag newspapers and schoolteachers think they can take on the might of the British Empire? Ha! They ought to be taken out and shot like the rabid dogs that they are, spreading their filthy disease. Mark my words, each and every last one of them will be routed out and dealt with as they should be.'

She could feel his eyes penetrating her head as she kept her eyes downcast. 'Good. Now hear this, ladies. I do not wish to discuss this matter again. Everyone –' He paused for emphasis. 'Every single person in this building is here at my pleasure. I will not hesitate to remove anyone who purports to support this scurrilous nonsense. Is that clear?'

'Yes, sir.' Mary tried to keep the tremor from her voice.

'I was addressing everyone in the room.' His voice was icy. 'Do I make myself clear?'

'Yes,' Mrs Grant answered.

Mary didn't risk glancing in her direction. The master was not just making a point. He wanted to humiliate his wife by berating her in front of the staff. Mary hated to see the mistress humbled like this.

She stacked the tray as noiselessly as she could and escaped to the kitchen. Mrs Kearns was chopping vegetables for dinner when she looked up and saw Mary's stricken face.

'God Almighty, child, you look like you seen a ghost!' she exclaimed.

Tears appeared unbidden in Mary's eyes. The housekeeper wiped her hands on her apron and crossed the room. Gathering Mary to her ample bosom, she led her to the table.

'What's happened, child? What has you so upset?'

'It's the master,' Mary managed to say.

Mrs. Kearns stiffened. 'Did he touch you?' Her voice was ominous. She obviously noticed the way the master looked at Mary.

'No. No, Mrs Kearns, he just was asking me questions about the Lockout and about independence. He knows, he does – I swear he does – and what's to become of us?'

Mrs. Kearns relaxed. She had feared the master had made some untoward advance towards the young girl.

'Now listen here to me.' The housekeeper held Mary's face in her two chapped hands as if she were a small child. 'The Volunteers know what he done to the mistress the last time. I made sure they knew it, and he's being watched. He might be all high and mighty, but his day will come. He has some dealings with that Captain Johnson, out of the Castle, who calls here late some evenings, and I'll bet they're up to something. The master'll get his comeuppance and, God forgive me, I hope I'm there to see it. In the meantime, you watch yourself with him. I know you're a bit innocent, but he's a horny auld goat to add to everything else, so be sure to keep well clear of him.'

Mary giggled at Mrs, Kearns's description. She was right, though – whenever he did look at her, which was very often, she hated how it made her feel kind of dirty. She pulled herself together.

'I'm fine, Mrs Kearns. Sorry for getting so silly about it. You're right. And anyway, aren't the men risking everything by standing up to their employers? So shouldn't we be tough as well? Though now that so many people are arguing over whether to join up and follow Redmond or stay at home and strike for our own independence, it's hard to see how we'll get anything moving.'

'Exactly!' Both women looked towards the door. Mrs Grant stood there, smiling. 'You have it exactly right, Mary. We must all make sacrifices, and there will be plenty more of them to come. Sometimes we will be humiliated, abused, perhaps even imprisoned, but that is as it may be. We must – all of us, men and women – stay united and indivisible. This recent split between those who followed Mr Redmond and his instructions to join up with the forces of the Crown must be the last schism among us. It is simply not good enough for petty squabbles to exist between us. We have lost many of our number, gone to the other side and wearing British uniforms. It is a misfortune, but there you have it. They believe that they are furthering the cause of Home Rule, and they must reconcile their actions in their own conscience. Those people are no longer our concern. Now is the time to unite and conquer. We, the women, have an important role to play and must stay strong and stoic in the face of the enemy. And that enemy does not always wear a uniform, but is just as deadly – perhaps even more so.'

The three of them stood in the kitchen, united in their beliefs that transcended class and station in life. They were not servants and mistress, but three women, each determined by their common cause.

'Now, Mary, word must be delivered to the general council that something may happen. My husband did not mean to prewarn us. He thinks I am too frightened of him to continue my efforts, but the fact remains that he has done us a great service. The leaders must be warned, particularly

Pearse and Plunkett. He mentioned newspapers and teachers, did he not? Mary, I need you to get a message to someone… But to whom?' The mistress drummed her fingers on the table, deciding who was best.

'Well, ma'am, I am due to meet Rory O'D-wyer today. Do you remember him, from the day at the pier? I could ask him to deliver a note…' Her voice was hesitant. She was wary of admitting that she had arranged an outing with a man.

Mrs. Grant seemed to take no notice of that aspect, instead crying out, 'Perfect! Rory will be able to get word to the highest echelons of the Volunteers. Well, better than a note, just tell him, Mary. You heard what the master said as well as I. He'll know what to do, I'm sure. Now run along, dear, there's no time to waste.'

Mary ran to her room and quickly changed out of her uniform. She'd bought a new dress for the picnic and had spent the previous night worrying that it was a bad decision. He had seen her only other good dress, and while the mistress often gave her items she no longer wore, Mary never had the courage to wear them. Anyway, up until now, the only places she went were to Mass on a Sunday and maybe for a walk with Eileen afterwards, but only every second week when she had the afternoon off.

The dress was of emerald green, and the lady in the shop said it was perfect with her colouring. She'd enthused about how the shade brought out the colour of her hair and her green eyes. The waist was cinched in and the sleeves stopped at her wrists with lace on the cuff. The skirt was at least three inches above her ankle, and beneath it she wore kid-leather button-up boots the mistress had given her months earlier.

She gazed in the looking glass as she fitted her cloche hat and put on her coat. She felt vaguely ridiculous, but there was no time to change it now. Rory had written a lovely note – the first and only letter she'd ever received in her life – telling her he'd meet her at the General Post Office (GPO) on Sackville Street at 1 pm sharp, and that he was taking care of the picnic. Just bring herself. She smiled at the memory because in brackets he added, 'I know what you women are like about timekeeping!'

She was determined not to be late. In the kitchen, Mrs Kearns sat alone, the mistress having obviously gone back upstairs.

'Well, you're like a fashion plate, so you are,' she remarked. Mary didn't know if this was a good or a bad thing, since any efforts to improve one's appearance were discouraged as vanity and sinful when she was in the orphanage. 'Mind you, don't let that young man of yours get notions now, do you hear me? Them fellas in the Volunteers think they are cock of the walk – some of them – and a girl has to make sure she stays respectable, and not be seen to be behaving as anything less than a lady from a good God-fearing house.'

Though there was warning in Mrs Kearns voice, her face was kind. 'I'm very fond of you, Mary, so be sure to take care and be a good girl.'

'I will, Mrs Kearns – of course, I will. I don't want to go the same way as my mother, and the bad is in my blood, I know, but Rory is a good man, and he's Eileen's brother. Aren't you always saying how well brought up she is? Sure they're out of the one house, so he's a gentleman too.'

The old housekeeper shook her head. 'The rubbish you come out with sometimes...I just don't know. "The bad is in your blood", is that what them nuns told you? You don't know what went on with your poor mother, the blessings of God on her wherever she is. Don't ever let me hear you saying that kind of auld codswallop again. "Bad in the blood" indeed. You are a fine girl, and please God you'll be a grand wife for some good man when the time comes. But this world 'tis a dangerous place, never more so than now. We none of us know what's ahead, but 'tis going to be bloody, I know that. But 'twill be worth it, and 'tis the likes of young Rory will make this a better country for us all. Sure, listen to me and all my auld ramblings. Go on off up to the zoo with Eileen's brother and enjoy it – God knows ye'll all have to grow up sooner than ye should if things go the way they are headed. Go, let you, or you'll miss the tram, and there's few enough of them on a Sunday.'

Mary felt a rush of affection for the old housekeeper. Nobody in her life had ever said a kind word about her mother. Mrs Kearns had been like a mother to her since she got to this house, and she knew that she meant a great deal to Mrs Kearns too.

'I will, Mrs Kearns, and thank you for saying that, and for looking out for me. I'd never do anything to let you down.'

'Sure I know it well, *a chroí*. 'Twas a good day the day you landed in here. Now get out before I go to meet him meself, and wouldn't he be thrilled with this auld broiler hen as his company for the day? Be sure to bring your muffler, though. 'Tis bitter out there.'

* * *

MARY STOOD up to get off the tram on Sackville Street, and her stomach was in knots. What if he wasn't there? Or what if he was and she could think of nothing to say? *This was a terrible idea*, she thought.

As she alighted from the vehicle, there he was. 'Well, would you look! Aren't I the luckiest man in Ireland to spend the day with such a girl as yourself on my arm, Mary Doyle? You look beautiful.'

Mary smiled and blushed, unused to such compliments. No one had ever said she was beautiful before! Mrs Grant oohed and aahed over her colouring, and Eileen said she wished she was tiny like Mary, but she had never actually heard the words 'You are beautiful'.

'Hello, Rory,' she managed to reply. 'You look very beautiful too.' The words were out and she realised how ridiculous it sounded. She coloured deep crimson. 'I…I mean, you look well. I meant to say you look well. And fine. I hope you are. Fine, I mean.'

*Just stop talking*, she berated herself. *He must think I'm a little unhinged.*

'Aah, Mary, 'tis only me – a big thick ignorant eejit up from the country, like yourself. Not that you're thick or ignorant. I just meant you were from the country too… Oh Lord, can we start this again?'

He looked as flustered as she did. They stood in the street with the biting wind whipping up the remaining leaves of autumn, and people walked purposefully all around them, head down to get out of the cold. Rory and Mary laughed.

'Now, Miss Doyle, I have a plan. 'Tis different to the first plan because when we arranged to go to the zoo, I thought it was going to stay warm enough, but one of my areas of expertise is, in fact, zoo animals. And I know for a sure and certain fact that no animal with a hair of sense would dream of coming out to be admired today, even if it was by the lovely Mary Doyle. So here's my proposal. Why don't we make our way to a nice warm hotel, where we will hopefully not be arrested today, and –'

'Rory, before that, I have to give you an important message, from Mrs Grant.'

His demeanour changed from joking fun to instantly serious. 'What is it?'

191

'Well, over breakfast this morning, Mr Grant was saying how the British are going to strike at the movement for independence, and be brutal when they do. He specifically mentioned teachers and newspapermen. Mrs Grant thought he might have been referring to Mr Pearse or Mr Plunkett, and she felt they should be warned.'

Rory's face darkened. 'Thank God you and Mrs Grant had the sense to get a message to us. We'd be lost only for people like ye, and that's the truth. You see, there's been rumours, all right, but nothing concrete. We'll have to get word to them, straight away. Come on.' He tucked her arm in his and headed for Liberty Hall.

As they walked down Sackville Street, a truck full of RIC drove slowly beside them, their weapons cocked and ready. Rory immediately changed the subject and started telling her a long story about a chef who got a job in the Royal Marine who couldn't boil an egg. But everyone was so fond of him, they all covered up for him. The owners took weeks to discover the truth, by which time the chef had learnt the basics from the kitchen staff. Rory squeezed her arm and Mary laughed and chattered back animatedly. They looked like a young couple courting. The truck pulled up directly in front of them as they walked, blocking their path.

A policeman jumped down and took out his notebook as he stood ahead. 'Name?'

Mary was terrified, but managed to remain calm.

'Joseph Murphy,' Rory answered.

'And you?' the policeman asked, nodding at Mary and writing furiously.

'Teresa Lane,' she replied without hesitation – and with more confidence than she felt.

'Address?' The policeman looked Rory straight in the eye.

'Well, we're from Tipperary, but we're up visiting Teresa's aunt in Kilmainham. She's not too well, you see.'

'Address in Tipperary?' His eyes never left Rory's face, as if trying to place him.

'Queen Street, Nenagh, and Teresa's from Duggan's Lane. That's in Nenagh as well.'

There was nothing objectionable in Rory's tone. He spoke clearly and respectfully, as befitting a country boy up visiting Dublin. Mary marvelled at his performance.

Addressing Mary this time, the RIC man continued his questioning. 'And this aunt of yours.

What's her name and address?' Again the same stony stare. This was her turn to act.

'My aunt is Mrs Kitty Lane and she lives at number 11 Kilmainham Cottages.' Her voice was steady and clear. She remembered the address Kilmainham Cottages because Mrs Grant's cobbler lived there.

'And where are you two off to?'

'We've never been to Dublin, sir, and my aunt wanted us to see a bit of the city before we went home. She told us to get the tram to Sackville Street and walk around the place a bit, to see it, like.' Mary remembered her Tipperary accent from her days in the orphanage and broadened her vowels slightly.

The policeman nodded and turned back to his truck without another word. The truck moved off and rounded the corner.

When it was safe to do so, Mary allowed herself to breathe normally.

'Well, we'll have to speak to Mr Yeats about putting you on the stage, Miss Doyle.' Rory grinned. 'That was some performance! "We wanted to see a bit of the city..."' He mimicked her broad Tipperary accent.

'I don't know that I'd have been so brave if I'd a note in my boot,' she breathed in relief.

'You would, of course. You're made of tough stuff, Mary Doyle, like I'm always telling you. It's one of the reasons I like you so much.'

They walked along in the direction of Liberty Hall as the wind gusted mercilessly up the River Liffey. Mary felt alive and strangely exhilarated. She'd lied to the police and Rory said he liked her. As he chatted away and they walked along together, she felt a joy in her heart she'd never experienced before.

# CHAPTER 16

*T*he blazing fire in the dining room of the Gresham Hotel on Sackville Street warmed her as Rory spoke to the waiter. By the way they greeted each other, they were clearly friends. Perhaps the man was a Volunteer as well – it was possible. The message had been delivered to someone in Liberty Hall and Rory seemed happy that the right people would hear it. She didn't dare hope that their day would be resumed after that, but she was delightfully wrong. Rory announced that instead of freezing themselves to death in the zoo, they would go to this lovely hotel and have afternoon tea.

The ambiance was further enhanced by the presence of a string quartet in the corner of the room, but when the waiter came forward and asked if he could take madam's coat, Mary felt quite foolish. Surely he must know she was only a servant girl, not a lady.

The waiter led them to a table in the corner, from where they could observe the entire room. Couples, men in morning suits, and elegantly dressed ladies all chatted amiably in the sumptuously decorated room. The walls were covered with teal and gold silk wallpaper depicting birds of paradise, and heavy lead crystal chandeliers sparkled. The cutlery, glassware, and linen shone, and the gentle hum of background noise was soothing. The only other time Mary had been in a hotel was the day in Kingstown, so she never imagined anywhere could be more glamorous than the Royal Marine Hotel, but she was wrong. This place was breathtaking.

Rory took off his coat and handed it to a waitress. He wore a smart tweed suit – the only one he owned, according to Eileen. His snow-white shirt was starched, and he wore brass collar studs and a wine-coloured neck tie. *He really is so very handsome*, Mary thought. His hair was black, like Eileen's, and curled slightly where it met his shirt collar. She suspected that like his sister's, it would be corkscrew curly if he left it to grow. She wondered at his skin tone, much darker than hers. Women had noticed him as they walked across the room, his tall muscular frame filling the space around him. Beside him she felt like a dwarf, and his azure-blue eyes twinkled with merriment.

'Rory, surely you can't afford this?' she whispered, once the waiter had left them with some beautiful leather-bound menus.

He winked at her and leaned over the table to whisper in her ear, 'Of course I can. The Defence of Ireland Fund is paying. Sure we must keep the ground troops fed and watered.'

Mary was horrified. She knew the Volunteers and Cumann na mBan collected money, but it was for guns and things, not for the likes of her to be dining in places like this, aping her betters.

Rory laughed. 'If you could just see your face! I'm only pulling your leg. I've been working up here in Dublin for three years, and all I do is work and well… You know the rest of what I do, and so I decided it was time to treat myself. And what better way than afternoon tea in the Gresham with the most beautiful girl in Dublin?' Seeing the worry in her face, his jokey tone changed. 'Please just enjoy it, Mary. Don't worry about the cost of it. I have enough for it, I promise you, and I really do want to treat you.

'Twill take all the good out of it if you can't enjoy it too.'

He put his head to one side and gave her a pleading smile. She melted, incapable of refusing him anything. 'Very well, but the next time, I'm paying. I get paid too, and apart from my contribution to the fund, I've nothing else and no one else to spend it on.'

'So there's going to be a next time then, is there?' Rory was teasing. She was going to have to get used to this.

'Well, that depends. If the cakes are as good as Mrs Kearns's, then I'll consider it,' she remarked primly.

Though the conversation flowed effortlessly between them, Mary noticed that Rory's eyes constantly darted around the room, and he checked the door every time it opened. On one occasion a group of British officers walked in, and Rory and the waiter exchanged glances.

'Everything all right?' she asked, stopping her funny story about Mrs Kearns telling Jimmy off when she saw a shadow cross his face.

He leaned over and held her hand on the table.

'Yes, I think so. I'm just a bit wary after earlier with that RIC man. John, up there –' He nodded in the direction of the waiter '– he's with us, so he knows the regulars. He seems to think they're fine.'

Suddenly the whole situation became very real. They weren't playing at this. Mrs Grant was always telling Mary that things were going to get serious, even more than they were already, and that they must be ready.

'I know it's dangerous, Rory, but you will try to be careful won't you?' Mary tried to hide the worry in her voice.

He just nodded, and went on quietly so only she could hear. 'I will. Especially now I have a lovely girl waiting for me. You will be my girl, won't you, Mary?' The normally confident Rory looked vulnerable.

'I'd love it!' she answered honestly. He grinned and leaned his knee against hers under the table. It was a most intimate gesture, but instead of terror, Mary felt a warm glow. He went on, speaking quietly and holding her hand. To anyone they were a courting couple, whispering sweet nothings.

'Look, the worst thing that could happen for the moment is they force through conscription, though that seems unnecessary at this stage, seeing as so many of our lads joined up anyway. Sure you can't blame them, I suppose. They need the money and they trust Redmond when he tells them that if we fight for the British, they'll give us Home Rule.'

'Don't you think that they will?' Mary asked.

Rory considered his answer for a moment. 'Well, it's not that I don't believe him. It's just that for me, and for a lot of us, Home Rule isn't enough, even if they did give it to us. We want to be free, totally and completely. Free of Britain forever with no ties to her in any way. What Redmond and the Irish Parliamentary Party are offering is a kind of independence, but we'd still be beholden to them. Sure, they'd let us determine ourselves up to a point, but we would still be subjects of the British king. I can't accept that. I never will.' Determination burned in his eyes.

She knew she shouldn't ask, but she couldn't help it. 'There's going to be a move made, isn't there?'

'Mary, we can only live one day at a time. We have to get rid of them, we just have to. We deserve to be a self-determining people, and generations of men who went before us believed that too. Maybe ours will be the generation to achieve it, maybe we won't. But I'll tell you this – we will die trying to free our country if we have to.'

Another girl might have begged him not to get

involved, or to avoid danger, but Mary knew that Rory O'Dwyer was true to his word. None of them wanted to die, but if they had to, then die they would.

She told Rory about the attack the master made on Mrs Grant, and for a moment she saw the fury blaze in his eyes.

'They're nearly worse, you know, Mary, than the British – those Irishmen who are in cahoots with the Castle. He's an informer, I'm sure of it, so be very careful of him. One or two of our lads worked for him in the factory and he was always nosing around and asking questions. He's a dangerous man with a lot to lose, but if he ever says or does anything to you, I need you to tell me, all right?'

She nodded, but vowed to stay out of the master's way as much as was possible.

Rory insisted on seeing her home all the way to the door of the Grants's house. She would have liked to ask him in for a cup of cocoa, but she wasn't sure that would be allowed. Mrs Kearns didn't mind Eileen calling in the evenings – in fact, she quite liked the company – but a young man was a different matter.

'Well, Miss Doyle, it was my pleasure.' Rory

bowed theatrically and kissed her gloved hand. She felt silly but thrilled at the same time.

'Thank you, Rory. I had a lovely time.' She smiled.

'I say, you there!' A loud male voice coming from behind made her jump. 'What on earth do you imagine you are doing loitering outside my home?' Mr Grant got out of the carriage and Jimmy looked sheepish.

'Get away from my housemaid at once, and leave this place before I call the police.'

Rory bristled. Mary found herself deeply embarrassed at the way Mr Grant spoke to Rory, but also prayed that Rory wouldn't do anything to upset her employer.

Mr Grant stood in front of them both and spoke sharply to Mary. 'Get inside at once. This type of behaviour will not go unpunished, let me tell you. I'll deal with you myself later.'

Dismissing her, he turned his attention to Rory. Mary went down the steps into the trades-man's entrance, but waited inside with the door slightly ajar to hear the exchange.

'Identify yourself,' Mr Grant demanded.

'*Rúaraí O'Duibhir is ainm dom*,' Rory replied in Irish.

'What? Speak properly! Who are you? I advise

you not to try any trickery with me, young man. You do not know who you are dealing with.'

'Oh, I know who you are, all right. I know exactly who you are,' Rory said quietly. 'Don't you worry about that.'

'Are you threatening me?' Grant's voice was icy. 'You come to my house and attempt to molest one of my servants, and now you are threatening me? I ought to have you horsewhipped.'

'Mary is not *your* anything. She may work in your house, but you have no ownership over her. I saw the way you looked at her, and let me tell you this, Mr Grant.' Rory sneered as he spoke. 'If you touch so much as a hair of her head, you will regret it. You and your friends above in the Castle are being watched. You might think you have powerful friends who'll protect you, but don't you forget, so do I...and so does Mary. And our connections aren't bound by the same rules as your friends are, if you get my meaning. Am I making myself clear, Mr Grant?' Rory spoke in a voice Mary barely recognised – cold and threatening.

Grant puffed up like a bullfrog. 'What do you mean I am being watched? How dare you! You are one of them, aren't you? A troublemaking fool, lapping up all the lies that Sinn Féin – that excuse for a political party – wants to throw at you. I'm warning you, if I ever see you around my property again, I'll shoot you myself.'

Rory laughed into his face. 'Times are changing, squire, and you're a traitor to your own people. You've lived all cosy with the crowd inside in Dublin Castle with your "Rule Britannia" and "God Save the King", and you line your own pockets by fair means or foul. But your king won't be much use to you when our day comes, squire, no indeed. And there'll be a few question marks about your contracts, maybe? I'm sure if the British Army went digging into the paperwork of the supply of uniforms, they'd be interested in what they'd find. Enjoy your position while it lasts, because your days are numbered. If they don't get you, we will. Now remember what I said about Mary. You're not the only one with powerful friends, you know. You don't scare me, and if you so much as even much as look in her direction, I will personally see to it that 'tis the last thing you ever do. Cheerio now.'

Rory turned and strolled nonchalantly away, whistling 'God Save the King' as he went.

Mary ran to the kitchen, praying Mrs Kearns was there. She was and Mary blurted out the whole story.

Mrs Kearns sighed heavily. 'Rory is foolish to take the master on. He's a right nasty piece of work if ever there was one. I always suspected there was something going on with the books, though. That Johnson is a right piece of work. Did I ever tell you what he said as I was I showing him out one night? I was getting his coat and sez he to the master, "Grant –" Sez he, and his big plumy accent up on him "– that's a fine filly you have there –" Talking about the mistress, of course "– but she needs a tighter rein. If you can't manage her, I'd be happy to break her in for you. She'd be a quiet little mare once I'd be finished with her." The master was raging, of course, but he was beholden to Johnson so he just had to take it from him. Johnson looks at the rest of us like we were something he picked up on his shoe. He's the right match for our fella above then. He gives me the shudders, so he does. There's something sinister about him too. We'll just have to hope that Rory's threats will be enough to keep him away from you.'

That night Mary lay awake, unable to sleep in her cosy little room. She was frightened of the master, and she hated the way he looked at her. She felt dirty after any encounter with him, but she smiled when she thought of how Rory defended her. She would have to steer well clear of Johnson. He sounded awful, and she hoped she wouldn't have to answer the door to him when he called. Nothing could take away her joy, though. No one had ever stuck up for her in her life before, and to think the handsome Rory O'Dwyer was on her side gave her a thrill of excitement.

# CHAPTER 17

Mary and Mrs Kearns sat at the table in the drawing room staring in disbelief at the mistress. She surely couldn't be serious?

'Look, ladies, I know it's dangerous. I've thought of the consequences and I'd do it alone if I could, but I need your help.'

Since the night of the attack, things had changed between Mary, Mrs Kearns, and the mistress. Around the master they maintained the respectful distance befitting their stations in life, but when they were alone, they were friends and allies. Mrs Grant took to eating in the kitchen when the master was out, and often the three women would sit by the fire in the evenings discussing the political events of the day. Sometimes Eileen joined them as well, and the mistress was impressed with her commitment to the cause of Irish freedom.

That evening the mistress had asked them up to the drawing room, where a fire blazed merrily in the grate, and they ate toasted crumpets with their tea.

'But Mrs Grant, what you're suggesting is…' Mary was incredulous.

'Dangerous, mad, all of those things. I know that. Look, Mary.' The mistress cut across her, anticipating her objections. 'None of the jewels he buys me are because he feels anything for me. It's all just showing off. My idea is simple. I get paste replicas made of all the jewellery I have – not all at once, obviously, but over time – and we sell the originals. The movement has friends in America, where there are plenty of buyers for that sort of thing, it seems. We'd have to be very careful and ensure none of the real pieces ever appear here again. The money we can give to the Volunteers. Edward will be bankrolling the Irish Republican cause unbeknownst to himself. Think of the satisfaction we'll have as he rants on with his supercilious lectures about "our boys" on the Somme. And we needn't stop there. The house is bursting with valuable artwork, antiques – all that rubbish that he thinks makes him look superior to others. I'll find someone to make copies of it all. I already know of an expert jeweller who has been making paste versions of ladies' pieces for years. So many people are financially suffering, even people Edward knows through business, but they don't want to lose face by not having their finery on display, so necessity is the mother of invention. This chap – he's a Jew from Austria, I believe – is a genius. You bring him the piece, ostensibly to be cleaned, and he makes a replica that is as close to perfect as can possibly be achieved.'

Mary had told her weeks earlier about the conversation between the master and Rory, and what Rory said about the military contracts.

'Just think, ladies. We know he is operating some kind of swindle with that oily toad Johnson, so he won't want any attention drawn to his affairs. There are hundreds of ways we can swindle him in return. Mrs Kearns, it's time we started being a little more creative with the household budget as well. The potential for a little fundraising there is as yet untapped. All we have to do is be clever, be cautious, and not rile him up so that he throws any of us out. Well, ladies, what do you think?'

Mary and Mrs Kearns looked at each other. The cause desperately needed money – the master was a criminal anyhow, and a thoroughly horrid man to boot – and the mistress was clever enough to make it work.

Mary smiled conspiratorially at her two unlikely friends and said, 'Let's do it.'

In the weeks that followed, Mary regularly went to the little jeweller's workshop off Mountjoy Square with pieces to be cleaned. A few days later she would collect the originals and the replicas, and then she would give the original jewels to a man in the movement who had connections in London and the United States. Mrs Grant was very careful that her pieces would never be seen in Dublin society, in case the master recognised them and put two and two together.

The amounts generated were considerable. Everything they were raising was accepted gratefully by the movement, and they were delighted to contribute to the cause. One by one Mrs Grant's diamonds, rubies, sapphires, and pearls were replaced with glass and paste, while the master was none the wiser.

# CHAPTER 18

Scarlett pressed the doorbell of Eileen's house on a bright Sunday morning. She was going to Lorena's for lunch, but she decided to check on Eileen first.

'How are you, Eileen?' She smiled as the woman gave her a warm hug.

'I'm fine, Scarlett, and thank you again for everything you did – cleaning up all the mess, but also, more importantly, finding my flag. It means a great deal to me and to lose it... Well, it would be unimaginable. Now, have you time for a cup of tea or are you in a rush?'

Scarlett could think of nothing that she would enjoy more than to sit in Eileen's sunny kitchen, so she accepted the offer. 'I'd rather coffee, if it's not too much trouble.' She grinned.

'Oh, I'm sorry, my dear. I used to have coffee here. A friend of mine liked it, but she has since passed on, so I don't have any reason to have it in the house.' Eileen looked genuinely put out.

'Don't worry, tea's fine.' She reassured her though she hated it. She had a brief flashback to Dan throwing a mug of hot tea at the wall, narrowly missing her, because Lorena hadn't left the teabag in the cup long enough.

'How have you been?'

'Oh, I'm fine. It could have been much worse. You hear such awful stories and people really are kind. There's a young couple across the street – I babysit their little boy sometimes if Bianca, that's the mother, is delayed coming home. Well, her husband Carlos is a builder and he fixed up all the things they broke, and the place is like it was before. Anyway, enough about me and my tale of woe, how about you? How are you doing?'

Eileen's blue eyes were innocent, but Scarlett had a feeling that Eileen knew about the thing with Charlie. She struck her as someone who kept abreast of current affairs.

She hated the idea that Eileen would see her as the home-wrecking sinner Lorena did, but she needed to be honest. 'Do you know who I am?' Scarlett asked.

'Well, I know you are a very kind-hearted person who came to my rescue in my time of need. But if you're asking do I know about the affair with Charlie Morgan, then yes, I do. But Scarlett, my dear, we all do stupid things, often in the name of love. How are you bearing up?'

Scarlett found herself feeling emotional for the first time in over a week at this woman's kindness, especially since she felt that she didn't deserve it. 'Ok, I guess. The press seem to have lost interest, so I can at least get around without being harassed, but its hurts like hell – if I'm to be honest about it.'

'I can imagine it does.' Eileen patted her hand and then busied herself with making tea. 'It's hard to deal with betrayal.'

'Charlie didn't betray me, though, not really. He had no option. He'd never deliberately lie or hurt me like the press are trying to make out. I know it looks like that, but it really isn't. We love each other, but he is so conscientious that he would be throwing away all the good work he's done on issues that really matter if we were to be together.' For some reason, she was anxious that Eileen didn't think badly of Charlie.

'Well, Scarlett, if I've learnt anything from all my years on this earth, it's that things are rarely straightforward. People see what they want to see and hear what they want to hear. And no more so than in matters of the heart.' She placed a tray of tea things and little homemade cupcakes on the table. Scarlett wasn't sure if she was referring to her or not, but decided to leave it. Nobody knew what she had with Charlie, so they couldn't be expected to understand.

The two women chatted for ages about this and that, and Scarlett was amazed to find how well read and aware of everything Eileen was. She knew about Scarlett's journalism award and was able to discuss the details of the pieces she wrote around 9/11.

She seemed to have a great network of neighbours who helped her out, but she, in return babysat, watered plants when people were on vacation, and was even involved with a paired reading programme for children with special educational needs in the local library. For a lady her age, she certainly led a full and rewarding life.

'Did you ever marry?' Scarlett asked. There were no wedding photos, apart from the one of Eileen's parents, nor pictures of babies in the collection she had tidied up after the burglary.

'No, dear, I didn't. I do regret that now. It would be lovely to have grandchildren around me.' She smiled wistfully.

'Why not? If it's not too personal a question...' Scarlett was curious about this sprightly little old lady. She seemed much more together and capable today, now that the effects of the break-in were wearing off.

'My parents loved each other so deeply, with all of their hearts and minds, and I guess nobody ever made me feel like that. The way my mother felt about my father was so intense, and I was waiting to feel that. I realise now they were young – so very, very young – and idealistic. I had a few boyfriends over the years. Fewer, these days, of course.' She grinned mischievously. 'There were a few opportunities, but I always thought, *No, it's not like how Mam described her and Dad,* so I let them go. Mothers don't always know best though.'

Scarlett glanced at her watch. She would need to get going soon to be at Lorena's at one. 'Tell me about it!' She sighed ruefully. 'My mother and I don't exactly get along. I'm an only child and my violent alcoholic Irish father is thankfully no longer here. He died. He didn't move out of state or anything.' She smiled. 'So it's just me and

Lorena. She's a bit of a religious nut. Well, actually more than a bit, of late, I think. I try to limit our time together to very tiny bursts because we drive each other crazy, but I've got to go there for lunch. She's been calling me every day to tell me she's praying for me. And this afternoon, apparently I'm to be the subject of an exorcism, to rid me of the demons, so that's something to look forward to!' Scarlett rolled her eyes.

Eileen smiled at Scarlett's face. 'Religion sure has a lot to answer for in the world, doesn't it? But I will tell you this, Scarlett: You only get one mother, and no matter what the relationship between you, you'll miss her when she's gone. You never really get over it, actually.' Her blue eyes gleamed with emotion.

'Hmm. I guess so.' Scarlett was being polite. Though she didn't like what it said about her, she couldn't imagine herself being devastated when Lorena went. Life would be a whole lot easier in so many ways.

'I know so.' Eileen nodded. 'Cherish this time. You can't imagine what it'll be like when it's gone.'

'So if you didn't spend your life raising a family, what did you do?'

One of the things she really liked about Eileen

was how direct she was. You could just ask her a straight question and get a straight answer, without any religious mumbo-jumbo or political spin. It was refreshing.

'Well, I suppose my family background was one of fighting oppression, if that doesn't sound too much like boasting.' She smiled. 'I've tried where I can to make life a little more fair, I suppose.'

She argued vehemently in favour of universal healthcare packages, explaining how all over the world, the battles that had been won for equality and freedom were being eroded in front of their eyes. Not by imperial powers this time, but by the faceless financial institutions who put profit before people all over the so-called 'developed world'.

'Hey, Eileen, you're not some sweet little old lady, are you?' Scarlett teased. 'I'm guessing you were a bit of a firebrand in your day.'

'Well, I don't know about that.' She smiled. 'But I spent my early life working for the Transport Workers Union of America. There wasn't much room for sweet ladies, old or young, in that kind of organisation. I was brought up to believe in equality – that work should be rewarded and profits shared. That women and men are equal, and that rather than being in competition with each other, the most effective way to make social progress is through cooperation. Not an idea that appeals to the powerful, then or now, as it happens. Nothing changes, really, just the names and the faces. There will always be greed and those willing to exploit others to get what they want. And hopefully, there will always be those willing to stand up and fight. Because fight you must. The powerful will never volunteer to relinquish power – it must be taken forcibly from them. It's the only way.'

Scarlett was fascinated by the passion behind her words, which were totally belied by her slight physical presence. 'But surely negotiations, or reaching a compromise, is better than all-out war?' she asked.

Eileen nodded, delicately wiping her mouth with a napkin. 'Ideally, yes, but if you are dealing with those who see exploitation and injustice as acceptable, then trying to reason with them is a waste of time. They got what they have through savagery, and it will often take savagery to take back what is rightfully the property, land or human dignity of someone else. You see, Scarlett, to defeat any enemy, one must first understand them – think like them, so you can beat them on their own terms. When you get inside their head, then you find their weak spot, their Achilles' heel, then you stand a chance of victory. Even if the enemy is significantly stronger and better resourced than you.'

'Is that what happened in Ireland? With the English?' Scarlett was probing, thinking of all the photographs and memorabilia in the living room.

'Yes, ultimately, of course that's exactly what happened. But not before they subjugated the population for nearly 800 years. So many revolts over the centuries, so much bloodshed, but all to no avail. After the Rising, well, things changed then. New ways of thinking, new ways of fighting back.'

'New in what way?' Scarlett asked.

'Oh, just a different approach. Too long to go into now, but the thing was that key people realised the same old tactics that had failed so often before must be abandoned.'

Scarlett looked at the Waterford crystal clock sitting on Eileen's mantlepiece, and realised she had to go. 'Time to face the music, or worse!' She was dreading going to her mother's. 'I'd love to stay here chatting all day, but there will be hell to pay – literally – if I don't show.' She smiled at her own joke.

Eileen remained serious. 'Scarlett, you are a good person. Don't let anyone tell you otherwise. You made a decision out of love, and things didn't go the way you planned, but that doesn't mean you are bad. Try to go easy on your mother. I'm sure she loves you, but when religion gets a grip on people… Well, it's hard for them to see clearly sometimes.'

Scarlett wished for the hundredth time that her mother were more like Eileen.

'Thanks, Eileen. I know she does love me, and I guess I love her too, but sometimes I don't actually like her all that much. She's got this priest that she hangs out with. I'm meeting him properly today, and now she's talking about going to Mexico with him, doing some kind of extreme pilgrimage or something. I know I should intervene, but it's easier just to stay out of it.'

Eileen nodded knowingly. 'My mother and I were very close, extremely so, but there were days when we could have happily strangled each other. We had different ideas about things, and it's really because of her that I never married. She would never have stopped me – nothing like that – but her marriage to my father was held up as the ultimate, and I never thought I'd found that. Maybe she should have advised me otherwise. I don't know, but all I'm saying is mothers are just human beings as well, fallible human beings who make mistakes. But I know everything my mother did, rightly or wrongly, throughout my life, was because she thought it was the right thing. I'm sure your mother is just the same.'

'Thanks, Eileen, for the tea and everything else. I've filed my copy on the burglary already, but I was wondering if you'd tell me the story of your family? I'd love to hear it, if you wanted to…'

Suddenly Scarlett felt stupid and gauche, like a teenager again, desperate for a date. She realised that she just wanted to maintain a friendship with Eileen, but it was weird. How do you say 'Let's be friends' to a ninety-something-year-old lady? She just knew she didn't want to leave and not have a reason to call at this warm, welcoming little house again. In the whole sea of crazy that was her life, this was a little island of calm acceptance and she hated to leave.

Eileen seemed to read her thoughts.

'Well, I'm here most of the time, and I can never thank you enough for all you've done for me. I'd be delighted for you to call anytime you have a moment. The story of my family is quite a tale, I can tell you! Now you'd better get going.'

She ushered Scarlett to the front door, handing her jacket to her.

'Don't you have a scarf? Or a hat?' she asked, concerned. 'It's freezing out there with that wind. Here, let me find you something.' Before Scarlett could protest, Eileen was opening a little closet under the stairs, and from it she took a beautiful dark-green fine-knit wool scarf with gold flecks. She wrapped it around Scarlett's neck and patted her on the back. The gesture was so caring and gentle that Scarlett felt five years old again. Instinctively, she kissed Eileen on the cheek and left with a heavy heart, dreading what faced her.

# CHAPTER 19

HOLY THURSDAY, 1916

'*O*uch!' Mary yelped in pain.

'Oh, for goodness sake, Mary Doyle, you're neither use nor ornament today. No wonder you cut yourself – you're a million miles away! Here, wrap this around it before you drip blood all over the carrots.'

Mrs Kearns led Mary to the sink and wrapped her finger in gauze and a bandage.

'I'm sorry. You're right – I'll concentrate better, I promise.'

The housekeeper put her heavy calloused

hands on Mary's slight shoulders and spoke directly to her.

'I know you're worried, and frightened, we all are. None of us knows what's going to happen, but something will, and sooner rather than later, I think, so we must stay strong. And if your man above –' Her eyes gestured towards the Grants's private rooms upstairs '– gets a sniff that anything is not as it should be, he'll be on to his friends in Dublin Castle like a flash. You're fierce jittery altogether and he'll spot that if he sees you, so you need to settle down, all right?'

Mary nodded. Last night she, Eileen and Mrs Kearns sat in the kitchen while the Grants attended a dinner party in the neighbouring wealthy suburb of Foxrock. The three spoke about the sense of anticipation. Something was definitely about to happen, they all agreed.

Eileen was in on the swindle they were running on the jewellery, and recently the mistress had found an artist who could produce credible replicas of the artwork the master had dotted throughout the house. He considered himself a man of high culture and loved to show off his collection, but actually, the mistress assured them, he knew nothing about art. He'd never notice if they were replaced with good copies. So Mrs Grant was systematically, and with great attention to detail, divesting him of that wealth as well. Though the thought that the master was unwittingly helping to arm the very people he despised gave the women a thrill, they remained deeply cognisant of the fact that if they were caught, they would face deadly consequences. This was not a game, but it gave the mistress a reason to stay with him and endure his daily ritual humiliations.

She rarely attended meetings these days, preferring to send the girls and Mrs Kearns to avoid further conflict in the house. Mary reported back to her the details of the discussions, but Mrs Grant was also very connected to the upper echelons of the Volunteers, so she was kept abreast of events. She regularly attended the Abbey Theatre, where Lady Gregory and William Butler Yeats were firmly establishing a National Theatre, celebrating all aspects of Irish culture. The movement towards independence was being fought on many fronts, she would regularly tell Mary.

The last Cumann na mBan meeting Mary attended had been different in tone from all previous meetings. Usually the talk was divided between matters of principle, such as suffrage or Home Rule, and practical issues of first aid training, driving and, in recent weeks, shooting. Recently however, the discussions became less abstract and more urgent. The sense of impending action was palpable. She and Eileen had been thrilled the month before when they were part of a group taken high up into the Dublin Mountains and shown how to fire a rifle.

She, Eileen, and ten other women had waited near Wynne's Hotel early on Sunday morning. Three cars arrived and they were bundled in and driven out of the city, past the small poor houses of the city centre, past the smoke-producing factories, and then finally leaving behind the beautiful detached houses of the wealthy in the leafy suburbs. The landscape had reminded Mary of Tipperary, rural and peaceful compared to the urban energy of Dublin.

They approached the shooting area through muddy lanes where the cars dropped them at an open field. She and Eileen instantly recognised Rory. He greeted them in a friendly way and introduced himself as their instructor, but treated her and Eileen the same way as the other women, giving clear instruction in marksmanship. Only as Mary held the rifle to her shoulder did he come up behind her and place the butt of the gun under her arm. 'The recoil of these old things will really hurt if you have it against your shoulder bone,' he whispered. 'Move it down slightly, you'll absorb it better.' She tingled where he touched her on the upper arm as he adjusted the position of the gun.

After that first lunch in the Gresham, he wrote regularly to her, but despite the fact that they lived in the same city, it was difficult to make time to see each other. She had every second Sunday off, but Rory was often down the country. He never wrote anything about his Irish Volunteer work in his letters for fear of them being intercepted, and when they did manage to meet, it was often rushed or cancelled at the last minute. She knew from his letters how he felt about her. He was always honest and open about that, but she would have loved some time with him. On Sundays, she watched with envy the couples walking arm in arm in the park, chatting away without a care in the world. Mrs Grant and Eileen, and even Mrs Kearns, were understanding, but they all told her how Rory was doing very important work and 'We all have to make sacrifices.' She knew that, and made those forfeits happily, but she wished sometimes they were just an ordinary couple with time for courting.

Mrs Kearns's voice broke into her thoughts.

'Now so, bring up the breakfast there to him. The mistress is out at early Mass, so she'll have hers when she gets back.'

Mary's heart sank. She hated serving the master when Mrs Grant was out. He always managed to make her feel uncomfortable. He seemed to think his wife had given up on her political life after the battering he had given her, but he did, from time to time, bring up the subject in Mary's earshot. She would have preferred anything else than serve him alone. Since the night of the run-in with Rory, he had watched her closely, and her flesh crawled beneath his malevolent and sinister gaze. She knew he despised her, but obviously the conversation with Rory had struck a chord with him, so he rarely spoke to her.

'And Mary,' Mrs Kearns added, 'in and out nice and quick now, d'ya hear? Don't be dilly-dallying with him.'

Mary looked incredulously at Mrs Kearns. 'I certainly won't!' she blurted out indignantly.

'Good girl! If you're not back in three minutes, I'll send Jimmy up on an errand.'

Mary took the tray firmly in both hands and walked upstairs. She took a deep breath to steady her nerves before entering the room. The master was sitting at the dining room table, fully dressed.

'Aah, Mary, have you brought my paper?' His tone was so unusually cheery and pleasant that Mary instantly felt fear dance up her spine.

'Yes, sir,' she responded, handing him the freshly ironed *Irish Independent*.

TWENTY CRIMINALS QUESTIONED IN DUBLIN CASTLE

The headline screamed the news. Mary tried to ignore it as he rattled the paper while she poured the tea and placed his toast and marmalade on the table in front of him.

'So, Mary, looks like the chaps in Dublin Castle are doing a good job rounding up these hooligans and corner boys that are threatening to disrupt our lives, what?'

'Yes, sir,' she replied demurely as she placed the last item from the tray onto the table. He knew well her connection to Rory, so he was clearly goading her.

'I hope a young girl such as yourself is never drawn into this nonsense, now. You have kept very unsuitable company in the past.'

Mary felt her heart pounding. Despite threatening to deal with her, he had never said a word until now. Perhaps she was foolish to think Rory's standing up to him and telling him that the

Volunteers knew about his dealings with Dublin Castle had scared him off.

'I read an article last week about how these groups – claiming to want Irish independence and all that rubbish – were targeting the young and undereducated of the city and filling their heads with this dangerous talk. If anyone approaches you suggesting you get involved in anything like that, it is your duty to inform me. Is that clear? I'm sure any previously unsuitable people have now been eradicated from your life. It would have been prudent to do so, and you don't strike me as stupid.'

'Yes, sir.' Mary felt like she'd been in the room for hours. She tried to slow her pulse and to act normally. She could never tell with the master what he was really saying, but there seemed to be a subtext to everything he said. She backed away from the table. It took all her resolve not to bolt for the door.

'Come here.' His voice was smooth as silk.

She returned to within two feet of the table, her eyes downcast.

'Look up, Mary. I won't bite.'

Reluctantly she raised her head slightly.

'I know you are not foolish enough to have anything further to do with that guttersnipe I saw you with last year, because believe me, he won't protect you... Not when you need it most,' he purred.

'No, sir.' She gulped silently, trying to swallow her fear.

'Come, come, now. I see the lad from the post office delivering letters downstairs after he leaves in our post. Now, Mrs Kearns is hardly in receipt of love letters at her age, and that clown Jimmy probably can't even read, so who are these letters for, I wonder?' His tone was playful, yet terrifying.

Mary thought quickly. 'I get some letters from a nun who used to be kind to me in the convent, sir.'

'Well, perhaps that is so, though why you should blush so deeply at the mention of letters from an old nun, I don't know.'

He stood up from the table and moved to where she stood. Mary was sure he could hear her heart pounding. Reaching out his hand, he lifted her face by her chin and looked deeply into her eyes. Mary tried to look demure but unafraid as his eyes raked her face, searching for something. His huge moustache covered his thin lips, and as he smiled at her, she noticed his little teeth – like a ferret's. His eyebrows sprouted long greyish black hairs and almost covered his small piggy eyes. Mary thought him repulsive. He moved his face closer to hers and she could smell egg on his breath. She was rooted to the spot, terrified.

Just then there was a knock on the door and Jimmy entered without waiting to be summoned, obviously on the instruction of Mrs Kearns.

'Sorry, sir, begging yer pardon, sir, but will you be needing the carriage this morning, sir?' Jimmy blurted out, clearly only slightly less terrified of the master than of the housekeeper, to say he managed to get the words out at all.

'What on earth do you mean, bursting in here like this? Who the hell do you think you are? Of course I need the carriage. Get out, you imbecile!' The master was fuming.

Mary took her opportunity and scurried out the door behind the petrified Jimmy and dashed to the safety of the kitchen. Moments later she heard the master leave by the front door.

'Are you all right, child?' Mrs Kearns had dispatched Jimmy to the yard with a clip round the ear for his trouble as she saw Mary enter the kitchen. 'You're white as a sheet.'

Mary took a deep breath. 'He asked me about the letters and who they were from. He sees everything, Mrs Kearns! What if he knows about the jewellery and the pictures and everything?' Terror filled her as she whispered urgently, 'He was going to try to kiss me. Only Jimmy came in...'

'Calm down, child, calm down! 'Twas only a matter of time. He's furious about the way Rory spoke to him, and he won't let it go. I don't know what we're going to do about this, but something will have to be done. He'll try again, but if you say anything to Rory, then you could make things worse.' Mary had never seen Mrs Kearns look so worried. 'Here, a letter arrived while you were upstairs.'

Mary sat in the easy chair beside the fire, trying to compose herself. The letter was from Rory and it made her heart sing. The previous Sunday they'd made arrangements to meet, but he sent a boy to the house at the last minute to say he couldn't come. She was bitterly disappointed, for she hadn't seen him since the day in the mountains, shooting, and that was with lots of people around. She felt selfish even thinking these thoughts and banished them from her mind.

*Dear Mary,*

*How is my best girl? I'm so sorry about last Sun-*

*day. I was all set to go to meet you when I was asked to do the afternoon shift here – one of the other lads was sick. I know you understand. I'd never willingly let you down, you know that, don't you?*

*I know it's Holy Thursday but I'd love to see you today, even for half an hour. Do you think Mrs Kearns would let you out? I need to talk to you about something. If you can, I'll be beside the bandstand in the park at three. I'll wait until twenty past, but then I'll have to get back myself.*

*Love,*

*Rory*

Mary reread the short note and decided she had nothing to lose. Mrs Kearns liked Rory on the occasions she had met him and she approved of him as a beau for Mary.

'Mrs Kearns, the note was from Rory. He wants to meet me today in the park, just for a short time. He says he needs to talk to me about something. I know I'm supposed to be here, but would it be all right if I went to meet him at three o clock, just for half an hour?'

'Summoned by the mighty Rory O'Dwyer, are ye?' But the housekeeper was smiling. 'All right, never let it be said I stood in the path of true love. Mind you don't say anything to him about his morning, though. Not till we've had time to think about it. That fella is so hot-headed, he'd come charging round here, and then where would we be? If the master knows anything – and we don't know that he does – he could have us arrested, and Rory too, so we'll have to play his game and see what happens. Rory can't afford to get caught up in anything with him at this stage. He'll be needed when the time comes, and him locked up would be no good to anyone at all. 'Tis the likes of that lad who'll get us out from under the British, you mark my words! Something's happening, Mary girl. I can feel it, and especially after all the talk at the meeting the other night. The whole city is on tenterhooks. So go and see him, and tell him he's in our prayers, but mind no one sees you, and make sure you're back before the master gets home. If anyone asks, especially that nosey Jimmy, tell them you're going on a message for me to get ribbon for the mistress's Easter bonnet. There's a new length of green satin ribbon in the dresser there. Put it in your pocket in case you're questioned.'

Mary felt a rush of love for the old woman. Running to her, all thoughts of the horrible Mr Grant forgot, she hugged Mrs Kearns.

'Will you get off me, you daft girl! And get on with peeling the spuds for the soup. There'll be nothing eaten in this house tomorrow but soup and fish, being Good Friday, so be sure to have plenty of it made.' The normal work of the morning began, but all Mary could think of was seeing Rory.

# CHAPTER 20

She ran into the park, her hair escaping from under her hat in the brisk April breeze. She passed a British patrol as she made her way in, and the way they looked at her made her shiver. Sometimes she looked at them, when she was stopped on the tram or something, and tried to imagine them as ordinary lads. Most of them were no older than Rory. Did they have mothers and sisters and sweethearts back in England? One time she mentioned her thoughts to Eileen and Mrs Kearns and they both admonished her. Mrs Kearns's uncharacteristically harsh words rang in her ears:

'They're soldiers of a foreign king, ruling our country by savagery and violence, and we have to get them out by whatever means are necessary. That's the only thought you need have about them, my girl.'

As she approached the bandstand, her heart sank. He wasn't there. Couples walked in the park, a woman passed by with a baby in a pram, and two little children threw crumbs for the ducks, but there was no sign of Rory. She leaned against a pole beside the ornate but empty bandstand, catching her breath. She jumped when she felt two arms go round her waist from behind.

''Tis only me.' Rory chuckled as he kissed her neck. She knew such public displays would earn Mrs Kearns's deep disapproval, but it was just so good to see Rory again. She wanted him to kiss her forever. They began walking in the bright sunshine and it felt like nothing could ever go wrong. They chatted about this and that, and she wondered what was so urgent that he had to see her, since he seemed so relaxed. A pair of young men came towards them dressed in British uniforms, but they spoke with Dublin accents. Rory began to sing softly,

*Come all ye scholars saints and bards,*
*Says the grand old dame Britannia.*
*Will ye come and join the Irish Guards,*
*Says the grand old dame Britannia.*

*Oh, don't believe them Sinn Féin lies,*
*And every Gael that for England dies,*
*Will enjoy 'Home Rule' 'neath the Irish skies,*
*Says the grand old dame Britannia.*
*Now Johnny Redmond you're the one,*
*You went to the front and you fired a gun,*
*Well you should have seen them Germans run,*
*Says the grand old dame Britannia.*
*But if you dare to tread on the German's feet,*
*You'll find a package tied up neat,*
*A Home Rule badge and a winding sheet,*
*Says the grand old dame Britannia.*

The soldiers stopped, recognising the jibe. They looked around them, fearful it was an ambush. Members of Sinn Féin, the political wing of the Volunteers, were everywhere, and the country was deeply divided. The press were full of John Redmond's entreaties for young Irishmen to do their duty and fight for England in Europe, but those who did were held in deep disgust by the Volunteers.

'If they are so anxious to shoot people and die, then they should be shooting at the English, not for them, and dying for Ireland,' Rory was often heard to say. It was the subject of their first argument as he expounded his views at the side of the range in the Grants's kitchen one night while

Mrs Kearns made them cocoa. Mary pointed out that some families were so poor that it was the only option. What else were they to do to feed their families?

'Aah, Mary, my darling, who is keeping them poor, though? The king himself, that's who. 'Twill never change unless we change it, and sending our fellas away to have their arses blown off by German lads, who we have no gripe with, is just compounding the problem.'

'You'll keep a civil tongue in your head, Mr O'Dwyer, if you know what's good for you.' Mary recalled Mrs Kearns speaking sharply to Rory, diffusing the situation, though Mary knew that Mrs Kearns wholeheartedly agreed with him. She had joined Cumann na mBan a few months earlier and was every bit as enthusiastic as the mistress was. Unlike Rory, though, she still didn't blame these boys for joining up. He and Eileen had grown up on a farm, and there was always enough to eat and a warm bed to sleep in. Sometimes he just didn't understand.

The soldiers passed and Rory stopped beside a side path into the woods. He put his arm around her and squeezed her waist. He looked deeply into her eyes and raised his eyebrows questioningly.

She knew she should stop him. That's what nice girls did, but she nodded and he led her wordlessly into a copse of trees. She was creating an occasion of sin, as Sister Benedict would have put it. She knew she was, yet she felt her breath quicken with excitement. He walked ahead of her, holding her hand until they could no longer see the manicured lawns and paths of the park. The sun shone and dappled through the leaves, and Mary wished the moment would never end.

Slowly, and without his usual joking, Rory unbuttoned her coat and slipped his arms around her tiny body, pulling her close. Lowering his head he tilted her face up towards him, and for the second time that day, Mary's face was just inches from a man's. This time the sensation was one with which she was unfamiliar. Heat flooded her body and she wanted Rory to hold her, touch her. She knew very little about men and women, apart from what she had learnt in the cell with the prostitutes of Dublin that night. She didn't think any of that information applied to her and Rory, but she did know that to do anything with a man was a sin, unless within holy matrimony, and then only for the procreation of children. Suddenly she knew why her mother had fallen foul of a man. If she felt about Mary's father the way Mary did about Rory, then she could, for the first time in her life, understand why she did what she did.

Almost without realising it, she found herself reaching up and putting her arms around Rory's neck, drawing him to her. As his lips touched hers, she felt weak and energised at the same time. She kissed him back, hungrily, hoping she was doing it right. He'd often pecked her on the cheek, or even a quick kiss on the lips if no one was watching, but she'd never been kissed like this.

He kissed her deeply and she wanted it to go on forever. She wound her fingers through his hair as he drew her even closer to him. She started as she felt his arousal against her stomach, but instead of moving away as she knew she should, she leaned her body closer to him. She could hear him moan with pleasure as his hands roamed all over her back and down onto her bottom. On and on they kissed, their bodies straining to join together.

Eventually – reluctantly – they drew apart.

'Oh, Mary, I wish we could stay here forever and let the rest of the world go to hell. I had to see you. I need to tell you something, but you can't tell a soul, not even Eileen.'

Mary nodded. This was not like Rory to be so serious.

'I need to tell you that I love you. I know we haven't had much time together. I know you've been so patient and that you understand why I can't spend as much time with you as I'd like to –'

'Of course I do, Rory,' Pure, unadulterated joy spread through her. Rory loved her. 'I love you too. No one has ever said those words to me in my life before, and I've never said them to another living soul, but I know I love you too, Rory O'Dwyer.'

'Aah, my lovely Mary! Please God, when this is all over, and we're free of the bloody British, we can settle down, get a little house and get married and have a family. Fine strong sons and beautiful daughters who'll look just like their mammy, and we'll teach them to be decent and honest and brave.'

'I'd love that,' Mary whispered.

'But it can't be now, that's what I came to tell you. I want to marry you. I'll never feel about anyone the way I feel about you, but I can't ask you, not yet. I don't want your name up with mine for your own safety. Do you understand? If anyone asks, you only know me as Eileen's brother, nothing more.'

Mary nodded. 'Do you know something, Rory?'

He nodded gravely. 'This weekend. It's planned for this weekend. The whole country will rise in rebellion. You can't tell a soul, Mary, promise me.' His eyes blazed intently at her as he cradled her head in his big hands.

'I promise,' she whispered. This was real… maybe this was the last time she would ever see him. The unfairness of it all stung her.

'Now I know there's no point in asking you to stay out of it. The women will be needed as well, and anyway, you've all been preparing for this for so long, but please, my darling girl, will you keep yourself safe in as much as you can?'

Tears stung her eyes. How cruel life could be! She had never known love in her whole life and here she was, aged just twenty-one years, and the man she adored was going to war.

'Aah, Mary, *mo chroí*, don't cry. Don't cry, my love. I'll do everything I can to make this a free country for our children to grow up in. We have to take this cup, just like Our Lord did. He couldn't avoid it, and he did it to save us, and what we are going to do is the same. Good men are leading us, and they're leaving their loved ones too. We are taking on the mighty British

Empire. The odds might be against us, but right is on our side, Mary, and we have to try. The alternative – consigning ourselves and our children to a life of penury – is unthinkable. I give you two solemn promises before I leave you. The first is that I will love you, and only you, to the day I die. The second is that I will do everything in my power to make that day many, many years from now. But Mary, if it's not, and I get killed, live your life. Do you hear me? Live your life, get married, have children. Be happy and know that I'm looking down on you and blessing you every day.'

They stood together, holding each other close.

'I have to go,' he whispered into her hair.

She held him even tighter, willing herself not to beg him to stay.

'I love you, Rory,' she said, looking up at him. 'Please be careful.'

He held her face between his hands and she could feel his rough, calloused skin.

'I love you too, darling Mary. Goodbye, my love.' He kissed her on the head, as a mother might kiss her child, and then he was gone.

# CHAPTER 21

EASTER MONDAY MORNING, 1916

'*R*ise *from your knees, oh daughters rise,*
*your mother still is young and fair,*
Let *the world look into your eyes, and see her*
*beauty shining there.*

*Grant of that beauty but one gleam, heroes shall*
*rise on every hill.*

*Today shall be as yesterday, the blood red burns in*
*Ireland still.*'

Mary gazed, mesmerised, at Mrs Grant. The poem, written by Susan Mitchell, had appeared in the Cumann na mBan newsletter earlier in the month, and it had stirred them all to hear Mrs Grant recite the words aloud in the kitchen. While Mrs Kearns, Eileen and Mary stood there, resplendent in their uniforms, she felt the weight of history heavy on her shoulders.

The uniforms were of rough material, but they felt wonderful. They would change into their Red Cross uniforms later, but for the march, they wanted to be part of the military, with the men. Mrs Grant looked particularly magnificent, so used were they to seeing her in chiffon and lace, but she stood proud in her khaki jacket and hat and long skirt. Mary's favourite part was the badge – a little rifle with the letters *C na mB* wound around the weapon. Every time she looked at it, she felt a surge of pride.

'Ladies.' Mrs Grant addressed them. 'Today is a momentous day. It is an honour for me to have us serve together in defence of our country, alongside our men. Today we are not servants or cooks or ladies, but Irishwomen, undivided by rank or station. Now, let's go. Our orders are to present ourselves at Liberty Hall and get further instructions there. *Go n-eirí an tádh linn go leir.*'

They walked out quietly so as not to disturb Jimmy, who was polishing boots in the scullery. The master had left for work, despite it being a bank holiday, because as the war raged on in Europe, the demand for uniforms was almost insatiable and the master was making a fortune from it.

Their orders were to meet at Liberty Hall at 11:45. As they marched purposefully down the street, Mary noticed Mrs Grant glance wistfully back at her home once. No matter how things went today, there was a distinct possibility that she would never enter its doors again. Mary had her letters from Rory hidden under her petticoat, and the little medal Mrs Kearns had given her was around her neck on a chain – the only things of value she owned – and she too wondered what was to become of them all.

Eileen fell into step beside her as they walked purposefully towards the city with Mrs Grant and Mrs Kearns behind them. Mrs Carmody knew of Eileen's involvement, and while she was not a member of Cumann na mBan herself, and was very proud of her son who was fighting in the war on the Western Front with the Royal Dublin Fusiliers, she was a believer in women's suffrage, and so her maid's activities did have her tacit approval.

Eileen linked with Mary's arm and said, 'The mistress called me up to the study last night. I nearly had a heart attack. She never does that, so I was sure something had happened to Rory and that she had got the job of telling me.'

Mary breathed deeply. The mention of anything happening to Rory caused her to fret, but she had to stay strong. She was glad of Eileen's friendship at all times, but especially now, as she had no official link to him. Eileen was his next of kin in the city, so word of him would have to come through her.

'Don't worry!' Eileen smiled, squeezing her friend's arm. She knew how Mary and Rory felt about each other. Mary had confided Rory's declaration of love and his proposal to her friend on Thursday night. 'I'm sure he's fine.

'No,' Eileen continued, 'Mrs Carmody just wanted to say that she was very proud of me and that if I had to leave for any reason, she would understand, and that there would always be a job for me in her house! I know she couldn't say anything outright, but 'twas nice of her all the same, wasn't it? Poor Maura Hayes was dismissed from her place after her mistress got wind of her involvement with us. We're lucky to have our employers on our side, at least.'

'Yes, we really are. Though whether or not Mrs Grant will have a house to go home to after today is another thing.' Mary was preoccupied. All around them as they approached the city, groups of armed men and some uniformed women, Cumann na mBan members, were gathering.

'Surely the British in Dublin Castle aren't blind? Can they not see what's happening?' she asked anxiously.

'No – they think we're just going to parade. I heard one of the ladies say it at the meeting the other evening. They think it's better just to let us parade and be done with it. Are you nervous?'

Mary was, but she wouldn't admit it. 'No, I'm ready. You?'

'No! I'm ready too. We've been preparing for so long. It's time for action now.' They walked on in silence, Mrs Kearns and Mrs Grant talking quietly behind them.

At the headquarters on Brunswick Street, Mrs Grant went in to get their orders. She emerged after a few minutes with boxes of supplies and a handcart.

'The men and some of the ladies are marching from Liberty Hall. I'm sorry, but our task is a little less glamorous.' She smiled at the girls. 'Right. We're to report to the GPO – Pádraig Pearse is commanding there. We have bandages, ointment and disinfectant here, which we're to bring with us and set up a first aid station. Eileen and Mary, can you get the rest of those boxes there on the stairs? And Mrs Kearns, if you can help me get them into the handcart?'

For a few minutes they carried heavy boxes of bandages and loaded up the handcart as high as they could before setting off. They passed companies of Volunteers taking orders and preparing to dig in at various strategic points around the city. Mary wondered, for the thousandth time that morning, where Rory was.

She was interrupted from her thoughts by Eileen's good natured grumbling. 'God above! These boxes weigh a ton! Surely there must be more than just bandages in here?' And she heaved another box onto the handcart.

'They're flour bags from Boland's Mill. That's why they're so heavy,' Mrs Grant explained. 'The girls working there have been taking bags out for months and storing them here – unbeknownst to the Boland's, of course.' She smiled.

'I think that's about all we can carry for now. Well done, girls. Let's get to our position and hope we don't need to use all these bandages.'

As she turned to go, Mary noticed something shoved into Mrs Grant's belt that had not been there before: A Webley handgun. The reality of what they faced in the coming hours dawned once again on Mary. She caught Eileen's eye and drew her attention to the gun. They squeezed each other's hands in solidarity as they all manoeuvred the handcart over the cobblestones towards Sackville Street.

There were what seemed like hundreds of Volunteers and Cumann na mBan members taking over the General Post Office when they got there. As they entered by the side door, as they'd been instructed, a girl about her own age was being ordered to leave by a senior Volunteer. As the man marched off, the girl looked stricken and approached Mary.

'Aah, here, yez can't do tha'. Tha's me bike. I saved up for three years to buy tha' and I didn't know this was goin' ta happen. I'll only be a minute, please!' she pleaded with Mary.

Before she had time to answer, she heard a voice she knew behind her, 'Look, go on and get it, but be quick.'

Mary and Eileen spun round in the direction of the voice. She couldn't believe her eyes. 'Rory!'

'Hello, ladies, and welcome to the headquarters of free Ireland. Now I think ye are to set up a first aid station, is that right? Well, maybe upstairs at the back is the safest place for that, so find a corner there and get to work.' He winked as he gave them their instructions and gave Mary a quick squeeze as she passed.

'I saw that!' Eileen joked.

# CHAPTER 22

*E*ileen, Mary and Mrs Kearns strained to hear the voice of Pádraig Pearse as he read the Proclamation, declaring that Ireland was now, by order of the Provisional Government, an independent Republic.

The stirring opening words filled the men and women who heard him with resolve. Mary, who had never felt part of anything before her life in Dublin, found herself filled with emotion, all fear forgot. Though she had no blood relatives that she knew of, she was part of a family – this family of compatriots – and for a moment, she almost imagined the ghosts of heroes of the past were walking among them, giving them strength. Rory and Mrs Grant had given her books to read about brave Robert Emmet, the mighty O'Neill and O'-Donnell, the brave men at Vinegar Hill in 1798, all making their generation's bid for freedom from the hands of the oppressor, and now she felt their strength and approval. All the talk and meetings and endless lessons in bandaging and firing rifles were over, and the day had come. The revolution was a reality, and she, Mary Doyle – a nobody – was part of it.

'Irishmen and Irishwomen!' were called by Pearse to their nation's flag, to strike for Ireland's freedom. Mary and Eileen stood mesmerised as he looked so handsome and brave, saintly almost. There was something other-worldly about him. Perhaps the fact that he was a poet and a scholar rather than a soldier made him so. The other leaders, Connolly and Tom Clarke and MacDiarmuida, were different – brave and inspiring as well, but they seemed to be made of flesh and bone. Pearse was different. She said it once to Mrs Kearns, feeling a little foolish to be going on with such fanciful notions, but to her surprise, the housekeeper agreed with her.

Pearse stood for everything she hoped Ireland could become. He, and the country he represented, recognised her as an equal with the men who stood beside her. She felt so deeply now, as a result of all the people she'd met and loved since arriving in Dublin three years earlier, that she wanted to be part of a society where all children were cherished equally. She had never felt like she had power before in her life, since her very existence was the result of a sinful act, and she was a worthless drain on the nuns' resources, unworthy even of a family or a home. And yet now here she was, in the GPO in Dublin, her nation's capital city, taking an active role in fighting to free her country alongside her best friend and the man that she loved with all her heart.

The first aid station was set up, and other Cumann na mBan women came to inspect progress. James Connolly, leader of the Irish Citizen Army, was downstairs and had been heard arguing with some of the Volunteer officers, it seemed. He was a socialist, and also a supporter of women's rights. He wanted the women armed and fighting with the men, but Pearse wouldn't hear of it. He recognised women as equals on some levels and was happy for the women to be there, but only as cooks, doing first aid, and running messages to the other strongholds throughout the city. She smiled as she recalled Mrs Grant complaining about him a few weeks before when they had discussed his feelings on the subject. Rising up to her full five feet two inches, she had said imperiously, 'Chivalry is all very well and fine, when it comes to carriage doors and matters of little consequence, but it has no place in securing a nation's freedom.'

'At least Pearse lets us in,' Eileen whispered to Mary. 'De Valera is below in Boland's Mills, and he's refusing to allow any women in there at all!'

The shooting began that afternoon, albeit sporadically, as reports were coming in from all over the city. The British officers had gone to the races in Fairyhouse that day, leaving Dublin Castle with only a skeleton staff. It was a good day to strike. The news, brought by women couriers, was mixed. There had been a few victories, but as the night wore on, the by-now-startled British got more resources into Dublin. There was confusion down the country, but it seemed that, based on sketchy reports, Eoin MacNeill, the founder and chief of staff of the Volunteers, had countermanded the order to rebel, leaving battalions unsure of what to do next. Roger Casement, an ardent nationalist who was living in Germany, had been asked to procure weapons. He was arrested trying to bring in rifles, and MacNeill thought that without the supplies, the Rising would fail. The Volunteers were fuming at MacNeill's actions, but tried to make the best of a bad situation. The rebels had to focus on taking the city, and hoped to spread the Rising nationwide once the capital was secured.

Casualties were coming quickly now, and Mary and Eileen removed bullets and bandaged wounds as best they could. They were frugal with the supplies, fearing they would run out. There were a few doctors around for very urgent cases, but mostly they were left to themselves.

Mrs Kearns came up from the makeshift kitchen every few hours bearing hot soup and sandwiches when she could, and she greeted the girls warmly each time. Mrs Grant was acting as courier on a bicycle around the city, delivering messages between the various locations already captured by the rebels. Mary and Eileen marvelled at her bravery, but Mrs Kearns, who had known the mistress for years, was circumspect.

'She's a strong lady, right enough. Sure she's all in now anyway – that thundering so-and-so she married won't have her back now either way, nor us either, most likely. I just pray to God she doesn't get in the way of a bullet. God knows there are enough people being shot out there, and they only going about their business. Not to mention what would happen if she's caught, since there's no telling what they'd do to her.'

'They threw a lad out of a cart last weekend, on Leeson Street – the patrol had picked him up the day before. One of the Volunteers was telling me that even his mother didn't recognise him by the time they were finished with him.' Eileen shuddered as she spoke, her voice low, as wounded men were lying all around on makeshift stretchers. Some were half conscious, others agitated.

'We live in dangerous times, girls, and what can we do except keep on going? Now I'd better get back to my pot of soup below. I've a small fella coming with bread from a house up along, in a minute. Sure people are kind and we have right on our side, remember that! Now stay back from them windows, do you hear me?' As she spoke, a bullet whizzed past them, hitting a stone column three feet away. Squeezing their hands, she turned and was gone downstairs.

By Tuesday afternoon, the shelling was constant and the number of casualties ever-growing. A girl who had been acting as a courier down to Boland's was hit in the shoulder and was in terrible pain. They laid her down and managed to get a doctor to remove the worst of the damage, but she needed to be in hospital. Mary stopped two young lads, no more than fourteen, who were laying sandbags for protection.

'I need ye to carry a girl up to the hospital. She's badly hurt and she needs to be –'

'But Miss, we won't stand a chance out there if we have to carry someone. We can run between buildings and that ourselves, but the British are shooting anything that moves...' One of the boys was reasonable.

'All right... Can you get us more supplies? Bandages, disinfectant and anything else you can find?'

'Leave it to us.' And they were gone.

The hours wore on relentlessly, and despite their best efforts, some of the wounded died. Mary found that instead of being overwhelmed or distraught, she managed to remain practical, and with the help of Eileen, each did her job as well as she could. At one point Pearse himself came up and spoke to them briefly, thanking them for their commitment and offering encouragement. Eventually, other women came to help, allowing Mary and Eileen to sleep.

They lay down on some sacking near the back wall and felt the building shudder repeatedly, as incendiaries went off outside. Despite the mayhem surrounding them, Mary fell into an exhausted sleep, woken only occasionally by the screams and groans of the injured as they were carried, bleeding, to the first aid station.

The two other girls who had taken over were trying valiantly to cope with the casualties, coming now in ever-faster waves. One time, she and Eileen went back to their positions, feeling guilty for lying down when the others needed all the help they could get, but Countess Markievicz was on her rounds and insisted they leave the first aid station.

'You need rest, my dears. Otherwise you are of no use. Working while exhausted means mistakes, and we need to keep these men alive, so get some rest and we'll manage here.' Her tone, while kind, brooked no discussion. Gratefully, they returned to their makeshift bed.

Mary woke to a strange sensation. Someone was stroking her head. Forcing her eyes open, she saw Rory's dark features come into focus. He was sitting beside her on the floor. She sat up, but immediately panicked.

'What's happened to you? Oh, Rory, are you injured?' His uniform was filthy and blood ran down from a cut on his temple, and another over his eye.

'No, I'm grand. Just a scratch,' he said, but winced as he tried to smile.

'Here, let me see.' She got up and crossed to the first aid station and took some bandages and a basin of water. Gently she began to clean the cuts and noted with relief that he was right, the wounds weren't deep.

'What happened to you? Were you outside?' she whispered so as not to disturb Eileen.

'I was at Dublin Castle. We were hoping we could take it – what with all the officers either still at the races or sleeping off the effects – but we failed. Some others tried to get Trinity College too, but no good. Dev is dug in below at Boland's Mills, and Michael Mallin has Stephen's Green. The Four Courts and the South Dublin Union are ours as well, and we managed to do a fair bit of damage up in the Phoenix Park. So all in all, it could be worse.' He smiled and sighed, exhausted.

'It's going to get worse though, isn't it?' she asked, knowing the answer.

'Well, they're not happy, that's for sure. They think we have some cheek to demand our own country back, and when the mighty British Empire is riled, well...' He shook his head. 'You will remember our conversation, won't you, the day in the park?'

'Of course I will. But we're going to make it through this, Rory, I just feel it. Both of us. And then sure you can make an honest woman of me!'

Mary tried to inject her voice with humour. She knew from her meetings that the women had more to do than deliver messages and bandage wounds. Mrs Sheehy-Skeffington, and even the Countess, were constantly reminding them of the need to stay strong. She remembered the Countess's voice ringing over the crowd in Wynne's Hotel. 'Sisters in arms, it is absolutely imperative not to show weakness in the face of the enemy, but also, perhaps even more so, for our men who are being so brave. It is unhelpful and demoralising for them to see their women weeping or carrying on, making things even more difficult for them. Sacrifices are being made, and have been made for our beloved Ireland, and these pains have to be borne, however terrible, by men and women.'

*All those meetings about what we would do when the time came to make the sacrifices seem like a lifetime ago,* Mary thought. Now it was here, and those sacrifices were very real. She faced losing her home, her friends, her livelihood, and most of all, her future with Rory. It all seemed a lot to ask. She cleaned his cuts, and he winced as she dabbed disinfectant on them. She forced her thoughts away from the terror of anything more serious happening to him.

When she'd finished, he looked better. He took the cloth from her hands and placed it in the basin. He stood up and drew her into the shadows, behind a large pillar. Dawn was breaking, and the incessant shelling and gunshots continued relentlessly outside. She followed where he led until she felt the cold stone of a wall against her back. If the Countess were to come along now and find them, Mary dreaded to think of what would happen. Relationships with Volunteers were encouraged, but to be courting in corners while the Rising marched on bloodily would not be viewed favourably by anyone, she was sure.

'I love you, Mary Doyle,' he whispered in her ear as his arms went round her waist, 'and if God spares us, one day soon, you'll be Mrs O'Dwyer and we'll have a nice little house and ten babies.' He chuckled into her ear.

'Ten!' she whispered back, playfully punching him on the shoulder. 'What do you think I am, some kind of an old brood mare?'

'No, but I'm just thinking of all the fun we'll have making them.' He slapped her gently on the bottom.

'Rory O'Dwyer, I'll have you know I'm a respectable girl.' He stopped her protests with an urgent kiss. On and on he kissed her as she felt the chaos around them melt away and they were the only people in the world. His hands roamed all over her back and under her hair at her neck. She felt sure she shouldn't, but she held him tightly, praying the kiss could go on forever.

'Rory O'Dwyer! Has anyone seen Rory O'Dwyer?' An impatient man's voice cut through the early morning.

'That's it. I'm afraid duty calls!' he whispered. 'Mind yourself, my love. I'll pop back when I can. Stay away from the windows. There's snipers across the road.'

And he was gone.

# CHAPTER 23

Scarlett sat in her mother's small dining room, across the small table from possibly the creepiest man she'd ever seen. Fr Ennio reminded her of Mr Burns from *The Simpsons,* with his hunched back and shiny alabaster skin stretched over his small frame. Thin wisps of hair were stuck to his bald skull and his hands were like claws. His old-fashioned, full-length cassock, with red lining on the cape and ruby red buttons, made him look like the baddie in a kid's TV show. For the longest time he said nothing, merely muttered what sounded like incantations, as he fingered a rosary bead in his bony hand and refused to meet her eye.

Lorena was cooking something in the little

kitchen, leaving them alone. The sight of her mother when she had opened the door was a shock to Scarlett. Normally Lorena was beautifully dressed. She made many of her own clothes, but you could never tell – such was her expertise with fabric and stitching. Her auburn hair was always done perfectly and her make-up flawless. Her upbringing as a southern belle had ensured she was expert at grooming and deportment… and very little else. Even in the worst days of Dan's drinking, when they were close to being penniless, Lorena always made an effort to look nice. It was one of the many things she and her mother argued about. Lorena constantly bemoaned the fact that Scarlett seemed to live in jeans and T-shirts when she wasn't working. Today her mother's hair was lank and hung down her face, a face entirely bare of make-up, and she wore a long shapeless dress in a kind of beige colour with sleeves to her wrists. Scarlett barely recognised her.

'So, Father,' she began, 'my mother tells me that you and she have been talking about doing a pilgrimage?'

He looked up and his pale-blue eyes stared at her. Still he said nothing for a while.

Eventually, he spoke. 'You are filled with

demons. They battle for your soul. Satan is working within you. You must repent and do penance.' He whispered rather than spoke and his delivery was staccato. She fought the urge to giggle.

'Oh, ok. Well, I…' She was at a loss as to how to continue. What on earth was her mother doing with this guy? He was clearly crazy.

Sparing her the need to reply further, her mother appeared, cheerily announcing that lunch was ready. *At last*, Scarlett thought. She was determined to eat the food as quickly as was humanly possible and get the hell out of there. A niggling feeling at the back of her mind was telling her that she needed to do something about Lorena and this guy. He was clearly insane, but Lorena obviously thought he was wonderful. With everything she was trying to deal with, she just didn't need this too.

Her phone buzzed. A text from Charlie: *Hey Red, thinking about you xx*

She smiled. What she wouldn't give to spend the day in bed with Charlie, reading the papers, eating takeout and pretending the outside world didn't exist. She wondered for the millionth time where he was, how things were with Julia and what his plans were. Still, he wouldn't keep texting her if he was going to dump her, she reasoned.

Lorena placed a plate of food in front of her and she began to eat quickly.

'Scarlett! Please wait for the blessing of the Lord before you eat!'

Scarlett sighed and put down the fork and knife and bowed her head. How her mother had the ability to reduce her to a ratty teenager again never ceased to surprise her. The heat was turned up ludicrously high, even if it was chilly outside, and she could feel the perspiration between her shoulder blades despite the fact that she'd already removed her jacket and sweater.

Lorena had mentioned that she wanted to go on a trip to Mexico with the priest, but now that Scarlett had met him, she was sure that it was a bad idea. She tried once more to bring the subject up.

'Mom, about this Mexico trip. I'm not sure it's such a good idea. Perhaps somewhere a little less extreme would be better – Lourdes, maybe, or one of the other more recognised pilgrimage sites. There's loads of companies offering tours, you know, led by priests and everything –'

Fr Ennio interrupted her with his weird whispering voice. 'The path to the Lord, to true redemption, can only really be found through fasting and sacrifice. Lorena and I plan to fast at high altitudes in Mexico to try to gain closer association with God, for not only our own betterment, but also for the betterment of the whole of mankind. It has been known to happen at this holy site, that people can be brought by the Almighty, through protracted periods of deep, meditative prayer, into states of joyful bliss where it is possible to see the face of heaven. That is our goal.'

As he spoke, Scarlett observed him. He really was disturbingly peculiar. The way he spoke with such cold conviction was freaking her out. She had to get Lorena away from him.

'Fr Ennio is right, Scarlett. He alone knows the true path to redemption. He has the power of angels within him. He can combat the forces of Satan for the betterment of all mankind. I'm lucky to have been chosen by him.'

These weren't Lorena's words. Scarlett knew her mother, and however off-centre she was, she didn't normally go on with all this stuff about the forces of Satan. He and Lorena were obviously spending huge amounts of time together, and her conversation was becoming like a sermon on the gospel according to the weird priest. Scarlett couldn't figure out what his game was. Lorena didn't have any real money, because she only worked part time in a florist's, and Scarlett took care of her bills. So she was bewildered about the relationship that seemed to be getting closer and closer all the time.

'So, how many people are going on this trip to Mexico?' she asked, trying to sound conversational.

'Lorena and I will undertake this pilgrimage alone. But we will have the mighty strength of the Lord at our side,' Ennio lisped.

'But Father, with all due respect, depriving yourself and my mother of food at high altitudes over long periods of time would make anyone hallucinate. I'm not sure that what you are proposing is safe. Would you not consider going on a pilgrimage to a more recognised location? There are lots of places in Europe that might be easier on you and –'

'Scarlett, stop that immediately! Please, Fr Ennio, forgive my daughter. God knows I've tried to bring her up in the way of the Lord, but she is at constant risk of allowing Satan into her life. Scarlett, Fr Ennio is taking me to save my immortal soul from the fires of hell. Don't you realise how lucky I am to have him in my life? Without his spiritual guidance, I would have to spend all of eternity in the company of Satan! Only through Fr Ennio can I be saved!'

Scarlett watched this exchange with incredulity. Lorena really believed all this crap, and she had a slightly crazed look in her eyes as well. Scarlett had promised herself on the way over that she wouldn't lose her temper or be rude to anyone, so she was going to keep her promise. Her fear was that if this guy had a stronger hold on her mother than she first thought, she could drive her further away if she said anything derogatory about him. Scarlett hadn't seen her for several weeks, and she could see she was right to be worried.

'But Mom, why would you be going to hell? You're a good person, you never hurt anyone...' Scarlett put her hand on her mother's tiny one, speaking gently to her. When Lorena answered, Scarlett almost didn't recognise her voice. She was despairing, pleading.

'You don't understand, Scarlett. I am a sinner. All my life has been sinful. I married a man in the eyes of the Lord, and I did not honour or obey him as I should have. Now that he is dead, I cannot repent the sin of being a bad wife.'

Scarlett let out a snort, all semblance of

keeping her cool gone. 'Are you serious? Where are you getting this crap from? You were a bad wife to Dan O'Hara? Lorena, have you lost your mind? He was a violent, useless, lazy drunk. The day he died was the best day of our lives, and you know it!'

'Scarlett! How could you say such a thing about your father?' Lorena was anguished: All colour drained from her face, her fists clenched. 'He was your father and my husband, and maybe if we'd all tried to understand and support him instead of –'

'Oh, for Chrissake. This is just garbage, Mother. Is it you who've been filling her head with this crap?' Scarlett turned her venom on Fr Ennio, who had started praying frantically, muttering incantations and making the sign of the cross on himself repeatedly.

Suddenly he stood up from the table. 'We must leave this place, Lorena, my child. Satan is at work here. He has possessed your daughter and he is working his evil through her. You are at risk – your soul is at risk, Lorena. Come with me now, away from this devil woman…' He held up the huge crucifix he had around his neck towards her in the way Scarlett had seen vampire hunters do in bad movies. If he wasn't so serious, she would have laughed at him.

He was pulling Lorena by the hand, trying to get her to leave with him. Scarlett stood between her mother and the priest. 'Ok. Enough! Let her go!' she found herself yelling into his pale face. Her tone brooked no argument. Scarlett towered over him and removed his hand from Lorena.

'I think you'd better go now.' Scarlett spoke quietly, realising how distressed her mother was. She was weeping silently and beseeching the priest with her eyes not to leave. It reminded Scarlett of the way she looked when Dan was bearing down on her before he attacked.

Lorena wrenched her arm away from Scarlett and turned on her in fury. 'You are the work of the devil. Fr Ennio is trying to save me, trying to re-move the sin from my body and soul, but Satan is at work. You –' She pointed at Scarlett '– fornicating with men! God knows how many. But not happy with that sin of lust on your soul, no, you had to commit adultery as well, breaking up a family be-cause of your uncontrollable carnal desires! You are a she-devil, the work of the beast. You are an abom-ination! Get out of my house!' Lorena's eyes were unnaturally bright and her body shook violently.

Scarlett was in shock. She had never even seen her mother lose her temper in all her life.

Fr Ennio witnessed the exchange and decided things were getting out of hand, so he left, declaring ominously, 'Satan is at work in this house!' Lorena stayed, facing her daughter alone. They stood like that for long seconds, neither knowing what to say next, both in deep shock.

Then Lorena ran to the window, watching the priest depart up the street and crying silently, her hands on the glass. Scarlett was stone-faced. Her memories of her childhood, while blighted by the fact that Dan was her father, were not all bad. She remembered the comfort of sitting on her mother's knee after the cops took Dan, looking at the old movie magazines. She remembered going to the movie theatre on 104th Street to see her namesake in *Gone with the Wind* – about a hundred times – and how, while on the way home on the subway, she and Lorena would speak bits of the script to each other.

Scarlett knew her mother had become more religious over the years, and even though she saw it all as mumbo-jumbo, she believed it was harmless and would often go into churches and light a candle for her mother. She brought her holy statues or biographies of saints for birthdays and

Christmas, and her mother always seemed touched that she had made the effort.

Scarlett knew that in recent years she had neglected her mother, and shut her out of her life while she built her career. And then, once she'd met Charlie, he took up all her time. She could never tell Lorena about him, so she chose to avoid her. A wave of guilt crashed over her, knowing she had allowed this religious fervour to get out of hand because it suited her to have Lorena so involved with the Church. The more energy she put into that, the less time she had for annoying her daughter. She felt wretched for ignoring her mother, but the way she had just spoken to her was deeply shocking.

It never occurred to her for one moment in her whole life that her mother didn't love her... until now. It shook her to the core.

Lorena seemed calmer now, but in a trance-like state, her arms wrapped round herself as if she was cold. She stood with her back to the room, gazing out the window to the street where Fr Ennio had run. She had rosary beads in her hand and was muttering prayers, Scarlett presumed. Even if she wanted to talk to Lorena, she doubted that she could, for she seemed so far away. She approached her, but Lorena seemed oblivious to her presence.

'Mom.' Nothing.

'Lorena, are you ok?' she asked tentatively. Her mother just stared out the window, her lips moving but the rest of her rigid. Catatonic, almost, despite the muttering. Scarlett knew that this was serious. She had no idea what was wrong with her mother, but she knew she needed help to deal with it. In the absence of any better idea, she called an ambulance, explained what had happened, and was reassured by the paramedic she spoke to that they were on the way, and that she had done the right thing. Scarlett began to clear the untouched plates from the table, scraping the uneaten food into the large bowl in the centre. She stacked the plates and carried them into the kitchen and began loading the dishes into the dishwasher silently.

Her mother would need clothes and a sponge bag if she was going to be admitted to hospital, so Scarlett went into her mother's bedroom. The sight that greeted her made her blood run cold. The room was literally covered with the most gruesome pictures of martyrs and saints that Scarlett had never seen before, and over her bed was an almost life-size statue of Jesus on the cross. Scarlett was shocked and terrified. What on earth was going on in her mother's head? She always had little crucifixes and holy pictures, but not these things, like something from a horror movie.

She tried to block out the macabre décor and opened drawers, taking out underwear, slippers and a nightgown for her mother. On the back of the door was her dressing gown. She'd had it for years, and Scarlett could remember the feeling of comfort it gave her as a child to rest her face against the soft old cotton as Lorena told her she was named after the most beautiful woman in the world. She put the dressing gown in the bag, along with some wash things, and zipped it closed. There was a prayer book beside the bed and a Bible on the nightstand but she decided Lorena had enough of that for now.

She opened the wardrobe to get her mother's coat and hat, and that was when she spotted the box. It was the one Lorena had kept hidden from Dan all those years ago, full of movie magazines that she and Scarlett used to look at. Tentatively she opened the box, half expecting its contents to have been replaced with more religious para-phernalia, but she was relieved to find it exactly the same – full of photos, magazines, and posters from the Golden Age of Hollywood. Closing the box, Scarlett hoped that maybe there was some of the old Lorena left, and that she could be found.

The sound of the doorbell split the eerie silence of the house. The paramedics had arrived.

'Is she going to be ok? Will I go with her?' she asked as they gently eased Lorena into a wheelchair and tucked blankets around her. Her mother obediently did as they asked, though she was totally disconnected from her surroundings.

'Are you family?'

'Yes, I'm her daughter. Where are you taking her?'

'The Payne Whitney Psychiatric Clinic – it's on the Upper East Side. Don't worry. She's in good hands now.'

'Should I come in the ambulance with her?' she asked, unsure of what to do next.

'Well, maybe if you follow in your car, that way it will be there for you when you need to leave?'

Scarlett nodded, relieved that someone seemed to be thinking clearly. They pushed Lorena past the door and Scarlett took the small bag containing her things. She watched as they opened the ambulance doors, and one of the paramedics sat in the back and strapped Lorena into a seat, talking soothingly to her all the time. She never looked at them or spoke a word, just kept on squeezing her rosary beads through her fingers and mouthing prayers.

Scarlett stood on the pavement, watching the ambulance pull out into the light Sunday traffic.

# CHAPTER 24

'I'm sorry for just dropping by again like this, Eileen. I just didn't know where else to go.' Scarlett sat in Eileen's sunny kitchen while the older woman smiled kindly.

'Don't be silly, Scarlett, it's lovely to see you. I told you you're always welcome. How did it go with your mother yesterday?'

She placed a cappuccino in front of Scarlett.

'I thought you didn't have any coffee?' Scarlett asked, surprised.

Eileen looked abashed. 'Well, I hoped you'd call again, so after you left yesterday I went to the Vietnamese grocery store up the street and got some. I wasn't sure what kind to get, since I'm a dedicated tea drinker, but Zong, the girl that works there, is really helpful. She's doing a master's in history, so I help her out sometimes with proofreading and things like that. Anyway, she suggested I get this kind. She says everyone likes cappuccino. Is it all right?'

Scarlett was so touched at the small gesture, she felt a lump rise in her throat. 'It's great, thanks!' She sipped it, and though she would never normally order one, she found the sweet frothiness comforting.

'How about something to eat? Have you eaten yet?'

She suddenly realised that last thing she ate was the few bites of lunch at her mother's before everything blew up.

'I'm fine, Eileen. Honestly. The coffee's perfect.'

'Well, how about I make you a sandwich anyway. Grilled cheese? I think it makes almost everyone feel better.'

'That would be exactly what I'd love.' She felt guilty at accepting Eileen's kindness when her own mother was lying in a hospital bed due to her only child's neglect.

Eileen busied herself getting bread and cheese and Scarlett watched her. She really was very sprightly for her age, and totally different than the shaken woman she had met the first day after the burglary.

'So…' Eileen paused. 'Tough night?' She wasn't probing. Scarlett knew she would be just as happy to talk about the weather, but wanted to get it off her chest.

Scarlett felt so tired. Where to begin? She'd spent most of the night awake, waiting to get some diagnosis of her mother's condition. She sat beside Lorena's bed while she slept. The nurse had given her a sedative because she had become agitated, and they assured Scarlett that after that she would be fine, but Scarlett was reluctant to leave her mother. She looked so small and vulnerable in the bed. Over and over she berated herself for being so selfishly wrapped up in her own life that she had failed to look after Lorena. She eventually went home in the early hours, but couldn't sleep. She longed to call Charlie, just to hear his voice, but resisted. Instead, as soon as it was a reasonable time, she called Artie and told him what had happened. As usual, he was gruff, but she could hear the concern in his voice. He promised he'd use his connections to find out more about this Fr Ennio, and true to his word, he called her back twenty minutes later with what he found out.

One of Artie's friends was a rabbi who played golf with the bishop. It seems that Ennio had been removed from his parish a year ago after several complaints were sent to the bishop's office about his extreme views. The Church allowed him to stay in his house and gave him a small pension in the hope that he'd just live out his life calmly. They were horrified with the news of what he had done to Lorena, and the bishop wanted to meet Scarlett. That prospect was just too much to cope with on top of everything else. She'd eventually decided to get out of her house, as the walls were closing in on her. Artie invited her to lunch at his house, but she knew his kids and grandkids were coming too, and she just wasn't in the mood to socialise. So Eileen was the only other person she could talk to.

As she told Eileen the story, the reality of what had happened sank in. Explaining it as best she could to Eileen was helping her make sense of it in her own head.

She told Eileen about the shock of seeing her mother's bedroom and recounted the hurtful things Lorena had said.

'You poor thing. What a horrible thing to experience!' Eileen was sympathetic. 'Your mother must be a very ill lady to say those things. I know it's going to be hard to forget, but try to think of it as it being her, but not her – if you know what I mean. She is clearly being influenced by this priest, and I don't think, from what you told me about her, that she really meant those things she said. The thing is, usually faith is a good thing – at least, from where I'm coming from it is, anyway. But when you lose focus on the present, on the here and now, and your mind is taken over by what you imagine the spiritual world to be, then that's not living. And we are here to do just that – to live, and to try to be happy and be true to ourselves and those around us. You mentioned the fact that your father was violent. Maybe this was her way of trying to process all of that.'

'Maybe, but the thing is, it isn't just that,' Scarlett said quietly. 'I've ignored it for so long. I knew it wasn't right, but I thought that it kept her occupied and out of my hair. I really did think it was harmless. Also, I'm so angry at her, for so many things that I…'

'Why are you angry?' Eileen was gentle.

'Where to start? This stupid name, for starters. Why do that to a kid? I just don't get it. But I guess more for the fact that she could have left him, my father. She should have, but she didn't, and so I had the most horrible childhood. No fun, only fear. I would never put a child through that. I never said it to her – she's kind of vulnerable or something. It would have been like kicking a puppy. She was my mother – she should have protected me, and she didn't.'

Scarlett was surprised at herself. She had never verbalised these feelings before.

'Scarlett – it's a lovely name, by the way – you've had a terrible shock. You have enough to deal with in your own life right now, and now this. I understand how you feel, why you feel anger at her. Maybe it's time you gave yourself and your mom a break? This is hard, but maybe it will prove to be the thing you need to get things back with your mother. She does love you, I'm sure of it, and you love her too. But sometimes life just gets really complicated and we lose sight of what matters to us. Have you spoken to the hospital this morning?'

'Yeah, I spoke to the registrar. I called him as I was coming over here, but the main guy won't be there until tomorrow. She's ok – comfortable, is what they said. She did freak out in the hospital last night, and she scratched the nurse's face. But they sedated her and they're going to keep her mildly sedated until they can assess her fully.'

'And is there any sign of this priest?' Eileen asked.

'I need to speak to someone higher up in the Church, the bishop or someone, about him, I think. From what I can gather from Artie – that's my boss who owns the newspaper. I called him this morning because he knows the most unlikely people, and he found out this guy was sidelined and relieved of all his duties from his parish around a year ago. He was getting weirder and weirder, it seems, and the Church decided to take him out of the ministry after getting lots of complaints. The hope was that he would just toddle off into retirement, and the Church's intention were to house him and take care of him quietly. That plan backfired, and now he's a major headache for the diocese. I'm sure they're hoping that my mother is his only victim, but we have no idea. There may be other poor people under his influence as well. The most important thing to do now is track him down. He's not at his house, and he hasn't been seen since leaving my mother's house yesterday. Now it looks like we have to involve the police.'

'Does your mother have any money? Is that what he's after, do you think?' Eileen was pensive.

'No, that's the thing. Of course, your first

thought when something happens like this is that it's a scam of some kind, but Lorena has nothing really of value. She works in a flower shop part time and I help her out with bills and other stuff, so that's not what he's after. It's a mystery as to what's in it for him.'

She bit into the delicious grilled cheese sandwich and realised she was starving. Eileen put a large slice of homemade coffee walnut cake in front of her for afterwards.

'Well, is there a physical connection? I mean, is it an affair, do you think? Could that explain it?' Eileen asked.

Scarlett laughed for the first time since everything happened. 'No, definitely not! You should see this guy. He looks like Mr Burns from *The Simpsons,* all bent and skinny and bald and so creepy. No way. Lorena spends what little money she has on glamour. She loves clothes and jewellery and always has her hair done and her make-up perfect. She's a southern belle, through and through. Though I never saw her like she was when I got there yesterday – wearing a big, shapeless thing, her hair hanging over her face, and no make-up. In my whole life, she's been the one usually on at me for not dressing up enough. There's no way she's involved with him like that. Urgh.' Scarlett shuddered at the thought.

'Well, I do know they say that a sign of mental health issues is when someone loses interest in their appearance. I wonder what he wants... Maybe nothing. Maybe he's just crazy and really believes all that stuff,' Eileen wondered.

'Yeah, it's hard to know, isn't it? One thing I do know is that I'm going to track this guy down and make sure he doesn't do anything like this again. Who knows? He could have loads of old ladies under his weird spell. The Church will have to do something.'

On and on they talked all afternoon about everything and nothing. Eileen spoke about her own mother and the relationship they had – which was close, but not perfect, either. As Scarlett devoured another slice of the delicious cake, Eileen revealed it was her mother who had taught her how to bake.

As Scarlett was getting up to leave, her phone rang. It was Charlie.

'Hey, Red!' Her heart quickened – even the sound of his voice made her nervous with anticipation. Maybe he was going to suggest they meet. She'd risk it, even if they were being followed, just to see him again.

Eileen discreetly left the room to give her some privacy.

'Hi! How are you?' she asked.

'Ok, I guess. You know how it is. You?' He sounded strange, distracted.

'Well, things have been a bit stressful actually. My mother –' she began, but he interrupted her.

'Listen, Red, I can't stay on long. I gotta go in a second, but I just needed to talk to you.' Warmth flooded through her. He needed to talk to her.

She was about to respond that she needed to talk to him too when he went on, his voice low and urgent.

'I need you to promise me something. I'm so sorry for how everything turned out, you know that, right? But I need you to not react, ok? I'm going on *CBS Evening News* on Friday. Jordan Flint is interviewing me, and I'm gonna have to say some things that I don't want to say. But I'm not left with any choices here, Red – you get that, right? I'd never deliberately hurt you, so please just ignore everything…'

Scarlett was trying to process this as she was listening to him. 'Say what? What are you going to say? Something about me?' Panic was rising in her chest. She was trying to stay calm, but surely he wasn't going to do one of those confessional

TV interviews where he said he was a sex addict who loved his wife, or something like that?

'Look, I'm gonna steer it way from you as much as I can, but I guess they will want to talk about us. I have to say it was nothing. It's the only way I can recover anything from this. If you care for me at all, Red, you just won't react, ok? They'll be after you for a few days again, like when it broke, but you know how it goes. They'll leave you alone once something more interesting comes along. Can you do this for me?'

She couldn't speak. She had seen politicians and celebrities who had fallen from grace on these kinds of shows before, tugging the nation's heartstrings. She admitted to herself that she had never spared a thought for the other woman. Neither would anyone else, she realised. Through the haze of her confusion, she thought she could hear someone else on the line.

'Red, are you there? Red? Look, another thing – if you need money, I can get some to you. Are you even listening to me?'

She could hear the panic in his voice. Was he trying to bribe her to keep her mouth shut?

'Yeah, I'm here.' Voices behind him again.

'Look, I gotta go. I love you. Please just do this for me.' The line went dead.

# CHAPTER 25

Scarlett sat in the bright sunny office overlooking the hospital gardens, trying to process what she was being told.

'This is very complicated territory to discuss, because we are very reluctant to paint any firm belief in a religious idea as crazy. The last thing we want is to label anyone as insane because of their spiritual convictions. After all, few religions would stand up to logical reasoned explanation, but we do not dismiss as deluded those who believe in the resurrection, or transubstantiation, for example. And yet, we as psychiatrists know a significant percentage of patients fall victim to psychiatric disorders that include fixed and false beliefs, what we call *delusions*. They don't talk about the CIA following them, or extraterrestrials visiting them, but they're convinced they've been chosen by God for special missions, or are being told by God to fast, or they labour under the belief of actually *being* God. Religious delusions can afflict those who have expressed no prior deep religious faith, or they can befall those who are practising Muslims or Christians or Jews. I remember one man whose first episode of mental illness included arriving at the ER carrying a statue of the Virgin Mary, which he had stolen from a local church, believing he was receiving messages from her.'

Scarlett listened intently to the psychiatrist, whose voice was soothing and gentle. He looked like a kind old uncle with a green suit and a purple bow tie. His shiny bald head shone in the sunlight, and his large belly seemed to be putting undue pressure on his shirt buttons. She could imagine him as being very serene around people in distress, patients or their families, despite his garish outfit. His room was incredibly warm, and through the slightly open window you could hear voices from the garden below, where Lorena sat on a bench with a member of the clinic's staff.

She had seemed calm when Scarlett saw her earlier, but she looked much older and smaller, as if all the life was gone out of her.

'So, Dr Wells, is she depressed? Can this be reversed?'

'Delusions *do* sometimes occur in the setting of depression. Yet spiritual awakenings can occur at moments of desperation, too. And this is the tremendously difficult terrain we walk when we bring up the question of religious beliefs crossing the line into psychiatric symptoms.'

Despite his kind manner, Scarlett was getting frustrated with what seemed like fluffy answers.

Scarlett interjected, 'Ok, so she is having delusions, you think. Brought about either by depression or desperation. But what do we do now? Does she stay here, forever being medicated, or do we send her back home and hope she comes back to her old self?'

The psychiatrist smiled. 'I understand your frustration, I really do. It is extremely frightening and difficult to deal with a case such as your mother's. I understand you went to visit with her before seeing me? Well, you will have noticed that she is much less agitated, but she may have seemed a bit distant, unreachable?'

'Exactly,' Scarlett said, relieved. At least they didn't think this was a reasonable state for Lorena to be in. 'She appeared to be mildly pleased to see me and she spoke, but just about the garden and how pretty it was. She never mentioned the episode with Ennio, or how she spoke to me that day.'

'Yes, well, she remains mildly sedated, which explains her demeanour. I intend to reduce the dosage over the coming days, while monitoring her to see how she is coping with, "re-entry into the world," as it were. I am hopeful that she will recover from this episode, but there is undoubtedly underlying trauma there. I understand she had an abusive marriage in her youth?'

Scarlett nodded. 'My father was a violent alcoholic who regularly took out his rages on her.'

'And how did she cope with that?' His questions were gentle but probing.

'Well, she's not normally like she is now. Not just the religion, but everything. She's usually very glamorous, loves fashion and always looks well groomed. She always took her inspiration from the movies – the old ones, you know, from the Golden Era of Hollywood. And she had lots of magazines and things, and she would show me the pictures after my father had been arrested or just gone off drinking or whatever. It was like her escape. She's always been a little – I don't know, eccentric – but this is a whole new departure for her.'

Dr Wells chuckled. 'Aah, that explains your beautiful name then?'

Scarlett smiled. 'I'm used to it now, I guess, but yeah, she named me after the Vivien Leigh character. I've spent a lifetime explaining. It's been a pain, though, since I look nothing like my namesake.'

'I can imagine.' He smiled sympathetically.

Scarlett shrugged. 'As I said, I'm used to it now. But the thing is, she was always a little bit into religion. She was raised Baptist in Georgia, but I think all the flamboyance of Catholicism appealed to her, since she's very dramatic.' Scarlett added with a wry smile, 'So when she married my father, he was Irish and a Catholic, and she embraced it. But it was going to Mass on Sundays and dressing up for Easter and Christmas, that kind of thing, not like the way she has been recently.'

'So do you think anything might have triggered her relationship with this Fr Ennio? A reason why she moved towards him and away from the more standard Catholic Church? You mentioned she hasn't been seen at her local parish church for some time.'

Scarlett shrugged. 'I've no idea. I haven't seen much of her recently. When we talked on the phone, I knew she was getting a bit more into it, but I'd no idea it had come to this. I'm shocked, and I've no idea what to do next. I know you can't tell me exactly, but if I even had some idea where we might go with her…'

'Well, in my experience – and bearing in mind that no two cases are identical – I can tell you that sometimes the patient is fine, coming back to their old selves and no reoccurrences. Other times it leads to further episodes, which can be more or less severe. The key would be to ensure there is no contact between her and this priest. Maximum benefit can be gained by removing the person from the environment where the events that precipitated the episode took place, particularly in the early weeks after treatment, though this isn't always possible, of course.'

'Do you mean, like, move her from home, get her out of the neighbourhood?' Scarlett asked.

'No, nothing as drastic as that. Patients often do well after a little vacation, maybe. Somewhere away from the scene of the episode, where the potential triggers are limited. Somewhere that the patient can continue their recovery in the weeks after discharge from hospital. I have found that immediate replacement of the patient into the environment from which they came can lead to a regression – not always, of course, but sometimes. A little vacation, somewhere calm, can be like a stepping stone back into life, rather than plunging head first. But it's just a thought since I don't know if it is possible, or even something you would want to do. Meanwhile, you can think about it and we will continue with the course of treatment. I am hopeful to see some positive developments over the coming weeks.'

He got up and smiled. 'Now if you'll excuse me, I have to do my rounds. Please feel free to contact me should you have any further questions, and drop in to visit as often as you like. Feeling loved and wanted is absolutely crucial to your mother's recovery.'

He shook her hand warmly and ushered her out. Before she went back to face Lorena, she needed a moment to gather herself.

Charlie was doing the interview tonight. She hadn't decided whether to watch it or not, but she was dreading it. Artie had been calling for the past few days, so she decided to drop in to him after the hospital.

She spent the rest of the afternoon with Artie, drinking beer in his garden. Kathy was visiting a friend across town, so he was smoking incessantly in her absence. Scarlett tried to admonish him, but it was pointless.

Waving a cigarette in her face, he growled, 'Y'-know, kid, the only reason I put up with the nagging about the smokes from my old lady is cause there's somethin' in it for me, but I don't gotta listen to you, y'hear? So if you are comin' round here bein' all preachy, then you know what you can do. Now shut up and tell me what that jerk is gonna say on TV tonight.'

Scarlett sighed. 'I don't know. But I can guess it's not going to be good.' She told him about the phone call.

'You're worth ten of that worthless loser, you know that, don't you? Whatever he says, remember, people ain't dumb. He's saving his own sorry ass and people will see that.' He patted her hand roughly. She was touched at how protective he was of her these days. How strange that her two best friends were a chain-smoking old editor and an ancient old lady.

She told Artie the story of Eileen's flag – the bit she knew, anyway.

Artie listened. 'Hey, that might be something there. Sounds like an interesting story. Why don't you write it?'

Scarlett shrugged. 'I don't know. She might not want me to after she was so scared it had been taken. Her house is full of Irish political stuff, not shamrocks and all that, but actual photographs, and probably loads of other stuff to do with the Easter Rising in Ireland. She's a tough lady, even if she looks like someone's grandma. She doesn't have an agenda. She's perfectly happy to keep her flag and never tell anyone anything about it. I'd hate her to think I was just after a story.'

'Suit yourself. What are you doing for money?'

Scarlett hated the way Artie knew what buttons to press to drive her crazy. She fought not to rise to his bait.

'Not much. I wasn't at the *Globe Messenger* long enough to make any real money. I kinda went a bit crazy buying stuff at the start. I've saved some over the years, so for now that will do. Charlie offered…'

Artie crushed a cigarette butt into the patio and then immediately lit up another.

'He's that desperate, huh, paying you to keep schtum? The guy is even more of a lowlife than I first thought. Look, I'll lodge a few bucks in your account – just to tide you over, ok?'

She started to protest, but he interrupted her. 'Look, kid, I have it, you don't right now. Pay me back when you can. Now shut up about it.' He took a sip of his beer. 'Has the *Globe Messenger* contacted you at all?'

'No, nothing. I got a letter from the legal department requesting that I don't give any interviews about the thing with Charlie, and that if I mention the *Globe Messenger*, I am open to litigation. But apart from that touching little correspondence, nothing. One or two guys from the foreign office sent texts, but no. I'm a pariah, it seems.'

She knew that despite his gruff attitude, Artie cared about her and worried about her.

'But you gotta be entitled to something? Shouldn't you get yourself a lawyer and see what the game is? They aren't gonna want their name dragged through the media spotlight again, not after last time. Maybe they'll give you a payout just to shut you up.'

'Maybe. I'll think about it. I was so shell-shocked when it happened that I couldn't think of anything but how shameful the whole thing was. And now I've got this thing with my mother to sort out, and a job to find, and I'm just waiting for the fallout from whatever Charlie is going to say. But I'm tough.' She smiled. 'I'll be ok.'

'Attagirl' he said, clinking his bottle off hers.

# CHAPTER 26

Scarlett was looking at the photos in Eileen's small living room, and then she read the copy of the Irish Proclamation of Independence that was framed on the wall. To her surprise, the prose really moved her. She found profoundly uplifting the idea that a document, intended to be the declaration of a free country in 1916, would open with the lines 'Irish Men and Irish Women', when women didn't even have a vote. These people didn't just seek liberation from England, but they wanted a truly equitable and free society, where 'all children of the nation are cherished equally'. The leader of the rebellion, Pádraig Pearse, was a poet and a teacher, and it showed in this composition.

Eileen had called her cell phone as she was leaving Artie's to ask her to come over, and explained why she wanted to see her.

'Forgive me if I am being presumptuous, Scarlett, but I know the interview with Charlie Morgan is airing tonight, and I didn't want you to be alone watching it. I thought if you had no other plans, you could come over here and we could watch it together.'

'I wasn't going to watch it at all, actually, Eileen.' Scarlett's heart was heavy.

'Oh, dear, I know you must be dreading it, and of course you know best, but sometimes it's better to face our fears head on. At least if you hear for yourself his take on it, and see him saying it, it will make things clearer for you. You'll know exactly what you have to deal with.'

Scarlett knew she was right. She had to watch it.

As Eileen walked into the room carrying a tray, there was the unmistakable sound of the theme tune to the *CBS Evening News*. Scarlett felt sick with nerves as the voice of Jordan Flint filled the small room. She had met him a few times, and didn't like him. He was charming and good looking, but she got the impression that he'd do anything for a story.

'Welcome to *Evening News*. Tonight our top story: Congressman Charlie Morgan on his fall from grace. Then Lara Crosbie is reporting from Aleppo on the worsening situation in Syria, and finally, the nation speaks on the ongoing debates on Obamacare.'

His smile never faded as he turned to his guest. Charlie looked like his old self again, well groomed, tanned, and happy. The time out with his family had done him good. Scarlett's stomach lurched at the sight of him.

'Congressman Morgan, thank you for agreeing to talk to us this evening. I understand this is your first interview since the story of your relationship with the political analyst from a leading city newspaper broke.'

*Flint had to get in that he scooped everyone else.*

Charlie smiled, a totally fake smile, but Scarlett realised only she would know that.

'Yes, Jordan, I have been devoting my time to my family, who have been incredibly supportive during this very difficult time. But I felt the people of this country, those hardworking Americans who elected me, deserve to hear the truth.'

'And that truth is that you had an extramarital affair, and potentially compromised your position as an elected member of Congress...' Flint's

reasonable tone belied the sharpness of his ac-
cusation.

'Yes. I am guilty of betraying my beautiful
wife, who has been a rock of support, and my
wonderful family. But I must state this clearly: At
no time did I do or say anything that would, in
any way, compromise the integrity of our political system.' Charlie was adamant.

'Interesting that you should use the word *integrity*, Congressman. Don't you think the people
you represent deserve better from you? After all,
you were elected because people could identify
with you – the ordinary Joe image. People liked
and respected you. A hardworking family man,
upholding family values, and yet you proved to be
totally unworthy of that respect. You lied to
everyone,' Flint said.

Scarlett's heart went out to Charlie. It must be
horrific to have to sit there and take this conde-
scending crap from a guy who was acting like
butter wouldn't melt in his mouth.

'Well, Jordan, you are right. I have let people
down. My marriage is the most important thing
to me, and my children, of course. I wasn't lying
about that. Look, I'm not going to sit here and
make out like I did what I did because my wife
didn't understand me, or because I wasn't loved

as a child. The truth is, I was pursued relentlessly by a young woman who had her career in mind. I was flattered – of course I was. And as time went on and she became more persistent, I succumbed. Should I have? Of course not. I should have rejected her advances out of hand, but I'm weak. That's the reality. An attractive, career-driven young woman made me her goal and I fell for it. She was determined, and I wasn't strong enough to resist.'

Charlie spoke directly to the camera, and she could swear tears were glistening in his eyes. She felt like she'd been punched in the stomach. How could he say that? Making out like she was some kind of power crazy stalker. Eileen held her hand.

'So, Ms O'Hara, she really is the Scarlett woman?' Flint chuckled. 'She is the "bunny boiler" and you're the victim of her evil plan. Come now, Congressman, you surely don't think you can blame her for all of this?'

Charlie smiled ruefully. 'Of course not. We were both involved, but I have lost a lot more than Ms O'Hara. I was foolish and flattered, and I wasn't able to see what she was trying to do, which was further her own career.'

Flint looked incredulous. 'Are you seriously expecting the nation to accept that someone as politically astute as you was seduced by a self-serving young woman who set out to ruin you?'

Charlie ran his hand through his hair. 'I guess I am, because it's what happened.'

Eileen pressed the Off button on the remote.

'I think we've heard enough from him, haven't we?' She spoke quietly.

Scarlett tried to speak, but no sound came out. This was a nightmare, surely. Charlie hadn't just gone on national TV and said that it was all her fault? Like Glenn Close in the Michael Douglas movie – she couldn't think of the name of it right now. How could he do that? Then she thought back to the last phone conversation, when he begged her not to react to the interview. Sam Winters would have made him make the call. She was sure now that he was standing behind Charlie each time they spoke. He was protecting himself, and she was going to be his scapegoat.

'I never… That's a lie! I thought he loved me,' she croaked. She needed Eileen to know that she wasn't the horrible calculating monster she had been painted as.

'I know you did, Scarlett. He's a horrible, self-serving man and is not worthy of you, or of his wife, for that matter.' Eileen was gentle.

'He… He's not really like that. Not really. He's

kind and funny and…' She wanted so much to believe that. Her phone beeped.

*Sorry* was all it said. She threw the phone at the wall.

Eileen picked it up. 'Perhaps getting a new phone would be a good idea. And a new number? That way all those people who texted and called when the story broke won't be able to contact you. And neither will he.'

Scarlett knew Eileen was right. She needed to protect herself now, and the first part of that would be to cut off all communication with Charlie. She looked at the phone, her last link to him. Once she cut that off, she would have no way of contacting him…nor he her.

It buzzed again and she looked, disgusted with herself for hoping it was him. It was Artie.

*He's an asshole. You are great. A x*

Eileen held her hand as she cried.

She slept that night, eventually, in the pretty floral bedroom at the back of Eileen's house. She couldn't bear to be alone, so Eileen offered a bed for the night and she accepted gratefully. Eileen had been amazing, kind and gentle last night, and had allowed her to cry for as long as she needed to. Scarlett was so touched. When she had no more tears left she sat, drained, in Eileen's sitting room. Eileen held both her hands and looked straight into her eyes.

'Now, listen to me, Scarlett. I don't know much about relationships. I never married, but I did have a few boyfriends over the years. I do know this with absolute certainty: Charlie Morgan is not worth your tears. You're a lovely, kind, smart woman, and you're so much better than him, for all his money and power. I know you loved him – maybe a part of you still does – but honestly, you should try to put this whole sorry mess behind you. Put it down to experience and move on. Don't beat yourself up endlessly. You fell in love, and I'm not saying you are totally blameless. You did know he was married, but he was the one who made a promise to someone else and broke it. You deserve a man of your own, one who'll treat you properly. Now go on off to bed and try to sleep. Everything will look better in the morning, I promise. At least the press can't find you here.'

Scarlett slept all night and when she woke, she showered and dressed in the clothes she had been wearing the previous day. She'd have to go home, but the thought of the gathered media outside her house made her nauseous. She went downstairs. Eileen was sitting at the kitchen table drinking a cup of tea. She was immaculately groomed as usual, wearing a grey skirt and a pink blouse, and her silver hair shone. Scarlett noticed how Eileen's nails were always manicured, and her bathroom had some lovely skincare products. Taking care of herself was obviously important to her, and it explained how she looked so good for her age.

'Coffee?' she asked, smiling. 'Did you sleep?'

Scarlett smiled. 'Very well, thanks – that bed is so comfortable. Coffee would be great.'

'How about some eggs?' Eileen asked.

'I'm fine. I don't want to put you to any more trouble.' She was mortified about everything Charlie had said and that it was necessary for Eileen to comfort her.

'It's no trouble at all, dear. I'm making some for myself anyway. You'll need your strength. How are you feeling this morning?'

Scarlett put her face in her hands and sighed. 'Oh, Eileen, where to start? Embarrassed, ashamed, let down, heartbroken, like a complete fool… Take your pick. I know I said it last night, and I know it doesn't make what I did go away, but it really wasn't like he said. It was mutual. I'm not the kind of person that goes out to wreck other people's marriages just for the hell of it, or to advance my own career.'

Eileen filled the kettle with water and said, 'I know that. I know you're a good person, Scarlett, one who made a mistake. Very few can say they've never done that. As I said, I think the best thing to do now is forget about it. Throw your energies into something else and the pain will go away, the press will lose interest and you'll get your life back. And that starts with a good breakfast, so what about those eggs?' She smiled kindly.

'Well, thanks. Some breakfast would be great. Can I help?' She looked around the small bright kitchen.

'Sure,' Eileen answered. 'There's some bagels in that container there. You could toast them.'

After they'd eaten, Eileen announced, 'Now, let's turn our attention to something more worthy of our energies. I want to show you a letter I received a few weeks ago. I haven't replied yet except to say I had received it and would revert to them in due course, but I want to hear what you think about it.'

She handed the letter to Scarlett. The first thing she noticed was the letter was written on heavy embossed paper and a green harp emblazoned the top of the sheet. She scanned down to see who the letter was from. The words at the top were in another language and impossible to understand, but along the bottom was written *Department of An Taoiseach.*

'What's that?' Scarlett asked, pointing to the last word.

'*An Taoiseach* is the name of the Irish prime minister. It's pronounced Tee-shock. It comes from the days of Celtic mythology, when it meant *the chieftain.* A lot of public office positions within the Irish government use Irish language names from that era.'

Scarlett wondered how Eileen, who had lived all her life in America – as far as Scarlett knew – was able to understand this impossible-looking language. Dan had a few words in Irish – curses mainly, she presumed – but he wasn't much of a scholar, so Scarlett knew nothing really of the language.

'So this letter is from the Irish president?' Scarlett was confused.

'Read it,' Eileen said.

Scarlett read aloud.

*Dear Mrs Chiarello,*

*I sincerely hope this letter finds you well. It has come to our notice that some documents, letters and/or other items that made up part of the estate of the late*

*Mrs Angeline Grant of Strand Road, Glenageary, who died here in Dublin in 1960, may now be in your possession as a result of your relationship to the late Mary O'Dwyer of the same address. In the course of our current research on the 1916 Rising, to coincide with the centenary of that event, we are contacting anyone whom we think may have artefacts, photographs, letters or anything of that nature pertaining to the events of the Rising.*

*If you are in possession of any such material, and would be willing to allow it to be used as part of our research, then we, the Department of An Taoiseach, and the Irish people, would be in your debt.*

*In the event of your cooperation with the research, we would, of course, make any arrangements necessary to view and document the items, with no cost whatsoever to you. These items would remain solely your property.*

*I look forward to hearing from you,*
*Fiachra McCarthy*
*Department of An Taoiseach*

Scarlett stumbled over the last word again.

'Tee-shock,' Eileen repeated and smiled. 'It's a difficult language, I know, but it's beautiful and so expressive. Much more so than English.'

'Wow!' Scarlett was fascinated. 'Do you think it's genuine?'

'Oh, yes, undoubtedly. I believe it is because there's a telephone number on the letter, so I called and asked to speak to this man Fiachra McCarthy. He explained that he is heading up a research team on behalf of the Irish government to put together a big exhibition next year to commemorate the Rising. He explained that because there were so many Irish who ended up here, and all over the world, it was conceivable that there are bits of information scattered everywhere, and they are trying to gather it together. He knows it's a tough task, but they thought the only way to do it was to ask.' Eileen was circumspect.

'I never heard that name before.' Scarlett examined the name on the bottom of the letter, struggling to pronounce it. 'Is it Irish?'

'Aah, Scarlett, if you'd grown up in Ireland, you would know that name very well indeed.' Eileen chuckled. 'That name means *raven*, and it was the name of one of the sons of Lir, a king who, after the death of his wife married a woman called Aoife, in order that his daughter and three sons would have a mother. Aoife, though, was jealous of the love Lir had for his children, and so she turned all four of them into swans. Fiachra was one of the boys, and they were destined by her evil spell to spend 900 years on three seas. It's a very sad story, but every Irish child knows it.'

Eileen smiled. 'Maybe all Irish stories are sad. The story of the Rising certainly is. It must be a bittersweet task for these researchers to dig out all these letters and photographs and things. You see, this happened, not just in an academic way to be analysed and debated, but to real people, with real lives. People like my mother. I liked that Fiachra man. He seemed to understand that.'

'And do you have things they might like to see?' Scarlett asked.

The old woman thought for a moment. 'Yes. That flag, for a start. Also some photographs, letters – that sort of thing. They were belonging to my mother and father, though, and I have just inherited them. I explained to him that I needed time to think, and he was most courteous and kind. There is to be a gathering, in Dublin, where anyone who has anything they want to share is invited to attend. The items will be documented, photographed and so on, and the stories told for posterity. Then there's to be a large exhibition for the year of the centenary – if people are willing to lend their items to the Irish State. The thing is, my mother, Mary Doyle, was just an ordinary girl, born in extraordinary times. I don't mind sharing the photographs, even some of the letters, but the flag is special. My flag – well, her flag, really – is just a tiny part of the story, part of the whole experience of those who lived through the Rising, and of those who died too, of course. It represented something for those people in her life at that time, though it's not of national significance or anything. The thing is, I couldn't let it out of my sight again.'

'Well,' Scarlett exclaimed, 'surely in that case, you go with it! This guy in Dublin, or the authorities there in charge of this stuff, will understand. I'm sure lots of people are in the same position. They'd like their things to be part of the commemoration, but they are precious, and so they are wary of handing them over.' Scarlett was trying to figure out a way to help Eileen. She felt the woman wanted to participate in the remembrance, and for her mother to be represented there.

Eileen shook her head sadly. 'Twenty years ago, maybe, Scarlett, but I'm too old to make that trip at this stage. It's very far, and I don't have the stamina or the confidence I once had. That's what happens when you get old – your world shrinks. I just stay around this neighbourhood now. It's safer.'

'I could go with you.' Scarlett heard the words come out of her own mouth before her brain had even processed them. Initial horror at the madness of her offer immediately gave way to the hope that Eileen would agree.

Eileen said nothing for a moment, sitting calmly. Then she smiled. 'I believe in God, and that those who have died and gone before us are here with us. I've always believed that, but how you erupted into my life when I needed you most, I'll never understand. I do know you have your reasons that go beyond me and my flag, for taking a timeout, as they say. But I like you and trust you. If you want to accompany me and my flag back to Ireland, then let's do it.'

Eileen stuck out her hand and Scarlett clasped it, smiling and laughing as tears shone in Eileen's eyes.

# CHAPTER 27

*M*ary wondered if she would ever be able to hear properly again. The volume of noise inside the now-decimated General Post Office was relentless and deafening. The cacophony of continuous shellfire, gunshot, explosions, cries of agony and barked orders had been going on twenty-four hours a day. She and Eileen were exhausted, their uniforms filthy and encrusted with dried and fresh blood, and their hair hung limply, long escaped from neatly pinned caps. The British had put a gunboat on the River Liffey and were steadily smashing the city to smithereens. Mary felt like they wouldn't stop until every last man, woman and child in the city was dead. Reports from the couriers who were still alive were consistently dismal. They had lost again. The floor of what remained of the second storey was covered with bodies, some of them dead, others close to death, and yet others screaming for relief from the pain of their injuries, which was impossible to provide. Supplies were long since gone.

Eileen was cleaning the head wound of a boy, no more than sixteen years old, who was crying pitifully for his mother. Mary thought once more of Rory. Where was he? Mrs Grant was still alive, despite being injured badly by a shell blast when she was delivering a message down to Boland's Mills. She had managed, however, with the help of two teenage girls and a handcart, to bring up some fresh flour bags earlier, which they were about to cut up to use as bandages. Her former employer, now totally unrecognisable, was leaning against the wall, bleeding from a wound to her leg.

'Mrs Grant, let me see that, I want to clean it for you,' Mary said, grateful that the older woman was still alive at least.

'Oh, Mary, my dear, how lovely to see you! You and Eileen are doing so well, and the Countess was just saying to Pearse how you two are simply magnificent.' Despite the obvious pain, her voice was bright and enthusiastic.

'Well, we're doing our best. If we had more antiseptic, we could do more. Or if we could give something for the pain, but our supplies have run out.' Mary spoke as she cleaned Mrs Grant's wounds with a cloth and cold water. Her employer barely flinched.

'Well, at least that new load of flour bags means we have bandages,' Eileen called from where she was instructing two young girls on how to cut them for maximum use. 'Is it Friday morning?' she asked exhaustedly as she sat briefly beside Mrs Grant, having left the girls to their cutting.

'I've no idea,' Mary replied. 'I've lost all track of time. I was hoping to see Rory somewhere. Mrs Grant, did you see…?'

'All women downstairs now, please.' Tom Clarke was walking through the upstairs, carefully avoiding the many bodies lying on the floor. 'Pearse wants all the women downstairs, this minute, please.'

Mrs Grant inhaled and tried to get up.

'Stay where you are!' Mary exclaimed. 'Not injured women – I'm sure he didn't mean that.'

'Tom!' the mistress called as Clarke walked by. 'Tom!'

He stopped and looked down to where Mrs Grant sat.

'Aah, Angeline, 'tis yourself. Are you hurt?'

The three women looked at the man who was arguably the driving force behind the Rising. He refused any military rank and insisted on being called just Tom by all he came in contact with. He had been in prison for many years before the Rising because of his political stance on Irish Republicanism, and looked older even than his fifty-nine years. His wire glasses and bushy moustache almost hid his long, gaunt face. Mary remembered going into his tobacco shop months before for a message, and how she had loved the sweet unfamiliar aroma. She recalled the respect with which Rory spoke of him. How despite his unassuming presence, there was something fortifying about him. He made all those with whom he came into contact braver and more determined to succeed.

'Yes, Tom, a little, but I'll survive. Now, do we all need to go downstairs or can the girls bring the message up to me if I send them?' Mrs Grant was now gasping between words with the pain.

'Can you get down at all?' he asked kindly. 'If the girls help you?'

'Of course.' Clarke and Mrs Grant locked eyes. 'He's putting us out, isn't he?' she said.

Clarke just nodded. 'They'll let ye go. It's over now anyway. We want ye out and safe before we surrender.' He shouted to be heard over the din. Mary felt tears come to her eyes. It had all been for nothing. Tom Clarke noticed the disappointment and exhaustion on Mary's face and spoke directly to her. 'Don't worry – Mary, isn't it?' Clarke went on. 'We failed this time, but it's one step closer to victory. Next time we won't fail. Me and the others might not be around to see it, but you will, and your sons and daughters, please God. Don't forget, this isn't defeat; it's another step closer to freedom. The next generation will build on this and then…then there will be a free and independent Ireland.'

Something about the way he spoke, with his lovely Northern Ireland accent, made Mary believe him. He gave her hand a quick squeeze and was gone.

Mary and Eileen held Mrs Grant between them and made their way downstairs to the area where the leaders were deep in discussion, though conversation was proving close to impossible because of the constant noise around them as they waited for Pearse. Mary fought profound feelings of disappointment and despair. It was over – the Rising had failed. Pearse was younger than Tom Clarke – more popular, maybe – but it was the tobacconist that had the vision of a free Ireland. If he was saying it was over, then there was no hope. She thought of the men downstairs and in the garrisons around the city who had signed the Proclamation. They might as well have signed their own death warrants. Maybe he was right…maybe the British would let the women go, though they were furious that the women were involved in the first place, it seemed. But Tom Clarke; Pádraig Pearse, the schoolteacher; Joseph Plunkett, the dreamy poet, whose neck was in bandages before the Rising had even begun because he had to have surgery on his glands; James Connolly, who believed so fervently in the equality of men and women and was now lying down after being shot in the legs – all would all pay a heavy price for their actions. Thomas MacDonagh was down in Boland's with de Valera, and he was a signatory too. She remembered Eileen's remarks when she saw him at a meeting a few months earlier, about how handsome he was. Mary replied in a whisper that he wasn't her type, and Eileen had joked that she had passed the test. She only had eyes for Rory. If Mary couldn't see how good looking MacDonagh was, then she must be really in love.

Leaning heavily on his stick – needed because of childhood polio – another signatory, Seán MacDiarmuida, stood to the side, beside his mentor and dear friend Clarke. Mary wondered what they were talking about. What would she and Eileen talk about if they knew they were facing death together? What about the fate of Éamonn Ceannt, the last signature on the Proclamation? Would the memory of his heroism be a comfort to his wife Áine and their little boy when he was gone? He was holding the Marrowbone Lane distillery and the Dublin South Union with Cathal Brugha.

It all seemed so hopeless. Volunteers were lying sprawled on sandbags, and many were valiantly returning fire from the smouldering walls of the GPO. The only light was dim sunshine through the holes where the windows had once been, but sandbags were piled high to take the impact of the incessant gunfire, and so the whole area was in murky semi-darkness.

The discussions between Clarke, Plunkett, Pearse, MacDiarmuida, and Connolly were heated, and they roared to be heard over the noise. Women gathered all around, waiting to be addressed. Many were injured, and Mary thought how they were unrecognisable as the group of proud and well-turned-out Cumann na mBan members of the previous Monday. Despite their bedraggled appearance, though, there was a determination there as well. The men still stood and the women would stand beside them…to the end.

Pearse then stepped forward and spoke with intense passion to the crowd. He described the gallantry of the rebels who fought with fire and steel. As he spoke of this glorious chapter of Irish history, glass was smashing and fires were starting where shells landed. By now, most of the building was in flames. He praised the bravery and dedication of the women, and then he ordered them out of the building, instructing that they present themselves at Jervis Street Hospital. They were to bring as many of the wounded with them as they could, and have one girl out in front waving a white flag, which he said he hoped would allow them safe passage through the numerous checkpoints the British had set up all around the city.

Before they gathered their things to go, they all knelt on the glass-and-rubble–strewn floor and said a decade of the rosary. The men had their beads in their pockets; the women had theirs around their necks. A priest, who had come from a house in Moore Street, just adjacent to the building, gave the gathered crowd a hurried general absolution, and just for a brief moment, the shelling stopped. The Lord had absolved them of their sins, so no matter what came next, they were ready to face their Maker with clean souls. The sense of gratitude to the priest was palpable in the air.

Eileen caught Mary's eye. They would have to try to manage Mrs Grant between them, but of Mrs Kearns, there was no sign.

'You try to carry Mrs Grant and I'll look for Mrs Kearns,' Mary shouted, straining to be heard over the racket of the destruction all around. 'You're stronger than me.'

That was true. Eileen, raised on a farm, was as strong as a horse, and when Mary's arms ached with weariness, and frequently when her hands shook from overexertion from carrying and bandaging, Eileen had helped her.

All around, women were protesting, but there was no way to avoid leaving the men. Pearse had issued an order, not a request, and they had to go. Mary made her way to the makeshift kitchen area and found, to her surprise, large quantities of food. Not just bread and milk, either, but meat and fish and prepared dishes. She later learnt that these supplies had been liberated from Findlaters, the exclusive grocer shop, with a promissory note from the Provisional Government that they would repay it after the revolution. Apparently the kitchen of the Gresham Hotel was also required to throw open the larders to feed the rebels. Mary knew that the GPO was unique in that respect. According to the couriers going around the city, food was in terribly short supply in the other garrisons.

She pushed through the men gathered around, searching for Mrs Kearns.

'No, I've showed you before you, *amadán*! Are you deaf or what? You need to cut the bread thinner than that…' Mary heard her before she saw her, berating her underling in the catering section – a young Volunteer who was sheepishly trying to prepare everything exactly as she instructed.

'Mrs Kearns!' Mary yelled to be heard. 'Mrs Kearns, we have to go now. Everyone – all the women, we have to go on Pearse's orders before the whole building goes up in flames.' By now

Mary had reached her and was pulling on her sleeve.

'I have to stay here. Sure these fellas haven't a clue, and the men need to be fed. We're getting food down to Boland's and to Michael Mallin as well, not just here in the GPO, and these lads are grand, but they need to be told what to do. I can't go now.' Mrs Kearns was adamant.

'Please, Mrs Kearns, we don't have a choice. Pearse insists we go now. The building could collapse any time. There's fires everywhere and...' Mary tried to make herself heard, wincing as the acrid smoke stung her eyes.

Mrs Kearns drew Mary back into the recesses of the building, where the noise wasn't as deafening. She drew Mary close so she could hear.

'Mary, dear, I'm an old woman who lived under the hand of the English and the well-to-do gentry of this city all my life. My darling girl was taken from me by TB because we had no money for the doctor or the medicine she needed. The child of the woman I worked for then got it too, and they sent her to a sanatorium in Switzerland where she got better. That woman was a right auld rip too. She was horrible, not a bit like Mrs Grant. Why did her girl live and mine died? Because they and their kind – Irish or English, makes no difference – they were all the one. What divides us is them what have money and them what don't. These lads in here that I'm feeding, and some of them are only kids themselves, but they believe that my Kathleen was as important as that girl. Not more important, mind, just the same, and I don't care if I die trying to get that to be the way here. If I die, I can face my daughter in heaven with a happy heart.'

Mary was struggling to find the words. Mrs Kearns had only mentioned her daughter once in all the years Mary had known her, and even then only in passing. The sheer conviction and pride in the woman's eyes was deeply moving.

'I understand that, Mrs Kearns. I really do. I had nothing coming here and I now feel like I'm part of something, but we are no good to anyone dead. The food is all there, they can help themselves, and we'll be needed again. Please come with us. Mrs Grant needs us. She's been injured and Eileen and I can't manage her on our own.'

The mention of Mrs Grant seemed to change Mrs Kearns' mind. She was fiercely loyal to her employer and saw her as much more than just the source of her wages. There was a bond between the women that Mary could see was unspoken, but strong. Maybe it was because Mrs Kearns saw what went on that house with Mr Grant, or maybe because Mrs Grant was so different from many other ladies in Dublin at that time. Mary had noticed how some of the other women in Cumann na mBan, even though they were all supposed to be fighting for equality, were uncomfortable talking to people like her and Eileen. Social mixing between the classes was mostly unheard of, and it surprised Mary when she saw women – all supposed to be on the one side – still living out the age-old divisions even as the world was blasted to bits around their ears. Mrs Grant wasn't one bit like that, and Mrs Kearns and Mary loved her for it.

'Where is she?' Mrs Kearns asked urgently.

'At the other end of the building, but she can't walk. Eileen is with her,' Mary answered.

'Did ye bandage the wound?' Mrs Kearns's tone was businesslike, but Mary knew she was worried.

'Yes, but she's losing blood. We need to get her to a hospital.'

'Let's go, girl, we've no time to lose.' Mrs Kearns told the young boy who had been helping her to carry on as best he could, and together they battled through the scene of chaos and destruction all around them. Eventually they came to the part of the wall where she had left Eileen and Mrs Grant. They were still there, but by now Mrs Grant seemed to be lapsing in and out of consciousness.

'The others have gone, two groups of them, but I refused to go until ye got back. I think we will have to leave soon, though. The building is going to fall down, and Pearse and the others are preparing to evacuate as well. Tom Clarke just passed a minute ago and made me promise to leave in the next five minutes.'

Mrs Grant let out a groan of pain. Eileen soothed her and turned once again to Mary. 'I think we have to get her to hospital. We may be too late, but we'll try.'

'Right, girls.' Mrs Kearns was once again in charge. 'We haven't a stretcher and there's no time to make one, so you'll have to each take an arm and put it round your shoulders. I'll go in front and carry her legs.'

'But what about a flag? The others had white flags. If we go out without one, we'll be shot immediately.' Eileen's voice was breaking, exhaustion and stress finally showing on her normally calm and capable demeanour.

'One of the bags – we'll use one of the flour bags. They're white!' Mary cried, running back to the first aid station upstairs. Most of the injured men had been removed and she tried not to look at the dead bodies. The bundle of flour bags from Boland's Mills lay in the corner. She quickly grabbed one that had not yet been cut up for bandages. The long sharp scissors abandoned by the young girls who were charged with that task was still on the floor. Mary picked them up and ran the sharp blade down the seams of the bag, making a rectangle of white cloth. She looked around for something like a stick on which to tie the flag, and found, to her relief, a broom used earlier in the week to sweep away the shards of broken glass that were all over the floor.

She wrenched the brush off the handle with a strength she didn't know she had, but then was at a loss as to how to attach the bag. Men rushed all around her, shouting and firing through the windows, Others valiantly tried to put out fires. She took both the bag and the stick back downstairs, hoping Eileen or Mrs Kearns would have an idea.

'What are you still doing here?' Tom Clarke passed them and stopped, blood on his face as he tried unsuccessfully to douse flames with a bucket of sand.

'We're going now. I'm just trying to make a flag to wave when we go out. Mrs Grant is hurt, and we have to try to carry...' She tried her best to hold back the tears, but she was failing.

Smiling affectionately at them, he took the cloth and stick from her shaking hands, saying, 'Give it here to me.' Expertly he made a hole in two of the corners with a penknife from his pocket, and taking out his bootlaces, he used them to fasten the flag to the makeshift pole.

'But now you can't walk –' she began.

'Where I'm going, I'll have no need of shoes. God bless. Up the Republic!' He shoved the flag into her hands and was gone.

Half dragging, half carrying Mrs Grant, the four women managed to get out into Sackville Street. Mrs Kearns lodged the white flag in her belt to free up her hands to carry her mistress. Bodies littered the streets, and the once-imposing facades of the shops and businesses had been reduced to smouldering rubble. Across the street, a large barricade had been set up and was heavily manned by soldiers. The gunfire and shelling continued. They tried to keep low as they moved in the direction of a side street, out of the way of direct fire. The noise was deafening, and they were shocked at the scene of chaos and destruction on the once-magnificent street. Curtains blew out of glassless windows, and rooms were exposed as the walls had collapsed on houses and shops. Smoke and dust filled the air, making it difficult to breathe.

Progress down the street seemed fraught with danger, even with the flag, as the firing continued without interruption. There was no sign of the other women – gone to the hospital, probably – but the conditions in front of them meant it was impossible to try to cross the road. Mrs Grant was unconscious, and the bandage on her leg was now totally sodden with blood.

'We can't lift her any more,' gasped Eileen. 'She's a deadweight, and all the pulling is causing her to lose even more blood.' They looked at the mistress and she did appear to be in a very bad way. Mrs Kearns was carrying both her legs, but with each step, blood was seeping out of the bandage.

'Let's see if we can put her onto the flag and carry her that way,' Mary suggested as a bullet shattered a cobblestone two feet in front of them.

'Without the flag, they'll shoot us,' Eileen protested.

'Eileen, child of grace, they're shooting at us anyway!' Mrs Kearns shouted. She pulled the flag off its stick and laid it on the ground. As gently as they could, they laid Mrs Grant on the flag and

SHADOW OF A CENTURY

lifted it by the four corners. The injured woman's head hung down over one side and her legs from the knees down dangled on the other, but the flour bag held the weight of her middle and they were able to move her without jostling the wound.

'Jesus and His Sainted Mother, get in, let ye! Ye'll be killed stone dead out there!' a voice called from a shop door. They looked sideways in the direction of the voice. An elderly man crouched behind the door of what was once a jeweller's shop. Mary remembered looking at the beautiful things in the window one night when she was waiting for Rory, and he'd come up behind her and whispered, 'Which one will I get you?'

She remembered flushing with embarrassment that he would think her so presumptuous as to be looking at rings, and he laughed at her shame. 'You'll have a beautiful but tiny diamond.' He chuckled. 'I'd love to buy you the best one in the whole shop, but funds won't stretch to that. Anyway, a little one would look nicer on your little hands. That's why I had to find a girlfriend with small hands, to save me having to buy a huge ring!' She remembered how they giggled and laughed all the time. Where was he now? Alive? Injured? Or even dead, like so many young men?

'We've no choice. We can't get her to the hospital now anyway,' Mrs Kearns said grimly to the girls. 'And we can't go on carrying her like this.' They moved slowly with the weight of Mrs Grant between them to the door, still intact, and the man let them in. The front of the building was in ruins but he led them down a passageway into a living room behind the shop. Beside a fire, an elderly woman sat knitting.

They laid Mrs Grant on the couch and she moaned with pain.

'Have you any medicine, bandages – anything like that?' Mrs Kearns asked.

The old woman looked at her and then back to her husband. 'Did they come out of the GPO? What business had you bringing them in here on top of us?' The woman spoke in a strong Dublin accent and exuded resentment.

'Lily, they're women. They were getting shot at out there.' His voice was quiet, pleading for her to understand.

'They're troublemakers, is what they are, them and those high-minded fellas with all their talk. If they didn't start all this nonsense, then those soldiers would be in France or Belgium, and our Frank might survive and come home safe to us. Did you ever think of that?'

She took a framed photograph from the mantelpiece and thrust it into Mary's face.

'That's my boy, my Frank. He's in the Dublin Fusiliers fighting in Europe, and you and the likes of you are making things worse for him, and all the young lads like him. Did that ever enter your head, and you all about your bloody Republic? Did it? I suppose your lot would call him a traitor, wearing a British uniform. He's no traitor. My boy is the finest lad you'd ever meet – better than that shower of criminals and murderers inside in the GPO anyway. Do you know a baby was shot in his pram in front of his mother a few days ago? Did you know that, and ye blasting away at the whole city?' She spat when she spoke and Mary wiped her face.

'Lily, please.' The man was exhausted.

'I didn't know that.' Mary tried to steady herself.

'My husband's shop is in smithereens. I don't know how we'll ever recover from this, I really don't. My Frank had a fine business to come home to, after he does his time out there, and he'd look after us, but now what have we?' Suddenly, all the anger was gone and the woman faced the small group with her hands out in despair. 'What are we to do now?'

'Are we welcome here or are we not?' Mrs Kearns spoke sternly. 'For if we're not, then we'll go, but if we are, you'll have to help us with this lady here. She's very badly hurt.'

The businesslike way she spoke seemed to diffuse the awkwardness of the situation.

Lily looked at the mistress, who was moaning on the couch. 'Get Johnny Kearney. He's gone upstairs. I saw him come in the back a minute ago,' the woman said to her husband resignedly. He nodded and left. She went to the back pantry wordlessly, presumably to get some water. Eileen and Mary exchanged glances of panic. What if these people were informers?

''Tis done now anyway,' Eileen whispered pragmatically. 'Even if they are informers, what difference will it make at this stage? Either they're going to arrest us or they won't. Rory thought they'd let us go. It's the men they're after.'

'Rory? Were you talking to him?' Mary's heart was pounding in her chest.

'Sorry, I meant to tell you. When you went to get the flag, he came past us. He was fine – a few cuts, but fine. He was asking about you. I told him you were all right and that we'd take care of each other.'

Mary was dying to ask Eileen more about

Rory, but the man came back into the room, followed by a much younger man in shirtsleeves and flannels, carrying a medical bag. Relief flooded through Mary. A doctor, at last.

'Mr Browne, I'm not even qualified yet. You do know that, don't you? I'm only a student...' The young man tried to explain.

Looking at Mrs Grant, now ashen with very shallow breathing, he went on. 'I'll have a look, but I don't know how much I can do.' He spoke to Mrs Kearns, Eileen, and Mary. 'I'm a final year medical student,' he said, 'but this woman needs medical attention.' He went on to explain, 'Their son Frank and I are friends.'

'How long since this happened?' he asked as he began to remove the blood-soaked bandages.

'I'm not sure – earlier today, I think. I wasn't with her, you see,' Eileen said. 'She was a courier, on her bike around the city. She came in with her leg bleeding, so I just bandaged it to stop the flow of blood. The bullet might well be still in there.'

Johnny's hands worked deftly, and soon he was examining the wound. 'Yes, I see. I'll try to remove it and stitch the wound. She should have some morphine for the pain, but I don't have any. We'll clean it up and put some antiseptic on it, and bandage it, but after that, I can't make any promises. Maybe if it settles down out there, then ye can get her to the hospital. The main thing is to watch her temperature. If it goes up, then she's fighting infection and that's going to add to her problems.'

'Thank you,' Mary said. The other two women seemed in shock at the state of Mrs Grant's leg.

'The British won't just forget what you've done, you know?' The young man's voice was disapproving.

'Nor do we intend them to. We struck a blow for our country's freedom this past week. We are turning the tide of imperialism.' Even to Mary's ears, Eileen's words sounded hollow. It had all been for nothing. The Rising was over, the city in ruins. God only knew how many were dead and wounded, and the men who led them would pay a high price for their audacity. Maybe the women would too.

Johnny did the best he could, explaining that Mrs Grant needed blood and specialist care. All that night they sat in the living room. Kevin and Lily Browne had gone to bed, having shared a meagre supper of bread, butter and tea with them. Lily seemed to have thawed, and while they would never see eye to eye on political matters, they were able to chat about Frank and how he was getting on in Europe. Lily's favourite topic was the talents of her only child, so her monologue allowed the women time with their own thoughts.

Mary longed for another chance to ask Eileen about Rory, though she knew there wasn't really anything else to learn. The reality of the future seemed stark and grim as the small hours of the morning dragged on. Rory was in the GPO – either he would be killed or wounded or arrested when the surrender came. The surrender was inevitable. She recalled Tom Clarke's serious expression, and so it was only a matter of time. What the British would do with the rebels was what they all wondered and worried about, but felt unable to discuss, even with each other. There was a kind of stoicism ingrained into the women of Cumann na mBan, that the men must go through this and that their women must stand strong beside them. Mary recalled once more Mrs Sheehy-Skeffington lecturing them on how displays of tears and worry only added to the men's burden, and showed the enemy that their behaviour was impacting them. She had tried not to make Rory feel bad about what they were doing, instead reaching into her soul for strength to smile and be supportive. But now, in this strange house, with the gunfire and shells going off outside and Mrs Grant maybe bleeding to death beside her on the couch, it all seemed so much to bear. Mrs Kearns and Eileen were dozing and Mary once again laid her hand on Mrs Grant's brow, praying her temperature stayed normal.

The morning wore on and an eerie silence descended on the city. The gunfire and shelling, while not stopped completely, seemed to have been reduced. Sackville Street was in flames and the air was filled with acrid smoke and dust.

'What's happening, do you think?' Eileen asked. 'Will we try to get Mrs Grant to the hospital now?'

Mrs Kearns went into the now-decimated and looted shop, and the girls followed her. They looked out of what remained of the window. The trays of rings had vanished, removed to safekeeping, Mary hoped, by Kevin rather than by looters, and glass crunched beneath their feet.

A young boy ran past the window. Mary recognised him as one of the lads she had sent on errands while they were in the GPO.

'Donal!' she called.

'Yeah?' He was wary, but recognised Mary.

'What's happening, Donal?' she asked. The

boy's face seemed to crumble as he fought back tears of bitter disappointment.

'We got sent out with the ladies – anyone under sixteen – and the rest of the Volunteers had to evacuate the GPO last night. They moved into a house in Moore Street, behind ye there. The British had us beat by then and they wouldn't take nothing else, only an unconditional surrender. Commandants Pearse and Connolly signed it, and that's it.'

Mary grasped Mrs Kearns's and Eileen's hands. 'And the Volunteers that were left? Where are they now?'

'Being marched out in front of General Lowe. The commandants sent a woman, a Nurse O'Farrell, I think, out to meet him, and he said to her that if they didn't both sign an unconditional surrender, the shelling would start up again. They knew too that Commandant Connolly had been shot, and yer man Lowe said he'd have to be brought out on a stretcher, but he wasn't stopping nothin' till he seen the two of them.'

Mrs Kearns turned to the girls. 'Right. We need to get Mrs Grant to hospital, then we go out in front of the GPO and be with the men. It's what she would tell us to do.' Mrs Kearns went back into the house and asked Kevin if they could make a stretcher to carry her on. But at that moment, an ambulance passed.

'Stop!' shouted Eileen, standing in the path of the vehicle. 'Please, stop! There's a woman here needs to be treated!' she cried urgently. The ambulance was already full of people nursing various wounds, but the driver sighed wearily and went inside after Eileen. Kevin and the driver managed to get Mrs Grant into the ambulance and laid her down on the only space available on the floor. Mary tried to get in, but the driver stopped her, saying, 'I'll see she gets to hospital, but there's no room for able-bodied. I need to pick up as many as I can that need it.' Mary nodded and stepped off the running board.

The ambulance made slow progress because the road was destroyed, and as it moved off, Mary felt Mrs Kearns put her arm around her shoulders. 'We can do no more for her now, Mary, dear. Please God she'll pull through. If anyone is made of tough stuff 'tis herself, so we'll say a prayer and hope for the best.'

Through the chaos they heard the sound of rhythmic marching coming from Moore Street – battalions of Volunteers marching, grim-faced, some wounded, towards the GPO. They must have done it, the unconditional surrender! Mary and Eileen scanned the groups of men for Rory. Young Donal was right. Lowe wanted them all lined up together. One of the strengths of the movement was that the British could never figure out how many Volunteers, Citizen Army, and Cumann na mBan there were. The commandants were there with their men. Connolly was being carried on a stretcher and looked very pale. Joe Plunkett walked past them, straight and determined, though Mary thought he must be very weak by now. He had looked ill even at the start of the week. God alone knew how the events of recent days would have affected him.

The people of Dublin, now venturing onto the streets again, vented their anger and frustration at the state of their city on the lines of battle-weary men. Mary tried to will the Volunteers to have strength, to ignore the jibes of their fellow countrymen who didn't support the Rising.

They went back into Lily and Kevin Browne's house and gathered up their belongings. Mary folded the flag, now stained from Mrs Grant's blood, and placed it in her knapsack. The blood was drying and the holes made by Tom Clarke for his bootlaces were stretched and ragged. She tried to brush the dried blood from her clothes and fix her hair so it wasn't hanging in front of her face. They went in to the kitchen where Lily was making stirabout over the fire.

'Thank you, Mrs Browne, for your hospitality –' Mary began.

'Sure, I only did my Christian duty, the same as anyone would have. I hope your lady will be all right.' Softness crept into her brusque tone as she spoke.

'And I hope your Frank comes home in one piece,' Eileen said quietly as she went to shake the woman's hand. 'My brother Rory, Mary's fiancé, is a Volunteer, and my parents are worried sick the whole time between the pair of us. My mam says 'tis easy for us, playing soldiers, when 'tis she doing all the worrying.'

''Tis terrible times we're living in, and that's the truth of it,' Kevin said as he entered from the back yard. 'The city is in ruins. There's thousands dead, it feels like, and for what? Our boy fighting for a bit of land out foreign, your lot fighting over this auld island. In the end, no one wins. Isn't that the truth. No one at all...' he finished quietly.

'Well, thank you for everything.' Mrs Kearns was anxious to go.

'Should you not take off them uniforms ye have on ye? If ye go out now, looking like that, the British will know you're part of the rebels, and God knows what they'll do to ye.'

Mary thought Kevin was right. They'd managed to escape so far. To hand themselves over to the enemy at this stage would be stupid.

'I don't know. Maybe we should stand with the men.' Eileen was uncertain.

'Remember what they told us – avoid arrest if possible. We are more use to the men if we are free. At least this way, if Rory is put in gaol, we can send him things, visit even maybe. What good are we to him in gaol?' Mary was trying to be practical, though she understood Eileen's need to be loyal to the cause and the men who had risked so much.

'We haven't anything else.' Mrs Kearns was ever-practical. 'All our clothes are back at the Grants's house.'

With a dramatic sigh, Lily Browne got up. 'Stay there. We'll see what we have for ye.'

The women stood, unsure of what to do next. Perhaps something of Lily's would fit Mary and Eileen, being slim like herself, but the idea that the wiry Lily had anything to fit the buxom Mrs Kearns made Mary want to giggle.

When Lily returned with a selection of skirts and blouses and cardigans, the girls gratefully sifted through them. Embarrassed, because Kevin was still in the room, Lily gave him a shove. 'What are you hanging around here like a young fella for? Let the ladies get dressed without all in sundry gawping at them. Now Missus,' she said, addressing Mrs Kearns, 'I have this shawl. 'Tis floor length, and will cover most of you, anyway. Here, look,' she went on, pinning the huge black garment around the bulk of Mrs Kearns. 'They'll see no bit of the uniform this way.'

Mary and Eileen averted their gaze for fear of giggling at the sight. Mrs Kearns was not one to be trifled with, and the sight of Lily Browne, pulling and dragging her in different directions, was comical. They each chose a skirt, blouse and cardigan, which all seemed to be variations on the colour beige. They unpinned their hair and brushed the tangles and dried blood and dirt from each other's.

'I feel filthy.' Eileen groaned.

'Well, that's because you are filthy.' Mary smiled. 'But we are alive and out of enemy hands so far, so that's something to be grateful for anyway.' Eileen nodded at her friend, both knowing that Rory was to the forefront of their thoughts.

Lily brought in a basin of water and a cake of soap, and handed each of them a rough towel.

They washed their faces and hands and at least felt a bit better. Lily didn't give them any hats, and they couldn't imagine going out with their heads uncovered, even in these circumstances. Lily saw their dilemma and went upstairs muttering something about people who came from nothing having notions above their station. She reappeared with two headscarves, also browny-beige. The girls gratefully put them on and tied them under their chins. They giggled once again at the sight of each other, dressed like old women.

'Thank you again. We'll return your clothes as soon as we can.' Mrs Kearns spoke for all three of them.

'You're welcome.' Kevin nodded, opening the door.

'I'll say a prayer for Frank,' Mary added.

'And I hope your young man isn't blown to bits either,' he said quietly. 'I don't agree with your politics, nor the way ye've gone about it, but we all want the same thing, I suppose. A bit of peace and quiet and a few bob in our pockets, with our families safe around us.'

Out on the street, the devastation was total. Gaping holes where shops had once stood, soldiers everywhere and civilians caught in between.

The days when Eileen and she would catch the tram into the city and go window shopping, or for a stroll in the park, admiring the finery on the ladies, seemed a million years ago.

The sight of the Volunteers lined up outside the GPO with their weapons surrendered and thrown in a pile, under heavily armed guard, was a shock to them. The commandants were in front of their men. Mary spotted Éamon de Valera, who was a good head taller than the men around him. James Connolly was lying on the ground on a stretcher, obviously in terrible pain. General Lowe was clearly in charge, which was something that filled Mary with relief. Though he was un-doubtedly a loyal British officer, there was a kind of humanity to him that other officers lacked. His thin face was passive and he was renowned for doing his job efficiently, but without the vindic-tive streak seen in some of his colleagues.

Lowe stood in front with a plain-clothes of-ficer by his side, presumably from Dublin Castle, identifying particular men and speaking in the general's ear. Once selected, these men were dragged out of the ranks and put into a covered military truck. The crowd stood silently by, the resentment towards the Volunteers for what they had brought to the city hanging in the air like an invisible storm cloud. As she observed the reactions of those around her, Mary thought, *It is so unfair. These men sacrificed everything for people who don't even appreciate it.* Anger raged within her as she thought of how the passers-by had mocked and jeered Pearse and Connolly on Easter Monday as they read the Proclamation, and here they stood now with hatred in their eyes as these brave men faced charges of treason.

Her eyes raked the lines of Volunteers for Rory. Eileen and Mrs Kearns did the same, she could tell, but of him there was no sign. Once the British were sure they had the main ringleaders – twenty-five or thirty men in the truck, guarded by as many heavily armed soldiers – they drove off. The remainder were ordered to about turn and march in formation up the street. The crowds surged forward, and Mary and Eileen were pushed off what remained of the pavement and onto the roadway.

Despair was flooding through her. Where was he? She couldn't bear to imagine his body, lying inside the GPO now engulfed in flames. The fire engines were trying to put out the fires all over the city, but it seemed pointless.

As the Volunteers filed past, dejected and battered, she heard the sound of singing. *No, it couldn't be. Rory!* It began as a single voice from the centre of the column, but after a few words, he was joined by others.

*God save Ireland said the heroes, God save Ireland said we all, whether on the scaffold high or the battle-field we die, of what matter when for Eire dear we fall?*

The rousing chorus grew in volume and enthusiasm as the British soldiers shouted at them to shut up, firing shots in the air.

Mary was cheered to see some of the crowd joining in. Perhaps the Volunteers weren't entirely alone after all.

'Mary! Mary!' Her name was being called through the noise of shouting and singing.

'Rory?' She scanned the crowd.

'Leave him through to see his girl.' An older Volunteer, clutching a wounded head, shouted with a thick Dublin accent. Rory dodged through from the centre of the column to the edge, where she could see him. An officer marched between them, so she bobbed and ran to keep up, elbowing people out of her way as he went.

'Oh, Rory! I couldn't find you. I thought...' She could hardly get the words out.

'I'm grand. We're down, but we're not out, Mary, my love. Just you wait. This is only the first round.'

The officer then shoved him into the column again and roared at her to stand back or be shot.

Mary stood laughing, tears pouring down her face as the crowds following the Volunteers surged around her. Rory was alive, and more importantly, he wasn't in the truck!

*Maybe there is hope they won't realise how well connected he was*, she prayed. He was so young, they might just assume he was a regular and put him in gaol. They surely can't intend to execute the entire remains of the Irish Volunteers…

## CHAPTER 28

Mary and Mrs Kearns waited on a wooden bench. The peace and tranquillity of the hospital was in sharp contrast to the devastation and chaos outside. The nuns would allow no raised voices, no matter what the motivation, and the casualties were held in the emergency department, away from the quietness of the private rooms. The relief Mary felt at Rory's arrest – and their escape from any action by the British for their part in the Rising – dissipated during the night. Mrs Kearns had found them a room in a boarding house off Leeson Street, and as they walked through the ruins of Dublin that morning to find Mrs Grant, they talked about their options.

Neither she nor Mrs Kearns had anywhere to go. Eileen was lucky – her employer, Mrs Carmody, took her back, explaining her absence to her husband by telling him Eileen had spent the week caring for her sick mother. She and Mrs Kearns were homeless, and as neither of them could countenance returning to Mr Grant. Finding the mistress seemed the best possible use of their time. They thought she may have been brought to Jervis Street Hospital, so they decided to check there first.

The nun gestured to them to follow her and they were led into a darkened room. Mary marvelled at how quiet it was and how the mistress had a room to herself.

'Are you Mary?' the nun asked kindly.

'Yes, yes, I'm Mary.'

'Well, she has had surgery and the bone was reset. Whoever removed the bullet probably saved her life. She will be a little groggy as the effects of the anaesthetic wear off. Her husband specifically requested that she be allowed to rest and kept away from all the hustle and bustle of the public wards, but she was so agitated last night after he left, and she kept asking for you, Mary. I hope I've done the right thing…'

'Oh, don't worry about that, Sister,' Mrs

Kearns reassured her. 'Mr Grant is very protective, and he thought Mary was down the country. That's why he wouldn't have said for her to be allowed in to see his wife. I'll speak to Mr Grant myself later and explain everything. I'm his housekeeper. He'll be relieved Mary was able to make it in to see her.'

Mary and Mrs Kearns avoided each other's eyes for fear of giving themselves away. Mr Grant had been here, and he knew what had happened. The thought made Mary physically sick with dread.

The nun left at the sound of a ringing bell, and Mary and Mrs Kearns sat on either side of the bed. Mrs Grant was pale, with her hair brushed out. It made her look so much younger. She slept peacefully, her skin ashen against the starched white sheets.

'Mrs Grant,' Mrs Kearns spoke gently. The mistress's eyes fluttered and she tried to speak, gesturing that she wanted to sit up.

They helped her into a more comfortable position and gave her a sip of water.

'He knows!' she rasped. Gesturing for another sip of water, she winced as she swallowed it. From her first aid training, Mary knew that anaesthetic made the mouth very dry, which would explain the sore throat. She was trying to control her panic. What did he know? That they were involved in the Rising, or about the jewellery and paintings?

'He wants you both back, me also. Forget everything,' she whispered. Clearly, talking was a strain.

Mary looked confused. 'Does he know about the jewellery?' she whispered.

The mistress took a deep breath and shook her head. 'Just the Rising,' she rasped.

'Ma'am, do you mean the master wants us back at Strand Road, after everything that's happened?'

Maybe the effects of the drugs were making her delirious? If Mr Grant knew – and how could he not, given the situation – they assumed he would kill them with his bare hands rather than allow them back into his house. Even if he knew nothing about the selling of his precious things, he would hate it to be known that his wife defied him. He was connected to the British socially and in business, so he would take their involvement in the Rising personally.

'Yes. Here. Last night. Doesn't want talk. Wants to appear as normal. Afraid what it will do to him and his business, wife a Republican.'

Speaking was a huge strain on the mistress, her voice hoarse and straining to be loud enough to be heard.

On a strange level, it made sense. Rory had suggested to her on more than one occasion that Grant was an informer, and was being watched closely. The man was arrogant enough to believe his wife would never defy him, and so he imagined his was a loyal British household. Mary was sure that his associates would be appalled at the suggestion that the master couldn't control the women in his house. Maybe the mistress was right. Mary thought of her little bedroom, the only place she ever felt at home, and thought about how good it would feel to sleep in her little narrow bed. To wake to the sound of the milk cart in the mornings, to sit on the chair at the little writing table in her room and to write letters to Rory.

Mrs Kearns wasn't so enthusiastic. 'But ma'am, he'll kill you if we go back. You know what he did to you before, for even going to a meeting. What will he do now? No, it's too risky.' She shook her head.

Mrs Grant took hold of a hand of each of them. Breathing deeply to gather strength to talk, she simply said, 'More to do, more to take.'

She was right. While several paintings and most of the mistress's jewellery was now adorning the homes and bodies of wealthy Americans, there was still plenty to be taken. Just last week the mistress had told them how she was hoping to source an antiques dealer who could move on several small pieces of furniture and objets d'art that she could have replaced with copies. The movement desperately needed money, especially now, when so many families would be left without their breadwinners in the wake of the arrests.

To add to it, the three women had no other option. They were destitute. Everything they had raised they had already given to the Volunteers. There was no support available to them, since many of the men and women of the revolution were in custody, the movement in disarray. They had nowhere else to go. Unappealing as the prospect was, they would have to go back.

They sat all day in the hospital, looking up anxiously every time the door opened in case it was him, but thankfully he remained absent.

At around six o'clock, an exhausted young doctor came in. His dark hair flopped over his face, and his clothes and white coat were wrinkled and blood-spattered.

'Ladies, my name is Dr O'Leary. I'm sorry. Under normal conditions Mrs Grant would stay in hospital recovering for several weeks, but these are not normal conditions. We need the bed, I'm afraid. And as Mrs Grant is now over surgery and out of danger, all that remains is for her to rest and recuperate. I would imagine she could do that at home just as easily, perhaps even better, than here. Is that all right?' They could see he was suppressing a yawn, and a full day's stubble shadowed his jaw.

'You look like you could do with that bed yourself,' Mrs Kearns remarked kindly. 'When did you last sleep?'

He smiled. 'Before last Monday, it feels like.' He spotted the uniform under Mrs Kearns huge cloak and realised he was among friends. 'I was below, in Boland's with Dev, patching lads up. I only came back here yesterday because he ordered me out. Said I was more use out and working on our lads here than rotting in an English gaol. I suppose he was right, but when they marched the rest of them away...' Suddenly he looked very young and insecure.

'We're in Cumann na mBan.' Mary spoke quietly. 'We were in the GPO. We were late leaving and a man took us in and gave us clothes and looked after Mrs Grant, that's how we escaped.'

'But your man, her husband, he's not...' The doctor was confused. 'He seemed so concerned for her.'

'Yes, well... He's not to be trusted, but we don't have anywhere else to go, and with the mistress as weak as she is... That's why going back to his house is the lesser of two evils. He told the mistress here that all is forgiven, to come home, but I'm not so sure,' Mrs Kearns said darkly.

'Is it the only option?' Dr O'Leary was concerned. 'Mrs Grant will need really good care – and no upset – to recover from her injuries.'

'It looks like that anyway.' Mary sighed.

'Well, I don't know what can be done, but if you want, I can let whatever is left of the Volunteers know the situation. Maybe they can keep an eye on ye?' The doctor was at a loss. 'I'd offer, but I live in a room of a house with about six other fellows, and there just isn't space.'

Mary smiled. Even in this, the bleakest day of the movement, the rebels stood by each other. They weren't alone. They had support and they had each other. They'd be fine.

'Let's get you home, ma'am, to your own bed, and you'll feel much better. The master knows not to try anything. They haven't got all of us, and he knows that too. Dr O'Leary, do you think there's a way of getting us a way back to Glenageary? A motor car, or even a carriage?'

'That will not be necessary, Mary. Jimmy is outside with the car.'

They turned in shock to see Mr Grant standing in the doorway. He crossed the small room and sat beside his wife, taking her hand tenderly. 'I'm relieved to see you looking better, my dear. I was so worried. I understand that my wife is to be discharged, Doctor? Marvellous, it will be so lovely to have you home.' He smiled lovingly and patted Mrs Grant's hand as he spoke.

Turning to Mary and Mrs Kearns, he raised his hairy eyebrows. 'Well, then, shall we set about getting the mistress home? Mary, gather her things. Mrs Kearns, help me get her into that wheelchair there.'

As the women busied themselves, he spoke to the doctor again. 'Please don't trouble yourself with us any longer. My wife is not the only innocent bystander to be injured in recent days. Please, continue your valuable work, and thank you for all you have done for her. I don't know what I should have done if anything more serious had happened to her.'

Mary caught the mistress's eye and Mrs Grant just nodded.

The doctor seemed concerned and reluctant to leave. Despite the syrupy gratitude, he was being dismissed.

'Well, Mrs Grant, be sure to take it very easy and keep that leg elevated. You know where I am if you need me.' And he left.

The journey back to Strand Road was slow. So much of the city was in ruins, and flames still billowed out of some buildings. Mr Grant kept up a pleasant chatter, bemoaning the state of the city and enquiring after his wife's levels of comfort. Mary felt terrified; this was so out of character for him that she feared it was the calm before the storm.

Later that night, once the mistress was settled in her room – thankfully, the Grants had not shared a bedroom for years – Mary and Mrs Kearns sat in the warm kitchen. Mr Grant had gone to see a friend, he explained – another unprecedented action. He normally never informed anyone in the house, even his wife, of his movements. He expected the entire household to be available and ready for him at any time of the day or night he chose to appear. This new, considerate master was even more petrifying than the man she knew and feared before. Mary tried to dispel fears that he knew everything and was on his way to report them for theft.

She longed to hear word of Rory. She speculated about the fate of the leaders and those close to them. The absence of any contact with anyone from within the movement was so frustrating, but Mrs Kearns was right. The best thing to do for now was to keep their heads down and pretend everything was normal.

# CHAPTER 29

Mary served breakfast to Mr and Mrs Grant as the sun streamed through the dining room window. The mistress was improving steadily day by day, and was now able to manage the distance between her bedroom and the dining room with the use of two canes. Mary doubted the mistress would ever be able to walk straight again, though. Her leg was permanently twisted at an awkward angle due to the way the bone had broken, and the fact she endured it in that position for so long before it could be reset. Despite the pain of her injury, she made valiant efforts to never leave Mary alone with her husband. His considerate and almost loving demeanour hadn't slipped once in the week they had been back in the house.

'Mary, would you mind passing me the newspaper?' he asked in unctuous tones. Mary went to the side table, where each morning Jimmy placed the newspaper, freshly ironed to dry the ink. The headline caused her heart to thump in her chest so loudly, she was sure the Grants must have heard it. The headline screamed:

SEVEN LEADERS OF DUBLIN REVOLUTION
TO BE EXECUTED

Before she could turn around, he spoke again. 'That little alabaster and ivory statuette of the pony, the one I got at Sotheby's last summer. Have you moved it?'

Mary tried to keep her breathing normal. He was probably watching her for a reaction if he suspected anything untoward. She wasn't sure if he was addressing her or the mistress, so she waited. The statue was in the kitchen, being wrapped by Mrs Kearns for delivery to Mrs Grant's contact in the antique world. The mistress had been sure he wouldn't miss it, as it was kept on a shelf in the downstairs cloakroom, normally only used by guests.

'Oh, let me think.' Mary marvelled at her employer's calm, steady voice. 'Perhaps I did. I think I asked Mrs Kearns to clean it. I don't know where the dust comes from, but it is such an intricate little piece, I thought it would be best washed in warm soapy water. Mary, could you ask Mrs Kearns if it has been cleaned, please?' The mistress smiled pleasantly at her as she approached the table.

Mary couldn't read any more as she handed the paper to Mr Grant with shaking hands.

'I want to show it to a friend of mine in Dublin Castle, a bit of an expert in these matters. He thinks that I may have a more valuable piece on my hands than I first imagined.' He read the headline. 'Aah, yes. Well, what did they expect? Treason has to carry the death sentence. If people could just run around claiming independence and throwing the goodwill of their betters back in their faces, there would be chaos. They must be punished. Don't you think so, Mary?' Mr Grant's smile was broad.

Mary caught Mrs Grant's eye, who gave her an almost imperceptible nod.

'Yes, sir. I'm sure you are right,' she murmured quietly.

'Oh, I'm right, Mary. Yes. I forewarned of this

happening, but people will carry on with foolish-ness, even in the face of the best advice. Foolish people, hoodwinked by communists and trouble-makers. I think there must be a lot of people in this city feeling very stupid these days, as they ponder on how easily they were led. Playing dress up and acting like real soldiers, when in fact, they were being laughed at by the authorities, and rightly so. Utter nonsense from start to finish, and they deserve everything they get. Leaders of an empire must show strength and a hard line when it comes to this kind of rubbish.' He went on to read the paper, happily munching toast.

Mary retreated to the kitchen at the earliest opportunity and heaved a sigh of relief to be out from under the master's questioning. He was goading them, and he knew they were entirely at his mercy. Mrs Kearns had heard the news from the grocer's delivery boy moments earlier. Pearse, Connolly, Clarke and Plunkett from the GPO, and Ceannt, MacDonagh and Mac Diarmada, the other signatories of the Proclamation, all to face the firing squad. Even though they knew there was virtually no chance of them being allowed to live, to see it confirmed in black and white shook them to the core.

'Quick, where's the small statue of the pony?' Mary whispered urgently.

Mrs Kearns replied, "Tis wrapped up out in the scullery, ready for you. But you can't go now, he's still above. What if he sees you leaving?'

'He's looking for it.' Mary hurried to get it.

'O Holy Mother of God and all the saints, I'm too old for this. Quick, Mary, get all that wrapping off it. What did ye tell him?' Mrs Kearns panicked.

'The mistress was calm out, said it was after getting dirty upstairs and needed a good wash in warm soapy water, so she gave it to us to do down here. She never turned a hair.'

Just then the door of the kitchen opened to reveal the master standing there. Mary could never recall a time when he had entered that area of the house before. She walked calmly into the kitchen, the little statue in her hands.

'Aah, there it is, Mrs Kearns. Splendid. Have you cleaned it yet?' He examined the newly un-wrapped statue.

'No, sir. I was afraid to use the carbolic on it, sir, for fear 'twould damage it, so I was going to send Mary out for something milder this morn-ing.' Mrs Kearns was magnificent. Calm and courteous, as if she and the master chatted about the care of antiques every day of their lives.

'Very well, but I'll take it now anyway. I wonder, would you have something to wrap it in?'

Again, his tone was mild and genial. It was impossible to tell if he knew anything. Quick as a flash, Mrs Kearns went to the scullery and picked up the soft cloth the statue had been wrapped in only moments before.

'Would this be all right, sir?' she asked. 'Mary, go into the drawer there and get some string and some of that hemp wrapping the silversmith sent the cutlery back in last week. That will do nicely to protect it.'

Mr Grant looked around the kitchen, lifting up various tools and examining them while Mrs Kearns expertly wrapped the little statue for the second time that day.

Mary tried to go about her duties all day as normal, but her heart was heavy. The mistress knew the leaders personally, and was particularly fond of Tom Clarke, with whom she had a special bond. She had often had tea with him and his wife in the months leading up to the Rising, and she would deeply feel his loss in particular. Mary wished she could be of some comfort to her.

The mood in the city was changing. Over the

following days, she overheard the conversations in the shops and on the trams as she went about her errands for Mrs Kearns and the mistress. The near miss with the little pony statue did nothing to dampen the mistress's enthusiasm for what she called *her fundraising efforts*. As well as delivering and collecting valuable items, many of the errands Mary was sent on were spurious, as she was the only link to the outside world. The mistress and Mrs Kearns wanted to know what was going on in the city, but she always made sure to come back with a package or a purchase of some sort in case Mr Grant questioned her.

People were outraged at the treatment of the rebels, and their execution had a uniting effect on the city – even on those who originally opposed the Rising. Once the leaders had been executed, the British realised they had made a terrible mistake. They had made martyrs of them, and in so doing, had turned public opinion from resentment to support for the rebels. Tales of James Connolly, shot while tied to a chair because he couldn't stand, and rumours that Joseph Plunkett was allowed to marry his fiancé Grace Gifford the night before his execution in the presence only of soldiers, but was not allowed even a moment with his wife before being led to his death, captured the imaginations of the public.

The tide was turning against the British in a way unforeseen by even the most optimistic of the revolutionaries, and they were being proved right. Nothing would ever again be the same. Mary thought of Rory, cheerily shouting at her from the ranks as they were marched away that this was only the beginning. The next round would begin, and the next time they would win. The despondency she had felt two weeks before was dissipating, and a slow optimism and determination was replacing it. She longed to see Eileen, but was afraid to make contact because of Mr Grant's surveillance. She didn't want to draw her friend into anything that could prove awkward later. Eileen had managed to send a few notes, with the lad who delivered eggs to both houses, to the effect that she had heard nothing of Rory, but that no news was probably good news and to keep positive.

One evening, about a week after the executions, there was a knock on the window. Mrs Kearns and Mary both jumped in fright, as it was after ten o'clock and they were just getting everything ready for the morning before going to bed.

Lifting the curtain, Mary recognised with delight the dark hair of her friend.

'Eileen!' she exclaimed quietly, for fear of disturbing the Grants upstairs. She rushed to the back door and unbolted it as silently as possible. Instead of Eileen's usual cheery smile, her friend's face was ashen, her eyes red. Mary felt her stomach muscles contract. Something was wrong.

'What is it?' Mary could barely get the words out. 'Is it Rory?'

Eileen just nodded as Mrs Kearns drew her towards the range, on her way making sure the door into the passageway connecting the kitchen to the main part of the house was tightly closed.

Eileen's voice was barely a whisper. 'They sent someone round to the Carmodys. They want me to go to Kilmainham with them at eleven tonight. To see Rory.' Her words were stilted. They both knew what that meant. If she was being brought into the prison at night, then it could only be for one thing: to say goodbye.

'But why? They don't know anything about him. As far as they're concerned, he's just a regular Volunteer.' Mary was struggling to keep the panic from her voice. This couldn't be happening.

'Will you come? I told them I was going to get

you and to come back for us.' Eileen grasped Mary's hand.

Mary just nodded. She went to get her coat, all the while telling herself there must be another reason. They would never execute her Rory.

They left in silence, clinging to each other as they went out the door. As soon as they were outside on the street, Mary looked up instinctively to ensure she wasn't being watched. A cold realisation struck her. She caught Mr Grant's eye when he moved the curtain to look directly down on them, a horrible sneer on his lips. Instantly, Mary knew: This was his revenge. His revenge on her for defending the mistress, and his revenge on Rory for standing up to him.

She thought back to the night, so long ago, when Rory refused to be intimidated by the master. The plan to get them back into the house after the Rising was all for this. He had been biding his time to inflict maximum pain on them, and now his day had come. For a moment she feared he would try to stop them going, but then she realised he was relishing the prospect of her having to say a final goodbye to Rory. He was enjoying this, and he would no doubt enjoy goading her about it in the future. Eileen never noticed him, such was her grief, and Mary said nothing.

When they reached the back entrance of the Carmody house, the army truck was waiting, its engine idling. The soldiers helped them into the back and they set off.

The journey to the gaol in the back of the truck was cold and bumpy. They were driven into the yard of the prison and helped out. An officer came to meet them and asked them to follow him inside to a room where three women already waited. Mary recognised them as the wife and two daughters of Seán Dempsey, a friend and comrade of Rory's. Molly, Seán's wife, smiled bravely and nodded as Eileen and Mary came in. The officer left and the women were alone.

'Now, girls,' Molly began, addressing her own daughters as well as Eileen and Mary. 'We know why we're here, and what we have to do. We're no good to them crying and weeping. We've known from the start what the risks were, so we are going to go into our men and be strong and smile and love them and give them strength. We'll have all our lives for crying after they're gone. This is what we must do for them now. It's all we can do.'

Mary fought the urge to scream, to beg, plead with the soldiers to release Rory. Instead she nodded at Molly Dempsey and the older woman squeezed her hand.

The officer came back and called Molly and her daughters to follow him. Mary marvelled as they walked out, stoically dry-eyed.

Once they were alone, she and Eileen turned to each other. 'Will you come down to Limerick to tell my parents with me?' Eileen asked. 'They'll want to meet you. They know Rory wanted to marry you.'

Mary didn't trust herself to speak, so she simply nodded. She remembered the conversation in the woods when she promised Rory that she would live her life if the worst happened. Molly Dempsey was right – she had to be strong now. Rory would hate to see her upset, and she couldn't give the British the satisfaction. She hated them with such venom, it frightened her.

Lit only by a gas lamp, they sat – in the freezing cold room, despite the fact that it was mid-May – holding hands but saying nothing.

What seemed like hours later, the officer came back again.

'Ladies, if you'll follow me, please.' The politeness of the officer seemed ridiculous, given the savagery of what they were about to do, Mary resisted the urge to laugh. She remembered Rory telling her that he often got the urge to laugh in the most serious of situations and how it had got him into endless trouble in school. She must have caught it from him.

As he led them up stone stairs in the centre of the prison, Irene and Nora Dempsey, Seán's daughters, were coming down. The look that passed between the four girls spoke volumes, though not a sound was made. *Stay strong. Don't let them see how they have broken your heart.*

The officer opened a door on the landing and indicated that they should enter. Rory was sitting on a mattress on the floor of the tiny dark cell. The officer stood outside and closed the door, leaving the three of them alone. He had lost a lot of weight, and his hair seemed to have gone grey in the weeks since they had last seen him. His face was bruised and he moved gingerly, as if he was hurt. He stood up and the girls moved into the circle of his outstretched arms. They laid their heads on his chest as he held them tightly.

''Tis all right. 'Tis all right,' he said soothingly.

'How, Rory? We thought you were free…' Eileen asked.

'Edward Grant. He couldn't wait to go up to the Castle to his friend Johnson and squeal about me like the little piggy that he is. Sure, half the things they're pinning on me are total lies, but it doesn't matter. He was going to get his revenge on me for having the cheek to stand up to him, and all his connections. He has a lot of axes to grind – not just with me, but with his poor wife, and you girls as well. They told me 'twas him, so I know for sure. He wanted me to know who was behind my arrest. That Captain Johnson questioned me, and he was careful to point out the error of my ways when it came to Grant. Don't worry, though. He'll be dealt with too. Now, I don't want to waste one minute more on him.'

Releasing them from his hug, he put his hands on his sister's shoulders and looked deeply into her eyes. 'Eileen, my darling girl, you've followed me around since you could walk and I've led you astray right and proper, now haven't I? When you tell Mammy and Daddy, tell them I was happy to die, and that I'd do it all again if I had to. And that I love them, and all the small ones at home, and I always will. Will you do that for me?'

Eileen nodded, clinging to the brother she had adored since babyhood. He hugged her tightly and then let her go. Turning to Mary, he wiped the tears from her face with his thumbs. She tried to hold them in, but it was impossible.

'Mary Doyle, you'll remember our promise, now, won't you? Live your life, girl. I know you'll grieve for me – at least, I hope you will.' He managed a little chuckle. Even facing death, he was always a joker. 'But remember that someday, I want you to find a man – one who'll love you almost as much as I do. You are brave and beautiful and good and kind, and I feel so privileged to have known you.'

He led them to the back of the cell and whispered to them, 'Now listen carefully to me, both of you. I want you both out of Dublin as soon as you can. Now that Grant has got what he wanted, he has no reason to keep you, and I'm afraid of what he'll do. Don't even go back to that house for your things, Mary – it's too risky. And don't say a bit to anyone, not even Mrs Grant or Mrs Kearns. I don't want him going looking for ye. He'll be dealt with, as I said, but I don't know when. So in the meantime, stay below in Limerick with Mam and Dad, both of you. Will ye do that, promise me?' Both girls nodded.

Mary threw all caution to the wind. She needed to tell Rory how she felt. Normally she would never have spoken like that in front of anyone, even Eileen, but these were not normal times.

'I love you, Rory. You were all I ever dreamed of. In fact, I never even dreamed that someone like me would be loved by anyone, let alone someone like you. Thank you, Rory. Thank you for giving me a life.' She kissed him softly on the lips and released him. Eileen once more clung to him, and he rubbed her hair for a few moments until the door opened and the officer appeared once more.

'Time's up, I'm afraid.'

They looked back at the handsome, cheerful Rory O'Dwyer and smiled their brightest smiles.

'*Slán libh*.' Rory raised his hand in a wave goodbye.

# CHAPTER 30

'Ladies and gentlemen, please return to your seats and fasten your seatbelts, as there are ten minutes to landing. Aer Lingus would like to remind passengers that use of the toilets is prohibited until after the captain has switched off the fasten seatbelts sign, and the aircraft has come to a complete stop.' The soft Irish brogue of the flight attendant matched perfectly the rolling, fertile landscape below.

Eileen looked down on the land as the patchwork of green fields and wild ocean became ever closer, lost in silent contemplation. Scarlett wondered what she was thinking about. She had become silent since the first sight of Ireland. Scarlett often wondered why someone so deeply entrenched in Irish history and culture had never gone there before.

On the night they decided to make the trip, Eileen had told her a bit more about her background. She was born in 1922, which would make her ninety-three years old. Her mother was a woman called Mary Doyle, who worked for a couple called the Grants, and that somehow she was there in the GPO in 1916. Eileen promised to tell her the whole story when they got to Ireland.

Scarlett leaned over, pointing things out of the window to Lorena. It had been Eileen's idea to bring her when she heard from Scarlett about her mother's recovery.

Scarlett initially rejected the idea out of hand, and even though Eileen had convinced her, she still worried that she had made the right decision. Apart from anything else – like the fact that Lorena would drive her insane, and drive Eileen insane –Ireland was a Catholic country where she might actually get more fanatical. But it was not that kind of trip. They were meeting various academics and writers to discuss the flag, and there would be no place for Lorena in that. Plus, in reality, her mother was a loose cannon who could do or say anything. Though she was undoubtedly coming back to her old self, and she looked very glamorous, Scarlett had to admit that the new, saner Lorena was still a bit odd by anyone's standards.

Lorena had been so excited at the prospect of the trip that Scarlett felt she couldn't back out, despite her many reservations. On a few occasions before her mother was discharged, Scarlett had brought Eileen to visit. The two women, while they had utterly different personalities, actually got on very well. Eileen thought Lorena was hilarious and loved to hear her take on the activities of the celebrity world. Lorena wasn't a reader, not like Eileen was, but she loved the gossip magazines, so she kept them both entertained with stories of Botox gone wrong and the crazy things people do to get thinner. Whenever Lorena was irritating Scarlett, Eileen intervened and diffused the situation.

So far she'd been ok. Scarlett was prepared for her mother to have a breakout, to do or say something inappropriate, but so far she was kind and sweet and easy to please. In the airport, a chubby woman behind them in the security line – wearing a garishly coloured tracksuit and a bird's-nest hairdo – had stared at Scarlett and whispered something to her husband. Lorena overheard the name Charlie Morgan and the word *slut*.

She had whipped around, almost knocking Eileen over with her enormous fake Louis Vuitton carry-on, to face the woman squarely.

'Excuse me, ma'am. If you imagine for one moment you know anything about my daughter, or if you believe yourself to be so righteous that you can remark on the private lives of others –' Lorena's southern accent cut the air around them as gathered passengers stared '– then my heart goes out to you, sir. That's a terrible cross to have to bear, to share your life with such a judge-mental person.'

Eileen grinned delightedly, and the woman turned indignantly away and joined another line, dragging her bewildered husband with her. As she moved away, Lorena added, in her haughty tone, loud enough for other passengers to hear, 'Incidentally, dear, there comes a time in every woman's life when sportswear is no longer ap-propriate. Only those with the body of an athlete should wear the clothes of an athlete.'

Scarlett was mortified. Lorena patted her hand and then practically pushed her into the handsome customs official.

'Oh, sir, you can check my daughter through

first. You look strong enough to lift that big bag of hers. It's much heavier than mine. You know all the cosmetics and such these young *single* girls need.'

She winked on the *single* and laughed her flirtatious, tinkly laugh. Scarlett glanced apologetically in his direction, noting the wedding ring on his left hand. He smiled gently and went to deal with another passenger while his female colleague smirked at Scarlett's discomfort and patted her down. It felt like every passenger going through security was watching this pantomime. On the next belt, the exasperated customs official pulled all kinds of contraband from Lorena's bag.

'Mom!' Scarlett hissed over at her. 'I told you, no liquids and no sharp things.'

'But Scarlett, honey, who am I going to stab with this teeny nail file and scissors? And the water is for you. I know you get so hot. And I just had to bring my perfume. You bought it for me last Christmas, and I know how expensive it is, so I didn't want to risk losing it if our bags went missing,' Lorena argued reasonably as the security guard tried to put the items in the large clear bin beside him.

Eventually, and without Lorena's perfume and

nail set, they emerged from the security area. Scarlett was fit to scream. Eileen had placed her bag on the belt and it went through with no problem.

She couldn't help but think back to that last time she was in JFK airport, flying back from Washington, DC, after the midterm elections. She had covered the political campaign, a well-respected political journalist whose star was on the rise. *How far the mighty have fallen*, she thought to herself, as she saw her reflection in the window of a shop full of overpriced luggage. Here she was now travelling to the home of her drunk of a father, in the company of a mentally disturbed mother who was determined to find Scarlett a 'nice husband of her own,' and a very old lady who was carrying a bloodstained, hundred-year-old flag as carry-on baggage. How bizarre!

Settled in their seats, Scarlett had to smile at Lorena's enthusiasm for everything. She realised her mother had never flown before, and she was glad she was able to give her the opportunity, despite the drama at customs. Now that the wave of embarrassment had passed, Scarlett realised how nice it felt to have her mother stand up for her to that horrible woman in the tracksuit. The weeks in hospital had done her the world of good. She no longer prayed constantly, nor did she like to talk about Fr Ennio. Because Scarlett had more time on her hands, she had spent long afternoons sitting in the garden of the hospital, reading to her mother from celebrity biographies, or just chatting. It felt like a lot of the prickliness was gone from their relationship – they were just a mother and a daughter. They talked about Charlie, and Lorena was much more compassionate than she had been at the time the story broke. Gone were the recriminations and talk of sins, and in their place was an easy peace and understanding interspersed with indignation at how that low life had treated her darling daughter.

One day, when Lorena mentioned Vivien Leigh, Scarlett took the opportunity to raise the subject of how much she hated her name.

She explained to Lorena the difficulty of going through life with a name like Scarlett O'Hara – the jokes, the constant teasing. It had not been her intention, but as she spoke, all the resentment and anger came out and the floodgates opened. All the recriminations, buried for so long, flooded out. She railed against her mother for marrying Dan, for staying with him, for putting Scarlett through all that misery, and for never having the courage to leave, if not for herself, then for her daughter.

Lorena cried, not tears of self-pity, but tears of genuine grief for the life she and Scarlett could have had. She couldn't explain why she had stayed, but she apologised to her daughter for the mistakes that she made. She admitted she should have left Dan, but once she married him, her family told her she was on her own. They had hated him the one time they met him. She explained that she had no where else to go, no skills, no way of making money, and she feared that if she left him – if she failed to provide for her little girl – Scarlett would have been taken into care.

'I couldn't bear to lose you, Scarlett. I could endure anything but that, and I knew he'd never hurt you. He loved you. I remember that time I came to pick you up from that children's home in Queens, and you had such a nice time there that you didn't want to come home. They offered to me that you stay on for a while, but I couldn't do it. Maybe I should have, but you are the only thing in my life that I'm proud of. I should have let you go, let you be fostered by a nice normal family, but I was selfish. I needed you. I'm so sorry, Scarlett.' Her voice cracked with emotion.

'I would never have wanted to be fostered, Mom. I just wanted it to be just us, without Dan.' They sat in silence for a while, holding hands, each lost in her own private thoughts, trying to process what had just happened. Eventually Scarlett spoke, and surprised herself when she felt no more resentment. It was as if she had let it go in that outburst, and now she could see her mother properly – maybe for the first time. Lorena wasn't perfect. She had made mistakes and Scarlett did suffer as a result, but she knew that everything her mother did was out of love. Her only motivation was the love of her child.

She spoke quietly, still holding her mother's hand. 'I understand now a bit better why you did it. You were only acting out of love, and y'know, people make mistakes. I'm not exactly without flaws myself, so who am I to criticise you? I'm sorry I let you down, y'know…with Charlie and everything…'

Lorena held one of Scarlett's hands in both of hers, looking deeply into her daughter's eyes. 'I've always been proud of you, Scarlett, always. So you fell for the wrong man. I'm not in a position to berate you for that, am I?'

An easy silence settled between them as the gentle breeze ruffled the flowers in the hospital garden. They sat silently, letting go, at long last, all of the hurt.

'Why the name, though, Mom? Surely you knew what you were doing to me?' Scarlett asked, because it still rankled with her.

'I named you Scarlett O'Hara because, in my eyes, nobody, not even Vivien Leigh herself, was as beautiful as my baby girl. I still think that, and nobody ever will be.'

THE TERMINAL SEEMED to be like every other one all over the world: bright, smooth, light-coloured tiles and lots of plate glass. The customs and passport control was quick and impersonal. In a matter of minutes, they found themselves standing in the Arrivals area, waiting to be claimed like pieces of lost luggage. Eileen and Lorena both needed the bathroom, so she accompanied them. Eileen seemed sober to be in Ireland, but Lorena was blissfully unaware and chattered incessantly about John Wayne and Barry Fitzgerald in *The Quiet Man*.

When they returned to the Arrivals area, they found a tall, dark-featured man holding up a sign with Eileen's name on it. There was no way the guy was Irish, so he couldn't be this Fiachra Mc-Carthy who was supposed to meet them, could he? Lorena was telling Eileen about how the air was so fresh here and was gushing on about the inside of the airport terminal. Scarlett was trying to keep her irritation in check. Lorena was just excited, she knew, but her endless chatter was starting to get on Scarlett's nerves. She was about to point this out when the man turned and beamed at them.

'Mrs Chiarello?' He extended his hand to Eileen and she offered hers in return.

'Mr McCarthy. Nice to meet you at last.' Eileen was calm and gracious as always, the opposite of Lorena, who was now trying to get her cell phone to work by pressing buttons repeatedly. Scarlett wanted to hear what he said to Eileen, but her mother's frustration with the phone was drowning them out. Why this mattered was a mystery anyhow, as she only ever called Scarlett. So she resisted a sarcastic remark as she gently took the phone and got it working.

So the man talking to Eileen was, in fact, Fiachra McCarthy after all, though he didn't look like any Irishman she'd ever seen. He was tall and slim, in his mid-forties, she guessed, athletic looking, with jet-black hair and olive skin, and his face was lit up by warm, dark-brown eyes. He looked more Turkish or North African than Irish.

'Well, Mr McCarthy –' Eileen began to introduce them when he interrupted.

'Fiachra, please.'

Eileen smiled, as if these new ways of addressing total strangers by their first names was ridiculous, but she went on. 'Very well, as you wish. Fiachra, these are my friends, Scarlett and Lorena O'Hara, from New York. This is Fiachra McCarthy from the Department of An Taoiseach. It was he who first contacted me about the flag,' she added by way of explanation for Lorena.

'What a lovely name you have, sir. So unusual. How do you pronounce it again?' Lorena beamed as she shook his hand vigorously and her southern accent seemed even more pronounced to Scarlett, like she was putting on the southern belle act. *I must stop it*, she admonished herself, *or everything out of Mom's mouth will drive me crazy.*

Fiachra smiled and Lorena melted. 'Well, it's like "Fee-ack-rah." My mother wanted us all to have Irish names, and she's a big fan of Celtic literature so some of my siblings names are totally unpronounceable to anyone not Irish so I got away lightly. But working in the Department of

Foreign Affairs with a name like mine can be challenging as people try to pronounce it.'

Shaking Scarlett's hand, he turned his smile on her. She was waiting for the usual smartass remark that came after she was introduced for the first time.

'It's lovely to meet you, Lorena and Scarlett. Welcome to Dublin!'

Scarlett was amazed. No comment on her name at all. Either the guy lived under a rock and had never heard of the name before – which she doubted – or he was a most unusual person.

'Well, if ye are ready, I'll let ye get to the hotel. I hope you'll be comfortable there. It's not far, so I've organised a taxi. Maybe tomorrow, if you're feeling up to it, Mrs Chiarello, we can meet to discuss your flag? There is to be a meeting of minds, and of artefacts, on Thursday in the National Museum in Collins's Barracks. People from all over Ireland, and indeed, the world, are meeting to share what they have brought, and so the historians and organisers of the commemoration can catalogue it. As a project, it's huge, as you can imagine, so the first phase is to see what we've got, and maybe to see what the various things can tell us about the period. I really must thank you again for bringing the flag home. I can't tell you what it means to us.'

'I'm glad to be able to do it, but I wouldn't have been without Scarlett here. Regarding the arrangements, that sounds fine, Fiachra,' Eileen said.

He assisted them to the waiting cab and helped them load their luggage. Eileen and Lorena settled in the back, and Fiachra held the passenger door open for Scarlett.

'I'll see you tomorrow, Scarlett, if you're coming with Mrs Chiarello. She mentioned in her letter that you were assisting her?' he asked.

'Sure.' Scarlett smiled. 'I'm looking forward to it.'

# CHAPTER 31

'*Adhaoine uaisle, go raibh mile maith agaibh go leir dun teacht anseo inniu.*'

Scarlett was sitting beside Eileen as the leader of the Irish government addressed the gathered crowds. He was fair-haired, of average build, and spoke with a soft brogue rather than the more musical accent of the Dublin area she'd heard many times since arriving. He didn't have the shiny, polished look of American politicians. She thought he looked like someone who was real – someone for whom life was not a series of sound bites and snapshots. He seemed quietly confident and she found herself being well disposed to-wards him. The man was speaking in Gaelic, and

Scarlett hadn't the faintest clue what he was saying. Eileen, however, seemed entranced.

'Can you understand him?' Scarlett whispered in Eileen's ear.

Eileen just smiled and nodded. 'Perfectly.'

As Scarlett had come to expect, Eileen did not elaborate how a woman who lived her whole life in the United States could speak this language of Ireland.

To the relief of the gathered assembly, many of whom were foreigners, he reverted, after the initial address, to speaking in English.

'Ladies and gentlemen. What an honour it is for me to stand before you today. As Taoiseach of the Irish Republic, to welcome the descendants of those brave men and women of 1916 to our capital city is a highlight of my career. On behalf of myself and of the government, but most of all on behalf of the Irish people, I thank you all for making the journey. Many of you have travelled long distances to be here with us, coming from Australia, New Zealand, the United States, Canada, Japan, South Africa, Singapore, South America, Ghana, and from all over Europe. I'm sure you all had to go to considerable lengths to be here with us today, and we do appreciate it, very much.

'What unites the people in this room is that each of you has, through those who have gone before you, a connection to the events of Easter Week in 1916. Those people, the mothers and fathers of Irish democracy, gave everything they had to free our island of tyranny and maltreatment, with far too many paying the ultimate price. They were, to a man and woman, unwavering in their belief that Ireland was, and should be, a sovereign nation, free and equal with all the democratic nations of the earth. They fought and they died. Many went on to fight in the War of Independence between 1919 and 1922, and sadly, more again went on to fight in the subsequent Civil War. Our history is one of hardship, violence, loss and grief, but also one of bravery, tenacity and pride. Those men and women, whose blood flows in the veins of many of you gathered here today, deserve to have their contributions recognised. Through this initiative, to commemorate the 1916 Rising next year on its centenary, we hope to honour their work and their sacrifices. And not just the leaders, those names that, as Yeats put it, 'Stilled our childish play.' The names of Pearse, Connolly, MacDiarmuida, Plunkett, Ceannt, Clarke, and MacDonagh are commemorated and remembered daily in the place names of our streets, our public buildings, our bridges and our train stations. But I – and, I suspect, they too – would want us to recall to mind those who have perhaps been forgot by history. We hope that we can reignite the flame of remembrance to those men and women whose stories you each hold dear.

'A gathering such as this will no doubt give us many new and interesting perspectives on an era that was so fundamental to our country, then and now. You who have gathered here are part of something much bigger than any individual or group. You share in that history that they made – your mothers, fathers, uncles, aunts, cousins or friends. Whomsoever you are here to tell us about, are, I feel sure, looking down on us and wishing us well in our commemorative endeavour.

'*Go raibh mile maith agaibh go leir.*'

The applause went on for a long time as the Taoiseach smiled and shook hands with the team of academics and historians on the platform. The enthusiasm and nostalgia in the room was palpable. Scarlett looked around at the faces of those nearest to her. Jubilation, pride, loneliness, and relief echoed from face to face, and she found herself longing to know and tell their stories. Her eyes rested on Eileen, who was not clapping or cheering, but was standing silently with tears pouring down her face. A thought struck Scarlett: Their stories would make a great book!

'Eileen.' She touched the older woman's arm. 'Are you ok?'

'I wonder if he's right. I wonder, are they here, watching us? We've kept faith for so long, so long. I never dreamed I'd ever come back here, to this place.'

Scarlett was at a loss as to what to do. Eileen seemed to be talking to herself more than to Scarlett.

People were wandering around the ornate hall that was adorned with military pictures and memorabilia as the researchers set up tables and chairs around the room. Teas and coffee were being served outside in a little café attached to the museum, and Eileen had been given a table number to approach when she was ready, where her flag would be photographed and her story recorded. There must have been several hundred people at the gathering, and Fiachra had explained earlier, when they had arrived, that this event would run for four more days, such was the response to the call for artefacts. He seemed to be responsible for Eileen, while other official-looking people took care of others who were clearly here with the same purpose.

Sensing Eileen needed a bit of space, Scarlett led her friend to a table in the glass conservatory adjoining the café and settled her there while she went in to get them some tea.

'Well, Scarlett, how are things? Did you enjoy the Taoiseach's address?' Fiachra was in front of her in the long line for coffee.

'Oh, hello again! Yes, thanks, though I couldn't understand the Gaelic parts. Eileen can, though, which is amazing considering she has never been to Ireland, I believe. She was very moved by the whole experience this morning.'

Fiachra nodded. 'He's a great speaker, and this is a cause that is very dear to his heart, of course. He's a direct descendant of one of the signatories, and his family is steeped in the history and politics of this country. He's really driving this thing. There must be so much information out there...'

'Well, he did a good job of recruiting people,' Scarlett agreed. 'It's amazing the stuff that must be left in all the corners of the world. Still, finding people, contacting them and all of that, it's a huge undertaking for you.'

'I'm delighted to be involved. I studied history at college, and the decade from 1913 to 1923 really fascinated me. Since entering the civil service, most of what I do is administrative, and so this is something new and interesting. I'm looking forward to hearing Mrs Chiarello's story particularly. She's an impressive lady, isn't she? Have you known her long?'

'Well, no, actually. Only a few months,' Scarlett replied.

'Well, she seems to trust you. She strikes me as a good judge of character.'

'Yes. We had a kind of peculiar start. It's a long story.'

Fiachra seemed to sense it was not a story Scarlett was going to go into and changed the subject. 'So, did you all sleep well last night?'

'Oh, yes, and once I had my mother and Eileen tucked up, I went for a stroll around the city. It's a good-looking town, though there was a lot of partying going on,' Scarlett joked, remembering the groups of young people who were singing and revelling on the streets.

'I suppose you went into Temple Bar, so? That's the kind of touristy hang-out in the city. Big gangs of lads and girls from all over Europe descend there at the weekends for hen and stag parties.' Noting her look of confusion, he went on. 'I think you call them *bachelor parties*?'

'Oh, yeah, sure. I guess that's what I saw last night then. They sure weren't holding anything back.'

Fiachra rolled his eyes. 'Hmm. Yes, I can imagine. Please don't hold it against us. Most of us are fairly civilised. There are some really nice places to go in the city, and even a bit outside. How long are you here for?'

He seemed so relaxed as he smiled his thanks to the lady serving and went to a nearby table for milk and sugar. Scarlett wished she could talk to him for longer – he appeared to be very nice. She joined him, having got her drinks, and began adding milk to Eileen's tea.

'Two weeks – we are going to do what Eileen needs to do as regards her flag, and then we thought we might rent a car and take a bit of a tour around the country.' Scarlett glanced in the direction of Eileen, worried she had left her alone for too long, but she was deep in conversation with a man in military uniform and seemed perfectly happy.

'That's a great idea. I'm guessing with a name like O'Hara, you have some Irish blood somewhere along the line?'

Scarlett paused for a moment. Her stock response to that frequently asked question was that there probably was, and that she had no idea who they were or when they had emigrated to the United States. But for some reason, she had the urge to tell him the truth.

Fiachra took her pause to mean he had offended her and began apologising immediately. 'Me and my big mouth. I don't know how I ever wound up in the diplomatic business! I'm sorry, I shouldn't be so nosy…'

Scarlett put her hand on his arm. 'Relax. I'm not going to bite your head off. I was just deciding whether to tell you the official party line on my Irishness, or to tell you the truth.'

'And which is it going to be?' His eyes twinkled mischievously.

'Well, the truth, I think…if you want to hear it. But I'd better bring Eileen her tea, though she seems deep in a chat.'

He glanced over in Eileen's direction. 'She's in safe hands. Here, give me the tea and you hold that table. That's Commandant Seán Kelly. He's in charge of Military Archives here, so he'll be fascinated with her story.'

As Fiachra crossed the room, Scarlett watched him. He really was gorgeous, she admitted to herself. Since the debacle with Charlie, she'd decided she was sworn off men for good, but there was something about him – his unassuming manner hiding a quick intellect. He was obviously in a senior position, so was a political animal like herself, but he seemed very candid. After spending a lifetime with people who had an agenda, or their own cause to promote, she found him refreshing.

He was so kind to Eileen, never patronising her. But he did realise that at her age, there was a limit to how much energy she had. He had called the hotel yesterday evening and spoken to her just to check that she had everything she needed, and was waiting for her when she arrived this morning. Such genuine kindness was unusual in a politician, so she was impressed. He had a few quick words with various people as he made his way back to her. Clearly, he was someone people knew.

He sat down opposite her. 'I'm intrigued now, Ms Scarlett O'Hara. Tell me everything about your Irishness. You can trust me – I'm a politician.' He chuckled.

Scarlett thought again how un-Irish he looked, with his dark features and those chocolate-brown eyes ringed by the longest eyelashes she had ever seen. They seemed to be wasted on a man.

'You don't look very Irish yourself, I must say,' she joked.

'Well, I'm Irish, all right, but my parents adopted me from Romania when I was two and a half. I don't remember anything about my life before I came here, but judging by what I know of those places, that's probably a good thing. My mother had ovarian cancer as a young woman which, thankfully, she survived, but the treatment left her infertile, so they decided to adopt. They actually adopted four of us from the same orphanage in the end. I've an older brother and two younger sisters. We get some funny looks, all right, when we are out together, because Mam and Dad are both red-haired – like yourself, pale skin and freckles, the whole lot – and we are all dark then. You'd look more like their child than we do.'

Scarlett smiled. 'Wow, they sound like great people.'

'Aah, they're brilliant. We were so lucky, I can't imagine how different my life would be if they hadn't rescued me. I appreciate them now that I'm older, more than I did years ago. They sacrificed a lot for us, you know?'

'I guess. I wish someone would have adopted me!' Scarlett joked.

Instead of laughing along with her joke, Fiachra sipped his coffee and then asked, 'Why?'

Scarlett took a deep breath. She had never discussed her past with anyone. Nobody from her adult life apart from Lorena, Eileen and Artie had the faintest idea where she came from, but something about Fiachra made her want to confide in him. *Maybe it's the whole stranger on a train idea*, she thought. *Blurting out your deepest, darkest secrets to someone you know you'll never meet again.*

'Well, my father was Irish – not like fifth generation or anything, but actually from Ireland. Someplace around Mayo, I think. He came over to New York in his twenties and met my mother, a southern belle. Well, you've met her, and they got married and then had me.'

She paused, then went on. 'He was a violent alcoholic, and he made our lives hell until he was killed in a road accident when I was fifteen. The best day of my life. My mother loved the movies. She used them as a way of escape, I guess, and she loved *Gone with the Wind* best of all. So when she had a little girl, and she already had the last name of O'Hara, then Scarlett I became. Growing up with red hair and freckles and looking nothing like Vivien Leigh didn't help. So there you have it: The reason why I wish I'd been adopted.'

Fiachra seemed to know instinctively that her telling him this was a big deal. He reached over the table and squeezed her hand. 'Sometimes life deals us a bad hand, Scarlett, but then, every so often, something great happens to restore your faith in the world. You might curse your father, and you have a right to, but without him, bad and all as he was, you wouldn't exist.'

The normal guardedness with which Scarlett lived her life seemed to evaporate. 'Are you married?' she asked.

'No. You?' He was still holding her hand.

'No.' She smiled.

'Will you have dinner with me on Friday night?' he asked.

With her heart thumping and throwing her usual caution to the wind, Scarlett grinned. 'I'd love to.'

# CHAPTER 32

$\mathcal{M}$ary was walking back from the creamery along the quiet country road. She liked this part of the day best, because it allowed her to be alone with her thoughts. So much had happened in the weeks since the Rising, and her heart was heavy with grief. The O'Dwyers were so welcoming and kind to her, but they, like their children, were heartbroken. The loss of Rory was something they were all finding impossible to bear.

After that final goodbye, they did exactly as Rory asked, going back to Eileen's small bedroom at the Carmody house. By the time they got back from the prison, it was so late that everyone was sleeping. They slipped out early in the morning and caught the train to Limerick. Mary and Eileen had serious reservations about abandoning Mrs Grant and Mrs Kearns to the wrath of the master, but Rory had assured them that he was to be dealt with as soon as possible by the Volunteers. Once Mr Grant was gone, they would be safe.

Mary felt huge sadness at not saying goodbye to the two women who had come to mean so much to her, and she wished she could have gone back for her bundle of letters from Rory, but he had been insistent, and she wanted to keep her promise to him. The idea that she might never again open a letter from him, or hear his voice, or feel her hand in his filled her with all pervasive despair. When she was alone, she could allow the pain in, but when she was with any of the O'Dwyer family, she felt that they had more of a right to his memory than she did. After all, he was their son, their brother – and she had only known him for three years.

The newspapers were full of the executions, but she couldn't bring herself to read them. There had been no official communication to say Rory had been executed, but that meant nothing. They probably wouldn't bother to notify his family. She'd read about the execution of Seán Dempsey and immediately her thoughts went to his wife and daughters. But the British became concerned about the backlash of public opinion against them in the wake of the executions of the signatories, and so were only releasing very limited information. Some tenacious journalists were finding things out, but it was frustrating not knowing.

Yesterday, Eileen had pointed out a small section in the paper, detailing the discovery of the body of Mr Edward Grant in the Dublin Mountains following an anonymous tip-off. He had been shot at close range, and the police were calling it an execution. Her first reaction was one of relief, but that was closely followed by fear that it had taken the Volunteers too long. Rory seemed sure they would pick him up immediately after they left, but weeks had gone by. God alone knew what he had done to the mistress and the housekeeper in the meantime.

She had sent a postcard to Mrs Kearns, posting it from Kingsbridge Station on the day they left so it couldn't be traced to her, just saying that she was all right, and that she would be in touch. She hated the thought of the housekeeper worrying, but she didn't want to put her in even greater danger by allowing Mrs Kearns – the only mother Mary had ever known – to be aware of where she was.

As she walked along, she composed a letter in her head. She would write it tonight, knowing the master was dead and it was safe. Remembering that terrible night so long ago, she was glad that at least Mrs Grant would never again feel his fists. Mary dreaded to think of the fate of that kind, brave woman, the only comfort being that at least she had Mrs Kearns.

Days with the O'Dwyers passed in a blur, sometimes racing by, but mostly at a deathly crawl. Eileen was withdrawn and silent, dealing with Rory's death in her own way, and the younger children seemed wary of her. Mary tried to comfort her friend, but her grief made her un-reachable – a different girl to the carefree, viva-cious Eileen that she loved.

Mary knew she should be thinking of what she was going to do next. Going back to Dublin wasn't an option. Though Mr Grant was dead, that didn't mean she was safe. But apart from that, something much more painful was keeping her away. She couldn't bear to be in the place where she had been with Rory. It would be too hard, remembering at every corner the times they had when they were young and in love, and believed the whole world was theirs for the taking. They had thought that no matter what happened, they were invincible. *Maybe all young people think that – that's what gives us the courage to do the things we do.* Mary marvelled even more at the bravery of people like Mrs Kearns, and of Tom Clarke, who had seen so much more of life and probably knew better than she and Rory how it would all end, but went ahead anyway.

The sun was warm and she removed her cardigan as she walked along, mulling over her options. She had no reference, and while she knew Mrs Grant would give her one, she couldn't risk a new employer finding out her connection to the Grants, what with everything that had happened. A political past and links to an execution were not the attributes needed to be a good maid. Everyone in the townland in Limerick knew what she and Eileen and Rory had been involved with, and so any future employer in the area wouldn't have to do too much digging to find out. She could go to England, she supposed, but she hated the British with such passion, she couldn't bring herself to consider it seriously. America was somewhere she'd read about before the Rising, but the journey was so expensive...and anyway, she just couldn't motivate herself to go so far away, feeling as she did. Perhaps somewhere in the northern part of Ireland. Maybe she could get a maid's position up there, where the happenings in Dublin were remote and irrelevant.

Suddenly she was exhausted and despondent again. Whenever she tried to make plans, her brain refused to work. She just couldn't think about the future, because without Rory, she wished she had no future. She thought about all the bullets flying about during the week in the GPO. *Why couldn't I have got one of those? Then me and Rory would be together, and I wouldn't have to live each day alone.*

Such thoughts haunted her every day – always the same – and she wondered if she'd ever really recover from Rory's death. People always said that time heals, but she wasn't convinced. The pain was on so many levels. She felt it as a physical pain in her heart, literally, as if her heart was broken, but it was the mental pain that was the worst. The thoughts of long lonely years stretching ahead without him tormented her. Sometimes she wished she had never left the convent, never known him, because at least then she would never have discerned what she was missing. Throughout the day, she kept busy, helping on the farm and playing with the little ones, but once she went to bed, these thoughts went round and round in her head, refusing to allow sleep to come. Last night she had gone outside in the early hours of the morning, only to see his face every time she closed her eyes, smiling down at her, making her promise to live her life. There wasn't much room in the farmhouse, and she was sharing a room with Eileen and two of Rory's younger sisters. She needed to be alone with her grief, so she had slipped outside. As she leaned against the wall of the byre on the summer's night in her nightdress and cardigan, she felt her body rack with sobs. Loneliness and heartache crashed over her like relentless waves, and she felt she might drown beneath the horrific weight of it all.

Strong arms enveloped her and the sobs continued. Rory's father held her tight and rubbed her hair. "Tis better out than in, Mary girl. You'll be all right. Leave it go!'

For what seemed like forever, he rubbed her back and let her cry for Rory. Eventually, as the sobs subsided, he gave her his handkerchief. He took a small bottle out of his coat pocket, and taking the cork off, he handed it to her. She sipped it, and though the whiskey burned her throat, it warmed her. He drew her down to a low wall and sat down beside her. As the sun rose, nature's dawn chorus was commencing.

'He wrote to me, you know, all about you and ye'er plans together.' John O'Dwyer spoke quietly, not wanting to wake the household. She wondered why he was up and about at his time, then remembered Rory saying his father hardly slept at all. There were calves in the field nearest the house, and one of them was sickening for something. He was probably checking on her. Mary had liked him the moment she met him. He was quieter than Rory, but he was strong and solid, and was like a big warm blanket wrapped around his family. Not for the first time, Mary felt a pang of envy at the happiness and safety of their home. Rory and Eileen adored their parents, and once Mary met Peg and John O'Dwyer, she could see why.

'Did he?' she asked through her tears.

'He did. And he also asked me to look after you if anything happened to him. My son died for Ireland, and though our hearts are breaking at the loss of him, we will do what he wanted us to do. Now I know you were talking to Peg the other day about finding a job in one of the big houses around or something like that, but there's to be no more of that talk, do you hear me? You are my daughter now, the same as the ones inside, and no different. You'll stay here till you want to go. And if that time never comes, then that's fine with me too. I won't have any child of mine married off to some man who won't love her, nor sold into the service of the gentry. So you have a home here for as long as you want it. You're a great help to Peg around the place, and the small ones are mad about you. I know a bit about where you came from, and how hard it was for you growing up with the nuns. All I want you to know is that you are home now.'

Mary thought that might have been the longest speech she ever heard Rory's father make, but she knew that he meant it. Peg was so kind to her too, and the little ones were like the brothers and sisters she never had. The few times she had smiled or laughed, in recent weeks, were when she was playing some game with them, or when they were making up stories to tell her. The nuns hadn't liked the children in the home to become friendly with each other, so people just stuck to themselves. Even now that he was gone, she could feel Rory's protection and love.

Mr O'Dwyer left to attend to his calves. The sun shone on Mary's face as she got up and kept walking along, the bright luminary doing its best to lift her spirits. Foxgloves and bluebells bloomed in profusion in the ditches, and it was hard to imagine that it was the same country that had been plunged into bloody revolution just weeks earlier. The attitude in the country was changing rapidly towards the rebels. Once, they were regarded as nothing but troublemakers and glory hunters, but now after the British so callously executed the leaders, the mood in the country had changed. They were heroes, deserving of honour and praise.

Last week she had been in the local draper's getting cloth for Peg when the girl behind the counter seemed less than friendly. By now it was all over the parish who she was.

'So you're the wan from Dublin that was around with Rory O'Dwyer, the Lord have mercy on him?' the shop assistant asked with a sneer.

Before Mary had time to answer, Mae Sullivan, the owner of the shop, called from the back, 'That's enough of your attitude now, Vera O'-Driscoll. That girl was engaged to be married to Rory, and if the cursed British hadn't cut his life short, he'd be introducing her to you as his bride,

God be good to him. So don't mind your auld jealousy at all. Rory O'Dwyer had no eye for you, and that's all that's wrong with you.'

Mae moved out from the bales of dark cloth, smiling all the while. 'Don't you mind the likes of her at all, Mary. There wasn't a girl for forty miles who didn't set her cap at Rory O'Dwyer, and he charmed them too right enough, but he was never serious with them. There'll be a few round about here who might be a biteen jealous that you were the one to get him, the poor lad. And sure isn't it obvious why he was taken with you, and you so pretty! Peg tells me you were there, above in the GPO and all?'

'Well, yes, just as a nurse. I'm in Cumann na mBan, you see, and that's how I met Rory, really...' Even mentioning his name gave her a sharp pain in her chest.

'Well, he was a grand lad and he growing up around here, and he did his family and his country proud. That's eight shillings and four pence, please, for the serge. 'Tis gone a ferocious price, but with the war on, 'tis close to impossible to get anything half decent. All the ships that used to bring in anything to Ireland are fighting the Kaiser now,' she added in a stage whisper, 'and the best of luck to him too!'

Mary felt the chastened Vera throwing daggers with her eyes as she left the shop with her purchase. Eileen had warned her of the reaction she might get from some of the local girls. Apparently everyone had their eye on Rory, and she heard a few whispers as she went up to receive on Sundays at Mass. It was one of the rare conversations they'd had since they arrived in Limerick. Mary missed the old Eileen, but she knew her friend was trying to be strong for her family, and the only way to do that was to withdraw into herself.

Eileen was spending a bit of time with Teddy Lane, the son of a neighbouring farmer who clearly loved her, but she wasn't capable of feeling anything but pain at the moment. He was patient and gentle, taking her for walks and bringing her things that might put the smile back on her face. He was a friend of both Rory and Eileen since childhood, and he seemed to know instinctively what she needed. Teddy made no demands on her, just a reassuring presence, walking beside her through her pain. Eileen had mentioned him a few times when they were in Dublin. She used to get occasional letters from him, and Mary thought that maybe, in time, Eileen could smile again, and his love might be reciprocated. Mary hoped, for Eileen's sake, that he would wait till she was able to face living again. Mary knew that for herself, there would be no other. She had promised Rory she would move on, but she knew in her heart that there was only one man for her, and he was gone.

As she entered the yard, she was surprised not to see the little ones playing around. On the fine days, Peg gave them little jobs to do in the mornings, like feeding hens or picking tomatoes or fruit from the bushes, but the afternoons were their own for roaming around the farm. The twins, Michael and Patrick, who were ten years old and always plotting some devilment, were no doubt off up the fields, and Kate, Eileen's younger sister, was probably helping a neighbour with her new baby. Kate, with her sweet gentle nature, had a great knack with babies, settling even the most fractious ones, and so she was in high demand around the parish. The smallest ones, Tim, aged five, and little Siobhán, who was only three, usually pottered around the yard with the dog. The border collie had had pups a week before, and their arrival was a cause of great excitement. Everyone was waiting each day for the puppies' eyes to open. The exuberance and giggles of Tim and Siobhán were what kept the family going.

Mary went into the kitchen to find the two smallest sitting up at the table, drinking milk. John, Peg, and Eileen were standing by the range, staring at a piece of paper. Mary's heart thumped in her chest. It must be the official confirmation of Rory's execution. Peg and Eileen were crying and John just handed the piece of paper to her. She looked down... Something was wrong. It wasn't the terse, typed document she was expecting, but a letter.

With shaking hands she began to read:

*Dear Family and Mary,*

*I realise this letter might come as a bit of a shock to you, and I would have written sooner if I could have, but they only let me have pen and paper today. As you know, I was to be executed for my part in the insurgence against the legitimate Crown forces in Dublin two months ago.*

*Well, the commanding officer in Kilmainham Gaol, after I pleaded my case, reassessed the evidence against me. Based on a lack of proof that I was a major participant in the rebellion, I had my sentence commuted to ten years in prison.*

*I am currently serving my sentence in Frongoch Prison, in Wales, and I am well. My health is good and I am in fine spirits. We are being treated well here,*

*with enough food, and we even get to play an odd foot-
ball match now and then.*

*I hope you are all well, and know that you are all
in my prayers.*

*Love, Rory*

Mary sat down heavily on the kitchen chair,
suddenly too weak to stand. She tried to gather
her thoughts. Rory was alive! She had to keep
saying it over and over.

'Rory is alive! Rory is alive!' Suddenly, she was
pulled into a hug as Eileen and her parents cried
tears of pure unadulterated joy. The nightmare
was over. Rory was alive!

'Can we write to him, do you think?' Mary
asked a jubilant John.

'Well, we can try, girl, we can surely try!
Though from the sounds of that letter, they read
everything. There's no way Rory would have
called those murderers "the legitimate Crown
forces." No, I'd say they are worried now, now
that everyone is getting behind the rebels, and
they want to smooth things over a bit. They're up
to their necks in it over in France and Belgium,
and the last thing they need here is more
shenanigans out of the Irish.'

'Ten years, he said.' Peg was fretting. 'Ten
years in an English jail for my boy…'

John held both his wife's hands in his and said softly to her, 'Peg, *a stór*, our boy is alive. He's alive, and we thought he was dead. Sure, who knows what's going to happen next. Maybe he won't serve the ten years, or maybe he'll be allowed to serve them here and we can visit him. The thing is, our child is alive.'

'You're right, John, I know you're right. I just want to see him, to hold him in my arms. I thought he was in heaven. I couldn't bear it. Having him in an English jail is better than that. Do you think he was being truthful, that they're feeding him and treating him well?'

Eileen couldn't stop smiling. 'Aah, Mam, don't be worrying. Rory is tough out. Sure they were living out rough half the time above in the Wicklow Mountains when the crowd in Dublin Castle were rounding them up. He'll be there with all of our own, and they'll look out for each other. I'll tell you what – why don't we sit down right now, the children and all, and write a big long letter to him. They might let it into him if the small ones write it.'

The atmosphere in the house was ecstatic as the farm labourers arrived for their tea and were told the great news. It went around the area that Rory was alive, and neighbours called with cake and whiskey, and the music and singing went on late into the night. Eileen even danced with Teddy in the middle of the kitchen, much to his delight. Mary had to keep reminding herself that Rory was alive – in prison, maybe for a long time, but alive.

# CHAPTER 33

*arling Mary,*

*I got your letter this morning, and the package too. I'm wearing the lovely* gansaí *you knit for me, and all the other lads are eyeing it up, especially now the nights are getting chilly! When I put it, on it's like having your lovely arms around me. I'll probably get a right doing from the lads if anyone reads this, but I don't care. You've no idea what it means to me to hear from you and all the family. I'm so sorry I had to put you through all that, thinking they executed me XXX XXXXXX XXXXXX XXXX.*

Mary wondered what Rory wrote next. The letters were heavily censored, so the prisoners had to be very careful in what they said, and even then, large portions were clipped neatly out. It was most frustrating. Peg and John had got a letter last week that was impossible to read, so little was left of it.

*Life here isn't too bad, so don't be worrying. In your last letter you asked me what we did all day, so I'll try to answer you. We are left to ourselves most of the time, and we take turns to cook and keep the place fairly tidy, though it does lack a woman's touch, I'll be honest. We play a lot of football and Michael Collins – do you remember him? A big lad from West Cork – well, he's doing great work organising us into leagues. I'm a Limerick man first and foremost, but I tog out for Clare and Galway too whenever I'm needed, though I draw the line at Kerry. We suffered too many championship defeats to those lads over the years! It's a great way to keep in shape, though, and to pass the time.*

*We say the rosary every night, and we have Mass here once a week. I serve the priest, a local man. It takes me back to my days as an altar boy at home. Apart from that, I read a lot – the other lads get books sent in and we share them around. In fact, if you could send us a few books, that would be great. Anything you can get, but history books and mythology are very popular. I'm reading all about Fionn McCumhaill at the moment, so again I'm reminded of my days as a boy in the National School with Master O'Donnell. If you see him around, tell him I was asking for him. I'm learning a lot in here from the others as well – Irish, history, even a bit of French, would you believe? There's a few lads in here are teachers, so we have classes, just to pass the time.*

*Keep writing to me. It makes my day when I get something from home, and especially one from you, my darling girl. I go to sleep each night praying for you. I can just picture you asleep in the girls' bedroom upstairs with Eileen and Kate and little Siobhán, and it gives me great comfort to know my family are looking after you for me until we can be together again.*

*Always yours,*

*Rory*

Mary folded the letter and put it under her pillow. She lay in bed wondering what life was really like for Rory. She knew he would never complain about the conditions, even if they were terrible. It was all part of the mindset, just like during Easter Week and the aftermath: Never let them know they are getting to you. She knew one thing for sure, if Collins was in charge in there, those lads were not sitting around just trying to pass the time. He would be preparing them for the next time – a future onslaught against the British. The football was a ruse to find a way to keep the men fit and battle ready, she was sure of it! The thoughts of Rory going to war again, risking his life again, filled her with a dark dread, but she knew that this was what would happen, whenever he was released. *He won't rest until Ireland is free*, she thought. She also knew for a sure and certain fact that she would support him and stand beside him, armed if necessary.

The Great War was raging and the losses experienced by both sides were so catastrophic that it was kept secret for fear of damaging national morale. She recalled a Cumann na mBan meeting back in 1915 when the speaker reminded the women of the quotation from Daniel O'Connell, known as the Liberator, the leader of Catholic emancipation, that *England's difficulty was Ireland's opportunity*. Well, she thought, the pressure put on England by the Great War could be no more difficult than at this present time. If there was ever a time to strike, it was now. The general opinion of people across the country was favourable to the rebels, since England was now stretched to breaking point, but the men remained locked up. Surely there were others, though, she mused – men who had not been rounded up after Easter Week? Perhaps it was time to do more than just write letters. She wondered how Eileen would react if she suggested starting a branch of Cumann na mBan down in Limerick.

'We'd have to be careful,' Eileen said when Mary suggested it the following day as they were milking the cows, 'but I agree with you. We could organise relief for the prisoners, maybe help out the families of those imprisoned or killed. On top of that, we have to keep up the anti-conscription battle. The English are getting desperate at this stage, since the war in Europe is disastrous, and they'll offer anything to get Irish lads to join up. Last weekend, Mrs Ryan from up by the church told me her boy Liam was going. I tried to talk her out of it, but she said he was determined. He wanted to get out from the farm and see the world, he said. 'Tis precious little of the world he'll see over there, but she said there's no talking to him. The recruitment officer was in Croom a few weeks back, promising all sorts of rewards for any fellow who'd sign up. It's high time those lads were reminded what country they're from.'

Mary was delighted that her friend was en-thusiastic. She wanted Rory to be proud of them when he got out – that they hadn't just sat and waited but had kept up the fight.

'Why don't we go up to Dublin, see if we can meet with the Countess and ask her what we should do next?' Eileen's face lit up with enthusiasm.

'We could even try to see Mrs Kearns and Mrs Grant. Oh, Eileen, I'd love to, do you think we could?'

Eileen was pensive. 'The only problem might be Mam and Dad. They've gone through so much already, maybe they will be against us getting involved again, and I suppose we can't blame them. But still, I think we should put it to them anyway. We'll wait until tonight when the small ones are in bed and we can talk to them together. What do you think?'

Mary knew that Peg would hate the idea of them being involved politically again, after everything the family had been through, but John would understand, and he would, in his own gentle way, talk his wife round. He was deeply proud of his children, and of Mary too, and he felt, if anything, even more passionately that the struggles of Easter Week and the ground that had been gained must not be lost due to complacency. Last night over dinner he was voicing his opinion that the war in Europe couldn't go on forever, and if there was to be another strike for independence, it would have to be sooner rather than later. Peg had looked disapprovingly at him and quietened him with a delicious bread and butter pudding.

The girls walked back to the yard through the fields, the milking done for another day, all misery forgot. It was like they were themselves again, chatting, confiding and laughing as they did in Dublin.

'What would Teddy make of you being involved again?' Mary asked, glancing sideways at her friend. Despite his best efforts to progress their relationship after the good news of Rory's relative safety, Eileen seemed reluctant. Mary couldn't figure it out. Teddy was handsome and kind and funny, he was a fine hurler – and Eileen loved hurling – and he clearly adored her. He would be a great husband, and wouldn't try to stifle Eileen's natural exuberance.

'What would he have any opinion about it at all for? Sure, what business is it of his what I do?' Eileen was adamant.

'Aah, Eileen, come on. This is me you're talking to. I know he's mad about you, and surely you have feelings for him too. What's stopping you?'

Eileen sighed and shook her head. 'He's great, and I do really like him. I don't know how I would have coped without him when we thought

Rory was dead, and he's nice looking and all that, but...'

'But what?' Mary probed

'Well, I'm not sure he fully agrees with the struggle. He thinks we're are grand as we are, under England, and that Home Rule would have been enough. He didn't say it out just like that, but I just get the impression that's the way he thinks. If that is the case, then we have no future together.'

Mary heard the regret in her friend's voice. 'But why don't you just ask him? Then at least you'd know.' Mary understood that for a marriage to work, there had to be agreement on the big things. She and Rory were absolutely on the same side and they understood each other. The passion and the commitment the Volunteers showed during Easter Week were infectious, and even now that they were away from all of it, her dedication to the cause remained just as strong.

'I'm afraid to, that's the truth. What if I'm right and he does feel like the struggle is a waste of time? Or worse, that the Volunteers were nothing but troublemakers, wreaking havoc for no reason? I don't know what I'd do then. I have always liked him. You know, when we were kids, he was there all the time, playing hurling with Rory and the other lads, but I knew he had an eye for me. Before I went up to Dublin, Mam and Dad would have thought I was too young to have any notions about boys. But when I was working in Carmodys, he used to write to me, and over time he starting saying things like he liked me and was looking forward to seeing me when I came home. I never told Rory because he'd have given me an awful time with the slagging and teasing, you know the way he is, but I was delighted, really. Him and Rory were the two that all the girls round here fancied, and sure you know that Rory is a desperate flirt, but Teddy is different. I remember when I used to take the kids down to the pitch, to watch them playing hurling, and all the girls wanted to be friends with me just so that they could be talking to Rory. And when the match was over, they'd crowd around him, but Teddy always spoke to me.'

'What would you tell me to do if it were me in that situation?' Mary asked her friend reasonably. There was a time when tales of Rory and local girls would have worried her, but she was happily secure in their love now. She knew exactly what Eileen meant when she said he was a flirt. Rory just loved people and loved making them laugh. She could easily see why all the girls were mad about him, but she trusted him fully, and when he said she was the one for him, she believed him completely.

'I'd tell you to talk to him, have it out and decide then, Miss Know-It-All.' She punched Mary playfully.

'So you know what you need to do then, don't you?' Mary smiled.

'Speaking of young men and their romantic notions, have you heard from my brother recently?'

Mary smiled. The O'Dwyers were so good, for whenever a letter came for her from Rory, Peg just put it on her bed and never asked her anything about it. It was like they respected their privacy, and while they shared all his news at the family dinner table the evening a family letter arrived, they allowed her privacy with hers.

'I got a letter the day before yesterday. He's talking about Michael Collins being in charge in the prison and organising them into leagues for a football championship. Reading between the lines, I think they are gearing up for the next round. He's reading a lot, history books mainly. I got the impression that putting them all in there together and having very little surveillance of what they're getting up to might be a bit of a stupid move on the part of the British. Collins, what little I know of him, is not the kind to let them sit around all day being lazy. No, I'd say they are getting ready to strike again, and I think we should be getting ready too.'

'Really? That's interesting. He doesn't say anything about that in his letters to us, but then he wouldn't want them worrying about him. Still, though, ten years is a long time, and who knows what kind of world they'll come out to?' Eileen was circumspect.

'Maybe it won't be ten years. That's what I'm hoping, anyhow.' Mary sighed. 'I miss him so much. I'd love to see him, even through the bars or from a distance. I know he's fine, but until I see him with my own eyes, I can't believe it.'

Eileen gave her friend's arm a quick squeeze as they entered the farmyard.

'Speak of the devil!' Mary murmured, spotting Teddy's bike leaning against the wall. 'Now's your chance to talk to him.'

Teddy emerged from the kitchen carrying a large box. 'Your mam is having a clear-out for the station Mass next week, and I arrived just in time to be the donkey.' He chuckled as he pretended to buckle under the weight.

'Teddy Lane, I've fed you enough dinners in

437

your life for you to be strong enough to lift a little box of ornaments and things, so no whingeing out of you! This house is going to be shining from head to toe before we have the whole parish in here for Mass next week, and if we have to stay up all night to do it, then so be it. Besides, don't you love showing off to these ladies how gallant you are?' Peg was joking.

'I only came up because my own mother is on the warpath about whitewashing the outhouses, so I thought I'd escape. Little did I know 'twas going to be out of the frying pan and into the fire! Anyway, I was wondering if you wanted to go to the dance on Saturday. Both of you, I mean.' He spoke from behind the big box. 'It's a fundraiser for the GAA Club, and they've a band coming from Galway, so it should be a bit of *craic*. I'll collect ye in the car and leave ye home safe after?'

Mary smiled at Teddy's enthusiastic grin. He really was trying so hard with Eileen, and he was very nice. She hoped her friend was wrong about his political convictions. He would be a perfect match for Eileen, hardworking and well off as well. She'd never have to scrimp and save and work her fingers to the bone, like most wives and mothers. He was one of the few people round there with a car, though he preferred the bike, he said, for day-to-day travelling. He brought his elderly mother and his sisters to Mass every Sunday morning in the car, and Mrs Lane nearly burst with pride when all the neighbours admired it. He had said he was going to build a brand new house on the farm and leave his mother and his sister and her family to live in the home place, the unspoken part being when he himself married. A lot of men would expect a new wife to come into the farmhouse where her mother-in-law already ruled the roost, but Teddy knew Eileen's fiery nature wouldn't stand for that. He was willing to do anything to make her happy.

Mary made her excuses that she had to help Peg with the big clear-out, leaving Eileen alone with Teddy. As she stood at the kitchen sink, she saw them walking up the lane, deep in conversation. She prayed that Teddy would be on their side and see how important the work of the cause was.

'Are they a match, do you think?' Peg asked Mary as she dried a precious piece of Waterford crystal she'd had since she married.

Mary wondered what she should say. Peg was a clever woman and knew her daughter well, but Mary valued Eileen's friendship and would never go behind her back.

'He's very nice and she likes him a lot, I know that,' Mary replied

'Aah, but I suppose she wants a young hothead who wants to die for Ireland, not a steady man with a fine farm who'd give her security and comfort her whole life?' Peg smiled wryly.

Mary caught her eye and smiled. 'Like Rory, you mean?'

'Oh, sure, my Rory is a law unto himself. You can't lead nor drive him – never could, even when he was a small lad. He has a way of getting what he wants. He's an awful rogue, you know? But he has a heart as big as the sun. Eileen's the same. She's a great girl, and there's more than Teddy Lane admiring her. I like him, though, and he'd be very good to her. But love is love, and if 'tis there, 'tis there, and if not… Well, there's plenty round here who married for reasons other than love, and sure the most of them worked out grand. I was lucky with John, and I'd not wish anything less for my children. My boy loves you, I know that much, and you love him too, so please God they'll leave him out and ye can marry. But I'm not afraid to say it, Mary – there's a part of me wants him to stay over there in that place, because I sleep easy in my bed knowing he's safe. If they leave them out, and there's talk of *It*, you know, then he'll get stuck right back into it all again, and maybe he won't be so lucky the next time.'

Mary nodded. 'That's exactly what he'll do, Peg, and like you, a part of me wishes he wouldn't and we could be safe. But we are so close now. We really rattled them last time, and the mood in the country has changed. People are behind us now in a way they never were. Rory doesn't want to be fighting just for the glory of it or anything. He dreams of a peaceful Ireland, where our children, if God blesses us, can grow up safe and happy and proud of being Irish. And I want that too.'

'Ye're well met so.' Peg smiled, but there was sadness in her eyes.

# CHAPTER 34

'Well, as I live and breathe, is it yourself?' Mrs Kearns wiped her hands on her apron and stared in amazement at the sight of Mary in front of her. 'I'd almost given up on you ever turning up again! Come in here till I have a look at you. The life is good to you, wherever you were then, and a fine colour in your cheeks and a bit of meat on them skinny auld bones of yours. Well, you're a sight for sore eyes and no mistake. The mistress will be over the moon to see you, so she will. We were always wondering what became of you.'

Mrs Kearns turned her around in the middle of the kitchen, admiring her as Mary giggled with delight at being home.

''Tis me, right enough. I was in Limerick, with Eileen and her family. We promised Rory that we'd get out of Dublin straight away, and we left that night they brought us into the gaol.'

Tears came to Mrs Kearns eyes. 'Rory, what a boy he was, God rest him. Ye were fierce fond of each other –'

'Oh, Lord, I never told you! I should have written but I just… That's just it, Mrs Kearns. Rory is alive! We thought he had been executed with the others, but for some reason the governor in Kilmainham decided that he was to be imprisoned instead. So he's in Frongoch with Michael Collins and the rest of them.'

'Aah, Mary! Really? Oh, thank God. I used to pray for him every night, along with Mr Pearse and Mr Connolly and the rest of them. Rory alive! That's the best news I've heard in months, honest to God it is. I guessed you were with Eileen. Mrs Carmody told us that you stayed in her house one night, so meself and the mistress figured it out that ye were together, and that gave us a bit of comfort anyway. We got the postcard, so we knew ye hadn't been picked up, at least. We wanted so much to get in touch with you, to write or something, but we were afraid to, in case it got you into trouble or led the police to you or something.'

'How is Mrs Grant? Will I call her to come down? I'm dying to see her too.' Mary looked towards the door that separated the kitchen from the rest of the house, recalling how many times she went through it carrying trays. The mistress would always be her employer, but after everything they went through together on Easter Week, she felt comfortable asking to see her.

'Poor Mrs Grant won't be able to come down, Mary, I'm afraid. She's all right, but she's not as you remember her. Sit down, child, till I tell you – better that you won't get a shock when you see her. I don't know if you know, but the night Eileen came looking here for you to go up to the gaol with her, the master was at home. Mary, this is going to be a bit of a shock for you, but he was the reason Rory was put in with them that were to be shot. He used his influence with someone high up, and after ye left, I waited up. I couldn't sleep a wink for worrying anyway, and then in the middle of the night I heard a desperate racket from upstairs. First it was that Johnson from the Castle, and he was livid over something. I only heard bits of it, but he was absolutely raging, and it was over the thing they had going with the uniforms. Something had gone badly wrong for them, and Johnson was blaming Grant. He left, and then 'twas himself, Grant, and he roaring at the mistress like a bull and then crashing furniture. She was screaming, and as you know, she wasn't a bit well at that stage, only out of the hospital after the gunshot wound she got Easter Week. He was after finding out about what we did – the jewellery and art and the rest of it. Don't ask me how, we were so careful, but he knew anyway. On top of that, someone was after him, threatening to expose the swindle he had going with your man Johnson, with the uniforms. That's why Johnson was like a demon. If the army found out what he was up to, he was finished.

'Well, I didn't know what to do. I was going to get the police, but sure they'd do nothing, so I sent Jimmy over to Moore Street. I knew some of the Volunteers that weren't rounded up were staying there, in a house owned by a woman I know from the markets, and I told him to tell one of the boys that Mrs Grant was in trouble and to come quick. Then I got my heavy rolling pin – you know, the marble one I use for pastry? – and I crept up the back stairs.

'Oh, Mary, the things he was calling her, and the kicking and the belting he was doing. He was like a madman.

'"I'll teach you," says he, "to be disgracing me in front of the whole city." He accused her of having something going on with someone in the movement, and that's why she was involved. He had a hold of her by the hair, and he kicking her around the room. Then he boasted 'twas him got Rory arrested, and that he would see to it that he was shot, and he'd make sure you came to a bad end as well. He never forgave you for stopping him the last time he had attacked her.'

Mary was trying unsuccessfully to hold back the tears. The poor mistress. They'd witnessed his violence once before, but the way Mrs Kearns described it, this one was much worse. Mary put her hand on the old housekeeper's arm, urging her to finish the story.

'Well, I was standing in the doorway, and he was after ripping her dress off and she screaming at him to stop. I could see the wound bleeding a lot from her leg, and may God forgive me, I thought he was going to kill her there and then, in front of my eyes. So I just ran at him and I gave him one savage belt across the back of his head with the rolling pin. He didn't see me or hear me come into the room, you see. I was sure I'd killed him, because he just went down like a bag of spuds on the carpet. I ran to the mistress and tried to calm her. She was shaking so badly, she couldn't even talk. I wrapped a blanket around her and gave her a big glass of brandy and there we sat, the two of us, just looking at him and not saying a word.'

Mrs Kearns shuddered. 'I don't know how long we were there – maybe fifteen or twenty minutes – when I heard voices, and up the stairs came two men with Jimmy. I recognised one of them from the GPO, but I never seen the other one before. They turned Grant over and he groaned, so he was still alive. They told us not to say a bit to anyone about what happened, and that they'd organise a doctor to come round to look at the mistress. Then they dragged him downstairs and took him away.'

Mary was struggling to take it all in. 'But how did he find out about the jewellery and the paintings and things?'

Mrs Kearns shrugged. 'Hard to know, but he found out somehow. He was like a demon, so he was. He'd hate to admit that he had been swindled by his wife and a cook and a maid, though.

That probably angered him more than the money, really.'

Mary nodded. Mrs Kearns was right. The master would never admit to being robbed in his own household, under his nose. 'And so a doctor came?'

'Yes, a lovely man from Westmoreland Street, and two ladies from Cumann na mBan as well. They obviously knew the whole story, so they helped me to get the mistress settled. When the doctor examined her, he said she'd have to go into the hospital straight away. She had lost so much blood and the bone that had been set was shattered, along with some other bones. He did for her good and proper, so he did.'

'Poor Mrs Grant, how could he…' Mary wept.

'They had to amputate her leg, and her spine was fractured too. He broke her cheekbone and her nose, and a lot of her hair never grew back, but she does have a wig if she needs to go out. She's in a wheelchair and her face is very disfigured, so try not to look too shocked when you see her.'

'I read in the paper that the police found his body above in the Dublin Mountains, but that was fairly recently,' Mary said.

'Oh, that was a good few weeks later. They

shot him in the end, but not before they nursed him back from the clatter on the head I gave him. They got him to tell them everything he knew about anyone of our side. He was up to his neck with that divil Johnson inside in the Castle, and he stood to lose everything because they were doing some very crooked dealings, it seems. We've made an enemy of Johnson, and no mistake. Yourself and Rory better look over yer shoulders, because he won't rest till he gets revenge. I've no sympathy for Grant, Mary, and I've no regrets about what I did to him. He was a horrible man who would have had Rory killed, and us too if he could. The Volunteers took care of him, and that's all we need to know about it.'

The two women sat in the kitchen, the clock ticking loudly and the embers glowing in the range. The smell of baking and roasting meat was still as she remembered it, and now this house was without the one person who had made her feel uneasy there. It was good news, but Mary just felt shock.

'Now, I'll go up and tell her you're here. She'll want to tidy herself up a bit, so let you hold on here, or go into your room. Everything is just the way you left it, and sure you can take your things or leave them. I never asked you –

are you just visiting, or are you coming back to us?'

'Just visiting, but I was hoping I could stay a few days while I'm in Dublin. Would that be all right, do you think?' Mary asked.

'You know better than to ask that now, surely? This was always your home, and now that we are shot of that weasel Grant, then we are as safe as houses. The lads call every so often to make sure we're all right. The mistress got the house and all his money, and he had plenty of it too, the auld miser, so we muddle along just fine the two of us. You are as welcome as the flowers of May and always will be.'

Mary sat on her small bed in her cosy bedroom. She was relieved to see nothing had changed. But the relationship between the mistress and Mrs Kearns was different. Mrs Kearns was the one leading the household now, it seemed, and Mary was glad that they had each other. It felt like a lifetime ago that she had left, going up to say a final goodbye to Rory. How everything changed. She opened the little locker beside the bed and took out the bundle of letters she had tied up with a gold ribbon he had bought for her one day at a fair. The little room felt familiar and safe. In the wardrobe hung her maid's uniform, her one good dress, her Cumann na mBan uniform, and the knapsack she used when she was in the GPO. She picked up the khaki bag and looked inside. There was the flag they had made out of Boland's flour bags, with Tom Clarke's help, to get them out of the GPO. It was folded neatly and still stained with Mrs Grant's blood from when they had to use it to carry her.

Mary sat on the bed, holding the flag to her chest. For her, it represented all the brave men and women who had sacrificed so much for the country. She carefully placed it back in the bag, along with Rory's letters and the little silver medal of St Ann that Mrs Kearns had given to her on her birthday. St Ann was the patron saint of mothers, and while Mrs Kearns gave it to her in memory of her mother, wherever she was, Mary knew that Mrs Kearns herself was the only mother Mary had ever known. The kindness she and Mrs Grant had shown to her was unprecedented in her life before she came to Dublin, and she loved them both dearly. Everything they endured together seemed, in so many ways, a lifetime ago. Rory calling for cocoa in the evenings, going to the park or the sea for a walk, window shopping with Eileen on their half days. It was another life.

A gentle knock on the door brought her back. 'She's waiting for you.'

Mary followed Mrs Kearns out into the passageway and up the stairs to the drawing room, so beautifully decorated with patterned wallpaper and all the furniture and ornaments blending perfectly. The heady perfume of fresh flowers was still there as well. Mary remembered the flower deliveries each day and the mistress matching the blooms to the various rooms in the house. Mary thought back to how she had marvelled at such luxury when she first arrived. In the convent, flowers adorned the altar, but never anywhere else.

She opened the door and looked in the direction of the fireplace. There was Mrs Grant, sitting in a wheelchair wearing a pink shawl around her shoulders. Her hair was coiffed perfectly, and if Mrs Kearns had not told her, Mary would never have known it was a wig. Her employer's face was filled with joy and tears as she stretched out her hands to Mary, who tried not to register shock as she walked towards her. Mrs Grant's beautiful features were gone, her face a collection of scars – some white where the skin seemed stretched too thinly over bone, others red and angry looking.

Her nose was crooked and her bottom lip was misshapen.

'Mary, my darling girl. What joy to see you again!' she exclaimed. Her voice was exactly as Mary remembered it.

'I know I must look a fright, but I'm lucky to be alive, so I have to keep telling myself that. And my guardian angel here, Mrs Kearns, makes sure that there are very few mirrors around, so I can cope with it. Anyway, that's enough about me. How are you?'

Her infectious good humour dispelled all horror at her altered appearance and Mary sat down beside her and began to tell her the story of everything that had happened.

'Oh, I'm so happy he didn't manage to have his way over Rory,' Mrs Grant exclaimed. 'What a relief! No one knows for sure how many of our men are in prison in England. They keep moving them around, it seems, though for what reason, we can't fathom. They move them, question them and then put them somewhere else. A sizeable number seem to be in Frongoch, though, so that's good that they are together at least. And Rory is there also! What splendid news. We were sure he had been executed, so I never thought to check. Oh, Mary, that really is marvellous news. I'm kept abreast of things through the ladies of Cumann na mBan, you see. They have been wonderful, and of course Mrs Kearns told you the fate that befell my husband? Yes, well… We won't dwell on him any longer than we must. He's gone, and good riddance. Now tell me, what are your plans? Are you coming back to us? There is always a home here for you, you know that, don't you?'

Mary outlined the discussions she had been having with Eileen and asked Mrs Grant's opinion on setting up a branch of Cumann na mBan in Limerick.

'An excellent idea, my dear – absolutely in-spired. The problem the last time was we had mixed messages going up and down the country. Next time, and believe me there will be a next time, we need the entire country to rise as one, to battle as a country, not just as a city. And while of course it saddens me to think you won't be here at my side, spreading the good work we are doing around the country is invaluable. Now, I'm going to tell you something that is not widely known, so please keep it to yourself for now. I have it on good authority that there is to be a release of Irish prisoners from English gaols in the coming weeks. It seems the British have no more reason to hold them, and there is pressure being brought to bear by our MPs that Irishmen are being held without trial in England. They are hoping that by releasing the Volunteers, they will reduce the animosity within the population, and more men will volunteer for the front. I'm hoping they have that wrong, of course, but whatever the motivation, it is good news for us.'

The idea that Rory would be released in the coming weeks filled Mary with excitement. 'All prisoners, or just some of them?' she asked eagerly.

'I have no idea, my dear. It's just rumour at the moment, but I shall make special enquiries as soon as possible. And in the meantime, you must meet with the top brass of the ladies to see about setting up new branches of the organisation. It's more important now than ever – we must build on the success of Easter Week to finish the job. Oh, Mary, I can't tell you how happy your arrival has made me! I couldn't be prouder of you, not even if you were my own daughter.'

Mary smiled and squeezed Mrs Grant's hand. Despite all that had happened to her former employer, Mary marvelled at how the other woman was as determined as ever to free Ireland. She seemed happier, even with the horrific injuries and scars, but then she had lived under the tyranny of the master all those years, taunted for her inability to produce children, forbidden from having an opinion, utterly undermined on every level. The wheelchair, the wig – things that to others might be seen as unbearable impositions in life – were, for Mrs Grant, liberating.

# CHAPTER 35

'*And* so Santie Claus will only come if you all go upstairs now and go straight to sleep. And no peeking out to see him, because he is fierce shy altogether, and if he saw you he might get a fright…and maybe he wouldn't come in at all.'

Four pairs of eyes, wide in awe, gazed at their father.

'But Daddy, what if he is hungry or thirsty and we didn't leave him anything?' Little Siobhán's voice was worried.

'Well,' exclaimed John, slapping his head theatrically, 'what would we do only for you, my little one? We nearly forgot! Run over there to

Mammy and see has she anything nice we could leave out for our important visitor.'

Peg gave them a freshly baked mince pie and a drop of *poitín*, which they carried reverently back to the fireside where their father waited.

'Will he like the *poitín*, Daddy?' asked Tim. 'I don't like the smell of it.'

John winked at Mary and Eileen, busy stuffing the turkey.

'Oh, he'll only have a small drop to warm him up. 'Twouldn't do to have too much of it, because poor old Santie might get a bit woozy in the head after it, and he might crash the sleigh! And he'll be delighted altogether with the mince pie, because your mammy makes the best mince pies in all of Ireland. Now, then, are we ready? The stockings are hung up and he knows who each one is for. So off to bed with ye now.'

Michael and Patrick, the twins, started to shepherd Siobhán and Tim upstairs.

As they reached the door, Siobhán piped up again. 'Daddy, what about Mary and Kate and Eileen? They have no stockings up. How will Santie know to leave them something?'

'Aah, we're too big to be getting presents from Santie, pet,' Mary explained.

'Indeed and ye are not!' John announced. 'Peg,

have we three more stockings there for Eileen, Mary, and Kate?'

Peg shook her head in mock despair as she rooted in the darning bag.

'Mammy, we need four more,' Michael said. The family looked quizzically at him.

'One for Rory,' he explained. The twins adored their older brother and the news that he was alive but that they couldn't see him was a source of great sadness to them.

John boomed, 'Of course we'll have one for Rory, and we can send him whatever Santie leaves for him when we write to him after the dinner tomorrow.' Peg looked gratefully at her husband as he put his arm around her shoulder and gave her a squeeze. He always knew exactly what to say. She missed her son desperately, and Christmas was especially hard.

'Kate will be home shortly. She's helping Annie Collins with her new baby, and then we'll have all the family – except our boy Rory – at home under our roof. A few months ago we thought the worst. I know 'tis hard on all of us to have Rory so far away, but he is alive, and that is what we must give a prayer of thanks to Our Lord and his Blessed Mother for, this night.' The family knelt together and prayed for a few moments, and Peg blessed herself and looked up at the picture of the Sacred Heart over the fireplace.

Mary helped get the children to bed. They were not normally so enthusiastic, but they couldn't get up the stairs quick enough, while Peg and Eileen prepared the vegetables for the feast next day. The pudding had been made in September and was wrapped in paper and muslin. After the turkey and roast potatoes and carrots and parsnips, it would be served with the cream from the top of the milk, to much anticipation. Though the O'Dwyers managed well enough, nine mouths were a lot to feed, and it was through the hard work and good management of both the house and farm that they were all adequately fed and clothed. Treats like plum pudding and roast turkey were reserved solely for Christmas.

Peg put the cork in the bottle of *poitín* and replaced it on the top shelf, having 'fed' the pudding one last time. Both the Christmas cake and the pudding had received a capful every two weeks since they were baked in the autumn. She disliked having the potent spirit in the house. It was made up the mountain by an old farmer, but it did make the pudding and the small Christmas cake especially tasty. It was illegal to distil it, and if the local constable called and suspected anything, it could mean trouble. She only used it for the cake, but still. She thanked the Lord frequently that John was an abstemious man, that he took a drop of whiskey or a glass of stout at a funeral or a wedding, but never really outside of that.

Mary reappeared in the kitchen in record time. Usually the children demanded story after story and seemed to be fascinated by life in the convent, so it often took half an hour to get them settled. But tonight they lay in their beds, eyes squeezed tight shut, willing the arrival of Santie Claus. As she kissed each one goodnight, she thought that if only Rory was here tonight, her life would be perfect. She loved this family, who had never made her feel anything but one of them. She had bought little presents for each of them when she was in Dublin, as she still had most of the wages she earned in the Grants's employ kept in the post office, and Mrs Grant had insisted on giving her some money when she left. When Mary objected, Mrs Grant explained that she was, as a result of the demise of the master, now quite a wealthy woman, and she wanted to take care of those who had taken care of her. She said she remembered clearly the night the master attacked her the first time, how it was Mary who had stopped him from killing her. She reminded her of the night Mary and Eileen carried her out in the flag, and everything they did to save her life. Mrs Grant told Mary that she thought of her as family, and wanted very much to help her in any way she could, now or in the future.

Mary tried to give the money to John and Peg for her room and board, but they refused and seemed quite hurt that she felt the need to offer it. She explained that she just wanted to pay her way, but they told her to save her money, that she and Rory would need it to get set up once he came home.

So she had to content herself with showing her gratitude and love for them in the thoughtful little presents she had got for each of them. She had hidden the gifts in the barn, since the twins were driving everyone mad all week looking for presents in every nook and cranny of the house. She finished the dinner preparations with Eileen, and afterwards, her friend went over to Teddy's to give him his present. She had bought him a really nice hat in Dublin and was dying to give it to him. Mary was so relieved things had worked out well between her and Teddy. Eileen explained how she had confronted him about her fears that he wasn't a supporter of the Irish Republic, and he said that while he wasn't active in the cause, those that were had his full support. He added that couldn't see himself fighting, as he was a peace-loving man, but that could change. He also told her straight that he loved her and would always support her in whatever she wanted to do. Eileen was delighted and admitted that she loved him too.

Mary wrote and told Rory about the blossoming romance, and he was really pleased, since Teddy and he were friends since boyhood. Now that the children were asleep and John and Peg gone to visit an elderly neighbour, she decided to go out and get the presents. Kate, having been up most of the previous night with the crying Collins's baby, had gone to bed as well.

Having the big warm kitchen of the house to herself was such a very rare event. She could never remember it happening before, so she was going to use the time to wrap her gifts and place them under the tree. The day she and Eileen went shopping, she bought a beautiful leather-bound notebook for Rory and had the shop engrave his name and the date on it. She had posted it weeks earlier, so she really hoped he got it in time for Christmas. She wondered, as she ran across the dark yard in the cold December chill, what

Christmas would be like in Frongoch. Would they have turkey or would it be just like every other day?

Emerging from the barn, both arms laden down with her gifts, she started in fright. A light was flickering in the lane. Eileen would be driven home by Teddy, so it wasn't them, and Kate was already home. Peg and John would come home across the field.

Rooted to the spot, she tried to think of what she should do. Mrs Grant had warned her that the master had powerful friends, and to be ever vigilant. Before he died, he threatened her constantly that he was going to destroy them all for humiliating him so publicly by their involvement in the Rising, against his expressed orders, and he included Mary in that. Though he was dead, she was wary. There was nobody to call as the twins were too young and Kate was only fifteen and very timid. She decided to run to the farmhouse around the perimeter of the large yard and barricade herself in.

The light was coming from a bicycle. She could hear the heavy breathing of the cyclist in the still night as he laboured up the hilly lane to the yard.

She got to the door and was fumbling with the

latch, which required a peculiar kind of push and pull at the same time to work properly. Her heart was thumping in her chest and she begged the latch, which was always a bit sticky, just this once to open without endless jiggling. The ticking of the dynamo on the bike was in the yard now and Mary stood frozen to the spot in terror.

'I can't believe nobody has fixed that latch. What have ye been at since I left?'

Mary spun around, dropping her bags and boxes on the ground. She must be hearing things. 'Rory! Rory, is it you? How did you get here? I thought you were –'

Rory threw the bicycle to the ground and put his arms around her and silenced her questions with a kiss. On and on he kissed her, holding her tightly. She kissed him back as the tears poured down her face. After what seemed like forever, he withdrew from her and wiped her tears with his thumbs, as he had done the night in the cell in Kilmainham. She looked up into his face – the face she wondered if she would ever see again. He was thinner, and older looking, but he was her own Rory. She couldn't believe her eyes.

'Hello, my darling Mary. You're looking beautiful, just like I pictured a million times in my head. I was released the day before yesterday, no warning or anything. They just let a good share of us out. I was determined to get home for Christmas, so I landed in Dublin yesterday and I got a train to Limerick Junction, but I had to cycle the rest of the way, as I'd no money and they had someone tailing me to see where I went.' He stifled a huge yawn.

'You must be exhausted, and starving too.' Mary was concerned, putting her hand to the three days of stubble on his face.

'I'd eat now, right enough. And then I'd love to curl up with you beside me and sleep for a full day, but I suppose my mother would have something to say about that!' He winked at her.

Mary chuckled. Despite the changed appearance, he was her old same Rory, cheeky and incorrigible.

'I'd love that too, but you're right, your mother would be horrified.' She grinned.

Giving into a huge yawn, he sighed deeply. 'Then the sooner I marry you and we can legitimately sleep in the one bed, the better. I suppose the priest wouldn't do it tomorrow?' He laughed. 'Where is everyone? I thought the fatted calf would be out and all.'

Mary explained where the adults were as they entered the kitchen. Rory looked around at the unchanged surroundings of his home and breathed deeply, the smell of baking and clean laundry a delight in his nostrils. He smiled as he took in the row of stockings, and especially the two at the end, of his own and Mary's, side by side.

'Tim wrote your name on yours.' She spoke quietly. 'They were so excited going to bed, but Santie will fade into insignificance once they realise you're home. They missed you so much, Rory – we all did.'

'And I missed ye. Honest to God, Mary, 'twas what kept me going in there, knowing that my family was here at home, and you with them, safe. And of course knowing that Grant got what was coming to him.' Rory's face darkened.

Mary led him to the range and sat him down, and was telling him all the news from Mrs Grant, and all the story of what the master did to her before the Volunteers came to get him.

Munching on brown bread and jam and swallowing from a huge mug of tea, Rory was appalled. 'What took them so long? Sure they could have lifted him the minute I was arrested. Every second after was an opportunity for him to do something terrible.' He was visibly upset that Mrs Grant had had to endure such torture.

'Well, the mistress told me they were watching him, as they needed to be sure who exactly his contacts were so that they could remove them too, if necessary. The Volunteers thought that even though the Rising did come as a surprise to Dublin Castle, they still knew too much about us, so they're trying to find the leaks and sort them out before the next strike. They were never sure if Grant was an informer, or if he was just in with Johnson on a swindle with the uniforms. Either way, he was not to be trusted. We need to eliminate as many potential leaks as possible.'

Rory held Mary's hand as she went to take his plate, and sat her down beside him. He looked deeply into her eyes before he spoke.

'I'd love you no matter what – you know that, don't you? But the fact that you understand that there has to be another round, that we must rise again, and sooner rather than later, while they are suffering such heavy losses in Europe, makes me love you even more. I won't go into it now. We'll just have a nice Christmas together, especially around Mam and the family, but when we were in prison, we were planning, preparing. Collins is a fox; he'll play them at their own game and win this time. He says we can't take them on in open battle like Easter Week. We haven't the resources, not anything, like enough money, but we know our country and we can bring them to their knees if we just go about it the right way. I'm going to be part of it, Mary – hopefully a significant part, as well. As I said before, I hope and pray with all my heart that we live and grow old together, but I need you to be totally sure what you're getting into. The next time, I'll be much more of a target and if they catch me, they'll finish me.'

Mary looked into the face of the man she loved. His once-jet-black hair was peppered with grey, despite the fact that he was only twenty-five, and his skin was paler than it used to be. He'd lost weight, and it aged him, too, but he was the only man she could ever imagine loving. He was funny and kind, caring and loyal, and above all, he was passionate about the Republic. She nodded slowly.

'I know exactly what I'm getting into, Rory. I knew before you ever came home that you'd be only here temporarily, if you managed to get out. When you wrote to me all about the football training and reading the books, I knew ye weren't just passing the time in there. Ye were getting ready. I won't pretend I'm not terrified – I am, absolutely petrified to tell the truth – but it has to be done, for us and for the generations to come.

It's as simple as that. It must be done and we must be the ones to do it, whatever the cost.'

The moment was interrupted by the sound of the latch being lifted as Peg and John crept in, not wanting to wake the household. They were shaking the sleet from their overcoats when they turned towards the range, and froze. Peg's hand flew to her mouth. She was speechless, while John recovered first and his face broke into a huge smile.

He crossed the room in two strides as Rory got up to greet his father. They embraced, John's rumbling chuckle filling the room. Mary's eyes shone with emotion as she watched Peg and Rory's reunion, witnessing the bond of love between a mother and her child. It was as if Rory were a baby again as she held him and cradled him in her arms. He comforted her as she wept tears of relief and joy.

'Rory, my darling boy. Oh, Rory... When we thought they killed you, I nearly... I...'

Rory, who was easily a foot taller than his mother, simply held her tight and said in soothing tones, 'I'm home. Mammy. It's all right, I'm home.'

# CHAPTER 36

'To Eileen.' Fiachra raised a toast with his glass of wine. 'If it wasn't for her and her flag, I'd never have met you.'

Scarlett smiled. 'She's really amazing. She's ninety-three – did you know that? The whole thing with the flag is fascinating. She told me a little of the story, but she's saved it up, the full story, till we got here, she said. I can't wait to hear it all.'

They chatted over three courses of the most delicious seafood and drank a little too much wine. Fiachra was such easy company; with him, what you saw was what you got.

She found herself blurting out the whole sorry

tale of Charlie, and if he knew it already, which she suspected he did, he never let on.

He reached over and placed his hand on hers. 'We all make mistakes. My sister, a font of all wisdom, says they're all the wrong one till you meet the right one. It's just unfortunate for you that you were both in the public spotlight. Loads of people make bad choices all the time, but usually they just have to live with the humiliation within their own circle. It must have been horrible for you, though – the press outside all the time, the whole nation watching on TV.'

He didn't judge her, nor was he overly sympathetic or sycophantic.

'How about you?' she asked.

'Aah, sure, Scarlett O'Hara, I've no time for women...' He chuckled in a mock stage Irish accent.

'Oh, that's how it goes? I tell you my whole sordid, sorry mess of a life and you avoid the question?' she challenged.

'Ok, ok,' he said, raising his hands in surrender. 'I was engaged about two years ago to a girl from France. I met her while she worked here at the French embassy, and we went out for about six years. She dumped me, out of the blue. Kind of, well... Out of the blue to me, anyway, though I since discovered she had been cheating on me for a lot of the time. Anyway, she ended it, left Ireland and is now married to the local count, or whatever, back in Gascony, and they have a baby. I was in bits, to be honest, and so I took some time out. Did a bit of travelling, had some brief and therapeutic relationships and then I came home. Now I'm over her and I can say that easily. Watch: I am over Monique Richard,' he claimed dramatically with a rueful smile.

'Did she break your heart?' Scarlett asked, looking over her wine glass.

'Yep. Absolutely, but the thing about hearts, I've come to discover, is that, just like ankles and noses, they heal. Even if you don't want them to, or think they never will, they do. And someday you wake up and the pain is gone. I'm there now, but how about you? Are you, do you think?'

Scarlett tried to visualise Charlie in her mind, tried to summon up his voice. She wondered if he had called or texted the phone sitting in her bedside locker back in New York. She was pleasantly surprised to find she didn't care. All she could see was the election poster, the one of him on the couch with his perfect family in his perfect house. He didn't occupy her mind any more, and without her realising it, just as Fiachra had said, the pain was gone.

'I'm there too! I didn't know I was until just this second, but I'm there. Mostly I just feel shame and embarrassment that I threw my career away for him.'

Eventually the staff started making moves like they wanted to go home, and they realised they had chatted non-stop for five hours straight – no awkward silences or small talk.

They reluctantly left the restaurant and went outside, intending to hail a cab. Scarlett wished the night would never end. The light pollution of the city was far away on the other side of the bay, and the inky sky glittered with stars. She shivered, the weak heat of the Irish sun gone. She had left her sweater back at the hotel at the insistence of Lorena, who had convinced her to go shopping for a dress for the date. Though Scarlett hated the idea of shopping with her mother, she found they actually had fun. Lorena had a great eye for fashion, and before the craziness of Fr Ennio, she used to buy several celebrity magazines each week. She convinced Scarlett to purchase a red wraparound contour dress from Coast. Red was a colour she always avoided because of her hair, but when she tried it on and walked out of the changing room, the saleslady and two other customers gushed with enthusiasm for how great she looked. All the stress of recent months meant she was lean and toned. Once her feet were in nude LK Bennet high heels, she felt attractive for the first time in months.

Lorena gave her a pair of costume jewellery pearl earrings, and she and Eileen chatted to her while Scarlett got ready. At the time he was to arrive, she sent them down to the lobby to keep him talking while she put the finishing touches to her make-up. When she stepped out of the elevator, Fiachra turned and smiled at her, and she could see he was impressed.

He was about to signal to a passing taxi when he stopped. 'I know you're cold, but if I gave you my jacket, would you like to walk along the seafront?' He looked young and uncertain all of a sudden.

'I'd love it!' She smiled as she put on his warm jacket, several times too big for her. She liked the faint smell of aftershave from the collar.

As they walked along, close but not touching, he pointed out features of the bay to her. She thought she could listen to his accent forever, which made her smile, in spite of the fact that up to very recently, it was an accent she only associated with Dan.

They came to a bench on a bluff overlooking the sea below. The gentle lapping of the waves and the distant rumble of traffic were the only sounds they could hear. The lights of the bay twinkled and bounced off the black sea.

'It's beautiful up here, isn't it?' Fiachra asked, sighing deeply as he put his arm around her on the bench, drawing her close to him. It seemed like the most natural thing in the world. She leaned her head on his shoulder, feeling happy.

'It really is. I knew Ireland was beautiful – everyone knows that – but I never had any interest in coming here, you know? Too many connections with my father, I suppose. He would get drunk, pretty much every night, and would keep the whole neighbourhood awake with his yelling about the Rising and the British and all that, cussing and then breaking into these stupid songs. I used to feel so scared when I was little, and then as I got older, I was just embarrassed. I knew everyone on the street talked about us, and looked the other way when they saw Lorena all bruised and battered as she shopped in the grocery store, but they hated more the fact that Dan O'Hara was their neighbour. Our street was full of people on the way up – second or third generation immigrants, a lot of Irish – and they didn't want to be associated with people like Dan. We were the stereotype and our neighbours wanted nothing to do with us. Who could blame them? He was such a jerk. I was angry for so long, at him, and at Lorena too for staying and putting up with him. She should have got us away from him, somewhere we'd be safe, but she never did. But the thing is... I don't know... Seeing Lorena so messed up these past few months has meant we've had time to talk things through, and we've put a lot of things to rest. Coming here, seems like...closure, somehow. Does that sound crazy?'

Fiachra thought for a moment. 'Not at all. Life's too short to have resentment or regret. It only hurts the person feeling it, not the person it's directed at. Your father is wherever he is now, and you've a life to live. I think it's great that you can let it go. Though it must have been terrible. I've always been proud of my parents. I suppose your mother just couldn't leave. I might sound like one of those TV psychologists now, but I think after years of living with abuse, it drains your confidence. Maybe she loved him at the start, and by the time she realised what he was really like, she had lost the power to do anything to change her situation. Your mother strikes me as a fragile kind of person. She was reared to be a lady – not like you.'

Scarlett laughed. 'Gee, thanks!'

Fiachra rolled his eyes. 'See? How the hell did I get a job in diplomacy? No, I don't mean that – God, no. I just mean you're tough, strong, capable, so you can't understand how your mother isn't like you. I was involved with a case a few years ago, when I was in the Department of Foreign Affairs, where an Irish woman was in an abusive marriage overseas. Her husband had taken her passport, and she was trapped. We got her out, but afterwards it turned out that he left to go to work every day, so she could have run – taken her chances that she would get some help – but she couldn't do it. She just couldn't, because this ape she married had such a hold over her that she was paralysed with fear.'

Scarlett sat in silence, thinking about what he said. Then he went on. 'I'm not claiming to understand. I'm really not, in case you think I have all the answers, but all that business with religion you were telling me about Lorena, she sounds like someone who needs a bit of help to get through life. She's lucky to have you.'

Scarlett smiled ruefully. 'I don't know about

that. A lot of the time, she just drives me crazy. I always get the feeling that I'm not what she wanted, that I didn't turn out like she hoped, or something. She wanted someone girly, who got married to someone nice and had two adorable children and a pretty house.' She shrugged.

'I don't know about that. When I was waiting for you to get ready, I had a chat with her, and she was telling me all about your career and how she is so proud of you. She was bursting with pride telling me about you, so I think you mean more to her than you think.'

'Really?' Scarlett was surprised. Lorena never said anything like that to her face. She was surprised at how touched she was by it.

'She was probably trying to big me up so that you'd fall for me and she'd finally marry me off.' Scarlett laughed.

'Well, it's working,' he said. 'I think you're great – so honest and straightforward. Some women are hard to make out. You feel like you're in a play and everyone's got the script except you, y'know? But I think there's a lot more to you than you allow the world to see, and I'm too old and too battered from this dating thing to play games. Scarlett, I really like you – more than I've liked anyone in ages – and I'd like to see you again. I'm sorry if I'm being a bit blunt, but flirting and being all mysterious isn't my strong suit. I can't play games, not any more.'

She smiled. She knew exactly what he meant. She absorbed what he said: He liked her. For the first time in her life, she felt someone liked her for who she really was. Charlie liked the sassy journalist who was fearless, and if she were honest, he probably liked the conquest. At that, a wave of self-disgust threatened to engulf her.

Fiachra was different. She found herself spilling out to him all the insecurities she had bottled up for her entire life. She couldn't analyse it, but it was like she was testing him. Telling him the worst so he knew, and then might back off now, rather than later, and leave her broken hearted.

'All those teenage years when girls were practising flirting and going on dates, I just wanted to disappear. I had this stupid name, I wasn't blond and tanned, I had this mad red hair and freckles, I was ashamed of my family, and I was only average at school. It was all crap. Then I got into journalism and I was finally good at something. I worked really hard – in a fairly misogynistic world, a lot of the time – and I did date a few guys then, but it was never sustainable. I guess I wanted to be taken seriously, not just some piece of skirt playing with the big boys. So I built this shell around myself. I could laugh and joke with the other journalists. I sat all night with them in countless hotel bars all over the city, going from one political crisis to the next, but I wasn't available, and they knew it. Charlie was the first man I ever really let in, and what a choice he was!'

She smiled ruefully. 'So I'm not very good at this. I don't know the rules of this game either. But I would like to see you again too.'

Fiachra took her hand and put it to his lips. 'How about we don't play at all? Let's just be straight and honest, and see where that gets us?'

Scarlett felt butterflies in her stomach. Was this really happening? 'Novel approach, Mr McCarthy, but in principle, I like it.' She grinned.

He drew her to him, kissing her softly. She responded, moving closer to him, and she felt herself succumb to the desire she felt for him. On and on he kissed her, as she was transported to a place where only they existed. She could feel her body reacting to him in a way she'd not felt for the longest time, and she hesitated. What if it all went wrong again? She just couldn't go through it again.

Fiachra sensed her hesitation and stopped. He

looked at her questioningly. 'Is everything ok, Scarlett?'

She could hear the defensive tone, obviously a wound from the long-gone Monique. 'Yes. I really like you. I'm just wary, I guess…'

'Whew!' He theatrically wiped his brow and nudged her playfully. 'I thought you'd decided I'm a rotten kisser or something. Though you'd be wrong, of course, because Jacinta O'Leary told me I was the best kisser in the whole of fifth class in St Joachim and Anne's National School in 1978, so I've always been confident in that department.'

She punched him gently on the arm and laughed.

When he went on, he spoke seriously. 'Look, I know. Do you think I'm not a bit scared too? You live in New York and I live here in a country you're ambivalent about, at best, and I'm not interested in just a holiday romance with you. I know I don't know you really, not yet, but I'd like to get to know you. Sure we can see where it goes from there, ok?'

'Ok,' She sighed and nestled into his arms as they watched the moonlight ripple on the dark sea.

* * *

THE NEXT MORNING, she was late down to breakfast, and Eileen and Lorena were almost finished with theirs. She ordered coffee. She would never understand the Irish obsession with tea and a cooked breakfast. The food in the hotel was delicious, and though she never had anything more than fruit or a bowl of cereal at home, she found herself looking forward to the sausages and bacon offered in the hotel restaurant. She even loved the black pudding, which apparently was made from congealed pig's blood, but if you could forget that, it tasted amazing.

'Good morning,' she chirped as she sat in the last vacant chair at the table.

'Good morning, darling,' Lorena drawled. 'How was your date last night?' She winked.

The usual exasperation she felt at her mother's constant enquiries about her love life was absent, and she felt instead a wave of affection for her. She knew Lorena would always drive her crazy, no doubt about that, but she just wanted the fairy tale for her daughter. Despite her own grim experiences in life, she still believed in the Hollywood happy ending.

'It was lovely. He's really great.. We're going to

try to spend some time together and see how it goes, but I really enjoyed it.'

If Lorena was amazed at this new, forth-coming Scarlett, she gave no indication of it. 'Oh, honey, that's wonderful! He seems such a nice man, and you looked a million dollars last night, didn't she, Eileen?'

'You looked lovely, Scarlett. Who knows, maybe the flag will be responsible for more than just commemorating the Rising. It's early days, I know, but you deserve to be happy. You have been so kind to me, and if it weren't for you, I would never have come home. So if this trip has some added benefits for you, then that's wonderful.'

Scarlett was moved by the way Eileen referred to Ireland as home, despite the fact that she had never been there until now. She remembered Eileen's reaction a few days earlier at the meeting when the president talked about all those who fought to free Ireland, and though she didn't really know the reasons for Eileen's reaction, she knew her feelings for this country were deep and complex.

*What an odd trio we must look*, she thought. But watching Eileen's response to being here, and seeing her mother return to her old self, she knew she had done the right thing. Scarlett thought back to that awful day with creepy Fr Ennio and realised she was over the hurtful things Lorena had said. That wasn't what she thought about her daughter, not really. She was just so influenced by that weirdo that she had been driven to the brink of insanity.

Scarlett had spoken to the bishop's office before they left New York, and was told that Ennio had been tracked down and was now in a secure psychiatric facility. The diocese wanted to know what action, if any, Scarlett or Lorena wanted to take. But when Scarlett raised the matter with her mother, she simply said that she never wanted to think about him again. Scarlett knew she was embarrassed by the whole episode, and if she wanted to forget it ever happened, then the psychiatrist recommended she be allowed to do just that.

Scarlett had explained to Artie the way her mother's house had been recently decorated, and he'd organised for his daughter, who was an interior decorator, to go in and give the place a makeover. Lorena was delighted with her little home's new look, all freshly painted in neutral creams and beiges with splashes of colour here and there in lamps and cushions. Artie's daughter even managed to source an original movie poster of *Gone with the Wind* to replace the macabre religious décor.

Lorena had invited them all to lunch the Sunday before they left for Ireland, and Scarlett hugged Artie gratefully in the little garden where he had slipped out for a cigarette. She even gave him a mint to hide the smell from his wife. Scarlett looked in the window at Artie's daughter chatting animatedly with Eileen, while Lorena offered delicious nibbles, and she thought how lucky she was to have these people in her life. In a weird way, the craziness of that whole thing with Ennio had brought her closer to her mother. If, this time last year, someone had said they would be on vacation together, and not killing each other every five minutes, Scarlett would have laughed. That whole thing was best left in the past. Fiachra was right – Lorena was fragile, and making her face difficult truths was cruel, so she continued her life as before…though without the creepy priest.

The waiter delivered her breakfast and as she began to tuck in, she was waiting for Lorena to make some remark about her eating such calorific food.

'I had that this morning, and my Lord, it was just about the best breakfast I ever ate,' she said, eying Scarlett's bacon. 'How do they get it all crispy like that?'

Scarlett grinned. 'I don't know. Happy pigs, maybe? So ladies, what's our plan today?'

Eileen sipped her tea and said, 'Well, there are some places I want to go. I spoke to Fiachra this morning, and he's going to take me. I told him there was absolutely no need, but he said he wanted to. I think he was hoping you'd come as well, Scarlett.' She smiled mischievously. 'And you too, of course, Lorena,' she added hastily.

Scarlett knew that Eileen probably wanted to visit a grave or a house, or something to do with her family here, and Lorena wittering on might be difficult to cope with, so as much as she would have enjoyed the day and longed to see Fiachra again, she decided there and then to let him take Eileen on his own, and she'd babysit Lorena.

But before Scarlett had a chance to tell Eileen her plans, Lorena burst in. 'Oh, Eileen, I'm so sorry, but do you mind if I don't? I saw some wonderful little stores with the most darling things when we were shopping for Scarlett, and I'd love a shopping day. I promise I won't buy much, but I'd love something for my living room, now that it looks so lovely. A little memento. All this culture and history is making me kinda dizzy. I know you guys love all this stuff, but it kind of leaves me cold. The past is best left where it is, in the past, but that's just me, I guess. And anyway, I saw an old movie house, just like the ones I used to take you to, Scarlett. I know those multiplex places are all the rage now, but I just love those old theatres, with the smells, and how you can be transported away to somewhere else...'

Eileen and Scarlett chuckled at her. Scarlett remembered so many afternoons at the movies with her as a kid, usually after one of Dan's attacks. She used to watch Lorena's face while munching popcorn and be amazed at how her mother was transfixed by the screen. The thoughts, however, of her wandering around a strange city on her own, especially one with so many Catholic churches, made Scarlett apprehensive.

'I don't know, Mom. You don't even know the city –' Scarlett began.

'I'll be perfectly fine,' Lorena interrupted. 'Scarlett, in case it passed your notice, I have lived all my adult life in New York, so I think I can manage to go into a small town like Dublin and do a little window shopping and take in a movie, can't I? I've checked it out, and I'm going to take the bus into the city. It goes from right outside the hotel, and I'll take a cab back here if I get tired. Now both of you go off with that gorgeous man and have a great day. Maybe now you can see what I saw in your father. In the early days, he was quite the charmer, let me tell you.'

She swept out of the dining room, in case there were any further objections, ready to launch herself on the unsuspecting shopkeepers of Dublin.

Eileen smiled. 'I know she's been through a lot, but she'll be fine, I'm sure. She can turn on that southern charm if she gets lost, and she'll have them eating out of her hand. She really is great company, you know – she makes me laugh so much. All the staff here are crazy about her. She and I went for a little drink to the bar last night, and she was flirting with the young barman, much to his delight. It was a lot of fun.'

'You have a calming effect on her, I think. I don't know why, but she doesn't make me so crazy these days,' Scarlett admitted. 'It was good to talk to her, when she was in the hospital, about everything.'

Eileen nodded. 'We can't hold bitterness forever. Get it out, then it doesn't seem so bad.'

Scarlett smiled. 'Tell me all about it! I blurted

out my whole life story last night – not the edited version, or the total fictitious version, but the real version. Dan, school, Lorena, Charlie, the works. Poor Fiachra!'

'So, is it a *thing*, as I believe young people say nowadays?' Eileen smiled mischievously.

'You're watching too much TV!' Scarlett chuckled. 'I think it could be, it's in the early days, I know. I don't want to get getting ahead of my-self, but he's nice.'

'Nice?' Eileen raised an eyebrow.

'Ok – hot and sweet and funny and gorgeous and I'm crazy about him, ok? Happy now?'

'And he's definitely not married?' Eileen was only half joking.

'Nope, definitely not. He was engaged a while back, but it didn't develop the way he wanted, so he's free as a bird.'

'Well, I'm delighted for you, I really am, and I hope it works out for you. My mother was a great believer in the uniqueness of Irishmen, and if you got a good one, then there was nothing like them.'

'Well, Eileen, my experience of Irishmen to date has left a lot to be desired, but I'm not letting the memory of Dan O'Hara take up any more space in my head. He's gone, and the past is in the past, so I'm just going to forget about him and live my life.'

Eileen got up to leave the table, and Scarlett noticed she was so frail. She often forgot just how old Eileen was, because she was mentally so sharp, but this trip really was taking a lot out of her.

'Are you sure you want to do this today, Eileen? Maybe you should take a rest – you look tired.' Scarlett was worried.

Eileen put her hand on Scarlett's arm. 'Scarlett, dear, I've waited all my life to do what I came here to do, and today's the day. I'm a very old woman, and I've lived a full and happy life. I'm not saying I'm ready to shuffle off just yet, but there are some things that need to be done before I rest, and this is one of them. Will you help me?'

Scarlett squeezed her hand. 'Of course I will.'

# CHAPTER 37

iachra and Scarlett stood back as the small figure of Eileen made her way to the memorial. The trip to Arbour Hill on the north side of the city was done mostly in silence, since Eileen was lost in her thoughts, and they didn't want to disturb her.

On the way, Eileen asked Fiachra to stop at a florist's, where she bought three large wreaths and a bunch of lilies. She asked Fiachra to put them in the trunk of the car without an explanation. The first stop was a memorial across from a modern-day prison.

'What is this place?' Scarlett whispered to Fiachra as soon as Eileen was out of earshot.

'It's the place where the leaders of the Rising were buried, though that's not really accurate. After they were executed, they were thrown into a mass grave and quick lime poured on their bodies. This place used to be a British barracks. They were all sentenced to death here and shot. The writing on that wall up there, can you see it? It's the Proclamation of Independence. There's a commemoration here every Easter, and the Proclamation is read aloud. The green rectangle is where the bodies were thrown, and the names of the leaders are engraved all around the kerbstone.'

Eileen carefully laid seven lilies on the edge of the memorial. Then she beckoned to them to come up. 'There's one each for the seven men who signed the Proclamation. I promised my mother I'd do it someday, and I thought I had let her down. But Scarlett, because of you, I've been able to keep my promise. My parents knew them all, you know, but my mother always talked about Tom Clarke. He was a lovely man, she said. It was he who helped them get out of the GPO, her and Eileen, Mrs Kearns and Mrs Grant.'

Eileen looked at the face of her young friend. 'You came to me looking for a story, and instead you got me and all my baggage, as us Americans say. So maybe now I should tell you the story, as much as I know it, anyway.' Scarlett linked her arm and led the old woman to a bench under a tree.

'My parents were both in the GPO. They were only sweethearts then. My father was a Volunteer and my mother was a maid in a house here in Dublin. She was also a member of Cumann na mBan, and she, her employer Mrs Grant, her best friend – who was my aunt, Eileen – and the housekeeper in the Grants's house, Mrs Kearns, were all there. My mother and Eileen had set up a first aid station, and Mrs Kearns was cooking for the men and women inside the General Post Office. Mrs Grant was a runner – that meant she was delivering messages all over Dublin between the various buildings they held. My mother often told me that when they tried to get out, Mrs Grant was so badly injured, she had to be carried. Pearse ordered all the women out, in the hope they would be spared, but my mother and her group missed the main evacuation of the women and were facing out into the street where the British were firing indiscriminately. There were lancers on horseback, and incendiaries going off everywhere. The whole street was in flames. Well, you've seen the pictures. They were looking for some way to get out, and to get to safety, but with Mrs Grant so badly hurt, it was looking very bleak. They had been using flour bags from the mills down at Boland's as bandages, so they got the idea to make a white flag out of the flour bags to wave as they tried to leave the General Post Office. Tom Clarke – he was one of the signatories buried over there – came by and helped them. He took off his own shoelaces and tied the flour bag to a broom handle. He and his wife Kathleen were good friends of Mrs Grant, and my mother said she remembered saying goodbye to him that day. Of course, he was executed, along with all the others. My mother knew his wife well afterwards. They were involved with helping the families of the men who were in prison, or shot. He never knew it, but she was pregnant during the Rising, with their fourth child, but she didn't tell him when they brought her to say goodbye. She didn't want to add to his worry. She lost the child not long afterwards, poor woman. So, even after everything, the women, and the men too, of course, endured. They remained loyal to the cause and the belief in equality. They believed in the Proclamation.'

Scarlett and Fiachra sat silently with her as they looked back towards the monument.

'It really was so far ahead of its time, wasn't it?' Scarlett said quietly. 'You know – talking about men and women of Ireland, even before women had the vote, and cherishing all the children of the nation equally.'

'They were brave men, and educated men, and the women who stood beside them were strong and determined. Some said it was foolish, that they could never win, but Kathleen Clarke told my mother that when they took her in to see Tom, the night before they shot him, a soldier was with them the whole time, and only one candle to light the cell. He said that the leaders could die happy because they knew the first strike had been made, and the next one would be successful. They were so selfless.'

A few raindrops began to fall as they walked back to the car.

'So, Eileen, where would you like to go now?' Fiachra asked as he helped her buckle up.

'We have a few more stops to make, but perhaps a cup of tea first?'

Fiachra smiled delightedly. 'I'd murder a cup too. Come on, Eileen, we'll get this one addicted between us.' He chuckled, nudging Scarlett playfully as she settled into the front seat of his car.

Scarlett retorted in mock distain, 'It's a vile substance. I don't know what you people see in it. Take me somewhere I can get a latte and we'll stay friends, ok?'

# CHAPTER 38

'I've told you before, I haven't seen him in months. He had no work here and he went to England. I had a letter from him about two months ago, from Birmingham.' Mary rooted in her bag, determined to stop her hands from shaking. She proffered the letter, postmarked Birmingham.

'Right. You say your husband wrote to you on… Let me see…' The officer put on his glasses '…the 5th of November 1920, and you haven't heard from him since?' His voice was quietly threatening. This was the infamous Johnson, the most sadistic officer in Dublin Castle. She had seen him once or twice, coming to the house late at night to meet with the master before the Rising. She understood that this wasn't a chance arrest. He knew well who she was, and he wanted to hurt her. He specialised in interrogation, stopping at nothing to get the information he was after. He had been known to extract fingernails, even to rape women who would not speak. Mary was terrified of him.

She had been questioned about Rory's whereabouts before. She'd been beaten up once during those interviews, threatened, screamed at, but she stuck to the story. The IRA, as the Volunteers had been renamed under Michael Collins, were clever. They had friends of the organisation in England post letters to the wives and families of soldiers, allegedly from them, to use as evidence that the men were not even in Ireland. It had worked for a while, but now the authorities were wise to it. She was telling the truth that she hadn't seen Rory in weeks, though. He was down the country, training groups known as Flying Columns.

Collins was an expert strategist and stuck to his policy that open warfare was a waste of resources and men, and ultimately not winnable. The way to beat the British was to use guerrilla tactics, so the men lived on the run, wore no uniforms and relied on the kindness of the people for food and shelter. They attacked police barracks in the dead of night, relieving them of their weapons and any intelligence they had gathered. British patrols were constantly ambushed. Collins had moles everywhere, and people said he even had his people inside Dublin Castle itself. Mary could well believe it, for Mrs Grant had been telling her only a few days before that a whole shipment of rifles, intended for the British Army, were intercepted by the IRA between the docks and The Barracks. After a bit too much to drink in the Hibernian Hotel, the junior officer who was held responsible for the cock-up was bewildered, and was heard complaining to his comrades that the only people who knew about the shipment were inside the Castle's walls. The barman was IRA, so the news got back quickly to Collins.

Mary had been so busy that she had become used to life without Rory. Though she missed him desperately and longed for some time with him, she knew he was doing what needed to be done, and she understood it and supported him completely. Kathleen Clarke had kept her busy since she and Rory married in February of 1917 and moved back to Dublin. He needed to be in Dublin to be with Mick Collins, who was managing the war from the snugs of pubs and people's living rooms. Tom Clarke's widow had taken on responsibility for the families of those dead or in prison, and Mary was tireless in her efforts to help. She had asked Mrs Grant for her old job back, and her former employer was thrilled to have her, but the reality was Mary was no longer a maid. They lived very simply these days, but it gave her a place to call home and an alibi if she ever needed one.

Despite her Republican connections, Mrs Grant's standing in society still meant something, so Mary was, to a certain extent, protected. At least she had been – until the IRA had stepped up the campaign in recent months. Now the British were suffering heavy losses, and like cornered rats, they were nervous and at their most dangerous. Innocent people were being picked up for questioning every day, with no reason at all, and the city was gripped with fear. Often they would get news of a body thrown on the street after an interrogation, usually dead. Before she was picked up, she had been getting ready in her little bedroom to go to the station, because she was going to visit the O'Dwyers, and hopefully be here for the birth of Eileen and Teddy's first baby. They were married two months after Rory and she, but she joked with Eileen that there wouldn't be any O'Dwyer babies for a while. She'd have to see her husband for more than ten minutes at a time for that.

It seemed like a lifetime ago that soldiers had come to the back door of the Grants's and dragged her out into the lorry. Had it really only been that morning? Mrs Kearns remonstrated with them as best she could, but they had orders to pick her up, and they were not going to be dissuaded. Johnson had her put into a cell where she nearly went out of her mind with worry about what they were going to do to her. Eventually, she was brought here, to this interrogation room.

Johnson threw the letter on the floor of the interrogation room and slammed his fist down heavily on the table in front of Mary. Grabbing her by both ears, he pulled her face close to his. His breath was sour, and little globules of spit landed on her face as he spoke. 'You listen to me, you stupid Fenian cow. I know perfectly well that Rory O'Dwyer isn't in England, so enough of your lies, do you hear me? I swear to God, if you don't start telling me the truth, by the time I'm finished with you, that bastard won't even recognise you. Am I making myself clear? Those animals have a lot to answer for, and believe me, I will make them pay. You remember Grant? Your old employer? Well, he was a friend of mine, and I do not appreciate what your husband's friends did to him, so I'm going to personally make sure both you and he suffer, do you understand?'

He released her throbbing ears and slapped her hard across the face. She fell from the chair and hit her head on the flagstones. She managed to get up, but could feel the warm trickle down her face from where she was bleeding. She sat on the chair again and tried to focus. She must not say anything, no matter what happened. She'd been interrogated before and withstood it. She could do it again. She tried to picture Rory's face, Mrs Kearns, Eileen, Mrs Grant, Tom and Kathleen Clarke, Pádraig Pearse, the O'Dwyers. She summoned the strength of them all to her. Johnson was one of Grant's associates, and she knew he was involved with all sorts of scams with him. The execution of the master would have meant the end of his lucrative little sideline, and he was furious. He had been biding his time to get his revenge.

'Now, we'll begin again. Where is Rory O'Dwyer?' His voice was singsong and mocking.

'I don't know. England somewhere.' Mary's voice came out as strong as she hoped.

The thump to the side of her head left her reeling. The room spun and she felt nauseous. She felt the blows of his heavy boots kicking her in the kidneys and back as she covered her head and curled up her body away from the blows. She felt herself being dragged up by her hair. The seconds ticked by while she waited for what was to come.

'Nice hair. I bet he likes to run his fingers through it, does he?' The voice was soft, gentle.

Mary opened her eyes to see something metal and shiny in front of her face. It was a knife. She couldn't register shock. He shoved her head down onto the table and began to cut off her hair. She was detached from the sight of her long red hair falling to the floor. She felt the metallic taste of blood in her mouth, and something else – a tooth. No, two teeth. She felt with her tongue for the gaps, hoping it wasn't her front teeth. Finished with cutting her hair, he pulled her upright and held a surprisingly ornate mirror up to her face. He must have come prepared.

One eye was almost closed and the area around it swollen, blood flowed down the right side of her face, and her hair, what was left of it, was in tufts off her scalp. She noted with relief that her front teeth were still there.

He walked round to his side of the battered table again and sat down. Reaching into his pocket, he pulled out a pair of pliers. Mary shuddered in terror, but was glad she had taken the advice of other women who'd been interrogated and had cut her nails as short as she could. He would have a difficult job finding enough nail to pull. As he examined her hand, the door opened.

An older man, with a neat grey moustache, entered the room. 'A word, Johnson, if you please.'

The captain smiled at her and said in mocking tones, 'If you'll just excuse me a moment, Mrs O'Dwyer, I won't be long.'

He went outside the room as Mary waited, trying to gather her strength. She said a quick prayer to Our Lady for the resolve to endure whatever was to come. And another to Rory, to be beside her.

The door opened again and this time there was no sign of Johnson, just the older man.

'You may go,' was all he said as he held the door of the cell open.

Mary did not wait for further instructions and stumbled after him and out the gate of the Castle onto the street. She knew she must look a sight and wondered how she was going to get home.

Suddenly, she heard a voice: 'There she is!' and Mrs Grant's car pulled up on to the footpath. Jimmy and Mrs Kearns got out, and between them, they got her into the car.

'My darling girl, what did he do to you? You poor child.' Mrs Kearns was distraught.

'I didn't say anything,' Mary whispered. 'He kept asking me about Rory, but I never said…'

'I know you didn't, pet, I know you didn't. We'll get you home now.'

Mary woke up in the guest bedroom of Mrs Grant's. It was dark outside, and she had no idea how she had got there. She felt awkward in this ornate room, wishing she was downstairs in her own little bed.

Every part of her hurt as the memories of her time at Captain Johnson's mercy came back to her. She realised she was one of the lucky ones. He hadn't even got into his stride by the time that other officer came in and interrupted him.

She tried to turn and see the clock on the bedside locker.

'Shh. Don't try to move, darling. Do you want a drink?'

Mary thought she must be hallucinating or dreaming. 'Rory?' she croaked.

'Yes, love, I'm here. My darling girl, what did

he do to you? I'll kill him…' Rory was sobbing. She had never seen him so upset. He looked dreadful, unshaven and exhausted, and he'd lost even more weight since she'd seen him last.

'I'm all right, really I am. I must look desperate, though.' She tried to smile. She was so happy to see him.

'You are beautiful. You are the most beautiful woman in the whole wide world, Mary O'Dwyer, and there's nothing anyone can do to change that. Oh, Mary, I'm so sorry. I'm the reason they did this to you. I should have been here to protect you. When Mrs Kearns got word to me that they had you and that it was that bastard Johnson was questioning you, I got Collins to use his influence. We have people in the Castle, and while it was hard, he got you out. He normally wouldn't do it, but I begged him and he managed it. Threatened one of them with something, I think. I don't know exactly what, obviously, but I don't care.'

Mary nodded and summoned up all her energy to speak. 'He was just about to do something – I don't know what – but this other man came in, older, with a head of grey hair and a moustache, and he just told me to go. He wasn't exactly happy about it, but I didn't ask any questions, I just got out of there as fast as I could. Thank God Mrs Kearns and Jimmy were there, the state of me…' Suddenly the reality of her ordeal dawned on her, her missing teeth, the cuts and bruises and all her hair gone. Every inch of her body ached. Rory hadn't seen her in so long, and now she looked like this. Sitting up, she caught a glimpse of her face in the mirror of the dresser opposite.

'Dear God!' she exclaimed, hardly recognising herself.

'You'll heal, pet, and your hair will grow back. I know you must be in shock now, and I can't say anything to help. In fact, I can't even stay. I promised Mick that I wouldn't stay here for fear they'll come looking for me. I'm putting everyone in danger just by being here, but I had to see you. Johnson won't like being overruled like that, so it's just too dangerous for me – or you, for that matter – to be here. He's not only lost a fortune now that Grant is gone, but he knows that we know about the thing he had going. If the army were to find out, he'd be in serious trouble. He needs us out of the way.'

There was a knock on the door, and Mary started in fright. 'Shh, pet. It's all right – the lads are outside, keeping lookout. We're safe for now.'

Mrs Kearns wheeled Mrs Grant into the room. 'I'm sorry to disturb you, Rory, but instructions are for you to leave. There was an ambush out Wicklow way somewhere, and they are scouring the city looking for anyone that they can pick up. Patrols are everywhere, so we need to get you away.' Mrs Grant took in Mary's stricken face.

'I know, Mary, my love, but he has to go. It's not safe for him, or for any of us, for Rory to be here. Collins only barely allowed it in the first place.'

She turned to Rory. 'Don't worry about her. We'll take care of her.'

Rory stood up and went to the window, peeking out from the side to see what activity was on the street. He gave a slight wave, obviously to one of his comrades, to indicate that he was on his way.

'Right. Listen carefully.' He reached into his jacket pocket. 'This is a ticket to Liverpool, and enough money to buy a ticket to America. As soon as you are anyway able, you have to go, Mary. Promise me you'll send her?' He pleaded with Mrs Grant, who nodded.

'America! I'm not going to America! Not without you, Rory, I can't go –' Panic was rising in her. Surely Rory wasn't sending her away to America all on her own!

He sat on the side of the bed and clasped both her hands in his. 'Mary, this is the last time I'll ever make you promise me anything. I've done nothing but make demands and put you in danger since you laid eyes on me. You don't deserve any of this. You are so brave and kind, and I love you with all my heart and I always will, but please do this one last thing for me. I just couldn't bear it if he got his hands on you again, and he'll try, I know he will. Mrs Grant has addresses of people who'll help you when you get there, people who support us. And I swear to you, I'll do everything I can to get you home the minute it's safe. We're close, Mary, we really are close, and any day now Lloyd George is going to give in. He has to – the British losses are too heavy.'

The room stilled, and suddenly the quiet night was a cacophony of shouts, vehicles and shots being fired as a roadblock was being set up at the other end of the street. Rory could still escape out the back, but only if he went now.

'I have to go. I'll try to see you before you go, my darling Mary, but if I can't, know I love you, and I'm thinking of you and praying for you every day of my life.' He kissed her tender face gently and was gone.

Mary sobbed as Mrs Kearns rubbed her back and Mrs Grant held her hand.

"Tis for the best, Mary, you know it is, but I know you'll be heartbroken to leave him.' Mrs Kearns was soothing, though Mary knew she was hiding her own anguish.

'When do I have to go?' Mary asked, knowing she sounded like a small girl, not a woman of twenty-five.

Mrs Grant spoke gently. 'Soon, but let's not worry about it tonight. We'll get you patched up a bit first, but Rory is right, Mary. That Captain Johnson will come looking for you again. He doesn't like unfinished business. He must suspect that I know as well, though maybe not. My husband probably told him that I was unaware of anything, but he knows you and Rory know what he was up to, and so he won't rest until you are eliminated. We are going to put the word around, Kathleen Clarke is taking care of it, that you are gone down to Rory's family in Limerick. That should give us a bit of breathing space for a few days, and then we can get you on the boat.'

'A few days!' Mary couldn't disguise her horror.

'The alternative is much worse, my dear, I'm sorry to say. You heard Rory – you know what's been going on. Things are getting very difficult, even for the innocent bystanders, let alone those with known connections to the Republican Movement. He'll follow you over there, and you'll have a wonderful life together. Think of that – you can go ahead, get yourself set up. Money will be no problem, I assure you of that, and you'll have made a lovely home for you both by the time he joins you.'

Mrs Grant was trying to be positive, Mary understood that, but then another horrible thought came to her. 'But what about you, Mrs Kearns, and Eileen and her baby, and the O'Dwyers? I don't want to leave you all.'

'And we don't want to lose you either, child. You're like a daughter to myself and the mistress, and we love you like you were our own flesh and blood. That's why we have to get you out, until this is solved one way or another. Johnson won't give up. He lost too much when Grant died, and Rory is too connected. He's Collins's right-hand man, and if they catch him... Well, you know what will happen. He needs to stay on track and focus on the job, and if he's half worrying about you, to add to all his other worries, then the risk of him slipping up and getting caught is bigger.'

Mary wanted to beg them to come with her, to promise they'd visit, but she knew it was a promise they couldn't keep. The mistress was too frail to travel, and Mrs Kearns would more likely agree to go to the moon as go to America. When she said goodbye to them, it might be forever, and they all knew it.

The days dragged and flew simultaneously. Eileen had her baby, a boy she called Rory Óg, and they were both well. Peg and John had come up to Dublin to visit Mary, and to say goodbye – something that wrenched at her heart. They couldn't hide their shock at her appearance and Peg tried unsuccessfully to hold back her tears. They held her tightly and told her it was all going to be all right, but like Mrs Kearns and the mistress, none of them was sure it was true. The fighting was intensifying all over the country, and martial law had been imposed in several counties, making travel close to impossible. The fact that Rory's parents had made an effort to see her under such difficult conditions touched her heart.

Ten days after her release from Dublin Castle,

Mrs Grant told her she was booked on the mail boat the following morning.

'I'm sorry just to tell you, you're going like this, as if you have no say in the matter, but I promised Rory, and you would never think it was the right time.' Though her tone was firm and brooked no argument, Mary could hear the kindness and loneliness behind the words.

Travelling in the depths of winter, alone, and looking worse, if anything, now that the bruising on her face was all shades of yellow and purple, filled Mary with dread. She knew the mistress was right, but it didn't make leaving the only life she had ever known any easier. She had hoped Rory could have come to see her, and she knew he would if he could, but the thought of going without seeing him gave her a stab of pain.

'There is some good news, though.' Mrs Grant smiled. 'Jimmy is going to take you in the car to a house in Westland Row. The doctor that came out the night Mrs Kearns clobbered the master with her rolling pin – I'm sure she told you about that? His is a safe house, and you will spend the night there before going to the boat for six a.m.'

Mary was perplexed. 'Why?'

'Well, if you don't want to spend the night

with your husband...' Mrs Grant was mischievous.

'Rory is going to be there?' She couldn't believe it.

'Yes. You're to meet him there at seven this evening, so you'd better get your things together. Now, I want you to take these.' She handed Mary several heavy velvet bags. 'There's a lot of jewellery there, most of it quite valuable – the few things I haven't sold for the cause. Don't worry, I have no attachment to them. They were either too difficult to replicate, or pieces that would have caused a stir if seen on someone else. I also have asked Mrs Kearns to sew some cash into the lining of your suitcase, in case you are searched. It's not illegal to carry money or jewels, but we don't want anyone drawing attention to you for any reason. When you get to New York, I will arrange to have someone meet you off the boat.

'Now, then –' She handed Mary a piece of paper '– once you are settled in, go to this address. This man will give you cash for the jewellery, and I've written – he is expecting you. I've never met him, but he's a friend of a friend, so I know he can be trusted.'

Mary tried to protest. 'I can't take all of this –'

'Mary, the death of my husband left me a

wealthy woman, as I explained. He bought me the finest jewels money could buy, not because he loved me, but because he wanted to show off to the world how rich he was. These things are meaningless to me, but if I thought that their sale could help you to set up a life in America, aah, what sweet revenge that would be. He hated the fact that he couldn't make you cower, Mary. I saw the way he ogled you, but you never showed fear. He hated that. The night you stood up to him and defended me, he was livid. A mere maid daring to defy him was something from which he never recovered. Your upbringing taught you to be quiet and subservient, to apologise for your existence. It is a testament to your own strength of character that you shook that off and became a brave, strong woman, a woman I am proud to know. That strength – or, in his eyes, that audacity – combined with Rory's refusal to bow and scrape to him meant he hated both of you. You can be sure that the venomous treatment you experienced at the hands of Johnson was at his behest. But the wonderful thing is, he's dead and you are both alive, so use his money to build your life, Mary. I have no need of it. Mrs Kearns and I have more than enough to see us out, and it would mean we would worry a little bit less about you if we knew you at least had a roof over your head and enough to eat. Please take it.'

Mary didn't trust herself to speak. This woman, who had taken her on as a maid when she had nothing, no experience, no friends, had given her a life. She introduced her to the cause of Irish Republicanism, she taught her how to stand up for what was right, she supported her, rescued her and loved her for eight years. Mrs Grant had given her opportunities a girl from an orphanage could never have dreamed of, and now she was saying goodbye. Mary threw her arms around Mrs Grant and hugged her while the older woman rubbed her back.

'I'm going to leave you now, and I won't see you again before you go. I have some people to meet, so take care, my dear girl. Your country and I are forever in your debt. If you achieve nothing further in life, and I very much doubt that will be the case, never forget that you fought in the GPO, that you were there when Pearse read the Proclamation of Irish Independence – that you are a part of the history of this country. Future generations will know of us and our actions, and realise those were the first tentative steps of a newborn nation. Be proud, dear Mary, and be happy.'

Tears glistened in her eyes. She then wheeled herself out the door without looking back.

Mary took a deep breath and went downstairs. As promised, Mrs Kearns was sewing bundles of cash into the lining of a suitcase. She was moaning that the fabric was too stiff for the needle and that it was taking too long, but Mary knew the old housekeeper was dreading her departure as much as she was.

'I'll just go in and gather the rest of my things so,' Mary said. She was meeting Rory at seven, and it was already ten past six. She stood in the little bedroom that she had slept in since she arrived in Dublin in 1913. She remembered so many nights, tucked up in her cosy little bed, reading her books by a gas lamp the mistress had given her. The lovely white eiderdown, embroidered carefully with blue forget-me-nots that Mrs Kearns had made her one Christmas, still covered the bed. She opened the drawer of her little locker and took out the bundles of letters from Rory. There were so many – some long missives, others notes scribbled on the backs of envelopes. She had kept them all. There were some photos too, a lovely one that Mrs Grant took on the morning of Easter Monday when she was all dressed up in her uniform, one of her and Eileen on the carousel in the Phoenix Park, looking carefree in summer frocks. A picture of the O'Dwyer family and another of baby Rory taken by Teddy and sent to her in a card from himself and Eileen, one of Mrs Kearns and Mrs Grant in their Cumann na mBan uniforms, taken at a meeting one night, and one of her and Rory on their wedding day in February 1917.

Their reception had been held at Rory's old place of employment, and the place she had first met him, the Royal Marine Hotel in Dún Laoghair. Mrs Grant and Mrs Kearns were as proud as punch, and the O'Dwyers all came up from Limerick for the day. Michael Collins was there, and Kathleen Clarke gave her a beautiful tablecloth as a gift. Several IRA and Cumann na mBan people were there as well. It was the happiest day of her life. She finally belonged somewhere. There had even been a Mass card from Sister Margaret in the convent, to whom Mary wrote every Christmas. They spent their three-night honeymoon in Connemara, and Mary hoped she would be pregnant afterwards, but alas, no. She longed for a child, a baby of her own, but her time with Rory since they married had been so infrequent, and often only for a few minutes. Their opportunities to be alone together were rare.

She carefully put the letters and photos into a big envelope and sealed it. In the wardrobe was her Cumann na mBan uniform. Of course, it was too bulky to carry, and she would have no need of it where she was going, but she carefully removed the badge, the design of which she had always loved: the initials of the women's movement, *C na mB*, looped around a rifle. She placed it in one of the velvet jewel bags the mistress had given her. It might've been just brass, but it meant more to her than all the diamonds in the world. She wore her wedding ring, and around her neck, the medal of St Anne, given to her all those years ago by Mrs Kearns. There were some books – a poetry book of W.B. Yeats that Rory had sent her a few months ago, and finally, the flag.

She realised that bringing a soiled, dirty flour bag across the ocean would be seen as the height of foolishness in some people's eyes, but she didn't care. Tom Clarke made that flag for them, and gave them his shoelaces to tie it to the broom handle. The bags came from Boland's, a mill that was being held by Mr de Valera, and she and Eileen had made hundreds of bandages with them. She carried the mistress, with Mrs Kearns and Eileen, out of the GPO, and it was Mrs Grant's blood on it. It represented everything about her life since she arrived in Dublin. It may not have meant anything to anyone else, but to her, it would always be precious. She carefully folded it and went to the linen cupboard. There she found a small sheet and wrapped the flag carefully. Then she went out to the kitchen to get the suitcase.

It was on the big table, where she and Mrs Kearns had chopped, kneaded, mashed and rolled for hundreds of meals. The housekeeper was nowhere to be seen, so Mary took the case to her room and filled it. She put in the few dresses she had, her spare shoes and her extra cardigan. She would wear her woollen dress and her winter coat and hat for the journey. The clock on the wall of the kitchen said half past six. It was time to go.

'Mrs Kearns,' she called. 'Mrs Kearns, are you here? I'm going now.'

She went out into the back garden. Jimmy would park the car at the back entrance to the house to avoid any confrontation with the soldiers. Mary spotted her, examining the contents of the potting greenhouse. She grew vegetables and herbs in there, and it was her pride and joy, though very little was growing now, in the bitterly cold month of January. Mary stood there for a moment, just watching her and committing her to memory, and eventually touching Mrs Kearns on the shoulder. She turned and Mary saw the tears flowing unchecked down her old face. In all they had endured together, she had never seen Mrs Kearns cry. She was usually so stoic and full of common sense.

Mary put her arms around her and held her close. 'How will I manage without you?' she said through her own tears. 'I've come to think of you as my mother. I never had one, you know, and now I'm supposed to leave the only one I've ever known. How am I supposed to do that?' Mary asked her.

'You'll be grand, Mary. You're strong and you've a good head on your shoulders,' Mrs Kearns said. 'But I'd be telling you a lie if I didn't admit that my heart is broken. God bless you, my darling girl, and I wish you all the luck in the world. I'll pray for you every night, and for Rory too, that ye will be together again, and that this will all end and maybe ye can come home to us. But if you don't, remember this, that you gave me more than I ever gave you, and I'll die a happy woman for having you in my life. Now be off with you, and see that rascal before you go. Write to us, Mary, and let us know you're all right, won't you? We'll be worried sick.'

Mary nodded and released her. Mrs Kearns put her hand on top of Mary's head and said a prayer. 'Our Lady of the Wayside, for the love of the child in your arms, take my Mary by the hand and lead her safely along the road. Amen.' Then she nodded and turned, and headed back to her kitchen.

# CHAPTER 39

'This is Shanganagh Cemetery, Eileen.' Fiachra parked the car. 'It's fairly big, so do you know where to go? Or will I try to find someone to help?'

Eileen smiled. 'I think I'll find it. Come walk with me, you two. This is the cemetery where Mrs Grant and Mrs Kearns are buried. Mammy was devastated when she got the news – she always hoped she would see them one more time, but then I suppose international travel wasn't what it is today. I often offered to go back with her, but she always refused, saying she just couldn't. I never pressed her on it, but I think when Mrs Grant died, and she got the telegram, I suppose it was from Mrs Kearns, she was inconsolable. I grew up with these people – though I never met them, they were as alive to me as the neighbours down the street. Mrs Grant's health was never good, but she lived until 1960, which was a grand old age. When Mrs Kearns died a few months later, Mammy was amazed to learn they were almost the same age. She always thought Mrs Kearns was older than *the mistress*, as she called her. They wrote all during their lives, and I would get presents from them on my birthday and Christmas.'

Scarlett and Fiachra each linked one of her arms as they went into the graveyard. 'I think it's down here,' she said, and Scarlett knew her well enough by now to know she was probably right.

'There it is.' They stopped and read the headstone.

*Angeline Grant*
*1875 - 1960*
*Beloved friend of Beatrice Kearns and Mary O'Dwyer.*

The two women obviously were buried in the same grave, because underneath it on the same headstone was written.

*Beatrice Kearns*

## *1874 – 1960*

Eileen sighed, her voice cracking with emotion. 'There should be something about Mammy underneath hers as well, but no one knew to do it, I suppose. Mrs Kearns really was like a mother to her – she loved her so much, and she always felt terrible about not coming back. But she just couldn't.'

Fiachra put his arm around Eileen. 'We can get it inscribed, no problem. Look, there's loads of room – we can put it right.'

Eileen looked up at him, eyes shining with emotion. 'Do you think we could do that?'

'Definitely.' He smiled and Scarlett marvelled at how Eileen instantly trusted him. He was just a genuinely good guy.

As they stood at the grave, she told them the story of the flag and what Mary Doyle, Eileen O'Dwyer, Mrs Grant, and Mrs Kearns endured during Easter Week together in the GPO, and why it was of such importance to her mammy. Finally Scarlett understood how crushed Eileen would have been if the thieves had taken it.

Eileen laid two of her wreaths on the grave and Scarlett and Fiachra stood back to let her have a moment alone. Scarlett reached up and kissed him on the cheek. He turned and smiled. 'What was that for? Not that you need a reason, of course.'

'Just for being so great to Eileen. She really trusts you, and I'm glad.'

'She's a smart cookie, that one. She might be getting on in years, but she's a sharp as a razor. I think it's great that you got involved with her… Imagine, without you, she would never have got to come here and do all of this. You should be proud of yourself, Scarlett. I mean it.'

As they walked back to the car, Eileen said, 'There's just one more place I have to go.'

# CHAPTER 40

*T*he house on Westmoreland Street, owned by a Dr O'Reilly and his wife, was often used as a safe house by Collins and his men. The doctor worked at the Arbour Hill barracks and was seen by the British as being loyal. Mary went in the front door the moment the maid opened it.

'Thank you,' she said to the young girl who took her coat and hat. She looked so innocent and trusting – Mary remembered a time when she looked like that too. The girl tried unsuccessfully to hide her shock at Mary's battered face, but Mary saw the flash of horror in the younger girl's eyes. How much she knew, Mary had no idea, though as a maid in a safe house, she would have to have some inkling as to what went on there. As she led Mary down the hallway into a large drawing room, voices came from behind the door. The girl knocked gingerly and opened the door, indicating that Mary should enter.

There were three men standing at the fire-place while applewood logs crackled merrily in the hearth. They each held a glass of whiskey, and as they turned to face her, Mary recognised two of them. Rory rushed over to her, taking her suit-case and leading her towards the fire.

'Mary, this is Dr O'Reilly – this is his house – and you know Mick.' Rory smiled.

Mary had never met Michael Collins before, though she had seen him several times. He was tall and handsome and seemed to exude energy and good humour. He extended a huge hand to her, after crossing the room in two strides. 'Well, 'tis lovely to finally meet you, Mary. Rory never stops talking about you, and he has us driven cracked, if the truth be told.'

He chuckled and gave Rory a friendly punch on the shoulder. 'I'm sorry you had to endure that Captain Johnson. He's one of the worst of them. And he was involved in some way with your former employer, who was dealt with, so he has a crow to pick with you and he won't let it go. I know you're not happy about going away, but honest to God, 'tis the safest thing for you, and for Rory. Your country has asked an awful lot of you, Mary, I know it has, and you've done your best every time, but 'tis time to leave it to others now. If I could get Kitty to go, believe me I would, but she's a stubborn woman and she won't do as I ask. There's a bounty of 10,000 pounds on my head, and you may be sure there's one for Rory as well. Johnson knows who you are now, and he's like a bear that he was overruled. I was able to do it once, to get you away from him. That other fella was up to something he shouldn't have been with a certain young lady of my acquaintance, and I had to threaten to expose him to his wife. That's the only way I got you out, and I wouldn't be so lucky the next time. You are in real danger. So will you go, Mary?'

Mary looked into his open, boyish face and wondered how anyone ever refused him anything. He had all the charisma and enthusiasm people said he had, but there was a soft kindness to him as well. He was capable of orchestrating a crippling war on the British through analytical and decisive action. He sent young Irishmen out on manoeuvres in the knowledge that, for some of them, at least, they wouldn't come home. But it had to be done. Rory often told Mary that Collins went very silent after the IRA suffered losses. He took each death personally, and felt responsible for every one of them.

'I'll go, but can you get Rory to send for me as soon as you can?' she asked. She knew she shouldn't ask, because he had important work to do here, but the thoughts of being thousands of miles away from him broke her heart.

'The minute this is over, I'll buy the ticket myself. Wild horses won't keep him from you, Mary – I'll have no need to instruct him. He'll be out of this the second he can, for like all of us, he's had enough. We share the same dream: A country of our own, where we rule ourselves and we can live in peace on our beautiful island. We won't fight one minute more than we need. But I need him now, and I'll try to get us all through this, and hopefully he'll be safe. He's a bit like a cat, this fella. He has more than one life, you know.'

He winked at her, and drained his glass. 'Now 'tis time I was gone. Thanks for the hospitality, as usual, Maurice, and tell Jenny that fish pie was the best I ever had – high praise from a West Cork man, I can tell you! Now so, good luck to ye.' He shook their hands and was gone.

'You're very welcome here, Mary.' The doctor

was a quietly spoken man, the total opposite to Collins. 'Now I'll leave you two alone. I have to go out on a sick call anyway. My wife left some pie in the larder for you if you're hungry. Rory, you know where everything is, so just help yourselves. And the very best of luck to you, Mary. I know you are probably worried about the bruising on your face, by the way, but it will be gone in a week or two. It's a sign of good healing.' He gave them a kind smile and left the room.

'Are you hungry? Do you want tea?' Rory was anxious to make her as comfortable as he could.

'No, I had a big lunch at the Grants's, and Mrs Kearns has been feeding me like a prize pig since I got back from the Castle,' she joked.

Rory held out his hand and Mary placed her small one in his. He led her up the stairs to a bedroom at the back of the house. The room was dominated by a large bed, covered with a handmade patchwork quilt. A fire burned in the small grate. Rory closed the curtains and turned the gas lamp low so the flickers from the fire danced on the walls. Mary sighed and wished with all her heart that she could stay in this safe cosy place with him forever. She wouldn't have to leave and he wouldn't risk being shot or arrested every day.

'What a lovely room.' She smiled at him. 'Do you often stay here?'

'A fair bit, but we have lots of houses we go to. 'Tis best not to have a pattern, and people are very kind. We're well looked after, Mary. Don't worry.'

He kissed her battered face then, tenderly. 'Does it hurt?' he asked.

'Not as much – it looks worse than it feels,' she whispered.

'You are beautiful. Always were, and always will be.' He led her to the bed and helped her out of her dress. They made love slowly and with such tenderness that Mary felt her heart might break at the thought of leaving him. They both tried to block out the fact that they were to be parted once more in a matter of hours.

In the small hours of the morning, they lay wrapped in each other's arms, chatting quietly. They talked about everything: about John and Peg, and the children, about their new nephew, Rory Óg, as he was being called, to distinguish him from his uncle, and how it was great for Eileen and for Peg and John that she was so close. Kate was doing marvellous things with her little nephew and was planning to go to Dublin in the summer to study midwifery. Rory told Mary that his sister had been nervous telling him of her plans, thinking he would hate the idea of her being in Dublin, but he would be glad to have a sister in the city again. He really missed Eileen. Mary suggested that she could stay with Mrs Grant, and Rory said he'd ask her. The idea that Rory could just call in to Mrs Kearns and Mrs Grant sent a stab of pain through her heart. Coping without Rory all the time before was made possible by the knowledge that she could sit by the range in the kitchen, or upstairs with the mistress at night, and have a cup of tea and a chat. Or work hard to ensure the families of the men who had died were taken care of – there was always so much to do. Now how was she to fill her days?

Eventually the time came to go. Rory walked to the boat with her as dawn broke over the city, and stood beside her as she queued up to go up the gangplank. As the purser called her forward to check her ticket, she clung to Rory, only releasing him when the woman behind her, who was travelling with several children, urged her on.

'The minute it's over, either way, I'll send for you. I promise,' he whispered urgently.

'You'd better, Rory O'Dwyer. I need you.' Mary was mock stern through her tears.

'I need you too. Goodbye, my love. I'll see you soon.'

She handed the man her ticket and turned to catch one last glimpse of her husband. He looked so forlorn standing on the quayside…so alone.

The journey was uneventful. She got a ticket to New York in Liverpool, leaving four days later. She checked into a boarding house Mrs Grant had recommended until it was time to go. She was nauseous and miserable during the Atlantic crossing, despite having a second-class cabin to herself, and when she arrived in New York, she was washed out and exhausted as she shuffled with the others through the endless procedures on Ellis Island. Everything was so big and loud, and every language on earth seemed to be babbled in the cavernous immigration hall.

Normally, second-class passengers didn't have to go through the health inspections, but there was a fear of cholera, so she shuffled along with the rest of the people. She looked with pity on those who had travelled in steerage, often not knowing a single word of English, and many of them were so young and bewildered looking. She was grateful at least for the money in her suitcase and the fact that someone was meeting her. The idea of trying to get around on her own in such a strange place was terrifying. Rory had ensured everything was in order, all her papers, and after a few hours and checks, she found herself on another boat to the shore, where she was deposited on the quayside.

'Hey, lady, you got somewhere you wanna go?' A man wearing only an undershirt and a vest appeared to be offering his services with a horse and cart. He had a gold tooth, something Mary had never seen before, and she hated the way he looked her up and down suggestively. She tried to ignore him, standing on the quayside, feeling bewildered and alone. Finally, she heard her name being called.

'Mary O'Dwyer? Mary O'Dwyer?' She turned to see a man dressed in a beige overcoat and wearing a hat. Whoever he was, he looked an altogether better prospect than the man with the cart.

'I'm Mary O'Dwyer,' she answered quickly.

'Are you Rory O'Dwyer's wife?' His accent was unmistakably American.

'Yes,' she said, unsure of herself.

'Ok, then! Welcome to America! Give me that suitcase there and come with me.' He took the heavy case and he walked ahead of her, elbowing his way through the densely packed quayside. He led her to a car, bigger than any she had ever seen in Ireland, and opened the door for her.

'Er, thank you for meeting me.' Mary instinctively trusted him, but everyone had warned her to be careful in New York, where there were plenty of unscrupulous people waiting to prey on recently arrived immigrants.

'No problem, we've been expecting you. I'm Sean Chiarello. My mother was a Deasy from Cork and I'm married to an Irish woman, so I'm more Irish than Italian despite the name. My mother knows Mrs Grant, who contacted her and asked me to meet you. My mom is a fundraiser for Cumann na mBan over here.'

Mary relaxed for the first time in weeks. If this man was connected with Mrs Grant, then she was in safe hands.

As they drove through the streets of the biggest, noisiest place Mary had ever seen, she tried to take it all in. She had been below deck, throwing up, as the ship approached New York, so she had missed out on the first sight of the Statue of Liberty.

Eventually they pulled up at a large house, with steps up to the wide front door. It reminded

Mary of the lovely houses on Merrion Square, or St Stephen's Green, in Dublin. A black woman answered the door and Mary tried not to stare. She'd only ever seen black people in books. The woman took Mary's suitcase and her coat and led her to the sitting room upstairs, where an elderly woman sat at a writing desk.

'Aah, you must be Mary.' She smiled in welcome.

'Yes.' She was unsure of what to say. 'Thank you for arranging someone to meet me. Your son told me you are a friend of Mrs Grant?'

'Well, not exactly, dear. We are both involved with Cumann na mBan, but I have never had the pleasure of meeting her personally. We do, however, have several mutual acquaintances. It was through one of those that I received the message to meet you.' There was still a slight trace of Irish in her accent, but Mrs Chiarello gave the impression of a very-well-got American lady.

'Now, my dear, let me get you some coffee or tea. Or perhaps you would like something more substantial?'

'No, thank you,' Mary said. 'I'm fine.' She was unsure what she was doing here. Was she to stay here with these people, was she to work for them?

'Sit down, Mary,' Mrs Chiarello said, leading her to a beautiful wing-backed chair by the fire.

'I… I'm afraid I have some very bad news for you, my dear,' the woman began. Mary felt her blood run cold. Her throat constricted and she could hear drumming in her ears.

'I received a telegram a few days ago. Mrs Grant intimated I should tell you everything. There's no easy way to tell you this, but your husband Rory was picked up by the British two days after you left. He was taken to Dublin, where he was shot and killed. The officer in question said that he was interrogating your husband when he attacked him, and the officer shot him in self-defence. I'm so very sorry, Mary…'

Mary was numb. The woman's voice crashed over her like waves on the ocean. Once before she believed Rory was dead and he came back to life – *Michael Collins had said he was like a cat, he had more lives left. This woman has it wrong. Rory isn't dead, he's injured, maybe. Johnson will have seen to that, but he isn't dead.*

Mrs Chiarello handed Mary a telegram. It was from Mrs Grant and it said exactly what this woman had said. It was true so. Mrs Grant would never lie to her, nor get something like this wrong. It was true: Rory was dead. Gone…forever. The words swam in front of her eyes, refusing to penetrate her brain.

The woman then gave Mary a newspaper, *The Irish Echo*, which carried the story of Rory's murder. Painstakingly she read the way Rory's body was dumped on Dame Street, almost unrecognisable, the report explained.

'I want to go home,' was all Mary said.

'I'm afraid there was another telegram, insisting that under no circumstances are you to return to Ireland. It was signed by Michael Collins himself. It is too dangerous for you, because this Captain Johnson is determined to find you as well. In fact, even here you are not safe. He is apparently a man of considerable influence. This has apparently gone far beyond the Irish struggle. He has a vendetta against you and your husband. It seems he lost a lot of money as a result of the death of Edward Grant, and things have gone badly for him since then. In addition, his superiors seem to have become aware of some irregularities in his dealings, and he is currently under investigation. He holds you and your husband responsible.' Mrs Chiarello sighed.

'Now, I know this is so much to take in, but I am going to make a suggestion. Many people, when they arrive to this country, take a new name. In fact, the staff at Ellis Island, I believe, have a suggested list, as so many of the foreign names are too difficult to pronounce. I think we should change your name. You are welcome to use ours, Chiarello, and it would then be most unlikely this man or his associates will be able to find you. They will be looking for a Mary O'Dwyer, not a Mary Chiarello.'

Mary's head was spinning. *What is this woman talking about? First she says that Rory is dead, then she is going on about changing my name?* Mary felt it must be a nightmare and that she would wake up any moment in her little bed in Mrs Grant's house.

Mary sipped the brandy Mrs Chiarello gave her, with *Rory is dead, Rory is dead,* going round and round in her head.

'I want to send a telegram. Is that possible?' Mary asked.

'Of course, my dear. To whom do you wish to send it?' The woman was anxious to do anything to help this distraught young woman.

'Mrs Grant.' Mary knew her voice was flat and distant, and that she should thank this woman for her kindness, but she couldn't.

The woman rang a little bell and the maid reappeared. 'Abilene, can you fetch the telegram boy as quickly as possible, please. Now, Mary what do you want to say?' The woman poised her pen on a clean sheet of paper.

'I want to come home. MC says no. Please! M,' she dictated. She needed to be with her people, to be with John and Peg as they buried their boy. To feel their love around her. She couldn't stay in this strange place, alone.

'Very well, Mary. It will be sent right away. Now I think you should have a lie down.' She rang the small bell again. The maid appeared once more. 'Aah, Abilene, can you ask Dr Bozek to come up now?'

Mary looked worried. What was going on? Everything was moving too quickly around her, and she couldn't take it in.

'You have had a terrible shock, and a horrible sea crossing. You need rest, and I've asked the doctor to come and give you something to help you sleep. Please don't worry now. We will take care of you.'

The days turned into weeks as Mary recovered in the Chiarellos's home. Mr Chiarello, who insisted on being called Remo, was a jolly Italian who loved to cook at home, even though he owned a whole string of Italian restaurants. Carmel Chiarello was kindness itself, but nothing could take away the pain in her heart. They fed her up on food she had never tasted, gnocchi in a sage and butter sauce, which was delicious; rich lasagne with meaty tomato sauce; spaghetti with cheese; and Remo gave her huge bowls of gelato for dessert.

Mrs Grant had written and begged Mary to stay where she was. Apparently Johnson had received a dishonourable discharge after the details of his nefarious dealings had come to the attention of his superiors. He arrived at the Grants's house one night and threatened them at gunpoint. By the time they managed to let the IRA know, he was gone, seen off by Mrs Kearns with the mistress's Webley revolver, but he was still at large. The fear was that he had gone to the United States in search of Mary. He was crazed with anger and bitterness, it seemed, and blamed Rory and Mary entirely for his downfall. It was vital that she remain out of sight.

Mary signed the papers to change her name, feeling like she was letting go of the last vestiges of her marriage and her life at home. She felt numb. The initial distraught feeling of despair had gone, but in its place was a cold, empty ache.

One morning, several weeks after her arrival in New York, Mary realised she was pregnant.

She was nauseous all the time, and her period was late. Carmel arranged for the doctor to confirm the good news, but Mary just nodded as he congratulated her. The feelings of joy and excitement she knew she would have felt if Rory was by her side were absent. She sat with her hands on her still-flat belly in the bright sunny bedroom Carmel had given her at the front of the house. She cried silently as she looked, unseeing, out onto the street in this strange city. The Chiarellos were kind, but they were strangers. They were doing their best, but to have a hopelessly despondent girl, now pregnant, in their house, must be a strain. She wondered what would become of her and the baby, alone in this big city. She couldn't stay with the Chiarellos forever. They had their own children and little grandchildren to consider.

Despite everyone begging that she stay, she decided to take her chances and go home. She would go through the pregnancy in New York, and once the baby was born, she would board a boat for Ireland. If she were honest, she cared little for whether she lived or died at this stage now, anyway. *Let Johnson catch me. Let him do his worst – at least that way I'd be with Rory.* She would go back to Dublin. At least she was married and would have the respectability of being a widow, not like those poor girls who found themselves pregnant without having wed. Mrs Grant and Mrs Kearns would help her rear the baby, and she could spend holidays with the O'Dwyers in Limerick. Rory's son or daughter would be reared by people who loved him or her, and if Colonel Johnson had his way and he killed her, their child would at least have family around. If he found her here, the child would end up in an orphanage, just as Mary had done, and that was a fate she would wish on no child.

No, the only thing to do was to have the baby, and then go home and face whatever might come. At least she had enough money to rent an *apartment*, as they called it, and see a doctor about delivering the baby, and then she would go back. Despite their dire warnings to stay where she was, she knew Mrs Grant and Mrs Kearns wouldn't turn her away, not if she was standing on the doorstep with a baby in her arms.

Abilene knocked on the door and entered. She had been so kind to Mary in the past weeks that Mary wished she could reciprocate the other woman's warmth, but she felt frozen inside.

'Miss Mary, there's a letter for you.' Abilene had started addressing her as Mrs O'Dwyer, but it seemed wrong to Mary. Abilene was much older than her, and after all, they were both servants. She asked to be called Mary, but Abilene said that it wouldn't be right, so they settled on *Miss Mary*.

'A young man come by just now with this letter. He said it was delivered to some other address in Staten Island, but they sent it back to Ireland, since they didn't know where you were. It's been readdressed to here.'

The envelope, well battered, had an address scribbled out, and the Chiarello's address written alongside. Abilene held out the silver platter bearing the letter to Mary.

She couldn't move. Even the effort to raise her hand and take the envelope seemed too difficult. She recognised the writing immediately.

Sensing her distress, Abilene took the envelope and opened it, putting the pages into Mary's hands. She led her to the fire and sat her down.

The words blurred in front of Mary's eyes, and her hands shook so badly she couldn't focus, but she took a deep breath. She wiped her eyes with the sleeve of her blouse and read.

*My darling Mary,*

*I'm just back in the doctor's house and I'm looking at the bed. The fire is still glowing, and I think I can smell you from the pillow. I'm not ashamed to say I held it up to my face for ages when I came back, trying to relive our last night together. Was it only a few short hours ago we lay there in each other's arms? Letting you go up the gangplank this morning was the hardest thing I've ever had to do. I was trying to let on that I was fine about it, that it was for the best, but deep down, I wanted to grab you by the hand and pull you back to me. I know what they say is right – that bastard Johnson won't be happy till he sees me dead, and you with me – but honest to God, Mary, I feel like just going up there and roaring at him to come out and face me. Let him do his worst, whatever he thinks he can do to me. But to protect you, I think I could have the strength of ten men.*

*May God forgive me, Mary, but I'd put a bullet in his skull as quick as look at him. I've never felt such murderous hatred for anyone, but I can't even think about what he did to you, my sweet, sweet girl. The rest of them, sure they're just doing their jobs, and we have to fight them but I don't hate them. I just want them to go home. Johnson, though... He's pure evil.*

*You never asked for this, this life of fear and violence. I wanted to give you so much, you know? A home, children, a lifetime of love. I'm not a violent man. I hope you know that – in fact, I hate it. I hate all of it and I'm so tired, Mary, but we have no choice but keep going. It has to be this way, us taking them on, despite the bloody and sometimes almost unbearable consequences. You should see what they've done to some of our lads below in Cork. Having to give the broken, battered bodies of boys – and that's all some of them are – after they've been interrogated and their bodies dumped for us to pick up, back to their mothers to bury, I just can't describe it to you. But there's no going back, for if we back down now, they'll enslave us forever. 'Twill all have been for nothing. And they won't forget, no. We'll pay for having the cheek to demand to run our own country. One of the many, many reasons I love you is that you understand that.*

*I made you promise me, before Easter Week, that if anything happened to me, you were to live your life, get married, have children and be happy. I still want you to keep that promise, Mary, though I pray every night that we may grow old together. I know how lonely you'll be over there in America – at the start, anyway. I'm sending this letter to one of the addresses I gave you. I'm not exactly sure where you are, but I hope they are kind to you and that they'll be able to get this to you. Write back to me as soon as you can, and send it to Mrs G's. I'll call in from time to time to check on them anyway.*

*Please don't even think about coming back. We are close to victory, Mary, I know we are, and with Collins in charge, we'll finally get what we always dreamed of. I'll send you the fare home the minute it's safe, but I mean it about not coming back. None of this is worth it for me if anything happened to you.*

*I've no news to tell you, sure I only saw you this morning, but I miss you so much 'tis like a pain in my chest. I'm just going to throw myself into getting this job done as fast as we can.*

*I'm going to do every single thing in my power to get you home safe, and we'll have a great life together, if God spares me. Home to a new, free Ireland, where we can live and love for the rest of our days. I'm starting to believe what Mick says about me – that I'm like a cat, with more than one life.*

*So, my darling girl, mind yourself, and I'll try to mind myself too, and we'll be together again.*

*I love you always and forever,*
*Rory*

Her body wracked with tearless sobs while Abilene cradled her in her arms.

THE BABY WAS BORN in October, in the Chiarellos's house. They refused to listen to Mary's protests that she should get an apartment of some kind, and took great care of her as her pregnancy progressed. She gave birth to a little girl who she called *Eileen*, in honour of her aunt and Mary's best friend. She wished she could be called *Eileen O'Dwyer*, but she had promised Rory she would stay safe. Now she had to keep his daughter safe as well. Every time the baby smiled, she saw Rory, and she realised he had never really left her.

A truce had been signed in Ireland. But as soon as it had, trouble broke out again. Collins had given six Ulster counties in the north to England, it seemed, and half the IRA members were appalled. De Valera raged against his former friend and comrade. Collins claimed it was a start, the best that could have been achieved, but it divided the country. Eileen was disgusted with the agreement and sided with de Valera, claiming Collins was a traitor to his country. Mrs Grant and Mrs Kearns, on the other hand, were loyal to Collins. Apparently the housekeeper and Eileen met at a Cumann na mBan meeting, and sharp words were exchanged. Mary hated the thought that her friends were so deeply divided. Her instinct was to trust Collins, for she was sure that's what Rory would have done, though Eileen didn't agree. Mary remembered the night in the doctor's house in Westmoreland Street when the big, handsome West Cork man held her hands and looked into her eyes and she thought he could be forgiven anything. She was wrong.

Reading their letters, each side full of contempt for the other, Ireland felt less and less like somewhere she wanted to be. She was tired of it all, of this endless war. And as the months went on and Eileen grew to recognise her surroundings and come to love the Chiarellos, New York became home. Sean called often with his daughters, who doted on baby Eileen, and soon these people became her family. With every passing week, further news came from Ireland of all-out Civil War. The English were gone, at long last, but at least under them, the country had been united in a common goal. She cried at the thought of everything Rory and men like him died for, all reduced to dust as Irishmen turned on each other.

On 22 August 1922, word reached America that the anti-treaty side had shot Michael Collins and killed him in his native Cork. Mary got the news from Carmel, who came out to the garden where Mary was playing with little Eileen on a blanket. Then and there, she knew. She would never again go back.

# CHAPTER 41

'The Republican Plot in Glasnevin Cemetery is a Who's Who in the struggle for Irish independence. The biggest memorial is, of course, to Collins, though Daniel O'Connell's tomb is fairly impressive,' Fiachra explained as they went in the gates. 'But they're all here: Kevin Barry, a young medical student executed by the British; Brendan Behan, the writer; Roger Casement; Cathal Brugha; Harry Boland, Collins' best friend who took the other side in the Civil War. Over there is Charles Stewart Parnell, and that's de Valera's spot. My dad used to bring us here when we were kids, and he always used to say there must be desperate fighting and arguing going on with all those lads buried here together.

It's as much a visitor attraction now as a grave-yard, there's even a museum and shop and café here. A million Dubliners lie in this place and it's meaningful and special for locals and tourists alike.'

Scarlett and Eileen smiled as they weaved through the headstones, pausing here and there to read inscriptions.

'There's Rory O'Dwyer, he was one of Collins's right-hand men, he –'

'He was my father,' Eileen said quietly.

Scarlett and Fiachra stood in stunned silence.

'He was picked up by the British. There was a particular officer who had a gripe against my parents, and he had my father arrested, tortured and shot two days after my mother left for America. They dumped his body on the street. She had been interrogated earlier and badly beaten up, and everyone felt it was safer for her to get away from this Captain Johnson. My father was to send for her as soon as it was safe. What neither of them knew at that stage was that she was pregnant with me. She got the news of his death when she landed in New York.'

'Oh, Eileen, how awful! I'm so sorry, your poor mother...' Scarlett looked at Eileen in sympathy.

'Mrs Grant, she had connections everywhere, so she asked a woman who was a Cumann na mBan supporter to meet my mother and break the news to her. She was a Carmel Deasy from Ireland, but she married an Italian, Remo Chiarello. I called them Uncle Remo and Aunt Carmel all my life. They were wonderful to us. We took their name when we got there, as a precaution. At first, my mother really wanted to go back, but we settled there and she was just tired, I think, tired of all of it. The fighting, the killing, and maybe she couldn't go back to where she was with him, my father. It was too hard for her, she said.' Eileen closed her eyes briefly.

'She qualified as a nurse in the States. She loved nursing and had a good life, but she never saw any of them again. She kept in touch with the two old ladies, Mrs Grant and Mrs Kearns, until they died, and, of course, the O'Dwyers, my father's family. I have lots of cousins in Limerick, my dad's brothers' and sisters' children. I've even had some of them visit when they came to the States on student vacations over the years. My mother and Eileen stayed in touch until she died of breast cancer in 1944. If my mother was ever to consider going back, it would have been then, to attend the funeral, but what with the war, in-

ternational travel was impossible. I remember we had a Mass said for her in New York, and my mother cried and cried. She was a tough lady, not given to overly emotional outbursts, so it was a shock for me. I didn't really understand. I was in my twenties then, and caught up in my own life, I guess.'

'Did your mother ever remarry?' Scarlett asked.

'No. There was only ever one man for her, and that was Rory. She loved him to the day she died.'

'And how about you – you never married either?' Fiachra was curious.

'No, I never did. I suppose I grew up hearing about this great love story between my parents, and I guess I just never felt like that about anyone. I do regret that now, I think. They were so young, so very young, and living in wartime... Well, it heightens everything, I think. They loved each other, I don't doubt that, but maybe she should have tried to meet someone. She had lots of admirers. She looked a little like you, Scarlett – the same beautiful red hair and complexion, but she was tiny. I have had a great life, though, so don't pity me. I spent my career doing things I cared deeply about and I had a great social life, I still do, and my mother and I were best friends.

She made sure I knew all about my heritage. She taught me Irish, we read poetry, sang songs of Ireland, so even though this is my first time on the soil of Ireland, I've always felt it in my heart.'

Scarlett and Fiachra smiled at Eileen's philosophical attitude. She exuded common sense, and despite a husbandless, childless life, you didn't feel sorry for her.

'We are going to give you some time here,' Fiachra said, touching Eileen's arm. 'We'll be in the coffee shop over there when you're ready, ok?'

As they sat in the bright coffee shop, they watched Eileen through the large plate glass windows. Fiachra was right, tourists and locals alike mingled in this place, where the bones of those who freed this country rested side by side...and Eileen O'Dwyer said hello and goodbye to her father.

# CHAPTER 42

The sumptuous surroundings of the State Apartments of Dublin Castle looked wonderful as the gathered crowd took their seats. Each group checked where they were to sit, and Fiachra led Eileen, Lorena and Scarlett to their allocated places. He kissed Scarlett on the cheek as she sat down, and she was touched by the gesture. After being hidden by Charlie for so long – a guilty, sordid secret – it felt good to be with a man who wanted to broadcast to the world that they were a couple.

They'd had a wonderful ten days of touring Ireland. It really was a beautiful country, and they even visited the O'Dwyer cousins in Limerick.

They were invited for afternoon tea, but didn't leave the house until three a.m., and had to return to the hotel by taxi, as Scarlett was incapable of driving after enjoying their hospitality. Lorena was in her element, flirting outrageously with the men. She still had a thing for Irish guys, it seemed. The food and drink were seemingly endless, as more and more cousins arrived to meet Eileen.

Fiachra was very busy with the commemoration preparations, but he drove to meet them several nights, getting up early to drive back to Dublin. If Lorena or Eileen were shocked by his overnight presence, they gave no indication of it.

Today was the official ceremony where the artefacts, which by now had all been catalogued, and the stories recorded on video for posterity, were to be given on loan to the Irish State. There was going to be a huge exhibition set up in one of the conference centres in the city, and everyone was going to be able to see the collection for free for the duration of the year 2016, the centenary of the Rising.

Eileen had her flag, still in the cotton sheet her mother Mary had wrapped it in the day she left the Grants's home for good. As the benefactors were handing over the artefacts, they were to go up on stage, where eventually there were to be press photographs. The president of Ireland, the Taoiseach, as well as several dignitaries of various kinds, were already in place on a podium to the left of the stage, to watch the proceedings.

Last night, Eileen had asked Scarlett to go up on stage on her behalf. She was afraid she wouldn't make the stairs.

'No way,' said Scarlett, smiling at Eileen's surprise at her refusal. 'That's your flag, and it's yours to hand over. I'll go up with you. I'll carry you if I have to, but you are doing this yourself. I will be right there beside you every step, and you'll be fine.'

Eileen smiled, put her arms out to her and they hugged. 'I never had kids, as you know, but if I did, I'd want them to be exactly as you are. Thank you, Scarlett. From the bottom of my heart, thank you.'

Fiachra crouched down beside Eileen as she sat in her seat. She looked lovely in a gold dress and coat, which Lorena had helped her buy in a very expensive but gorgeous shop in Galway. On her lapel she wore her mother's Cumann na mBan badge.

'So, wait till your name is called. Then you just walk up to the right there, up the stairs. Scarlett will be with you, so don't worry.' He patted Eileen's hand and winked at Scarlett before he went to help another benefactor.

Lorena squeezed Scarlett's hand. 'Isn't this exciting? It's worth it to come for the fashion alone!' Lorena had gone all out and looked amazing in an aquamarine dress. She radiated health and happiness, and Scarlett was filled with love for her.

'Scarlett!' she hissed. 'Look at that green dress on that woman with the ash-blond hair.' She nodded ahead and to the left. 'She's a little too busty for it, but it would be beautiful on you.'

Scarlett shushed her, in case she was overheard. Lorena's whispering was louder than most people's talking.

Lorena had been a revelation on the trip. She was no longer religious, it would seem. She hadn't been inside a church since the Ennio episode, and she just adored everything about Ireland. She shopped until there wasn't a dollar left on her credit card, which was paid by Scarlett anyway. And how they were going to get all the stuff home, Scarlett had no idea. Lorena looked lovely, back to her old self – still capable of saying completely the wrong thing, but she irritated Scarlett less. She couldn't decide if it was that Lorena was easier to deal with or that Scarlett herself was mellowing.

Last night, she confided in her mother, the first time in years, that she had made a big decision. She was going to move to Ireland for six months. She was covering the commemorations for an Irish newspaper in New York. She had emailed Artie to see if he could pull any strings, and he did. The money was small, but it allowed her and Fiachra some time to see if this relationship was going somewhere. She really hoped it was. Artie's daughter and her family were going to rent her house, since their apartment was to be redeveloped, so everything was falling into place. She just had to go back to New York for a few weeks to get everything fixed up, and then she was coming back. Lorena was thrilled, and told her that Fiachra was a keeper if ever she saw one. She promised to visit, and to bring Eileen with her.

Scarlett watched the procession of people, all carrying their artefacts to the stage. Eventually she heard, 'Eileen O'Dwyer-Chiarello.' Fiachra had changed the name on her donation as a surprise for Eileen. The old lady grinned broadly as her eyes shone with emotion. Scarlett took her arm and slowly walked up on stage to bring Eileen's flag home.

# GLOSSARY

**Irish Volunteers** – The men who volunteered to join the armed Republican cause, set up in 1913.

**IRA** – Irish Republican Army. An Act of Dáil Éireann turned the Volunteers into the IRA 1919. Commonly known nowadays as the 'Old IRA', not to be confused with the Provisional IRA, a terrorist group operating in Northern Ireland since 1969.

**Dáil Éireann** – The Irish Parliament, located in Leinster House, Dublin.

**Taoiseach** – Leader of the Irish government.

**President of Ireland** – A nonpolitical appointment; Ireland's head of state.

**Cumann na mBan** – Women's Army set up to

operate independently, but in support of the Volunteers.

**The Lockout** – The official reaction of the Dublin merchants to those who joined the first trade union in 1913. They were locked out of their places of work without access to either wages or social welfare. It caused widespread destitution. At the time, Dublin had the highest infant mortality rate in Europe, and the second highest in the world.

**Pádraig Pearse** – The leader of the Irish Volunteers who read the Proclamation of Independence outside the General Post Office, (GPO) on Easter Monday, 1916.

**Jim Larkin** – Founder of the Irish Trade and General Workers Union. Hated by the industrialists – in particular, William Martin Murphy. Larkin rallied the workers during 1913 Lockout.

**James Connolly** – Leader of the Irish Citizen Army, a socialist movement. He was an agitator during the Lockout and one of the signatories of the Proclamation of Independence. He was shot after the Rising while tied to a chair, as his leg was injured during the fighting.

**Éamon de Valera** – A leader of the Volunteers, but not a signatory of the Proclamation. He was not executed because he was an American citizen, and to do so would have caused an international incident. He went on to lead the first Dáil and remained a colossus of Irish politics until his death in 1975.

**Michael Collins** – A young Volunteer, imprisoned in Frongoch, Wales, in 1916, and went on to be Minister for Finance in the first Dáil. In reality, his role was as a military strategist and Director of Intelligence, and he was responsible for the success of the War of Independence. He lived openly, but with a huge price on his head. The British never had a clear photograph of him, so he was never arrested. He was shot during the Civil War in 1922 in his native Cork, aged just thirty-two.

**Kilmainham Gaol** – Where the Volunteers were incarcerated immediately after the Rising, and where the leaders were shot.

**Frongoch** – An internment camp in Wales, where the Volunteers were incarcerated until Christmas 1916. While there, plans were made for the War of Independence.

**Eoin MacNeill** – Chief of Staff of the Irish Army who countermanded the order to rise in revolution on Easter Sunday 1916. This order caused widespread confusion and meant the Rising was restricted to Dublin, rather than a nationwide action. The Volunteers did not trust him, so did not inform him until the last minute of their plans for revolution.

**(Sir) Roger Casement** – An Irish man who worked as an Anglo-Irish diplomat. He retired from the consular service in 1913 and became involved with the Irish Republican Movement. He procured weapons from the Germans to be used against the British in 1916. The First World War was raging, so the arrangement suited both Ireland and Germany. He was captured by the British and put ashore at Banna Strand, Co. Kerry. He had his knighthood stripped, and he was subsequently hanged for high treason.

**DMP** – Dublin Metropolitan Police.

**RIC** – Royal Irish Constabulary, the pre-partition Irish police force.

**Dublin Castle** – The centre of British administration in Ireland.

**Countess Constance Markievicz** – née Gore-Booth. One of the founders of Cumann na mBan, the wife of a Polish count. A friend of W.B. Yeats. First woman in the world to be elected to Parliament.

**Liberty Hall** – A building in Dublin that was the centre of the trade union movement, and later one of the administration centres of the Republicans, and headquarters of the Irish Citizen Army.

# ACKNOWLEDGMENTS

This story was a labour of love for me. In literature, the futility of war is a recurring theme, and a popular one. War is a destructive, violent force that destroys people and countries, and yet, without conflict, and the blood that was shed on this island, the reality of my existence as a citizen of the Irish Republic would be unlikely.

The notion of giving your life for a national cause forms part of the literature, poetry and song of virtually every civilisation on earth, but to actually do it – to be willing to die, to leave all that you love so that others might enjoy a level of freedom denied to previous generations – is something that must give us pause for thought, whatever the cause.

I am grateful for the fact that I have never had to say goodbye to someone I loved before sending them to war, but researching this book has given me an insight into that most tragic of partings. The unimaginable pain of mothers, in particular, who have spent their lives protecting their children, to then knowingly allow them to go where they could be wounded or even killed is, for me, and I imagine all mothers, inconceivably horrific.

Mine is a typical Irish family. My great-grand-father, Pierce Kearns, was a stretcher bearer with the Royal Dublin Fusiliers on the Western Front during World War One. My great-grand-uncle, his brother, was in the Irish Republican Army. Another grand-uncle on another branch of the family tree was imprisoned for Republican activities during the War of Independence in the early twenties. In the 1950s, when opportunities for advancement or employment were few in Ireland, my aunts and uncles, like so many young Irish people, went to England in search of a better life. They settled there, and that country was good to them. My cousins are British and proud, and so they should be.

My family is more the norm than the exception. The centuries-old relationship between Ireland and Britain is bloody and complex, and our stories are inextricably linked. Throughout the centuries, so many lives were lost on this island, and they were all, irrespective of nationality, some mother's child.

This story is told from the Irish perspective, and from the point of view of those who fought and died that we could be a sovereign nation, and is dedicated to them.

I would like to express my thanks to my editor, Helen Falconer, without whom this story wouldn't work.

To my dream team of first readers – Tim, Beth-Anne, Hilda, Joseph, Jim and Tracey – who each help me in your own unique and invaluable way.

To Vivian, my sincere thanks and gratitude that you never retired your red biro.

To Millie Samuelson, whose generosity to a total stranger will never be forgotten.

To my family, friends and readers who have encouraged me to keep writing, your unfailing enthusiasm for my stories really is the fuel for the fire. Thank you all.

My children, Conor, Sórcha, Éadaoin and Siobhán, still my greatest achievements.

And finally, to the piper – the reason for it all.

\* \* \*

I sincerely hope you enjoyed this book. If you did I would appreciate it if you would write a review. To hear about other books from me, special offers and to download a free novel please join my readers club at www.jeangrainger.com

It is 100% free and always will be.

If you would like a sneak preview of another of my books, *So Much Owed*, read on!

# SO MUCH OWED - CHAPTER 1

## 20TH JANUARY 1919

Solange Allingham gazed out of the window of the black Morris Oxford at the sodden fields. The endless journey through England by train and the choppy crossing to Ireland had barely registered with her. She could feel nothing except a dragging despair, deep within her. Even the rhythmic slosh of the wipers of the car seemed to beat out the mantra, 'Jeremy is dead, Jeremy is dead.' They had been planning to buy a vineyard in the Dordogne, after the war; they had been going to have a huge family – three boys, three girls. *Jeremy is dead, Jeremy is dead.*

Gradually, the green rolling hills of the south eastern counties of Wexford and Waterford gave way to rugged, stone-filled fields. She kept on catching distant glimpses of a grey, cold ocean. Beside her, Richard drove in silence, his vivid green eyes focused on the wet road ahead, his sandy hair neatly cut and combed. How he and Jeremy had been such good friends amazed her. Her Jeremy had been always so bright and funny and full of life. This quiet, shy Irish doctor entirely lacked that sort of charm. When he spoke, it was always slow and deliberate. He was painstakingly methodical in his work, irrespective of any chaos that surrounded him. Yet she had seen injured soldiers stop screaming in agony when Dr Buckley spoke to them or touched them. 'The gentle giant,' Jeremy had dubbed him, and he was indeed big – well over six feet tall, with a deep voice she knew his patients found reassuring.

'Not long now. We'll be in Skibbereen by six, I should think. I hope you aren't too uncomfortable?' His eyes never left the road.

'No, thank you.' She hesitated, seeking the English words. Her mind felt like it was wrapped in wet cotton wool, and all she really wanted to do was sleep. 'I am fine.' In the weeks since Jeremy had died, she had barely spoken, in either

her native French or her husband's English. Not that she had learnt much English from Jeremy – he had always said he was too romantic and passionate to be Anglo-Saxon and so spoke in French to her most of the time.

All the nurses had been in love with the young doctor with his thick, wavy hair and warm, hazel eyes; he had flirted outrageously with all of them, but they knew there was nothing in it: he only had eyes for Solange Galliard. He had pursued her relentlessly from when he was first assigned to the hospital, ignoring her protests that she was engaged to Armand De La Croix, the son of a local banker. Jeremy saw this as no obstacle whatsoever; she simply had to break off the engagement and marry him instead. It was impossible to do anything else, he'd claimed – she had bewitched him with her deep azure eyes and her black corkscrew curls, forever threatening to liberate themselves from the starched white veil of her nurse's uniform. He told her regularly that she occupied his every thought, waking and sleeping, and, despite herself, she had fallen in love with the incorrigible English doctor. When he talked, he made her laugh till tears flowed down her cheeks, and when he touched her she tingled with desire. She had married him and was the happiest girl on earth.

Back in 1914, the war had been seen as something to be over by Christmas. The girls had giggled with delight at the vast numbers of handsome soldiers arriving daily. It had all seemed so romantic, the men so gallant – a bit of a lark really, as Jeremy termed it. How wrong they all were. The fun and high spirits of those early days had quickly given way to scenes of unprecedented human misery. Those scenes would haunt all those who witnessed them for the rest of their lives.

Solange wondered if Jeremy would even recognise her if he were to see her now. Grief had taken its toll on the curvaceous body he had loved; her once round cheeks were hollow, and dark shadows circled her blue eyes. At twenty-six, her jet-black hair had become suddenly threaded with silver hairs. The person she had been before the war seemed a distant stranger to her now. She suspected the carefree girl of her youth had died along with that whole generation of young men. All gone now, and Jeremy gone with them.

'There is a rug on the back seat if you're cold,' Richard's voice interrupted her reverie.

'No, thank you. I am fine.' She realised her answer was a repetition of her response to his earlier enquiry so she added, with an attempt at enthusiasm, 'Ireland is a very pretty country. Quite like Brittany in places, I think.' She knew her voice sounded flat and colourless. She couldn't help it.

He nodded thoughtfully. 'Yes, I'm glad you like it. Though of course, when the sun shines it's much better. When we were students in England, Jeremy often came here on holidays. He complained that it never stopped raining. I tried to get him to consider moving here after the war, but he said he would rather get a suntan in France than rust in Ireland any day.'

They both smiled at the memory of him; his presence was almost tangible between them in the car.

'Thank you for doing this for me,' Solange began again. 'You have been so kind. I cannot imagine how it would have been if I would have stayed in France. I don't know if I can survive now, but at least here has no memories. I will try to be of service to you and your family.'

Richard drove and sighed deeply as if weighing up how best to phrase what he was going to say next.

'Solange, I'm not bringing you to Dunderrig to be of service to us. I am bringing you to be a member of our family. Please understand that. It's your home for as long as you want it to be. We, Edith and I, don't expect anything from you but I, we, both hope that coming here will help you. I can't imagine how hard it must be, considering all you have lost. Not just Jeremy but your parents, your brothers. It's almost too much to bear. We just want to help, in any way that we can. Jeremy would have taken care of Edith had the situation been reversed. We talked about it, you know. What we would do if either one of us didn't make it. I know if it had been me who was killed then you and Jeremy would have helped Edith. So please, you are family as far as we are concerned. You don't owe us a thing.'

In the four years she had known Richard Buckley, this was the longest speech she had ever heard him make. His voice was cracking with emotion, and it was clear his offer came from the heart. She hardly knew what to say – she sat in silent gratitude as he drove the narrow, twisty road.

'Down there is Skibbereen, but this is where we turn off,' he said, taking a slow right at a sign-post marked 'Dunderrig'. 'I wrote to Edith to let her know we were arriving this evening, so she will be expecting us. Though naturally, she has been very tired of late.'

'Of course. She had only a few more weeks to go?' Solange enquired politely.

'Two weeks, perhaps. No more than three. I would have given anything to have been here to help her. She has suffered badly with sickness throughout this pregnancy. And she had to cope with the loss of my mother and father too, within a few days of each other. Thank God, the influenza spared my wife, if not my poor parents. She has had so much to cope with.'

'It will feel strange for you to be home and not to see them. Even as an adult, you are never ready to lose your parents.' She was conscious that her voice had grown heavy with her own pain and made an effort to be stronger for him. 'But you must be very excited to see your wife after all this time?'

'Yes, I am.' A brief smile but nothing more.

She glanced at him, questioningly. Richard very rarely mentioned Edith. Solange had often speculated with Jeremy about what kind of marriage the Buckleys had – practical, passionate, romantic? When she wondered what Mrs Buckley was like, Jeremy told her that he had met Edith only briefly and explained how he had dragged his shy best friend to a dance while they were still at the medical college in England; to his surprise Richard had spent his evening talking about Ireland with a cool but beautiful blond from Dublin. Only weeks later they had qualified, and Jeremy had signed up for France, and met Solange, while Richard had gone to work as a doctor in Ireland and had ended up marrying the Dublin girl. Solange's only knowledge of Edith was based on the photo Richard had of her on his desk in the hospital; it showed a tall and elegant woman, beautifully dressed. She also knew that Richard had seen his wife very briefly, eight months before, when in Dublin on leave – a leave that had been cut short before he'd been able to travel home to Cork to visit his parents, then still alive and well. Poor Richard. 'And are you also excited to become a Papa?'

'Yes. I am.' The same answer, but this time the smile was warmer.

THE HOUSE WAS SET back from the road and was impressive in its size and architecture. While not a *château* by any standard, it still seemed to be a very large house for a couple to inhabit alone. It was built of a buttery stone with limestone edging, and, despite its grand size, appeared welcoming, with lights blazing in each window, promising a warm and inviting end to her long, tiring journey. The tree-lined avenue passed through gardens that were beautifully kept, even during their winter sleep. Large sections of the housefront were covered with crimson-and-gold creeping ivy, and as they drew level with the large, bottle-green front door – the car's wheels crunching on the gravel – Solange admired the blood-red Poinsettia spilling from pots in wild profusion on either side of the door. Perhaps Edith was a keen gardener. She hoped so because she loved gardens too – it would give them something to talk about.

Richard opened the car door and offered her his arm to assist her out. Standing, she found she was stiff and sore, and suddenly longed for a bath and a good night's sleep. As he opened the front door, a plump, matronly woman with iron-grey hair and a currant-bun face came hurrying from the back section of the house.

'Dr Richard, you're home! You're as welcome as the flowers of May. Let me have a look at you! God in heaven, you're skin and bone! We'll have to feed you up. Oh, 'tis wonderful to have you home, so it is. I can't believe 'tis two years since you set foot in Dunderrig. Wouldn't your mother and father be just delighted to see you, God rest them, home safe and sound. They never stopped worrying about you, God be good to them.' Tears filled the woman's eyes.

Solange stood by as Richard put his arms around the grey-haired woman and held her tightly.

'You were so good to them, Mrs Canty. My mother's last letter told how much ye did to ease my poor father's passing, and how skilful ye were at nursing her herself. I can't believe she won't be in the kitchen or he in his surgery ever again.'

He spoke quietly. Their loss was shared. Mrs Canty was clearly much more than a house-keeper; more like one of the family. After a few minutes, he stepped back and indicated Solange.

'Mrs Canty, this is Madame Solange Alling-ham, Jeremy's wife.'

The woman hurried towards Solange, dabbing her eyes with the corner of her apron.

'I beg your pardon, I didn't see you there. What must you think of us at all? You are very welcome to Dunderrig, pet, and I'm sorry it's only me here to greet ye. We didn't know exactly when to expect you, you see. My Eddie is out and about somewhere, and Mrs Buckley is upstairs having a lie down. She's been very out of sorts all day.'

She took Solange's hand while sadly shaking her head.

'I remember your husband well – a lovely lad and no mistake. He was like a ray of sunshine around the place when he used to visit. Dr Richard's mother, God rest her soul, used to knock a great kick out of him altogether – the antics and trick acting out of him! I was so sorry to hear he had been killed, and ye only a young couple starting out in your lives. 'Twas a terrible thing that war. So many grand lads like Jeremy, gone forever.'

The woman spoke so quickly that Solange struggled to understand her – but she could tell enough to be moved by the kind way this woman spoke about her dead husband and warmed to her at once.

'Thank you, Mrs Canty. Yes, my husband spoke often about the happy times he enjoyed in Ireland.' Solange hoped her English was clear enough.

Whether Mrs Canty fully understood her or not, she seemed satisfied with Solange's halting answer. 'You're very welcome here, especially now. God knows, with the new baby arriving any minute, we'll be all up in the air soon. I'll tell you Dr Richard, she's not great at all today. I've been trying to get her to eat a bit all day long, but she's not having a bar of it. You'd think she'd be all excitement over having you home after all this time! Normally women get a bit of a boost just before, you know, getting things ready for the baby and all that, but she just lies in bed, the only thing she's interested in is writing letters…'

'Thank you, Mrs Canty, that will be all.'

Both Richard and Mrs Canty turned with a start, and Solange followed their eyes to the top of the stairs from where the cold sharp voice had come.

'It is perhaps not so inconceivable that I would not wish to eat, given the standard of cuisine in this house. Please attend to your duties.'

The haughty tone brooked no argument. A tall, blond woman was descending the staircase, which curved elegantly around the walls into the large square entrance hall. She was dressed in an ivory silk gown, over which she wore a contrasting coffee-coloured robe, and she moved remarkably gracefully, given the advanced stage of her pregnancy; despite the large bump, she was slender, almost thin. She looked pale and tired, but also something else. She seemed to exude distain, not just for the verbose Mrs Canty but for her entire surroundings. She certainly seemed to show no delight at the safe return of her husband.

'Edith, you look wonderful, blooming. Mrs Canty was telling us you haven't been well? It's so good to see you.' Richard crossed to the bottom of the stairs, offering his hand to assist her down the last few steps. She allowed him to take it and turned a powdered cheek for him to kiss, but Solange could see her actions lacked enthusiasm. Richard must have noticed it too. Having pecked his wife lightly, he released her limp fingers and retreated a few steps, looking around him, clearly searching for something else to say. His eyes alighted on Solange. 'Edith, this is Solange Allingham, Jeremy's wife.'

Edith Buckley heaved a huge sarcastic sigh as she approached Solange. 'Yes, Richard, I did gather who this was. You wrote to me several times to tell me she was coming, and it is not as if Dunderrig is such a hive of social activity that I would confuse the guests. Mrs Allingham, what on earth possessed you to leave France for this godforsaken place?'

Uncertain how to respond, Solange silently extended her own hand, but Edith ignored it.

'Oh, well, you're here now, so you will have to make the best of it. Presumably you will either expire from boredom or food poisoning, but if you are determined to take your chances... Oh, Mrs Canty, are you still here?'

Mrs Canty marched off furiously to the kitchen, saying loudly how someone had to prepare a 'good, wholesome meal' for the poor travellers. Richard seemed unsure what he should do next. He made to put his hand on his wife's back, but the look she gave him was so frosty, he changed his mind.

Solange hurried to lighten the mood. 'Madame Buckley, I must thank you for inviting me into your home. Please believe me, after the past few years in France, a quiet life is something I wholeheartedly desire, so do not be concerned I will be bored. Besides, when the new little one arrives it will be a very busy household. I hope to be of some service.' She tried to infuse her voice with gratitude and friendliness, to bring some much-needed warmth into the situation.

Edith shrugged. 'I suppose so. But I warn you, it will all seem deathly dull. I am sorry about your husband. Still, if countries insist on colonising smaller nations then war must be an inevitable outcome.'

Solange was nonplussed. Was Edith saying that Jeremy deserved to die because of the past decisions of English and French rulers? Surely she could not be so callous. She glanced at Richard, who had coloured with embarrassment.

Nonchalantly changing the subject, Edith addressed her husband, 'Richard, please contact Dr Bateman to come out. I'm not feeling well, and I need to consult him. I'm going back to bed. Welcome home. Please don't disturb me until he arrives.' She turned away.

Richard followed his wife across the hall to the foot of the sweeping stairs. 'Perhaps it's something I can help you with? It is rather a long way for Bateman to come...'

'Richard,' Edith said wearily, without looking back at him. 'While I accept you are a doctor, you are not *my* doctor. You have been conspicuous by your absence throughout my confinement, so it would be wholly inappropriate for you to involve yourself in my care at this late stage. Please contact Dr Bateman as soon as possible.' Moving wearily but not slowly, she climbed the stairs.

'Very well. If that's what you want, then of course I'll contact him – and then maybe we could have tea?'

Richard was almost pleading. But Edith had already disappeared into a room on the second floor, and his request was met with the closing of the door behind her. He turned anxiously to Solange.

'She is very tired. And she is so devoted to the cause of Irish independence. She didn't mean anything against poor Jeremy. Her opinions... She is not a supporter of the Allies. But of course, she doesn't support the other side either. I'm afraid I have to leave you a moment to call Dr Bateman. Can you take a seat here, until Mrs Canty returns? She will see you to your room and feed you to within an inch of your life, and hopefully, you'll start to feel normal again.' Then he backtracked, as if worrying that he had sounded as crass as his wife. 'I mean obviously not normal, not after everything, but maybe you can feel just a little better. Welcome to Dunderrig.'

While Solange waited for the housekeeper's re-emergence, she studied her new surroundings. The entrance hall was warm and welcoming, in stark contrast to its mistress. It was as generously proportioned as any reception room and carpeted with a rich red-and-gold rug. The furniture – a hall stand, a writing table and chair, a loudly ticking grandfather clock, and the upholstered chaise longue on which she had seated herself – were all highly polished. Oil paintings – landscapes and horses, mainly – adorned the silk-covered walls. The cantilevered staircase had a deep pile runner at its centre. A passageway led from the hall towards the back of the house. It was down this that Mrs Canty had disappeared and, based on the aromas of baking, it was connected to the kitchen. To her left and right were four large oak doors, also richly polished and all closed. Richard had gone through one of them into what was clearly a doctor's surgery. Why had Edith insisted Richard call her a different doctor? If she, Solange, had been pregnant with Jeremy's child, her husband would have been the only doctor she would have trusted to attend her.

She glanced up to the second floor. The mahogany banister became a small but ornate balcony for the rooms above, all the doors of which opened out onto the landing. The effect meant the entranceway felt like a stage and the upper gallery the viewing point. Solange felt exposed and wished that Mrs Canty would re-appear. She dreaded the possibility of Edith's return.

'Aah Lord, did he leave you here all on your own? Where's he gone to, in the name of God? I don't know what's happening to everyone in this house, honest to God, I don't. God knows, in the mistress's time, Mrs Buckley now, I mean old Mrs Buckley, Dr Richard's mother, no visitor would have been left alone in the hall, but I don't know, things are very different around here these days. Poor Dr Richard, home after that terrible war, and you'd think his wife would be happy to see him anyway.'

The housekeeper's voice dropped to a whisper as she pointed theatrically upwards while ushering Solange down the passageway into the kitchen.

'She's a bit of a handful, and she can be very cutting when she wants to be. Poor old Dr Buckley and the mistress, God be good to them, nearly drove themselves cracked trying to please her, but the day young Dr Richard left her here in Dunderrig while he went off to the war was a sad day for this house. At first he'd taken work in Dublin to please her, but he couldn't rest easy when he heard from your husband about all the terrible goings-on at the front, and in the end nothing would satisfy him but to follow Jeremy to France. He thought his wife would understand how she would be better off waiting for him in Dunderrig, and maybe, look after his parents for him. But she stayed above in her room with a face that'd turn milk sour. Sure, even when the poor doctor got the flu earlier this year, and we lost him, and the mistress less than a week later, not a budge out of herself above! And there were never two kinder people, God rest them. They were lovely, lovely people. I know she's from Dublin and not used to life in the country, but she's stuck in something to do with the Rising and all that nonsense. Her father was some kind of a bigwig professor in the college up there, and he knew them all, Pearse and Yeats and all of them. We're not fancy enough at all for her, to my way of thinking. Sure, she just writes letters all day and gets letters back, too. I don't know whom they're from, but 'tisn't right for a married woman to be going on with that kind of thing. Though I keep my own counsel because of course Dr Richard won't hear a word against her. He was forever writing to us to make sure she was all right, and what have you, and Mrs Buckley decided he had enough to worry about over there so she told him 'twas all grand, but I'd say he got a bit of a land when he met her above in Dublin. Though she came back expecting, so I suppose they must have worked it out some kind of a way.' She softened, and chuckled.

Solange found herself standing in the middle of a warm, cosy kitchen that looked out onto a cobbled courtyard. The stones shone in the wet twilight of a winter's day.

'Now you poor misfortune, you must be perished alive after sitting in that car for so long. My husband Eddie – he does the gardens, you see, and a bit of fetching and carrying around the house – he drove it down to the boat yesterday and got the train and bus back, so 'twould be there for ye when ye got off the boat, and he said it was cosier on the train by far. Sit down there, let you, and I'll get you a bowl of soup to warm your bones. Were you ever here in Ireland before?'

Mrs Canty's patter was so like a babbling brook – comforting and restful, whatever its content – it took Solange a second to realise she had been asked a question.

'In Ireland? *Jamais*…I mean, No, never. Jeremy always said he would bring me here when the war was over but… Well, that was not meant to be.' Solange tried to recover, but Mrs Canty noticed the break in her voice. Turning from the large range, she crossed the floor and took Solange by surprise by enveloping her in a warm hug.

'Your husband was a grand lad entirely, and I'm sure you brought him great joy in his short life. 'Tis better you had him, even for a short time, and had the happiness of a good marriage than years stretching out without it.' And she nodded knowingly again in the direction of upstairs.

Anxious not to take sides, Solange said, 'Perhaps things will be better after the arrival of the new baby? Madame Buckley is probably just tired. I do not know myself as I have no children, but I imagine the last weeks can be exhausting. So perhaps once the baby is born safe and well, Madame Buckley will feel better?'

'Hmm. I don't know about that. I was never blessed with children either, but I know plenty of mothers, and none of them are like herself above, I can tell you that.'

Mrs Canty placed a steaming hot bowl of creamy vegetable soup and a slice of brown soda bread thickly spread with butter on the table in front of Solange. After the deprivation in France, the richness of the food was glorious. Realising that she was very hungry, she ate greedily while Mrs Canty continued in the same vein.

'I don't know what to make of her. She arrived here with all her grand notions, but then she didn't change one thing about the place. I mean, even before she was expecting, you'd think a young bride coming into a place, especially a place like Dunderrig, would want to put her own stamp on the house. But 'twas as if she was a guest, and one that mightn't be staying at that. Very vexed she was with Dr Richard, over him joining up, I suppose, but 'twasn't as if she was heartbroken without him. Sure, she has no *meas* on him at all, she treats him no better than an auld stray dog. His parents now, the old doctor and Mrs Buckley, they idolised young Richard. He was their only one, you see. They nearly went out of their minds with worry when he went over there to France, and who could blame them? Sure what has France to do with us here?'

Suddenly remembering that Solange was French, Mrs Canty corrected herself hastily, 'Not that we thought the other side should win or anything… But it's just they were so worried, and him the only son of the house and all, but when they heard he was going to be with Jeremy, well that made them feel a bit easier in their minds. They were mad about Jeremy. We all were.'

'My husband loved you all, too. And he never wanted Richard to leave his parents. In truth, he was angry when Richard followed him. He didn't want his friend to be in danger, even though when Richard came, Jeremy was so happy to see him and so glad to have the help of such a good doctor.'

Remembering her young husband's concern

for his friend, Solange felt very far from home, and from him. Jeremy had been the essential link between her and Richard; in Amiens, she had only ever met the Irish doctor in Jeremy's company. Richard had never called on her separately or even chatted to her apart from a polite enquiry after her health. Yet here she was in Richard Buckley's house, in this foreign country so far from anything she'd ever known, and without Jeremy. Perhaps this had been a terrible mistake. Yet there was nothing left to which to return. Maman and Papa both gone, Pierre and Jean-Paul too, and the city in ruins. You can't ever go back, only forward. She had no choice. Richard had saved her from a life inhabited only by ghosts. At least here in this strange place she could be of use – help with the new baby, and begin again. Richard had thrown her a lifeline, and though at the moment drowning seemed like a more appealing option, she knew that she could and would survive.

'NOW PETEEN, WE'D BETTER get you to bed,' announced Mrs Canty as she ushered Solange upstairs and into a pretty room overlooking the garden. The walls were covered in exotic bird of paradise wallpaper, in royal blue and gold, and on the teak double bed lay a beautifully embroidered cream bedspread. There was a large matching armoire and chest of drawers and a full-length mirror stood on a stand. The room was pleasantly warm and scented by a bunch of snowdrops arranged in a cut-glass bowl on the dresser. Her bags had been delivered to the room, presumably by the reticent Eddie, whom she still hadn't met.

'*Les fleurs*…the flowers. They are beautiful.'

'Oh that's himself, my Eddie, he grows them. Winter and summer he has flowers growing. He has Latin names for everything; you'd be demented trying to remember them all. There's nothing he can't grow, that husband of mine.' Her voice glowed with pride. 'Now so, let you have a good sleep, and we'll see you tomorrow sometime. Don't be in any rush to get up now, do you hear me?'

Solange slept fitfully, despite the comfortable bed. She tossed and turned and dreamed of France, and of her parents – though never of Jeremy. That often struck her as strange, how his loss was like a large gaping hole of pain in her every waking moment, yet once she slept, he never entered her dreams. The countryside was so quiet; only the crowing of a rooster in the early hours disturbed the peace. Lying awake, she decided to make the best of this situation. She would do her utmost to be a good friend to Richard's wife. Though Mrs Canty seemed a kind person, there was probably not a woman on earth whom the housekeeper would have thought good enough for her precious young master. And although Edith had seemed very cold and even rude to her at first, Solange acknowledged that if Jeremy had brought a young widow into their home, she too would have been cautious at first, however much she trusted her husband.

As dawn crept across the sky, she dozed off into a light sleep. She was disturbed by a piercing shriek from across the hall. Dashing out of bed, she threw on her dressing gown and ran in the direction of the sound. She found herself at the door of Edith's bedroom and hesitated, unsure if Edith was in there alone or if Richard had already joined her. A second later, another loud scream rent the air. This time, tentatively, Solange opened the door. The room was in complete darkness; she moved in the direction of the bed.

'Madame Buckley? Are you well?' The words sounded foolish to her ears, but she didn't know what else to say. Moving towards the curtains she pulled them half open, allowing in sufficient dawn light to see Richard's wife alone in bed, a terrified expression on her face.

'Something…something is happening,' Edith gasped.

Solange ran to the bed and, gently moving back the covers, discovered Edith's waters had broken. Her nightgown was soaking as was the sheet and presumably the mattress beneath. Despite the pain, Edith was clearly mortified by the mess and was trying to cover it with her hands.

'Please, do not worry, Madame,' Solange said soothingly. 'This is normal. Your baby is now coming. Please stay calm and I will send for your husband…'

'No!' Edith screamed.

Solange was unsure if the woman's cry related to Richard or to the pain, but Edith was holding her hand so tightly it would have been impossible for her to move away from the bed anyway.

'No,' repeated Edith, this time as a hiss. 'Not Richard. I don't want him seeing me like this. Not Canty either. Get Dr Bateman back.'

'But Madame, I think there may be no time to send for him. I'm sure your husband will be here any moment.'

Where was he? No one could sleep through

these screams. Solange took a deep breath; she must stay calm.

'If you will permit me to examine you, I think we will find that the baby is almost here. Please do not worry, everything is going to be fine.' Solange was trying to measure the time in between the waves of pain that seemed to grip Edith with such savagery. She'd been present at many deliveries and could tell that this labour was very advanced. Had Edith been having contractions for hours and said nothing until she could bear the pain no longer? Was she that resistant to her husband's presence?

'Please Madame, please try to relax. I know it is difficult but please trust me, it will hurt less if you...' frustratingly the English would not come to her... 'breathe slow and deeply,' she finished, relieved to have recalled the words. 'If you can try to relax, you are doing so well and then the baby will be here very soon, and all of this will be over, I promise.'

Edith's response was another high-pitched scream. Mrs Canty appeared at the door in her night robe and bonnet. 'Oh Lord above! It's time, is it? Dr Richard's gone out on a sick call, tonight of all nights, and he only in the door. I don't even know where he is. What should we do?' Mrs Canty's voice was rising to a crescendo of panic.

'Please, don't worry, everything is perfectly normal. I have delivered many babies before.' A white lie – she'd only ever played a supporting role, and that was when she was still in training – but she had to calm the old housekeeper down. 'So Mrs Canty, if you can just help me by… No, there is no point now trying to get towels under her. I think the baby is coming soon. Please, go and wash your hands and sterilise some scissors in boiling water and bring them back to me. Now, Madame, please just breathe, *oui*, yes, very good, you are doing everything beautifully, and very soon you will hold your baby in your arms.'

Edith's breathing became deeper and more even as she locked eyes with Solange. Then she screamed again.

'Now, Madame.' Solange attempted to infuse her voice with both kindness and authority. 'The next time you feel the pain you must push down very hard. Your baby is almost here. Just a few more minutes and all this will be over, everything will be well. Just keep your energy for delivering your baby. You are doing very well.'

It seemed that Edith was coming to trust her. As the next contraction came, she gripped

Solange's hand tightly and pushed with every ounce of strength she had.

'Now Madame, the next one will be the one to deliver your baby. Try to pant, like this…' Solange demonstrated and Edith followed her instructions. The next contraction began to build. Solange moved to the foot of the bed. Between Edith's legs, the head of the baby was crowning.

'Now, just push very hard, and the little one will be here.' The infant came slipping from Edith's body into Solange's arms. 'Oh Madame, a little girl, a beautiful little girl!'

She cut the umbilical cord with the scissors and handed the wailing child to a tearful Mrs Canty, who wrapped the tiny body in freshly warmed blankets. Minutes passed as Solange waited for the placenta to follow. Surprisingly, Edith's contractions continued without abating. The pain should have ceased with the delivery of the child, but she seemed to be still in full labour.

'What's happening?' Edith gasped, terror in her eyes. 'Why is it not over? You said it would be over once it was born!'

Solange fought the urge to panic. She looked again between Edith's legs and was astonished to see another head crowning. 'Madame, please do not worry, but there is… Yes, there is another baby. Please, you must push once more.'

With a loud cry from Edith, the second infant slipped out quickly and easily and was also deposited into the waiting arms of Mrs Canty.

'A little boy! Oh, Madame, how wonderful for you!'

The two placentas followed and finally Edith lay back on the pillows, exhausted. Solange helped her into a more comfortable position, murmuring soft, soothing words in French. Then she changed the sodden sheets and replaced Edith's nightgown with a fresh one. Throughout this process the new mother avoided her eyes as if acutely embarrassed by what had just happened. She appeared very self-conscious of her body, even in front of the woman who had just witnessed her giving birth.

Mrs Canty was busy wrapping up the babies and cooing over them. 'Oh holy Mother of God. Oh Missus, ye have a pair of beauties here and no mistake.' She was wiping away tears as the lusty wails of the newborns filled the air. Solange took them from her, wrapped in their warm blankets, and brought them to the head of the bed, preparing to place them in their mother's arms.

'*Félicitations*, congratulations, Madame, they

are beautiful. I am sure you and your husband will be very proud of them.'

Edith looked down at her two babies, and to Solange's dismay, turned with difficulty onto her side, away from them.

'Please take them away, I need to sleep now.'

'*Oui*, Madame, of course, but perhaps you should feed them first? Then I can take them and bathe them?' Solange suggested.

'No, I shan't be feeding them. Please attend to them and do not disturb me.'

'But Madame, how will I…'

'Canty knows where everything is.' And Edith settled down to sleep.

'I wasn't sure she'd go through with it,' Mrs Canty whispered as she and Solange were wrapping up the infants once more, having put napkins on them. 'But by God, it seems she is. She had some bottles and tins sent over from England a few weeks ago. Nestlé, it says on the labels. She told me that's what the baby – well, I suppose it's *the babies* now – anyway, that's what we're to feed them. Not nursing her own babies, did you ever hear the like…'

'Please, just leave.' Edith's voice had regained some of its lost strength.

AN HOUR LATER, AS Solange sat dozing in

the rocking chair with both babies asleep in the smart new bassinet beside her, Richard burst into the kitchen. 'Oh Solange, thank God you were here. Eddie only just found me! I was up the mountain at Coakley's farm. I should have left a note, but I thought there was still weeks to go... I'm so sorry you had to manage on your own, but thank God you were here. So where is he? Or she?'

The news that there was not one baby but two filled Richard with joy. She had never seen this quiet man so animated and excited. She thought of Jeremy and how he would have loved the children they would never have. So often in bed they had discussed names for their children. She, favouring English names to match their surname, he arguing for French. He had loved France and everything about it. Most of all, he had loved her.

'Did you have no idea?' she asked Richard as he stood gazing down in amazement at his sleeping twins. The babies were sharing the bassinet; there was only one of everything for the moment.

'No. Bateman never spotted it, I suppose. Sometimes it can be difficult, depending on what position the babies are lying in. Edith must have got a real surprise.' He gently stroked their heads.

'Well, *felicitaciones*, Richard. They are beautiful. Do you know what they are to be called?'

'Yes. We'd like to call the boy James, after Edith's father; that's what we'd decided if it was a boy. And Juliet, after my mother, if it was a girl. I suppose we will just use both.'

He was beaming but seemed hesitant, almost nervous, to pick them up.

'Go on,' she whispered.

'I'm afraid I'll wake them,' he replied.

Solange reached in and gathered the tiny babies up, placing one in each of his arms. They stirred and instantly fell back to sleep. Richard Buckley looked at his children, and Solange saw raw emotion on his face for the first time since she'd known him. He gazed at their tiny faces and fingers, amazed at the miracle of life despite all his experience of death.

Eventually he spoke, 'Thank you, Solange, from the bottom of my heart, for delivering them safely and for taking care of them until Edith has had her rest.' He glanced at the bottle and tin of Nestlé powdered milk, still on the table. 'Poor girl, it must have been exhausting for her.'

'Of course,' she replied. 'I'm glad I was able to help. They are healthy little ones. They are enjoying the milk from the tins. I have never seen that before, but they are drinking it happily, so all is well.'

He said, clearly a little embarrassed, 'Well, to nurse twins would have been very difficult for her at first. I'm sure they will do wonderfully on the powdered milk, for a day or two. I can't tell you how grateful I...*Edith* and I...are for all your help. Now if you don't mind taking care of them for just a few more minutes, I've been in these clothes all night, so I just need to clean up. I don't want to asphyxiate my children. I won't be long.'

'Of course.'

'Was that Dr Richard I heard?' Mrs Canty came bustling into the kitchen, as outside, the winter morning was brightening up at last. 'He must have been over the moon with the little beauties, God bless them. Anything from herself above? Is she interested in looking at her children? Not a bit of it, I suppose, and you up all night. Here give them to me and let you go for a snooze.'

Solange looked down at the two tiny babies, still in her arms from where Richard had handed them back to her. They slept soundly, their little fists bunched up tight. They were so pure, so innocent; they knew nothing of ugliness or brutality. For the first time since she had heard the news of Jeremy's death, she felt something thaw deep inside her.

All that morning, instead of sleeping as Richard and Mrs Canty insisted she must, she lay in bed thinking of the twins and hoping they were all right. When the quiet of the house was finally shattered by a newborn cry, she couldn't stay in her room. She went downstairs to help Richard who was attempting to feed one while the other bawled in the bassinet.

'Mrs Canty is just gone for a few messages, we need a few things from the shop. I told her I could manage but...' Richard was all fingers and thumbs.

Immediately that Solange picked up and cuddled Juliet, she stopped crying. She started to suck on her bottle and began drifting off to sleep again. Then she did the same with James, and soon both babies were fast asleep.

'You have the magic touch with them, Solange,' Richard whispered in awe as they slept cuddled up together.

Gazing into the crib, she said, 'I think they like to be near each other. They have been close for all this time and now to be separated – it must be a shock.'

'MADAME?' SOLANGE TENTATIVELY EN-

TERED the bedroom, having first knocked gently on the door.

Edith was awake and propped up on pillows reading a letter that had arrived that morning.

'Yes, Solange? Did you want something?' she asked, still reading.

'I was wondering if you would like to see the babies. I could bring them to you.' She had contemplated simply walking into the room with the twins but had thought better of it.

'No thank you, not just now. Are they well?' Edith asked as if enquiring about a distant relative.

'*Oui*, I mean, yes, Madame, they are very well and so beautiful.'

'Yes, I'm sure. I may come down to see them later. Although I'm sure they are better off not being disturbed from their routine.' Edith paused in her reading and looked up. 'Thank you for your assistance with the births. I am in your debt.' Her tone conveyed dismissal.

Still, Solange lingered. 'Madame, I am always happy to help.'

'Well, yes. It was good you were here.' Edith returned to her letter.

'And when you are ready for me to bring the babies to you...'

Edith looked up again with a sigh. 'Solange, not now, please. This is an important letter from an old friend of mine in Dublin. There are going to be changes in this country. Ireland may not remain the calm and peaceful place you imagine it to be. British imperialism will not be tolerated any longer. Now if you'll excuse me…'

This time, the implication that Solange was outstaying her welcome was too obvious to ignore.

# CHAPTER 2

*T*he weeks that followed were cold but bright. Solange wrapped the babies up well and took them for walks around the garden in their pram. The crocuses that bloomed in profusion around the trees delighted her. Her life had altered so irreparably and so often in these last months that she had lost all sense of continuity, and this garden gave her an anchor to cling to in an ever-changing world. It was a comfort to know that spring had come again as it had always done, irrespective of the turmoil in human lives.

Yet the main distraction from her own sorrows came in caring for James and Juliet. She was deeply grateful that the endless demands of two such healthy infants gave her so little time to brood over all she had lost. The twins seemed never to sleep simultaneously and were always hungry. Richard insisted that it was not expected of her that she care for them, but given the continued lack of interest their mother showed in them, there seemed to be no other option. He was so busy with the practice, and Mrs Canty, although a great help, had the household to run. Besides, Solange wanted to look after them. She could sit for hours just holding them and kissing their downy heads.

After Jeremy's death she had moved as if in a trance. Presumably she had slept and ate, but if so, she had no recollection of it. Life had stretched out in front of her as an endless colourless void of time without him in it, until she herself died. Over and over she thought how things should have been different. He was a doctor, not even on the front line, yet he was dead. She thought too of her Maman and Papa, so full of life and fun. Her mother's flashing eyes that could make her adoring husband agree to anything she wanted. Her father, who loved his sons and his only daughter with all his heart. But then Maman had got sick, and died – a simple cut on her foot that had turned to blood poisoning. Papa was killed a short while later, shot by a German soldier in reprisal for some imagined slight. Her older brothers had fallen at Verdun, dying side by side as they had lived since early childhood. To be left entirely alone in the world was a terrifying prospect. Yet in those early weeks, all she had thought about was how she could manage to live without Jeremy.

She was by no means over her loss; she doubted she ever would be, but the twins had become her new reality, and she adored them more with each passing day.

Sometimes she felt guilty for loving them as if she was their mother, yet Edith showed only the most cursory of interest in the babies. Once a day – or, on rare occasions, twice – she would descend into the kitchen to glance into their pram. She would enquire as to their health and whether they were eating or sleeping properly, but without any sign of genuine concern. She never picked them up or even looked too closely at them. It really was as if Solange were their mother and Edith a gracious employer enquiring after her housemaid's children; something to be done as a matter of form, rather than stemming from any real desire to know.

Richard loved the twins and often gave them their bottles; occasionally, he even changed a napkin – though not with much success. He asked daily if Edith had been down to see them, and if Solange thought that perhaps this was a question he should be putting to his wife, she gave no indication of it.

Time and again, Solange wondered how the Buckleys' marriage survived. Their union could not even be described as one of convenience; the entire household seemed to be a source of annoyance to Edith. Solange had long ceased to imagine that Edith's initial coldness to her had sprung from a natural caution; it was clear to her now that Edith's *ennui* extended to everyone in her life. Time and again she witnessed Richard trying to get closer to his wife, but each time Edith rebuffed him – avoiding him whenever possible and engaging in brittle conversation with him only when it was necessary. The letters kept on coming – two, sometimes three, a week, from her friends in Dublin, all of whom were, it seemed, involved in the struggle for independence. It was the only subject on which Edith seemed close to animated and, perhaps because her husband showed no interest, she would often explain to Solange certain points regarding Irish politics.

Last week, Edith had summoned Solange to her room.

'Aah Solange, thank you for coming up. I think we need to talk, to clarify some things. Tell me, are you happy here?'

Solange was nonplussed. '*Oui*...I mean, yes of course, Madame. I am very happy and grateful to you and Richard for...'

'No, I know that, but I think if you are happy to stay we should formalise the arrangement. I mean you are looking after the twins, no doubt admirably, and therefore, we should be paying you. It is not reasonable of us to expect you to work for nothing. Now if you don't wish to do it, then of course there is no obligation on you; we will simply hire a nurse to come in. Please don't feel pressured due to some sense that you owe us something. That is simply not the case.'

Solange stood there wondering what to say. The thought of anyone else taking care of the babies was abhorrent to her; she loved them so much. Also, she had very little money. Jeremy was due a pension, but the process of claiming it was taking a very long time. She did need something to live on, but she wondered if Richard knew about this arrangement Edith was proposing. He was always so adamant that she was a member of the family.

'Well, Madame, I do love taking care of James

and Juliet, so I am happy to do it. I don't know what else I would do if I did not do that. So yes, if it is acceptable to you and your husband then I would be glad of the job.'

'Good. That's settled then. Shall we say two hundred pounds per annum? And one and a half days off per week? Mrs Canty can cover your holidays. Of course, should you require more time off, please just ask and we will arrange it. I think that's fair.'

Solange was impressed – she hadn't expected this cool, indifferent woman to be so generous. A nurse generally earned only one hundred pounds and year, and one day off per month was typical. 'That is most kind, Madame, but please deduct from that my board and lodging.'

'No. That won't be necessary. Ordinarily that would be factored in, but these circumstances are far from typical. My husband promised your husband that we would be taking care of you and so we will. Now, there are some details we need to discuss.'

As part of her new role, Solange was to list all the items necessary for the raising of two babies. She should not be thrifty, explained Edith – just simply write down whatever she thought they would require over the coming months, and

Richard would see to it that everything was delivered. The babies were to be dressed exclusively from the Munster Arcade in Cork, or Arnott's in Dublin. Under no circumstances were they to be dressed in anything hand-knitted or bought locally. Prams and other paraphernalia were to come from Dublin also.

RICHARD SIGHED OVER HIS newspaper, as he ate his breakfast in the kitchen with Solange and the twins.

'I never realised when I offered you a life of peace in Ireland, how things would turn out here. This struggle between the British and the IRA is, I fear, going to get worse. God knows how it will end.' He looked pensive but then seemed to shake himself out of it. 'Still, it's a bright spring morning and hopefully someone will get a bit of sense and end this before it escalates. Now, will we take this pair for a stroll before I face the parish and their ailments?'

He pushed one pram and Solange the other around the path that encircled the house. The April sun warmed the old walls of Dunderrig and the garden had sprung to life. At nearly four months, the twins were thriving and loved to lie without blankets and furiously kick their chubby legs.

'They are so beautiful, *n'est-ce pas?*' Solange smiled. 'I don't know much about this independence war, I don't read the papers, though I should I suppose, but it just all seems so...'

'Pointless? Repetitive? Futile?' Richard suggested.

She nodded. 'After France and everything that we saw, war seems to be just waste. Nothing else, just waste. People, property, land, villages. I hope this is not the same fate for your home, Richard.'

Their relationship had become less formal in the past months. Richard would always be reticent, and she spoke as guardedly as he, but they enjoyed a good relationship. He was becoming more accustomed to fatherhood and was taking more and more of an active role in the care of his children. He'd even mastered changing their napkins. Nothing had improved with their mother, though she did still visit the kitchen once a day to glance briefly at them.

THE TWINS WERE BAPTISED in the local Catholic parish church, and on the morning of the christening, Edith arrived downstairs looking so glamorous that she took Solange's breath away. She had only seen the doctor's wife in nightgowns up to then and was amazed to see how elegant Edith could be with her hair pinned in an elegant chignon and wearing a beautifully tailored dress, cut daringly low at both front and back, with panels of cream sat alongside panels of ivory and white. Solange had never seen anything like it on a real person before, but she had taken to looking over various fashion magazines when Edith had finished with them. So she knew that since the war, when women had learnt to drive cars and wear trousers, they were reluctant to incarcerate themselves once more in torturous corsets and restrictive dresses. The post-war generation was raising hemlines and dropping necklines and, despite living in West Cork, it seemed Edith Buckley was not going to be left behind. For the first time, Solange could see why Richard had married her. She was so beautiful.

The twins were also dressed handsomely – Juliet in the simple christening robe that had been used to baptise at least four generations of Buckleys, and James in an identical robe made for the occasion by Mrs Canty. Both babies were wrapped in elaborately embroidered white blankets.

Mrs Canty told Solange she had overheard Richard and Edith arguing about the christening robes. Edith had wanted to order new ones from some French couturier based in Dublin, but for once Richard had put his foot down. Every Buckley baby was baptised in the family gown, and the twins were not going to be an exception. Mrs Canty delighted in telling the tale of how 'The One' – as Edith was unflatteringly called by her – got her comeuppance.

Richard made two trips in the car that day: the first, bringing Mrs Canty and her husband and a silent Edith to the church; the next, to collect Solange and the twins. As Solange entered the church with a baby in each arm, she felt the eyes of at least a hundred people upon her. Perhaps she imagined it, but it seemed as if they were more interested in her than in the babies. Edith and Richard sat side by side in the front pew, not touching, and next to them sat Dr Bateman and his wife, who were standing as the children's godparents. Once again Solange was struck by the peculiar ways of the Irish. These people were offering to be the babies' guardians in the event of their parents' death, yet here in the church on the morning of their christening was the first time they had ever even seen them.

Dr Bateman had called late on the morning of the birth to ensure Edith was well and that she had delivered safely. He had complimented Solange on her professionalism, and when she had asked would he like to examine the babies, he had stated that he was quite sure they were in excellent hands between her and their father, and promptly left. He had not appeared in Dunderrig since.

The babies were duly baptised, and afterwards Richard invited a select group of people – friends and family, Solange assumed – to the Eldon Hotel in Skibbereen for lunch. He'd pleaded with her the night before to come to the lunch, but she had refused. Edith wouldn't want her there – she was staff now, whether Richard liked it or not, and it wouldn't have been appropriate.

# CHAPTER 3

*R*ichard sat beside the fire in his study thinking about his wife. She had been bored and disparaging ever since her arrival at Dunderrig. He had hoped that the twins would soften her heart, but it hadn't happened. He tried to pinpoint the time when she had turned into this cold, snobbish person.

She had been such a beautiful, quiet, serene kind of girl. Such a restful person to be around, that he had decided only two weeks after meeting her at that hospital dance in England that she was the girl for him. He wasn't much of a dancer, but Jeremy had convinced him to have a night out. They had almost finished their training in Beauford Hospital, in Bristol, and Jeremy was planning to join up as soon as he qualified. There was a girl that Jeremy had had his eye on all week, and he was determined to have a crack at her. Richard was used to his friend falling for a new girl every few days; he also knew Jeremy would not let him rest until he agreed to accompany him to the dance. It was easier just to give in.

Richard had never had much success with girls. He had always envisaged himself married, but the process of becoming so seemed a bit of a mystery. There were a few girls at home in Dunderrig who were chatty and seemed friendly, but he was painfully shy and clammed up whenever a girl approached him. Since meeting Jeremy, it had become even harder for him to meet anyone – the girls were always dazzled by his handsome and vivacious friend, while he himself faded into the background.

He had seen Edith straight away when he walked in. He had plucked up the courage to speak to her after he heard her ordering a cup of tea in an Irish accent. She had been visiting an elderly relative in Bristol and had been convinced to attend the dance by her cousin. They danced several times that night, and Richard was sure he had never seen a girl as beautiful. They had gone to tea the following day and for a walk afterwards. She seemed to be happy to discuss issues of the day but rarely answered a direct question, and made very few demands on him emotionally; often they just strolled in comfortable silence.

Yet on their fifth date, as they walked through the Clifton area of Bristol, he had inquired about her parents. And after some hesitation, she had told him that her mother had died when she was still a child and that her father had become everything to her. Then, after much prompting, she told him her father's story. He had been a professor of English and History in University College Dublin, who regularly spoke out against the horrendous living conditions endured by the working classes. He had supported Jim Larkin in encouraging the workers' strike of 1913 and had been addressing a rally when a riot erupted between the crowd and the police. Badly injured in the ensuing melee, he had died a week later of his wounds.

The normally serene Edith became visibly upset as she spoke, and he realised then how difficult it was for her to discuss such emotional issues. There had been minimal physical contact between them up to that point, but there, in the middle of the street, he had held her in his arms and comforted her. That was the turning point;

she was so vulnerable and beautiful, and he decided he wanted to take care of her always.

After that initial fortnight in Bristol, they arranged to stay in touch when Edith returned to Dublin. He was working hard in the hospital, gaining experience before deciding his next move. He'd always intended to return to Dunderrig and take over the practice from his father, but the old doctor wasn't yet ready to retire and besides, meeting Edith had made him rethink. She seemed very settled in Dublin and so, after a few months of letters, and an occasional meeting, he had accepted a locum position in Kingstown. Edith had been so pleased. He had proposed in Stephen's Green, and she had agreed happily. He smiled ruefully at the memory. Nothing he did seemed to please her these days.

Those days in Dublin seemed a lifetime ago now. Edith had been happy and busy then; she had continued her interest in matters political, and he was so absorbed in his work that he was only glad she had a wide circle of friends to keep her occupied. Many of them were well-known literary and political figures – people who had known her father. Occasionally they came to the house for dinner or drinks; yet while Richard did his best, he found their conversation about the

Irish cause a little wearisome. It wasn't that he didn't care, but these academics and writers seemed so far removed from the common people they purported to represent. He contributed very little to these conversations, and he knew his lack of enthusiasm embarrassed Edith. They never argued, but he remembered one such dinner at a grand house in Ballsbridge, when he'd explained to an artist sitting on his left that while Irish independence was of course something to aspire to, it wasn't worth one drop of blood. He said that negotiation and dialogue was the only way and that he hoped a peaceful solution could be found.

He would never forget the looks from their fellow diners; it was as if he'd just said something incredibly rude or vulgar. Edith was furious with him and didn't speak to him all the way home. From them on he didn't attend those dinners – much to the relief of them both. They rubbed along well together, while not seeing too much of each other.

And that was where everything would have stayed, had he not received that letter from Jeremy describing the conditions in the hospital in Amiens. It was not in the true Jeremy style; his letters were usually about his passion for the gorgeous Solange. Before he'd convinced her to marry him, he had regularly asked Richard's opinion about how to get her to see him as someone serious, rather than a playboy. Richard found the idea of Jeremy asking *him* for advice ridiculous. Jeremy was the one who could talk to women. He himself could barely manage a romantic relationship with his own wife.

This latest letter was in a different vein, however, as Jeremy described the kind of injuries the young men at the front were sustaining and how supplies and staffing levels were woefully inadequate. He wrote too of the horrors suffered by so many Irishmen in the bloodbath of the Somme – many of them from the Munster Fusiliers regiment, from Richard's native West Cork. Suddenly, the idea of going to France, making a difference and helping his own countrymen seemed the logical thing to do. He asked his parents if Edith could live with them in Dunderrig while he was in France, and they agreed at once. The idea that his wife would refuse never crossed his mind.

'No,' she said calmly, when he had finished.

'No? No to what? To Dunderrig? Look Edith, I know you have your friends here, but I can't leave you here alone and unprotected.'

'It's true that I do not want to go to Dunderrig. My life is here. I am helping, doing something worthwhile, something my father would be proud of. But nor do I want you putting on a British uniform and fighting for their king.' She spoke slowly, but with steeliness to her tone he had never heard before.

'But Edith, my dear, I won't be fighting. I'm a doctor. I will be working in a hospital. Tending to the wounded. I don't have any political opinions about it; I simply want to help. Irish boys are out there too, you know, thousands of them. Please try to understand, I love you, but I have to go. And while I'm gone, I want you to be safe.' He was aware he was pleading.

She looked as if she was weighing up whether or not to continue. Her voice held a bitterness he'd never heard from her before. 'Yes, Richard. There are thousands of Irishmen fighting. Thousands of traitors to their own country. If they were so anxious to fight for something, then why not here, on their own soil, for their own people? You know how I feel about the British, and everything they stand for. Their puppet police murdered my father. Murdered him, Richard, for having the courage to speak out. I cannot support you putting that uniform on your back. Frankly, I'm shocked that you would even consider it. The

Rising might have ended in disaster, but we are not beaten. Already we are working on getting our men out of British gaols, and when they come home, I want to be here, in Dublin. *Here* is where you should be, looking after your own, not risking your life and wasting your skills in a country that has nothing to do with us. I am asking you, as your wife, not to do this.'

Richard felt as if he were seeing her for the first time – he had been so busy with the practice, he hadn't realised how deeply she had become involved with the Volunteers. Since the Rising the previous Easter, the city had been on tenterhooks. It seemed to him now that her support of an Irish Republic could only get her into trouble, and that it was more important than ever that she relocate to the peaceful backwater of Dunderrig while he was away in France and unable to protect her.

He tried at first to reason with her, 'Edith, I do understand your loyalty to your father. He was an honourable and brave man, but really, this is no environment for a woman, let alone one whose husband is away. I love you, and I want you to be safe. Please try to understand my reasons for going. I don't agree with war – I hate it, in fact – but medicine is not about ideology. The boys and men who are suffering need me to help them. I'm sorry you are unhappy, but I must insist that you go to Dunderrig. I would be out of my mind with worry were you to stay here.'

She looked at him with disgust, and from that moment on, she rebuffed all efforts he made to be conciliatory. They had driven to Dunderrig in silence a few weeks later, and everything he said was greeted with monosyllabic responses. His parents went to great lengths to make their daughter-in-law welcome, yet Edith showed them the same level of disdain she now did Richard. His father had taken him aside and questioned him what was the matter, had they done something wrong? Richard didn't wish to explain. He simply said that Edith would need to get used to country living, and that would take time – he was sure they would be a comfort to Edith, and she to them. Then, with a heavy heart, he set sail for England.

For him, the war passed in a haze of noise and blood. There was nothing glorious or noble about it, just the daily – and nightly – grind of trying to patch together the broken bodies with which he was constantly presented. He tried to get home on leave to see Edith, but he'd only managed it twice. He wrote long letters, but she replied only with short notes – answering all questions he asked her, but with absolutely no warmth. Still, she had met with unexpected enthusiasm the news that he was coming home on leave in the May of 1918, and announced she was coming to Dublin to meet him off the boat. He half-suspected his wife was more interested in seeing Dublin than in seeing him. He had heard from his mother that she often travelled up to the city, staying with friends overnight. He supposed there was no harm in it. It must be dull for a young woman to be stuck in a house with his elderly parents and no one her own age to befriend. He knew some of his old school friends' wives had made efforts to include her in their social circle, but it seemed she was still very much a Dublin girl. He told himself that when he returned home and the war was over, they would patch up their marriage, hopefully have children, and all would be well. By then she would have forgiven him.

They arranged to meet in the Bayview Hotel in Kingstown. They had often gone there for dinner in the early days of their marriage, so he hoped the location would rekindle their love. When Richard arrived at the hotel, around seven o'clock in the evening, he had expected to find her dressed for a night out. Instead, he was surprised to be greeted by his wife wearing a negligee and even more delighted to find her in an amorous mood. They'd made love quickly and silently. Richard would have liked to remain in bed with her, but she was determined that they go down to dinner. She never asked about his life in France. A group of her friends were waiting for them in the dining room. Hiding his disappointment, he made light conversation. His wife had taken up smoking and kept abandoning him for the terrace of the seafront hotel, yet he was so happy to see her animated and smiling again that he indulged her, and agreed to her suggestion that they stay in the hotel for a few more days before travelling to Dunderrig. Although his leave was suddenly cut short before he could get home to see his parents, he had returned to France with a lighter heart. In her next, very short letter she had told him she was pregnant. He was overjoyed, although worried that she herself expressed no pleasure in the news.

The deaths parents from influenza came as a shocking blow to him. It happened only weeks after he'd been in Ireland, and he was crushed not just by grief but also by guilt that he had been in the country but hadn't managed to travel down to

Dunderrig to see them. If he hadn't agreed to stay those extra days in Kingstown… He wrote long letters to Edith, describing his pain as best he could but, while she commiserated, he could tell that the death of the old couple meant much more to their housekeeper Mrs Canty and her husband Eddie than to his own wife. He longed to go home but could not get leave. John and Juliet Buckley were buried in the cemetery in the village without their only child there to say goodbye.

As the war wore on wearyingly to its end, the waves of wounded growing daily, Richard received a second, longer letter from Edith:

Dear Richard,

I hope you are well and that you will be home safely before too long. The house is very quiet without your parents, though Mrs Canty does her best to fill it with her relentless prattle. I am well, though I have been feeling quite nauseous. Mrs Canty's boiling of cabbage does little to help that situation. I have not been up to Dublin in some time, so I have no news about anything there. I am under the care of Dr Bateman from Cork. The child will be born in January sometime, he thinks. I hope you will have returned by then. I know we have had our differences,

Richard, but now that we are to be parents I think we should make the best of it for the sake of our child.

Fond regards,

Your wife,

Edith.

He felt great relief. *Fond regards...* Impending motherhood had clearly softened her. The war was in its final stages, he was sure of it, and he would return to Dunderrig, take over the practice, and raise his family with Edith. Everything would be all right.

CONTINUE READING BY CLICKING HERE:
http://
mybook.to/JeanGraingerSoMuchOwed

# ABOUT THE AUTHOR

Jean Grainger is a USA Today bestselling Irish author. She writes historical and contemporary Irish fiction and her work has very flatteringly been compared to the late great Maeve Binchy.

She lives in a two hundred year old stone cottage in County Cork with her husband Diarmuid and the youngest two of her four children. The older two show up occasionally with laundry and to raid the fridge. There are a variety of animals there too, all led by two cute but clueless micro-dogs called Scrappy and Scoobi.

Trials and Tribulations

**The Star and the Shamrock Series**

The Star and the Shamrock

The Emerald Horizon

The Hard Way Home

The World Starts Anew

**The Queenstown Series**

Last Port of Call

The West's Awake

The Harp and the Rose

Roaring Liberty

**Standalone Books**

So Much Owed

Shadow of a Century

Under Heaven's Shining Stars

Catriona's War

Sisters of the Southern Cross